# THE BLADES

The Stone's Blade : Book Three

# the BLADES

the STONE'S BLADE : BOOK THREE

# ALLYNN RIGGS

TimberDark
publications

timberdark.com

*The Blades* (The Stone's Blade, Book Three)

Published by
TimberDark Publications, LLC, 7683 E Costilla Blvd., Centennial, CO 80112
www.Timberdark.com

ISBN 978-0-9910002-4-1 (trade paper)
ISBN 978-0-9910002-5-8 (eBook)

Library of Congress Control Number: 2019909455

Interior, Cover Design, and Art by Nathan Fisher, www.ScifiBookDesigner.com
Edited by Melanie Mulhall, www.DragonheartWritingandEditing.com
Author Photo by Linda M Wilson, www.YourWorldOurLens.com

Printed in the United States of America

First Edition

19 20 21 22 23 24 SP 6 5 4 3 2 1

# DEDICATION

*For Bob*
*I love you to the stars and back.*
*Your support and belief in me has made this possible*

# TABLE OF CONTENTS

# ACKNOWLEDGMENTS

Amazement and wonder fill my soul when I consider how far the original story of *The Stone's Blade* series has come since 2012 when I decided that I would do whatever was needed to publish it. Now, with this third installment of the series, I just shake my head. I did not realize how much joy would become part of my life when I left a full-time job and, with the unwavering support of my husband, Bob, began this journey in earnest.

When I told Bob I wanted to change careers and focus on writing and publishing stories, his main comment was that we could do it, and we would do it right. I believe we have. In the past seven years, his emotional and financial support for what I am doing has kept me going. Even though he has not read any of the books, his enthusiasm for the story is infectious, and he often talks about my accomplishments and the awards the first two books, *The Blood* and *The Balance*, have garnered. He has soothed away the bad dreams and talk in my sleep when I am struggling against the characters or story line. He tells me everything will be okay, that I will figure it out, and that the story will be fine. He brings me lunch or dinner when I've totally lost myself in the writing and forgotten about the time. He reminds me to just get the words out, that I can always edit, that nothing will happen unless I write, and that I *must* write. He understands my need to write and unwaveringly supports my happiness. I would be miserable without him. He is my inspiration, my partner, my love. I cannot thank Bob enough.

More thanks go to my friend and editor, Melanie Mulhall, of Dragonheart, whose persistent coaching, cajoling, and encouragement push me toward excellence. I am continually learning the craft of writing from her. We are learning the ins and outs of writing a series together and are finding it a worthy challenge. This time, Melanie has brought in a new proofreader, John Wilcockson. He is looking forward to the fourth book—as we all are.

Beta readers Nancy Koos and Karen Dreher have seen multiple versions and are delighted in seeing the process a book goes through before it is published. I welcome their input and questions, which often lead me and the story in different and interesting directions.

Book cover and interior designer, Nathan Fisher, of Ideas Ablaze, has again created a breathtaking cover. The simplicity of this illustration belies the complexity of the scene he used, and it reflects the power of song and color that I saw when I wrote the scene. Again, I thank you, Nathan, for making my imagination visible.

9

Members of my Tuesday writing group have also had their hands in my writing process as we discuss techniques, writing resources, the similarities between widely different genres, and the pluses and minuses of traditional versus independent publication.

I thank the Colorado Independent Publishers Association (CIPA) for the continued support and encouragement since 2012. The networking available with service providers and other writers is outstanding, and the variety of programs presented at CIPA meetings enlightens and inspires me.

If you'd like to contact me directly, my social media platforms are below. If you enjoyed reading this book, please take a moment to write and post a brief review on Amazon, Goodreads, and wherever else you can. And tell your friends, coworkers, neighbors, teachers, and even a few enemies that they need to read *The Stone's Blade* sci-fi series. I thank you for your enthusiasm for this story. Now, are you ready for *The Seventh Stone: The Stone's Blade, Book Four*? It's coming soon!

Allynn@Timberdark.com
http://www.timberdark.com
http://www.timberdarkwriter.wordpress.com
https://Facebook.com/Timberdarkpublications

# THE PROPHECY OF
# THE BLOOD AND THE BALANCE
## (Also known as The First Song)

*Circle of Seven sing safe passage.*
*Divide by two and send in deep sleep.*
*The Blood and Balance shall each save one,*
*Awakening three to rejoice with time's message.*
*Time will soon come for reunion's leap.*
*Six will Sing joining three homes and suns.*

*Plague and sickness spur Stones to send*
*Singer and blade to chosen star unknown.*
*The Blood and Balance, in one birth two.*
*She, The Blood, to be aged by Time-Song's end.*
*He, The Balance, in time to heal first a Stone*
*Then home to awakened three to join anew.*

*One Stone healed, now three to find.*
*One southern, one northern, and one an island home.*
*Three to teach three then with their charges to share*
*The Song of Teaching to join separated kind.*
*Writings on walls and cloth the star path for the pilot are shown*
*A course to origin now healed and no longer bare.*

*With their charges, six of seven sent to distant stars,*
*new homes to protect and guide,*
*Await the One left behind its world-healing song near complete,*
*the plague a sign.*
*In time to welcome reunion and blending*
*of those sent safely away*
*Traditions of song and blade kept side by side*
*though three must hide*
*Until Stone and Pilot join with six opening star paths*
*in triangular line.*
*Each world its people a choice to go or stay.*

# CHAPTER ONE

The humming puffs of the hover-car soothed Isul Treyder's roiling thoughts as he arrived in Saedi City to the delayed meeting with Senator Nelham. Though no one else was in the vehicle, speaking aloud helped him focus on building up the proper amount of emotion for the upcoming meeting. The meeting should have occurred immediately after the sheriff's body was stolen from his laboratory, but with all the ensuing hullabaloo, there had been no safe time to meet. Because of that, he conceded that he shouldn't be too upset over the ten-day delay. It had certainly given him time to complete his operations in Wharton, which the senator did not know about. Treyder sighed and refocused on events prior to the raid on the laboratory.

Though he'd been shocked at first, Treyder was now grateful for the first visit to his office by the sheriff and the girl with her Southern escort. Their visit and questions had prompted him to remove his notes and drawings on the coma device from the Star Valley research center. Then, when the sheriff returned alone that evening to question him further, Treyder had seen the opportunity to test his new explosive-powered sliver blade. In so doing, he had gained another specimen for further testing. Outside of the noise and powder burns, the device had worked as intended, and the sheriff had lost consciousness quickly.

Moving the sheriff's body had been problematic without assistance, but that had been necessary. After dropping off the sheriff's body at the Saedi City laboratory, which he had been told was safe, and after he had given the senator directions for protecting the experiment, he had returned to Star Valley to get his personal items and several boxes of coma device research. Once back in Wharton, he'd shipped copies of the research to a third location, which only he knew. He was rather proud of himself for coming up with the third location in The Necklace Islands—just in case and just in time.

He grinned in self-satisfaction that, months ago, he had thought far enough ahead to have purchased the mine and hired the ready workforce in Wharton. Manufacturing and mining operations there were running smoothly now, and he was looking forward to seeing crates filled with boxes of the coma devices when he returned from this meeting. Plans for demonstrating them to the senator and the military elite were still being worked out. Perhaps he could schedule the demonstration with the senator at their meeting.

Treyder settled his hover-car into a parking slot in the darkest portion of the underground garage. The western hideout provided plenty of workers for building the devices, and the mining industry was reenergized because there was now a demand for the trace minerals usually dumped with other tailings. Treyder needed them to manufacture the coma device. No one would look for him there, and Treyder was confident it would take months for a connection to be made between the remote mining area's sudden growth and the experiments he was conducting. He would have all that time to perfect the mass delivery of the devices requested by Senator Nelham as well as finish his proposals for how it could be used in place of anesthesia in surgery. He finally had the upper hand.

Isul Treyder glared at the senator. "You said the lab was secure! If that was true, how did two individuals manage to get so close to it before being discovered—not by *your* guards, but by a lowly clerk. And let's not mention that *your* guards lost them by causing a ruckus in the street market. Not only that, but less than a day later, three or more armed warriors infiltrated the building and stole the sheriff and most of my notes! Including some that had your name attached."

At least the senator frowned at that last bit of news. Treyder smugly remembered he had backed up the computers from the now not-so-secret capital city laboratory just before his patient had been snatched back, presumably by his friends from Star Valley. Nelham had taken on the responsibility of safeguarding the laboratory and failed. Perhaps it would be enough to let him know that what had been taken would connect him to the lab and the coma device. The senator was pushing him for results too quickly. A premature release of the experimental coma device might make it more difficult for the senator to convince the military to use it in large quantities. Even so, Treyder was sure the military elite would see the advantages of the device if used sparingly, so Treyder would still gain the scientific acclaim, along with the financial boost he deserved.

He was conflicted about the prospect of entire battlefields of comatose soldiers, but he also needed to have his genius publicly recognized. How else would he be able to experiment on treatments that would save lives? Reslo and Shendahl Chenak had not supported his efforts, even after all the machines he'd designed and built for them over the years. And they had done nothing to help his wife when she lost the baby and lay in a coma for eleven years before finally dying. They and everyone else would finally acknowledge his brilliance.

Senator Nelham glowered back. "Whoever they are, they killed some of my guards. Do you know who they were?"

Treyder shook his head. He could not imagine how only a couple of people pulled off what he had to admit was a stupendously daring snatch-and-grab. "I was not present, remember? As you trusted me to bring you evidence of success, I trusted you to keep that same evidence safe. Less than thirty hours after the first intruders were chased away, the entire project was on hold. How in all the hells of Teramar did they get away, Senator?" For the first time, he knew he was on the right side of this blade. It was a powerful feeling. The fault lay fully on the senator's ineffectual security management.

"Did you or someone in your office have access to the files and blurt it out?" Treyder asked. "Did you want to take all the credit and renege on our agreement once you saw how successful the design was?"

There was a hesitancy in the senator's expression and the corner of his mouth twitched upward but was deftly camouflaged by a brush of the hand across his chin. Still, the act was too late for the twitch to go undetected by Treyder, and he wondered if the senator had only just now thought about that. Well, now that the idea had popped out of Treyder's mouth, he couldn't pull it back.

He'd be more careful in the future. Only the knowledge that he, Treyder, was the sole person with all the skills to manufacture and program the device would keep him alive. And Treyder knew that vital design information not only had never been at the Saedi City lab site, it was now not even in Star Valley. And unless the second coma device failed or had been removed, Treyder was confident that the sheriff would be in a coma until Treyder could show the surgeons where it was. Not for the first time, he wondered how the first recipient of the device—the girl—had returned to Star Valley fully conscious. Until he could figure that out, he had to keep a blade to the senator's heart.

"Well, what say you, Senator? Was this snatch-and-grab staged?" He was attentive to every muscle of the politician's face, searching for a lie.

"No. There is no evidence of how they got in or out. My troops even checked the roof. It was as if they appeared out of the air. They were there and then they were not." He shook his head. "It's most disturbing."

Treyder was curious now. "Are you still investigating?" According to some of the soldiers who had been on the roof and a few of the soldiers who had surrounded the building and covered all the entrances, the surprising snatch-and-grab had occurred without any evidence of building entry or exit.

But the security vid showed three individuals cutting the bonds from the sheriff, and after a brief violent encounter with a number of soldiers, they had taken not only the sheriff but also almost all of the written notes and several freestanding computers. Though the head and face were covered, he was confident one of the kidnappers was female, and he suspected her identity was Ani Chenak. He knew she was back from Southern, all healed up, but thankfully without memory of their encounter and fight in the cave that had given him the opportunity to cut her with the poison-laced blade and insert the first coma device.

But if he was correct and she was one of the kidnappers, he could not figure out how she had managed to pull off such a detailed and audacious caper in such a short time. "Do you know the identity of the two chased away from the lab prior to the snatch-and-grab?"

"Just a man and woman asking about you and a report I supposedly had requested. We have checked the surveillance vid, but the cameras were only inside the laboratory, and they never entered that space." The senator held his palm up, forestalling Treyder's next question. "That was remedied prior to the taking of the sheriff. More cameras were installed within hours. There was no way for anyone to gain access to the building without being seen."

With a nod, Treyder acquiesced this point to the senator. "Could they have come in from the roof? From another of the buildings?"

The senator seemed perplexed and irritated. He explained how detailed the examination of all surrounding buildings had been. They had looked for ladder marks, unlocked doors, scuffmarks, and anything else that might provide a clue. Unfortunately, in their search for the perpetrators, the soldiers had obscured any evidence in the stairway and on the roof. Treyder asked if anything unusual had been found.

After hesitating, the senator mentioned an incident on the roof that denied explanation. "The soldiers stated, without hesitation or variation in story, that once on the roof, all of their weapons were suddenly and violently pushed to the ground, and they could not pick them up for several seconds."

"Curious," Treyder said. It was the only thing he could think of to say. "All of their stories matched?"

"Exactly. Most were frightened by the incident. Some received minor injuries due to the abrupt involuntary movements of their blades."

Though he really didn't care, Treyder expressed concern about the injured while he began to speculate about what could have forced all the blades to the ground. It might be another way to stop a bloody war. "There were no cameras on the roof?"

Senator Nelham explained that the roof was not a logical way to enter the building because of its general inaccessibility. He repeated that roof access would have required creating a skywalk or roped ladder to the building from a neighboring one, and that could not have been done without notice. The senator had ordered interviews of everyone who worked in the surrounding buildings and even put up a substantial reward for information concerning the theft of medical research equipment. So far, there had not even been one false report.

A buzzing sound interrupted the senator. "Excuse me." He flipped the intercom switch. "Yes?"

"The emissary is here for her meeting."

"Have her wait, please."

"Yes, sir."

The senator gestured to a doorway that emptied onto a back stairway typically only used by cabinet members and apologized for the secrecy required in Treyder's departure. Treyder understood all too well and immediately added a note to himself to add such an escape route to his office in Wharton.

Before closing the door, the senator gave him a tight-lipped smile and apologized for letting the sheriff be taken. To make recompense, the senator offered him fourteen soldiers, volunteered by their officer to replace the sheriff in Treyder's experiments. He could collect them at the training depot on the southwestern coast of the continent. Treyder accepted an envelope with directions and contact information.

"General Wistoff is waiting for your instructions. He has told them only that they have *volunteered* for very special and secret duties that will prevent a war with Southern. Let me know when they have joined you in your new location."

Though there was no question in the senator's explanation, Treyder heard the underlying question about the new laboratory's location. Treyder made no response, and his hesitancy seemed to goad the senator into inviting him back into the room and handing over all the papers his guards had removed from the lab before the Saedi City police arrived. The senator hoped the documents, along with the new experiment subjects, would help Treyder catch up on the delayed research. He looked forward to hearing of results in the coming weeks because the time line for continued funding was approaching.

While Treyder considered how to respond, he opened the briefcase containing the documents and flipped through them. There might be enough to essentially start where he'd been interrupted. He tucked the briefcase under his arm and glanced at the senator, wondering if the politician would have returned the documents if he'd immediately thanked him for the volunteers. Treyder managed to express a modicum of gratitude for the documents and the offer of volunteers.

"I'll contact the general in a day or so, after I have readied the lab for the larger number of volunteers." He gave a sloppy blade salute as he stepped to the sterile concrete landing, stopping there a moment after the senator closed the door. Should he wait to see if he could hear any of the conversation between Nelham and the emissary? He considered the chance it might concern his projects and shook his head. As far as he knew, only the woman from Southern had direct knowledge of both who the specimen had been and what had been done to him.

Treyder sighed and took the stairs to the garage. He knew he should be happy to have the new specimens. Still, he wondered how the incompetent deputies in Star Valley figured out where the sheriff was so quickly. Had any evidence been left behind in his lab there? He quickly reviewed each step he had taken to clean up his office. Nothing glaring stood out and nothing linked the senator to either the laboratory or Treyder. Could he trust the senator to keep to his promise of anonymity until he was ready to release the full results of his findings?

Treyder knew he could turn the blade in the other direction and claim coercion on the senator's part if needed. He could say the senator was forcing him to develop the coma device for military rather than medical use and had demanded that a subject under its influence be brought to him for proof. He could protect himself. He already had several ways to disappear.

He tossed the satchel into his hover-car, and after peeling off the thin veneer of plastic coating that altered the color of the vehicle, he changed the identifying placard in the back window with another of the faux placards from a stack under the seat, exited the garage, and disappeared into the Saedi City traffic heading west. He needed to plan for the delivery of fourteen volunteers.

# CHAPTER TWO

The joyous three-note chord echoed inside Taryn's head. The tune seemed to warm his body. Two words repeated again and again: *Teramar! Reunion!*

He turned in place in the center of the chamber, alight with shades of amber, blue, and green. His gaze caught the Singers, Diani and Layson, wide-eyed in shock, and Ani was crouched at the base of the green Anyala Stone's pedestal, her head buried in Kela's fur.

"There are Stones on Teramar?" Diani's voice carried both skepticism and wonder as she stared at her Pericha Stone.

A six-tone harmony answered a resounding *yes* in Taryn's head. Everyone else in the room seemed to hear it, and even Kela wagged his tail in excitement. Taryn noticed that all three of the blades flashed in concurrence with the now iridescent Stones. Ani lifted her head and smiled at him. He realized her eyes matched the green of the Anyala Stone almost perfectly, and he wondered if a person's eye color had anything to do with the color of their

Stone. Diani's irises could have been considered amber in their deep honey color, flecked with brown and gold. He took steps toward Layson, curious to see if her eyes were the same shade of summer-sky-blue as the Kita Stone. Not an exact match, but they were indeed blue. He knew his own eyes were blue and wondered what shade of blue *his* Stone might be. He immediately couched that thought with a hint of hesitancy. It was completely out of context with what had happened over the last hour.

*It is not a requirement they match, Singer. Some of us are colors perhaps not possible in your species, and we would not want to limit our choices.*

Though the musical voice was warm and comforting, it was unnerving to *hear* something in his head that had not come through his ears. "Who said that?" He looked around the chamber at the confused expressions on everyone's face. They all shook their heads. They evidently had not heard.

*I, Pericha, answer The Balance's question.*

Diani chuckled. "Did one of the Stones sing to you, Taryn?"

Taryn tipped his head, rubbed a hand across the stubble on his scalp, and covered his confusion with a grin. "I guess so. I wondered, if I am to be a Stone Singer, would *my* Stone be the color of my eyes?"

"What was the answer?" Diani asked, smiling.

He repeated what he'd heard, but he was having trouble believing that a Stone had spoken to him alone. "So you all really didn't hear the comment?"

Diani's smile widened. She explained that the Singers typically only heard what the Stones sang if it was directed at them.

Diani admitted she used to think it was rare that a Stone would communicate with any other than their own Singer. Now she was not so sure. She gave recent examples, such as the meeting between the Anyala Stone and Ani's father shortly after he arrived from Teramar and with Renloret prior to his leaving Lrakira to pilot the rescue attempt.

"Does that mean they could sing to the entire population to explain things if they wanted or needed to?" Taryn asked.

The two Singers briefly stared at each other. Diani's sigh seemed to admit there were things about the Stones neither Singer knew.

Diani turned toward her Stone with a startled expression on her face. "Pericha says that long ago in our past, such a song was required to save us from an asteroid strike. It is adamant that while the Stones cannot stop certain things from happening—such as continental plate shifts or weather—in extreme circumstances, they can push time forward, as they did to age The Blood and The Balance on Teramar. However, they cannot reverse time." She raised one eyebrow briefly then frowned, as if she had just considered such a request and was disappointed.

"Oh." It was not his best response, but learning that some rocks were living creatures and able to communicate even with one person was a large blade to hone. To move through that knowledge to those same glowing rocks communicating telepathically with an entire world—tens of millions of people all at the same time—was almost beyond his comprehension. Then he realized Diani had said the Stones could move time forward. He glanced at Ani, surmising from her expression that she felt the same. They shared shrugs and tight-lipped smiles at the impossible possibility that had occurred—with almost disastrous results.

Standing in the chamber with the three Lrakiran Stones and their Singers, Taryn wondered if he was to become a Singer at all. Perhaps his role was only to save the Anyala Stone and thus prepare the people of Lrakira for the *possibility* of a male Singer. He had no intention of replacing one of the Singers in front of him.

Taking a deep breath, he shook his head to clear the multilayers of overstimulation and questions. He had to get back to being a sheriff, even if he was on another planet. "All right folks, let's focus on the immediate situation. I've pulled the blade from the rock and returned it to its rightful bearer." He nodded at Diani. "So, two questions: Is the rock going to live? Did it suffer any damage? I don't see any cracks or fissures." He cocked his head at Ani.

She ran her hand across the flashing green Stone, and the smile that lit her eyes was almost as brilliant as the Stone. "Anyala sings that there is much to be understood and learned. Because the Stones are so different from us, it was injured in ways only they can heal. It also says we should attend to the songs as the pilot has." She winked at Renloret. "It gives us permission to leave so it can complete its healing with the assistance of the other Stones. They will call us within a few days when it is able to communicate more fully." She chuckled. "It sings in Teramaran terms! It said days not sun-times."

Taryn placed his hands on his hips to keep from searching for his notepad. How was he going to remember all of this?

Ani walked to the center of the chamber and placed her arms

around him. "It is a lot," she whispered. "I'm glad I'm not alone on this journey. We'll get through this together, especially now that we are family. But even if you were not my brother, we'd do this together as friends."

She placed a kiss on his cheek before releasing him, and he recognized it as a sisterly action. A deep comforting hum followed her words.

"Together is good." He sighed and then looked at the Stones, their brightness ebbing just as adrenaline was seeping away from his body, leaving behind a weirdly satisfying exhaustion. He motioned for everyone to gather near the bases of the pedestals. Feeling like he'd just executed a triple-timed precision blade performance, he folded to the floor, drawing Ani down next to him. He patted the step on his other side and nodded to Diani. Her golden robe was cool where it touched his hand. The older Singer swung her waist-length braid of hair to her back, the glints of silver in it reminding him of his mother. *Melli*, he said to himself, trying out a new way of thinking about her. No, Mother or Nahnah. She would always be his mother. He felt Ani squeeze his hand and saw her nod. Perhaps the twin thing allowed her to know his thoughts.

The six of them sat in silence as the interior of the Stone Chamber returned to its usual lighting. The life lights in each Stone shone from single spots within each, but the Anyala Stone's hue was not as bright as the other two. Perhaps the creature was truly weak from its injury and needed rest and time to heal. Inside his head, the Stones' voices concurred in a calming whisper of a hum. He nodded. "A list."

"A what?" Renloret asked. Until then, he had been quiet but observant.

The sheriff in Taryn knew he could rely on the pilot's observations. With Renloret around, he wouldn't need a notebook, however much his fingers itched to write it down. "A list of questions."

"What would be your first?" Ani asked. When Taryn looked at her, she flicked her head at Kela.

Ah, a question from the dog. Should that topic be on the list? Probably not now. For some reason, he accepted the concept of a telepathic dog, but telepathic rocks were quite another thing. Taryn shared gazes with Kela. Intelligence resided in those icy blue eyes.

"Will the Stone live?" Ani glanced at Kela, evidently asking his question for him.

A cool green sound with exhausted undertones answered. Taryn rubbed the back of his neck and glanced at the others. They were all nodding. "All right, I'll cross that off my list."

"Number two?" Renloret asked with a slight grin.

"Why are there Stones on Teramar? Why aren't they here on Lrakira?"

This time the answer came in shades of blue and amber. Words formed alongside the tune. *Chosen by seven for safekeeping. Two new homes until first is healed. Three sent to each with charges to inspire, guide, and prepare for reunion and beyond. Lrakira's lacks healed by The Blood. The Balance, Anyala to save. Three to find and teach, then star path learned to first home, the pilot to guide. Choice to return for combined charges to grow forward in time.*

"Now I wish I did have my notebook," he muttered as he clasped his hands to keep from reaching to where there was no pocket or notebook.

Layson fished into her robe and handed him a thin, flat hand-size device. She pointed to a small pad on the top. "This way wakes it up. This puts it in sleep mode." Layson held up her hand to stop his question. She touched a button and the opaque screen lit up. There were symbols scrolling across the surface. "Repeat what you heard. It will record. You can scribe it down in your own words later. Return it to me when you can." She touched another button. Her voice issued from it, repeating what she had just stated. Taryn grinned, touched the first button, and sang the words.

Renloret and the Singers shared astonished looks. "They sang in Northern?"

This time it was Renloret who muttered. "I guess they really can choose who they want to talk to."

A tinge of smugness rose up and Taryn hid the smile with his speculation. "My first take on this is that three Stones went to Lrakira and three went to Teramar along with *their people*. This brings up a few more questions, but I think we should do as they request and leave them to finish healing the Anyala Stone. Renloret, get that book of songs you talk about. Between that and what we've just heard, I think we can come up with a clear list of questions." Offering a hand to Diani, he pointed to the door. "After you, Singer."

Both Diani and Layson paused to sheathe their blades before leading them out of the chamber, and Ani placed the Anyala

Stone's blade in the red silteene-lined storage box and tucked it under her arm. She followed the two Singers with Kela prancing by her side.

Taryn gave Renloret the lead and then closed the door behind them. With no one else to see, he watched Renloret hurry to Ani's side. When the pilot did not take Ani's free hand, Taryn thought of one more question he needed an answer to.

Once in the hall, to Ani's surprise, Taryn asked if there was a private room where he could talk to her, alone. The Singers stopped at the next doorway, announcing it was now Ani's office because she was the Anyala Stone's Singer. Taryn opened the door and ushered Ani in. Not to be left out, Kela pushed his way in as well.

Ani placed the blade box on the desk—*her* desk, not her mother's or her grandmother's.

The door had barely latched when Taryn tapped her on the shoulder. "Well, have you kissed him yet?"

She felt her face blush and cursed under her breath. By the blades, she wanted to smack the smug smile off his face. "After what just happened, that's the first question you can ask me?" How was she going to not answer? Was it time to admit her mistake?

Kela cocked his head, sending her his visual of a shirtless Renloret sliding down the alley wall, his head in his hands, seemingly devastated by her rejection after Kela had interrupted their masquerade as lovers to escape capture by the hired soldiers. She knew Kela was now sharing his memory of what he'd seen through her eyes and through their telepathic connection.

*Mistake?* His query was soft.

*You're the one who interrupted!* She tried to swat at him, but he ducked away.

Taryn laughed. "So, Kela. Did she?"

"Leave him out of this." She rounded on Taryn, her green eyes bright, almost burning in their intensity.

"Stop glaring at me. Did you or did you not?" His harrumph had a satisfied edge to it. "I think you did. We're not leaving this room until you tell me."

She wondered if she should tell him about the second kiss, the one on the cheek just before Taryn woke from the coma. No, he wanted the first one. And he would know there had been a first kiss. "You're not going to like it."

"Whether I like it or not, you will tell me. Start talking before I ask *him*." He moved toward the door.

Grabbing his sleeve, she pulled him back. "Oh, blades be damned, Taryn. All right, I'll tell you." She quickly sketched the deception in the alley after Renloret and she had located him in the laboratory.

"You mean you undressed in the alley and sexually assaulted him just to keep from being arrested?" His expression alternated between incredulity and disappointment.

"I said it was a mistake. But it worked, Taryn. We weren't arrested and we didn't do anything else. In fact, Kela was the one who interrupted just as things were getting interesting."

Kela gave her a "Who me?" expression, to which Taryn laughed again. "Now we're getting somewhere."

The interrupted incident in the alley blossomed to the forefront of Ani's memory: the taste of Renloret, the feel of his lips against hers, where she had allowed his hands to go—wanted them to go. Kela snickered in her mind. *Stop listening in, Kela.* He laughed it off from the other side of the desk where she couldn't reach him.

She couldn't hide her grimace. How had she gotten into this conversation?

Taryn laughed. "So you kissed him and wanted to do more, and Kela interrupted."

"We had to stop. Kela was correct."

Kela's head popped up from behind the desk. His head cocked and tongue lopped over one side of his lower jaw. *Finally.*

Ani pointed at him. "Stop listening!" His ears flattened at her admonishment, and he ducked out of sight again, snapping the mental door shut.

"How far would you have gone if Kela hadn't?" Taryn asked.

"That's private, and my little brother doesn't need to know everything."

He waggled his eyebrows. "Oh, come on, Ani. You'd tell your best friend, right?"

"Yes, but you're not my best friend anymore, you're my brother."

"Nothing more than some heavy-duty kissing? Even later?"

Blades, he was persistent. "No, there's been no time, Taryn. I mean, we had to plan and execute the rescue, heal you, and then get you to Lrakira. Exactly when was there personal time?"

"Why not on the journey to Lrakira? That took, what, at least a week?"

Kela's mental wall dropped, and he sent his support of the question with a laugh in her mind. Ani glared at him. Kela widened his eyes and tipped his head. *Well, why didn't you take advantage of the time?*

Ani tried to defend the lack of movement on the relationship by saying there were other things, such as her relationship with Yenne, that seemed more important at the time. A few breaths of quiet ensued, then Taryn asked how that had gone or was going. She admitted that Yenne was their father and that, in some ways, Taryn's behavior was like Yenne's. For instance, they both seemed able to accept odd things quicker than most people.

"Why isn't Yenne here?"

She watched Taryn reach his hand up to run through the hair that was normally there. He frowned at the two weeks of growth that had sprouted during the trip to Lrakira. Sadly, it would be a while before his hair was long enough to cut or shape as he liked it. She pushed away the trivial thought about his hair and focused on his question.

"I thought you would be overwhelmed as it was, what with waking up on another planet, learning that you're my twin, and understanding that you were supposed to save the life of an intelligent rock. Not to mention the fact that you are what you used to consider an alien. I figured it was enough to handle without adding your biological father to the brew. Particularly since your biological father was thought dead for twenty years and is not only alive but only about ten years older than you."

She paused and gazed about the room that was now hers with its heavy wooden desk and dark flooring. There were two chairs placed companionably in front of a fireplace along a sidewall. Stale ashes and partially burned wood reminded her of how much her mother had loved the old-fashioned heating method. Evidently, it was something Shendahl had passed on to her. Had her grandmother, Selabec, also once loved fireplaces? How old were those ashes? Months? Years? She felt a flicker of desire to try, one more time, to talk with Selabec.

"Does he *want* to meet me?" Taryn whispered.

She saw the anguish in his eyes. It seemed to match the heart sore that had settled inside her at the thoughts about her grandmother's refusal to see her as the promised granddaughter. Ani grabbed both of his hands and drew him to her. "Oh, Taryn. After I told him who his other child was, he sat beside your medical cubical at every unscheduled moment on the trip to Lrakira. A couple of times he was crying. I never felt like intruding."

She realized that she had not interrupted out of respect for their father's series of losses. First, he had left Teramar in the middle of an attack on their research facility. And the next thing he knew, his wife was dead, his brother was essentially missing, and his daughter had aged twenty years over a couple of months of his time. And finally, he'd learned that his wife had committed a lie of omission about birthing twins and had given his son to another family. "Perhaps I should have asked him to join us. My excuse was that we were all dealing with a lot of changes, Taryn. We still are." She felt her chin tremble and bit at her lower lip to still it.

They remained in the sibling embrace for several moments before she felt she could control her voice and release him. "He wanted to be there when you woke up after the removal of the coma device. I told him no." She wiped away the sudden tears that formed in her own eyes. "I'm sorry."

He turned away from her, went over to a window, and drew aside the curtain to look out. What was he thinking? He rubbed his palms across his face. She waited, counting the breaths. Then he pursed his lips, shook his head, and turned to face her. Smeared tears gave his cheeks a shine.

"I guess it was the best choice. You all knew I had to save the Anyala Stone first, right?"

"And you did, Taryn. You saved an alien's life."

"Yes, I saved the Stone, and now that we know the Stone will be okay, why don't we . . ."

She saw excitement brighten his eyes. He rubbed his hands together as he grinned. Oh, hells of Teramar, he was planning something he knew she would not approve of. She wanted to squash it before he could put words to it. But before Ani could refuse, he rushed on.

"Yes, why don't we all get together at an eve meal? You, me, Renloret, the Singers, and anyone else they might want to invite. Maybe even an alien or two. I can send an invitation to Yenne this eve. I could use a group around me when Yenne and I see one another so either of us can back away from the situation if we need to."

"Wish I had thought of that. I'm sure the Singers can set it all up."

Taryn stopped rubbing his hands together and placed them on

his hips. The expression on his face announced that his next idea was definitely something she was not going to like. "So, while I do that, you have time to tell Renloret how you really feel. You don't need to worry about me. I really am all right, Ani, and an official introduction to my father may take a few hours to get set up, so there's plenty of time for you and Renloret to do some much needed talking—and listening." He put a hand on her shoulder. "You need to listen to him. He loves you. Watch him. His eyes will tell you if he can't."

She nodded. "And how do you know that?" She glanced at Kela. He was smirking, again. *Don't say anything*, she warned. He wagged his tail.

"Because I'm the sheriff, and I'm observant." He winked at her, and she responded by rolling her eyes dramatically at his confidence in his skills. "Besides, the two of us have talked."

"You have?" Now she was miffed. Renloret had not said anything to her about that.

"Yes. But that is for you two to discuss." He squeezed her shoulder gently.

Could that mean trouble for her? She immediately felt a wave of reassurance with a hint of humor from Kela and sighed. All right, not exactly trouble, but perhaps too much explaining was in her future. Again, Kela's mental laugh softened her thoughts, and she sent him a mental message. *But I don't even know how I feel about him, so how am I going to explain anything?*

*Once you stop distracting yourself, you will know. Worrying about him rejecting you is distracting you.*

Blades, why was that four-pawed creature so right? Kela

laughed again, accenting his comment with a soft, rolling bark. He rubbed his head along her thigh. When she glanced down at him, he gave her a wink, and she ruffled the fur between his ears.

Her brother rambled on unaware of the silent communication. "Plus, while you two have a needed conversation I will have some time with Layson and Diani, acquainting myself with this alien world, which, so far, does not look all that alien, by the by. And because the Stones need a few days, we have time to lay out how we're going to handle some of the forthcoming changes." Taryn fished out the recording device Layson had given him and proceeded to tick off what she guessed was a list of things to do. When he was finished, he looked up at her and said that he wanted both of them to get bio-teachers.

"Really?" Her voice slid up almost an octave. "Don't you think that's too accepting of this situation?" Before he could launch off on more, she held out her hand. "Stop it! Just stop being a sheriff. For a few minutes, please, Taryn." She shook her head. "Blades, I don't know how you do this, but slow down and let me breathe, okay?"

Cocking his head to one side, Taryn placed his hands on his hips. He deliberately inhaled and exhaled slowly—and loudly—to tease her. She clenched her fists to keep from slapping him.

His smile faded. "Well, wouldn't it be easier to get an implant so I can learn Lrakiran quickly? If I'm going to communicate with these people about the idea that men can be Singers, I should be the one to get an implant if you don't want one. Not everyone on Lrakira is going to have one, and it shouldn't come through an interpreter, so it would be best if I have—"

"Fine!" She heard the irritation in her own voice as she threw up her hands. She squelched the sudden rise of bile at the thought of another machine in her head. "I'm sure all you have to do is ask and they'll be happy to insert a machine into *your* head. At least you have the option of *asking* for it." She didn't tell him that it would be a temporary thing and could be removed in a few weeks at a minimum and months or even years at a maximum, if Kela's report was correct.

"Sorry."

At least he sounded contrite. But he didn't stay that way for long. "Now, let's inform the Singers of meal plans and Renloret of your *needs*." He waggled his eyebrows as he firmly grasped her elbow and led her to the door.

She hung back, suddenly a reluctant and headstrong child, struggling against demands. "Can't the conversation with Renloret wait until after this welcome-to-the-family party you want to throw?"

"No. Now grow up, sister, and face the blade you have constructed." He levered open the door and shoved her into the hall.

She caught her balance and footing before she bumped into the wall opposite the door. Straightening her tunic, she flipped her loose hair to her back and plastered a smile on her face as the Singers turned to look. Renloret's forehead creased in a frown. She waved the trio off. "Sibling squabble."

Taryn smacked her shoulder lightly. "Yes, of course, a slight disagreement on how to proceed." He dipped his chin to Renloret. "Why don't you two take a walk? I have some things to discuss with these two lovely ladies." Offering his arms in escort position to Diani and Layson, he whistled to Kela, and the foursome sauntered away chatting amiably, leaving Ani and Renloret standing in the middle of the hall staring at each other.

Ani harrumphed at Kela's parting barb and pulled up the mental privacy barrier. "That sheriff has ordered us to talk, but I don't want to do it here. Let's walk."

## CHAPTER THREE

Renloret led the way out of the building and at Ani's suggestion, headed for the hilltop park where she had first discovered she was on an alien planet. He kept an eye out for the meat roll wagon where they had purchased food on their discreet first tour of Awarna. How long ago was that? It felt like sun-cycles, not just a few moon-cycles. He was heartened Ani was within touching distance, though he didn't dare cross that distance . . . yet. They climbed the hill, side by side, with an almost shy need for space between them, and he wondered what Taryn insisted she tell him.

The trees were naked of their leaves, allowing ample view of the intense blue autumnal sky. Renloret was grateful that it was not yet winter with its incessant rain. Even so, this late in the season, the weather was milder in Awarna than either Star Valley or the capital of Northern on Teramar, Saedi City, and jackets were not yet required. Occasionally, Ani puffed air out between her lips, perhaps expecting to see a condensation cloud. At the summit, they soaked up the afternoon light. Renloret watched Ani study the skyline. There was no fear in her eyes now. A slight smile appeared on her face as a shuttle launched with its bright trail noticeable in the midday light, and he began to relax.

"Is Awarna the capital of a province or the entire Lrakiran planet?" Her question and tone said she wasn't quite ready to talk about the real reason her brother had ordered them to walk.

"Both, really. It has the second largest space port on Lrakira, and most of the diplomatic services are based here."

"There's so much I want to know, to learn. Perhaps a bio-teacher would be . . ." She shook her head. "No, not yet." He noticed the shiver that rippled across her shoulders.

He wanted to reach out and sooth her unease. "Ani, you don't have to ever have one. You're doing well on your own." He knew she had been listening to some of the language tapes while on the journey from Teramar to Lrakira. He'd even overheard her humming some folk tunes on occasion.

He was very aware of the tension in her body, and she looked everywhere but at him. He cleared his throat, and she turned to him. Her head was cocked to the side, reminding him of Kela. A slow smile spread across her face and brightened those Anyala-Stone-green eyes of hers. Stones and blades, he wanted to kiss her. And so much more. He watched her inhale and exhale slowly. She seemed to be readying herself for something. He wondered how much longer he should or could wait, and shoved down the impulse to pull her to him. Instead, he matched her breathing rhythm to slow his racing thoughts and heart. He had to give her time. He could wait, couldn't he? He looked out at the far horizon.

A touch on his arm brought him around. He opened his mouth to speak, but she shushed him with three fingers to his lips before he could start. Her eyes were a stormy green now, and she was frowning. He steeled his heart for rejection. So much had happened in such a short time. And even though Taryn had hinted at a positive outcome, Ani looked down, clasping and unclasping her hands. He couldn't see her expression, but her hands were trembling. Had the kiss in the alley been a mistake? Had it broken the soul-bond he thought had been under construction? Why hadn't he openly pursued her, or at least told her how often he thought of her and how he couldn't see a life without her by his side.

She cleared her throat but kept her gaze on the ground. "I won't apologize for the distraction in the alley, only for the timing of it."

Though her voice was soft, he detected a hint of anger. The kiss had not meant the same thing to her as it had to him.

She folded her arms in front of her as if to protect herself from his reaction—or perhaps to keep from striking him. He prepared himself for either. Had he lost her because of his reluctance to voice his feelings? Raising his gaze to study the skyline again, he hoped she wouldn't reject him if he didn't look at her.

"Ren?"

She had never used the short version of his name before. What did that mean?

"Yes?" he whispered.

"That kiss. In the alley? You need to know that, at first, I thought I was just following orders from Taryn to kiss you at

42

the next opportunity. And though it was perhaps not the best time to do it, it did provide the needed distraction. And then I realized that I *wanted* to." Her words tumbled out. "And I didn't want to stop. I was thinking only of myself. Then to be caught by Kela made me aware of the wrongness of the situation. Even though the distraction worked, I should have stopped as soon as the guards passed on by. It was the wrong thing to do at the time. I should have stayed focused on Taryn. I didn't . . . don't want you to get the wrong idea about what kind of person I am, and I apologize for my behavior under those circumstances."

He frowned. Yes, he remembered his surprise when he had looked around the corner of the building just as the hired guards entered the street and heard Ani demand he remove his shirt. He had turned to see her pull off her leggings and boots and toss them into the trash receptacle. Her shirt was missing and she stood, brazen and defiant in her underclothing, her hand stretched toward him. "Give me your shirt," she had demanded. His mouth had gone dry in that instant.

But the ruse had worked. Their pursuers had thought them to be just another pair of lovers seeking the relative privacy of an alley. Nonetheless, the ardor of her kiss had nearly taken his breath away, and he licked his lips at the memory of it.

The roar of a shuttle landing edged into his thoughts, bringing him back to the now. He looked down. There were tears in her eyes and she was rolling her bottom lip between her teeth. Was she afraid he would reject her because she had told him that they would never talk about the deception in the alley? He knew in his heart that what had begun as a ruse had quickly melted into certainty, and he had reacted truthfully. He could not reject her.

"I've ignored my own heart. There is so much . . . I want," she murmured.

He touched her chin, inviting her to look at him. Her smile was tentative. He brushed strands of her hair away from her face and tucked them behind her ear, letting his fingers linger on her neck. She shivered beneath his touch.

"I confess, Ren. I've wanted to do much more for far too long." Her whisper shook him.

His hand moved to the back of her neck. She resisted slightly. Was this a warning that what he wanted to happen would not? She moved his hand off her neck and brought it to her lips.

"At first I didn't know what your Southern rules might be. Then, after realizing we both were from Lrakira, I didn't know if any kind of liaison would be sanctioned. I had a new role as Singer, and worried about doing anything inappropriate. Then . . . well, then all that other stuff got in the way." She released his hand to wave hers toward the sky. "And there's so much more I need to tell you and . . . now we're back here . . . and we have some time and—"

Stones and blades, he couldn't bear it any longer. "Kiss me, Ani." His voice was husky and his lips were oh so close to hers.

Their lips touched. Once. Twice. Tenderly, both questing, both giving permission. He closed his eyes to concentrate on the feel, the taste of her. She moaned. Blades, he wanted her. All of her. His hands slipped around her head, fingers lacing through her hair, pulling her closer. She placed both hands on his chest and slowly walked them up and around his neck, answering his request.

He felt her knees give way. They slowly dropped to the ground. Her tongue edged between his lips. Opening them, he accepted her invitation again. The kiss would be enough, for now.

Once around the corner and out of sight, Taryn slowed his pace. "So . . . my sister and I were talking." It felt only a little strange to acknowledge to his heart and mind that Ani was truly his sister. It would make her relationship with Renloret easier to accept, though he had already recognized their hearts were of the same blade.

"About which topic?" Layson asked. Taryn glanced sideways at the younger of the two Stone Singers. She appeared to be close to his age. He wondered if there was a minimum and maximum age for a person to become a Singer. Delighted by her strongly accented Northern words, he now understood the spell all the womenfolk in Star Valley had been under when Ani had introduced Renloret at the dance. It was not just the alien pilot's good looks. And if Taryn was honest and ignored the flicker of jealousy, he could admit that Renloret was quite the eyeful. It was also the accent, which by itself could bend an annealed blade. Now he chuckled at the thought that flashed through his mind. He'd only just met Layson, and it would probably be most rude to ask if she was promised to another. His heart could wait.

"What did you speak about?" This time it was Diani. She was the Singer for the saltren-gin-hued Stone whose blade had been used to injure Ani's Stone. Was that Kita or Pericha?

*Pericha. I am Pericha.* The warm tone of the amber Stone filled his head. He looked at the Singer. Had she heard?

Diani laughed. Evidently she had. "And I assumed Pericha would be too busy singing the healing song for the Anyala Stone to listen to me or anyone else. I believe that is the first time I have caught it eavesdropping. By the by, what is saltren gin? The impression I got of your thoughts from Pericha piques my interest, though I prefer Layson's teas. I am thinking we may be in need of a swallow or two before the sun-time is complete."

"Oh, this could become awkward," Taryn said. He brushed his hand across the stubble of hair on his head. He could feel the beginnings of a flush of embarrassment. Had Pericha heard and passed on his thoughts about Layson too? He didn't dare look at the younger Singer.

"Yes, I suppose so." Diani nodded. "And more interesting if we are to add three more Singers to the conversation, counting you."

"Hadn't Ani said she and Kela had developed mental blocks or walls so they didn't hear each other all the time?" Layson asked.

"Yes. Perhaps in a few days we should discuss such precautions with the Stones," Diani said. She placed both hands on Taryn's shoulders. "Now, what were you discussing with Ani?"

He sighed with relief. Either the Stone had not heard his thoughts or it was intelligent enough to only pass on certain things. "An introductory celebration. I would appreciate assistance in setting up a small gathering so I may officially meet Yenne. I am sure he is anxious to meet a child he didn't know he had. Ani said he is barely a decade older than us, so that may be a worry as well."

"Indeed. We have no explanation why we were not informed of S'Hendale's pregnancy and Ani's birth . . . and yours. I will tell you that twists in time are rare, and the consequences can be devastating. And though this twist hits on a personal basis, the commander understands. All that happened is fact now, and we will get through it." Her confidence was reassuring.

Taryn presented his arms again in escort and nodded toward the building's main door. "What is your recommendation for a place for meeting my father and what assortment of food would you serve at such an occasion?"

# CHAPTER FOUR

Wine and tea were placed on opposite ends of the table with a variety of foodstuffs piled high on platters between them. Taryn grinned at the display, which was so like those at community events in Star Valley. He wondered how the Singers had managed to know what would make him feel at home. It had only been two hours or so since he had been escorted to a residential room in a villa to freshen up and get in a short nap. He hadn't napped, but he appreciated the opportunity to just be with himself for a time.

Strolling along the immense spread, he tried to locate recognizable fruits. Only one caught his attention. Wasn't that the fruit Ani's uncle had sent his mother from Southern? He snatched a piece off the back of the stack. It certainly appeared to be similar, though these were not dried. He scratched the skin and held it close to his nose. Melli had used this fruit to make the preserves he'd spread on the breads she served with her teas that last winter. How was it possible that a fruit from

Teramar's southern continent was also on Lrakira?

Voices alerted him to the Singers' arrival. Layson entered the banquet room with a platter of bread. She held the door open for Diani, who carried a small cauldron. Both smiled widely at him. He stepped forward to take the cauldron from Diani. An earthy meat scent teased his nostrils, and his stomach rumbled. When had he last eaten?

Layson giggled as she made room for the stew pot. "It is a good thing we are to eat soon," she said. Her Northern was accented almost exactly like Renloret's. Again, he wondered if she was unattached.

Diani straightened the tablecloth, then she adjusted the wrap that twisted artfully around her neck and across her shoulders. "Does this meet with your approval, Singer Taryn?" With a tip of her head, she indicated the buffet.

Taryn hesitated, not sure how to answer. He nodded and smiled. "How did you know? We only talked about food and beverages, not . . . *this*." He spread his arms out to encompass the entire room. The food was laid out in the style of a Northern community gathering, like the spring event where he had played while Ani and Renloret had danced their newfound love. How long ago? How far away?

"We had assistance from Commander Chenakainet," Layson said. "He will be here shortly. He said something about appropriate libations."

Taryn chuckled. "Ani did say that when she and Renloret discovered that I was The Balance, they drank an entire bottle of twenty-year-old vaquin. It is a very strong alcohol made from the sap of a high altitude desert succulent. Yenne had perfected a distillation process before leaving Teramar. Once bottled, the liquid darkens in color. The older the vaquin, the stronger and darker it is."

"I should like to try it," Layson replied, her words muffled because she held a beaded hairclip between her teeth. She was standing in front of the larger mirror that covered one of the walls, smoothing the embroidered fabric of her gown across her waist. A flick of her fingers released the last wrinkle, and she removed the clip from her mouth and pinned her twisted braid into a higher position. "There." She tugged at a sleeve in final approval and turned, her eyebrows raised.

Swallowing against asking her right then if she was in a relationship, Taryn stumbled over his words. "Uhm, I'm . . . uh, perhaps I could have a bottle or two shipped from Teramar."

Layson laughed. "I would like that, Singer Taryn."

"Let's not use the title unless I really become one. We're only guessing at the moment."

A knock on the door announced the arrival of two men. Taryn noticed that one wore a jacket embroidered to match Layson's gown. He glanced at the Singer and watched her smile at the man's entrance. So much for being unattached. He shrugged mentally. He really wasn't sure he was ready to move on to someone else anyway. He was still getting used to the change of relationship with Ani. She had ended the romantic possibilities over a year ago, and he had reconciled himself to being her friend. That had ended up being a good turn of events. Being in a romantic relationship with Ani when they discovered they were siblings would have been more than awkward, it would have been alarming.

He turned to ostensibly study the layout of food trays. During the past year, he had been very aware that he was lacking that one person who would become part of his soul. And seeing how Layson looked at the young man who swept into the room with a smile only for her, Taryn found he was a bit envious.

In fact, he realized that he was envious of *any* relationship. That included his parents' relationship. And surprisingly, he was even envious of Yenne's relationship with Shendahl, even though the commander now knew his wife had died before he had a chance to return to Teramar. Taryn wondered how Yenne was holding up. He could not imagine being in similar circumstances. It was all disconcerting. He was determined to find and cherish such a relationship. He sighed and then smiled at the prospect of having two entire worlds to search for the right person. Surely there would be someone. At least he had managed to not ask awkward questions too soon.

Taryn turned back around and watched as Layson leaned close to the man's face and said something. They both glanced in his direction. Then Layson gathered the young man's hand into hers and pulled him forward. Taryn straightened his jacket, put on a smile, and offered a proper Northern blade salute, left hand to right shoulder.

"Taryn Avere, it is my honor my husband, Karvlet, to introduce." Her smile was all for the man at her side.

The Northern vocabulary was understandable, and Taryn was delighted by the unusual sentence structure. Hadn't Renloret's speech changed with each passing day? He assumed the longer a person had a bio-teacher implant, the shorter the time it would take to adjust, especially if that person was surrounded by native speakers. His understanding of the bio-teacher was that once implanted, the speaker spoke in whatever language was implanted, with an accent like any other person learning a new language until their tongues and mouth became accustomed to the new language. By now, Renloret's accent was barely noticeable.

Taryn nodded and gripped Karvlet's forearm in the traditional Teramaran Northern greeting. "Good eve, sir. My thanks for your attendance at this gathering." He listened closely as Layson translated to Lrakiran, now aware the man did not have a bio-teacher implant. There seemed to be more words than necessary, as if Layson was explaining something more. Karvlet frowned briefly, and Taryn saw the uncertainty in the man's eyes meld into an expression of surprise and awe. What had she told him?

Layson patted Karvlet's hand and shook her head, still smiling. He seemed to ask a question while perusing Taryn. She answered and then turned to Taryn. "My pardon, Taryn. He asks which Singer you replace. I have not yet explained all."

"I know less than you on the subject. I do not presume to replace any Singer. The Stones have only said that there are more intelligent rocks on Teramar, and I may be destined to be the Singer of one if we can locate them." There, he had put his thoughts on the matter into words. And those felt correct.

She translated, and Karvlet's stance relaxed as he sighed and offered what Taryn knew was a Lrakiran blade salute, right fist to left shoulder.

Diani arrived and passed a black band to Layson, who wrapped it around Karvlet's wrist. He immediately tapped the surface of it twice and paused, his head tilted a bit, and closed his eyes. After several breaths, he opened his eyes and offered a tentative smile to Taryn.

"My honor is yours, Taryn Avere. May the Stones bless your travels and adventures with music and color." Though the Northern was heavily accented, Taryn understood.

Taryn pointed to the wristband. "Ani said that a translation device has to be implanted in one's brain, but that is . . ."

Diani chuckled. "These are temporary translators used most often in political or social situations such as this gathering. True, the bio-teacher is not visible and thus is better for long-term use, especially when our travelers are in less than desirable or hostile surroundings, or more importantly, when they are on first contact assignment. The implants can impart permanent knowledge if worn long enough and are put to use in the specific foreign environment for a number of months. They are usually removed when the individual returns to Lrakira."

"Are they language specific?" He wondered if he could or should ask for one of the temporary devices. After Ani's reaction to the implant, perhaps a noninvasive item would be more acceptable. Besides, he planned to return to Teramar and would not need it there. Ani would be pleased to know that, though he was not yet going to tell her. At times it was best to keep her guessing.

"There are various types depending on the needs of the wearers. These only have your Northern language installed," Diani said. "I could get you one with Lrakiran if you desire."

"My thanks for the offer. I will think on it." Taryn glanced at a young servant who had entered the room carrying a massive tray piled high with fruit and a spouted pot, which dangled precariously from her fingers. "Excuse me." He nodded to the Singers and Karvlet and stepped in front of the girl, stopping her progress. With a smile, he gripped the handles of the tray and lifted it. He executed a shallow bow and tipped his head toward the banquet table. The girl returned his smile, curtsied, and then led the way.

Ha! She curtsied, to *him*! It reminded him of Ryken at the spring event when Ani introduced Renloret to Star Valley's residents. Ryken had curtsied to Renloret, and Taryn had expressed astonishment that a child he'd known since she was a babe had honored the unknown visitor with a rare curtsey. She had never curtsied to him or any other man he knew of. Now he could admit he had been hurt when Ani had explained that Renloret was a *handsome* stranger and by being Ani's escort, deserved to be curtsied to. He would have to tell Ani that here on Lrakira the youngsters were brought up properly. And on the way to the table, he realized that *he* was now the handsome stranger, even with a closely shaved head. At least he hoped the youth saw him as handsome.

The girl pointed at the one remaining space on the table for him to place the tray while she set the pot carefully on a heated stand.

"Traseevat," the girl said as she curtsied again. She turned and skipped away through the door.

"She said thank you."

Taryn turned at Diani's voice. "Traseevat?" He tried the word.

"Very good, Taryn. You may not need artificial assistance. That is my granddaughter, Juleen. The Pericha Stone believes she will be its next Singer. Considering how young she is, I can assume I will be around for a few more sun-cycles."

Taryn heard the maternal pride in the Singer's voice. "Is her mother not around?"

"Oh, her mother prefers to design and manage the construction of our starships. She is positively driven to do so. With the Stone's encouragement, she is doing what she loves. Something about a plan of some kind that is at least a generation or two in the future." Diani slipped her arm around Taryn's elbow and directed him to the man who had entered with Layson's husband.

"I'd like you to meet my husband, D'Marlos."

Taryn offered a Northern blade salute, and the man responded with a matched Lrakiran salute before presenting his forearm with a welcoming smile. The firmness of his grip telegraphed confidence and strength without being overbearing.

"Greetings, and welcome to Lrakira, Singer." Smoky grey eyes bright with mirth matched the smile.

Taryn raised an eyebrow in question. There had not been any hesitancy in the man's tone when speaking the title.

D'Marlos waved his hand. "Yes, my sweet Diani has explained about the possibility of male Singers. It is about time a man sings with the Stones." He winked and patted Diani's hand.

Diani's smile was gentle. "He's always wanted to sing with the Stones, but his singing voice is deaf to music. It cuts like a dull blade. Fortunately, he can hear and keep a beat, and drums are his musical outlet. Just don't let him sing."

They all shared a laugh. Though it seemed D'Marlos was easy with the barb, Taryn's laugh was carefully modest to avoid the possibility of embarrassing the man. He knew of several people in Star Valley who shared the same affliction. He had been taught to respect their personal talents in whatever craft they excelled or worked hard in just as he was for his perceived talents in singing and cyralist playing.

Layson and Karvlet joined the trio, bringing mugs of a reddish tea.

"Ani explained that the mother of your heart is a master tea maker. I offer this concoction in her honor. Beware. There is a surprising bite to it." Everyone followed her example as she raised her mug in both hands, nodded to Taryn, and intoned, "May the Stones bless the parents of your heart and your adventures."

Taryn smiled at the manner in which Layson had mentioned his mother. He would embrace the title of Melli as the mother of his heart. He joined in the slurping of the tea, suppressing a cough that threatened when he inhaled across the small amount he held in the cup of his tongue as Melli had taught him when trying a new beverage. A late sweetness followed, calming the hot spice as he swallowed.

A second mouthful confirmed the juxtaposition of spicy heat and honey sweetness. "My mother would be delighted to swap recipes with you."

Layson's smile grew wide. "Did your mother get the bag of tea I sent with Ani?"

Shaking his head, he explained that neither Melli nor Ani had mentioned it. The few days he'd been with Ani and Melli had been occupied by things far less leisurely than tea. He found himself thinking about the fact that the only mother he'd known—the mother of his heart—was not his birth mother. That Shendahl and Yenne were his parents and Ani his twin had been both a shock and something that made sense deep within him, all at the same time. And even having had little time to integrate it yet, he realized that he was lucky to have two sets of parents.

"Taryn?"

He felt a hand on his arm and turned to the speaker. It was Diani. "My apologies. I was just thinking about my mothers." Yes, two loving mothers. At Diani's concerned expression he added, "I'll be okay." Saying it helped. He swirled the liquid in the mug and took another swallow.

Both Layson and Karvlet had gone quiet at his words. He finished the tea and indicated the desire for more. Layson poured more of the hot beverage into his mug and topped off everyone else's.

Trying to lighten the mood his words had tamped down, he directed a smile at Layson and said, "You realize that you and the mother of my heart could open an interstellar tea house."

"Now there's an idea, Layson," Karvlet said. "How soon can we set up a meeting to discuss details?"

Taryn laughed. He'd been kidding, but only half kidding. As his parents would, Karvlet seemed to see the possibilities in it.

Layson touched her husband's sleeve. "Karv, let's not rush things. Taryn has only just learned of his identity, and neither parent of the heart knows. We must not catch them off their blade stance with such an offer. But I admit it is an intriguing thought." She turned to Taryn and with a wink, added that Karvlet was a business manager and had been trying for suncycles to get her to start her own teahouse, though the past suncycle—she corrected the term to Northern for year—she'd been learning to be the Kita Stone's Singer. She suggested that once he had shared his birth information with Melli and Gelwood, a trade business conversation could begin if they were interested.

Karvlet's expression softened. He bowed to Taryn. "Apologies. I forget the circumstances and rush to the future. Please pass on the possibilities when convenient."

A bark from Kela interrupted them. Taryn watched the canine stretch languorously before trotting to the door and sitting, tail swishing back and forth across the floor. Taryn left the group to stand next to Kela. "Is it Ani?" Now that he knew Kela understood every word, he didn't feel silly talking to Kela as if he were human.

Kela barked twice.

"Is Renloret with her?"

Another pair of barks. Kela's tail wagged faster. Taryn could hear footsteps approaching. A sudden fear chilled Taryn's body. "Is my father with them?" He could barely get the words out. Ani was correct. This was a huge change in his life. He'd been ignoring its impact—until now. He tried swallowing, but his mouth had gone dry.

Kela looked at him and shook his head, barking once. Taryn expelled air through pursed lips. No. Only Ani and Renloret. Not Yenne. Rolling his shoulders forward and back, he struggled to relax them. He suddenly questioned this whole celebration party. Could he leave? He took several steps backward. Should he?

Kela barked again, and Taryn looked down. Kela sat in front of him, one paw raised and his head tilted. The paw reached out and pressed against Taryn's thigh. A rumble issued from Kela's chest. Again, the canine's paw scraped. Taryn sank to his knees and embraced his furry friend.

"I'm afraid, Kela." A long, wet tongue washed his neck. Kela whined softly, and it comforted the roiling in Taryn's stomach.

"Kela! What have I told you about licking?"

Grinning, Taryn stayed crouched next to Kela and patted the canine on the head. "Thank you, Kela. Stick by me, okay?" He heard the rumbling response.

"Well?"

Taryn and Kela both looked up at Ani standing in the doorway, hands on her hips.

"Well?" she repeated.

Kela swiped Taryn's neck and cheek one more time and then bounced away out of her reach. Taryn stood and wrapped his arms around his sister.

"Don't blame him. He knows I'm nervous about meeting Yenne," he whispered.

He felt her arms worm their way around his chest, and she squeezed tight. It helped almost as much as the tongue-lashing he'd received from Kela.

"You? Nervous?" She chuckled. "You'll be fine." She pushed away and gave him her "let's be serious" look before patting his cheek and nodding. "Yes, just fine. At least you won't slap him as

I did at our introduction." Instead of explaining the statement as he had hoped, she looked about the room, her eyes lighting up at the sight of the tables burgeoning with food. "How many people are coming to this introduction? That's a lot of food!"

Laughing, he took her hand and pulled her toward the two Singers and their partners. After introducing her to Karvlet and D'Marlos, he looked back at the doorway. "Where's Renloret? Kela indicated that he was with you."

"Oh, he was, but he decided to check on Yenne, so he went back to get him."

"Why didn't you?"

"We tossed a blade and he lost." She tucked her arm around his and ushered him toward the table. "They will be here any moment along with some other guests—real aliens from what I hear." Her eyes were bright with excitement and curiosity.

"Real aliens? You mean like the Stones?"

"No, I mean the kind of aliens we were told did not exist," she whispered conspiratorially.

"With four arms, claws, wings, scales, and tails?" he whispered in return, knowing how rude it sounded. But wasn't that what the stories he'd grown up with said aliens looked like?

"Renloret said representatives from two worlds are coming. They aren't the most different, but they will help us get used to seeing other forms of intelligent life." She glanced down at Kela, who had followed them. "Evidently, some can be as alien as Kela," she added with a giggle.

Taryn saw Kela's forehead wrinkle before the canine shook his head.

Ani laughed. "He does not consider himself an alien."

"I guess I don't either, though knowing he can understand every word I say is a bit disconcerting." He rubbed the fur between Kela's ears in apology.

"Did Renloret describe them to you?

"Well, there are two individuals from the Caason Sector, whatever that is. They're reptilian with scale-like skin, and their eyes are big with oval pupils. Um, what else? Oh, tails! They have tails, Taryn! Other than that, they have two legs, two arms, and five digits each on their hands and feet. To be honest, they sound a bit scary to me, though Ren says they're a gentle, scientific people. Then there's an Ishan-Dru-something-or-other, who look more like us. They have long yellow hair, and their skin is so pale they're almost albino, except that they have dark eyes. Ren says they have ridges on their foreheads that make them look like they're frowning all the time." She paused. "Can you imagine *yellow* hair?" She was obviously more intrigued by the color of hair on one alien than a tail on another.

Taryn also noticed the shortening of Renloret's name and decided not to ask about it or tease her. But that brought up the one question he did want an answer to. "Did you?"

A frown creased her forehead. "Did I what?"

He looked toward the ceiling then back at her. "Kiss," he whispered.

A sly, slow smile crept over her face, and Taryn felt his jaw drop. "Oh, blades, girl, you kissed him. I mean, for real this time."

Ani shushed him with her fingers on his lips. "Quiet." She

pulled him away from the table and into a small alcove. "Yes, I did as you ordered. We walked and we talked. Well, I talked. I didn't give him a chance to say anything, Taryn. I kept apologizing and . . . then he kissed me."

He was mesmerized by the blush that lit up her whole being. A bit of sadness and a sense of loss snuck into his thoughts. It wasn't *him* she was thinking of, it was Renloret. He stopped the thought almost as soon as he had it. He was her brother. He smacked her shoulder and laughed nervously. "Well, congratulations. That's the way it should be!" He didn't know if that was how he should be reacting as her brother, but if she were a male friend, that was how he would have reacted. It was the best he could muster.

She rubbed her shoulder. "Taryn! What is wrong with you?"

He suddenly felt silly, and his face flushed with embarrassment. Evidently, that was the wrong way to handle the situation. How would she expect a brother to behave? He scrambled through a myriad of thoughts and actions then wrapped his arms around her in a crushing hug. "Sorry. I'm new at this brother thing. I'm happy for you. I know he loves you. And if he should ever hurt you, I will damage him."

He felt her chuckling. Good. He'd been the right kind of brother. Releasing her, he found a piece of dried grass in her hair as he brushed loose strands of hair over her shoulder. "Need more time to prepare for Yenne and the other guests?" he asked as he showed it to her.

Blushing, she slapped his hands away and began to braid the hip-length hair. When she finished braiding, she turned around. "Any more stray grass?"

He picked up the heavy braid and carefully inspected it. "Nope."

With a sigh, she turned to face him. "Good. I don't want to be the cause of any problems between Renloret and Yenne."

"Problems? What kind of—"

A commotion at the door announced the arrival of the alien guests, not Renloret and Yenne. Taryn stared at the alien beings as they trooped in carrying little pots and plates of food, then turned to see Ani's reaction. She was staring too. Taryn recovered first and smacked Ani on the shoulder again. She struck back almost as fast, flipped the braid to her back, straightened the hem of his jacket with a jerk, and pushed him forward.

"Time to correct our prejudices against the reality of aliens," she whispered.

She had pasted on a smile, though he could feel the insecurity edged with fear radiating from her. He noted that Kela had sidled close, as if protecting her.

A smiling Diani beckoned the three aliens to approach the group now gathered near the bowl of punch.

# CHAPTER FIVE

"Do you think this is appropriate attire for meeting my son?" Yenne asked. He adjusted the red and black waist jacket for the umpteenth time. Then, with shaking hands, he smoothed the newly trimmed beard and mustache.

Renloret knew the commander had decided to grow out the facial hair when he realized he might need a simple disguise if he was going to be back on Teramar. Renloret thought it might slow down the ability of old friends to recognize Yenne until his youthfulness could be explained.

Renloret stopped the laugh before it disrupted the tenuous rapport that hung between him and the commander. This was not the time to jest. Schooling his expression to seriousness, he walked around Yenne, stopping to pick an imaginary piece of lint from the back of his collar. "Yes, sir."

Yenne's shoulders dropped and Renloret heard him sigh.

"Taryn Avere is not the daughter I was expecting. Of course, I was not expecting Ani to be twenty-five either, so there is that.

But at least my daughter and I have had some time to start getting to know each other." A frown wrinkled his brow into a scowl. "Why aren't the Stones more concerned about this?"

Renloret considered his words. "The Stones don't necessarily think about individuals or even time as we do. I believe the Stones are surprised that the small length of time they intended to twist would impact the personal outcomes so dramatically. They are guardians and mentors, according to my great-grandmother. And they twisted time only because it was needed to speed the aging of The Blood to get the correct mix of hormones and trace elements in her blood to have an effective vaccine to cure the gravitas plague. They were caught off guard by Selabec's attack on the Anyala Stone. And while the First Song in the book warns of a Stone needing to be healed by The Balance, it hinted it would be some time after The Blood cured our people. Selabec's stabbing of the Anyala Stone near the end of the Time Song obviously pushed time further forward than planned, and so we have the current situation." Now that he'd put his thoughts into words they sounded logical.

Yenne nodded. "I suppose they could not control the people of Teramar any more than they could us. I suspect Selabec's behavior is rooted in a lack of communication."

Renloret had been thinking the same thing, but he was relieved Yenne voiced it first. "Would you care to explain, sir?"

The commander gave his reflection a rueful glance and pointed to the door. "Along the way, pilot. We're late."

Renloret stifled a chuckle. Being late was not unusual for him, but at least this time it was not his fault. He glanced at the timepiece at the base of the mirror. The off-world guests would already be there, and Yenne and he would be a few chimes late. He worried just a little bit about Ani's reaction to the aliens. Renloret was glad he'd been informed of the guest list so he could prepare Ani, and he knew she would tell Taryn. He smiled at the excitement he'd seen in her eyes when he told her there would two more *true* aliens at the event. She had teased that the Stones did not seem to be alien enough to scare anyone because they were just large crystals.

Yenne stopped at a small cabinet and opened it, revealing an array of bottles. He handed Renloret two and then grabbed two more for himself. Then he thrust out his chin, indicating the door. Renloret palmed the pad, the door slid open, and they both inhaled deeply before striding through.

The commander hesitated in his purposeful advancement when the dining room door was only a body length away. When he turned, as if to retreat, Renloret blocked him.

"It will be all right, sir."

"How do you know? He was five when I left and has known only Gelwood and Melli as his parents. And I never questioned that they were his parents. How can he be my son? How do you know he's accepting of this? *I'm* having problems accepting this."

"Because I know Taryn. He is not five years old, and you don't have to impress him or bribe him with sweets. He's an adult and the sheriff of Star Valley." He paused to let that sink in a bit.

"He's on the same blade in this, Commander. He knows who he is. His parents have raised him well. And now that I think about it, he is very much like you." He nudged the commander's shoulder to turn him about. "Don't expect him to be angry or upset because he won't be. He will be more concerned about Melli, Gelwood, and you. Taryn is more accepting of many ideas than Ani, and he already knows why you have not aged. I suspect he understands a little of what you have gone through these past weeks. He should not be underestimated."

Renloret smiled and gently urged Yenne toward the door. "Plus, he was the one who suggested this gathering. He asked the Singers to invite enough people so you two could move from group to group without all the attention being on your genetic connection. There will be time later for conversation between you." He glanced at the door. "For now, he wants to celebrate the extension of his family. I'll enter first if you like."

With a shake of his head, Yenne turned back to the door. "No. I can handle this. I am also an adult." He straightened his back, placed a bottle under his arm, and palmed open the door.

The conversations ceased as the door slid closed behind them. Renloret stepped to one side, giving the man some space.

No one moved for several breaths, and then Kela strutted forward, his tongue lopping over his lower jaw and his tail wagging jauntily. Kela sat before the two men, tipped his head to the side, and then barked, lifting one forepaw toward Yenne.

Renloret leaned close to Yenne's ear and whispered, "I think he wants to welcome you. You had best accept."

Yenne seemed to recover and reached down to grasp the proffered paw. Once Yenne released his grip, Kela stood and looked over his shoulder at Ani and barked again.

Her mouth spread into a grin, and she took Taryn by the elbow and marched him across the room to face his father. "Commander Yenne Chenakainet, as your daughter and The Blood, it is my duty to officially introduce you to your son, Taryn Avere, known on Lrakira as The Balance."

The words were in carefully pronounced Lrakiran. Renloret was proud of her efforts, even though she had been averse to the idea in the first place because she knew her father was fluent in Northern. But after Renloret had explained that there would be people present who did not speak Northern and might not be supplied with bio-teachers of any type, she had acquiesced and asked him how to say the correct introduction. They had practiced the statement numerous times on their walk back from the hilltop park.

Taryn executed a sharp Northern blade salute, adding an honorific bow of respect. As he straightened, he sent a sidelong glance to Ani, as though asking permission.

Ani nodded.

In Northern, Taryn said, "I am likewise honored to acknowledge our biological connection. When we return to Teramar, I will reintroduce you to the parents of my heart, Gelwood and Melli Avere. I'm sure you will have much to discuss. And may I say, you are looking well and fit for being dead these past twenty years."

Renloret noticed the twinkle in Taryn's eye and the slight upturn of the corners of his mouth. He saw an answering twitch in the corner of Yenne's. Then Yenne laughed out loud and reached over Kela to grasp Taryn's forearm in a Teramaran welcome grip.

"Well done and said, young man. Though in my defense, I

must say you've grown up rather fast over the few months I have been gone."

Renloret was struck by the sudden realization that the two men shared a family resemblance.

Diani approached with a tray of fluted glasses filled with a pale yellow liquid. "Please take one. The rest of us already have ours."

Taryn and Yenne chose theirs, and Diani offered the remaining one to Renloret. After setting the empty tray down, she motioned for Yenne and Taryn to stand on either side of her. "It is my pleasure to welcome The Balance, Taryn Avere, sheriff of Star Valley and blood son of Commander Yenne Chenakainet, to Lrakira. Be it known that the Stones have sung to us that the second part of the Prophecy of The Blood and The Balance has come to fruition. A statement has been prepared and will be broadcast to all Lrakirans. In short, Singers Layson, Ani, and I embrace the foretelling of a new era where, after one thousand sun-cycles, male Singers will be necessary to obtain and maintain true balance with our guardians. In the next few sun-times, after the Anyala Stone completes its own healing, we will have better understanding of the reasons behind the plague to which we lost so many."

There was a moment of silence as the tens of thousands of women and unborn who had succumbed to the plague were honored.

The Singer raised her glass to Taryn and Yenne. "May the Stones continue to bless you both with song, music, and color."

A chorus of "Stones blessings upon you" answered Diani's toast. Taryn shared a clinking of glasses in Northern fashion with Yenne, then both took the obligatory swallow. After a second swallow of the wine, Taryn offered his elbow to Yenne and escorted him to the food-laden tables.

Ani stood out of the way and watched, trying to ignore the flicker of envy. At least her brother had parents who were of an appropriate age. She was still uncertain of her feelings toward the father believed to be long dead whose image she remembered through a five-year-old's eyes. Her mood darkened in opposition to the celebration in front of her. She did not have the option Taryn was truly blessed with. Yenne's reaction to Taryn's dry humor indicated that they would get along fine and most likely become great friends. She, on the other blade, had no illusions of friendship with Yenne, even though she knew that he was her father. She tried to shrug the thought away and finished the last of the wine in her glass without tasting it.

*Can you not enjoy this moment?*

Kela's telepathic query startled her. She looked around for the canine. *I'm not sure. I'm conflicted, Kela. One moment I'm happy Taryn is adjusting quickly, the next I'm angry and sad because he has parents and my only family is an absent uncle I haven't seen in over a year and a father I thought died twenty years ago but is alive and only about ten years older than me. Plus, I know he's having trouble adjusting to being the parent of two adult children without the benefit of those twenty years we can never restore.*

*You have a brother, Ani.*

*Who used to be my best friend.* She allowed the bitterness to tinge her thoughts. *Everyone acts like this is normal. It's not normal. I may have to accept it, but I also don't have to like or enjoy it.* She folded arms across her chest.

*You're pouting.*

*Really?* She put as much sarcasm as possible into the single word.

*Yes. It proves you are a stubborn pup.*

She harrumphed audibly.

Kela turned back to her and winked. Then he licked his jowls and moved closer to the tables. *I could eat some of that stew.*

"Hells," she muttered under her breath. She set down the empty wine glass and obliged his request by filling a bowl to the brim and placing it on a large plate. Then she spooned roasted vegetables around the bowl and added three slices of bread. She lowered the plate to his view.

*Enough?* she asked.

*For now.*

Holding the plate prevented her from aiming a swat at him. He chuckled in her mind and sauntered to a corner and sat, waiting for her to bring him his meal. She rolled her eyes, followed, and set the plate on the floor a little harder than she intended.

*My thanks, Ani.* He wagged his tail in appreciation.

She sighed, told him he was welcome, and ruffled the fur between his ears. Taryn's laugh mingling with that of Renloret's caught her attention. "Excuse me, Kela." She straightened up and moved closer to the pair.

"Do you suppose that's what Kela sounds like to Ani?" Taryn was saying. He shook his head. "It must be amazing to hear that all the time."

Renloret reached for her hand and drew her to his side, welcoming her into the conversation. "Well? Does it?"

His hand was warm to the point of being hot, and she pressed her lower back into his palm. He answered her request with a slight squeeze. Oh, to be back on the hill overlooking Awarna kissing him. She cleared her throat. "Does what? What are you two talking about?"

"We were speculating about possible similarities between Kela's and the Stones' mental voices," Renloret said. "I was about to find you to ask."

His smile weakened her knees, and she slipped a hand around his waist. "They are similar, though each Stone's voice feels different from Kela's." She grinned at her brother. "And the Stones' voices are entwined with their music. I have yet to hear Kela really sing, at least in the way we think of singing. He usually howls."

Taryn nodded. "Oh, I've heard him howl. It is very different from the Stones, though he can get some amazing harmonics, which seem to tell a story without words. I should like to hear the Stones again."

"Have either Layson or Diani said anything? Are they all right?" Yenne asked. He had approached during the exchange.

Ani shrugged. "We were told it would be several days before the Anyala Stone would be able to fully communicate."

"We are to wait for their call," Taryn added.

"Well, then, I should like to properly welcome you to the confusion of our family." Yenne waved his hand in the direction of a table that was set with four tumblers and four bottles.

"Vaquin?" Ani asked.

Yenne shook his head. "Not so lucky. But as close as Lrakira can come." He opened one of the bottles. "I heard you and Renloret shared a glass of my last batch, Ani. You honored me. It was not wasted with such a discovery. I only wish I had been there to share it."

He poured out four servings three-fingers deep and passed them out. "I'm sorry for the confusion time has wrought with our lives and families. We all have much to reconcile, but I am both pleased and honored that you, Ani, and you, Taryn, are my children. That the time shift has rendered me younger than I would otherwise be in relation to you is something I hope we can all become accustomed to. Taryn, know that Gelwood and Melli are among my closest friends, and they have always been and will *always* be your parents."

His voice cracked, and he coughed. "Quick now, before I start crying." He raised the glass. "To Shendahl, my beloved wife whose choice, made under extreme circumstances and with overpowering love, has blessed our family."

Four glasses clinked and four people downed the Lrakiran liquor.

Both Taryn and Ani stifled coughs at the lung-clearing bite of alcohol. Patting her brother's back with her free hand, Ani held her glass out and managed to say, "Two fingers, for sipping."

Yenne poured.

"I'll second that." Taryn presented his glass for a refill. "It's not quite as strong as vaquin, but it is a close second. Did you distill it yourself?"

"No, dinshinga is commercially available in small batches, and it also comes from a desert plant. Very expensive, but I thought it worthy of this celebration."

Renloret nodded. "I agree with Taryn. Did Ani tell you that we didn't just share a glass, we emptied the bottle from your study?"

"Just the two of you? The entire bottle?" His tone was actually concerned.

Ani waved her hand. "Yenne, it was over a matter of hours, and we'd had a meal prior to absorb some of the side effects."

Sounding a bit indignant, Yenne replied, "Well, I guess that makes it all right, doesn't it?"

Taryn clapped his hands. "Ah, the parent rises to the occasion!"

Ani did not stop smiling as she studied her father's expression. Perhaps she should find a way to soften her brother's comment. She raised her glass again and pronounced, "To my father. May our relationship be strengthened by this . . . outrageous *time* of our lives." The others raised their glasses to her and sipped.

Kela chuckled in her mind. *Well said, little one. Now, may I have a taste?*

Ani tipped her head at Kela, who was trotting over. Diani's granddaughter had picked up his bowl and plate and placed them on a serving tray just outside the kitchen. The girl stood at the door, her attention to the rest of the room. "Yenne, Kela says he wants a sample as well."

"No reason not to share with everyone. I brought enough."

Yenne waved his glass in the direction of the kitchen. Juleen gave him a small salute and opened the door. Ani couldn't hear what she said, but Juleen held the door open and two servers marched in with short tumblers on trays. Yenne quickly opened the remaining three bottles and poured out generous shares. The servers then split up and moved among the people in the room. He then poured some onto a saucer and placed it on the floor for Kela.

When all had a drink before them, Yenne called for their attention. "As you may now know, this time in our history has not been without its mistakes and misunderstandings. We all have lost someone we love." His voice cracked again and he cleared his throat. For the first time, Ani reached out to squeeze his shoulder in silent support.

He patted her hand and continued. "It is through Renloret's efforts that The Blood was located and returned to Lrakira, thus ensuring the safety of our women and our future as a species. The Stones sang to us that The Balance would be needed to save the injured Stone. Renloret and Ani accepted the mission without hesitation and returned to Teramar to find and bring back The Balance. We assumed The Balance would be female, and we are still struggling with that misunderstanding. But we open our hearts and minds to Taryn Avere, sheriff of Star Valley, The Balance. Please raise your glass. To the Stones and their Singers, may they continue to sing."

A rousing cheer was voiced and all took at least a sip from their glasses. A few coughed at the unexpected rawness of the drink. Then the room was filled with conversation, and more food was added to plates and platters.

After the meal was completed, the two Caason Sector aliens approached and offered salutations. Ani elbowed Taryn in the ribs to stop him from staring at the long tails they held off the ground, though she was just as mesmerized by the nictitating membrane that swept across their unusually large eyes. She was fascinated by the color variations produced each time the membrane washed over an eye. The reptilian ambassadors displayed translation bracelets and worked hard to pronounce each Northern syllable of a practiced greeting. The results were somewhat stilted yet weirdly understandable. When the requisite greeting was completed, they offered their forearms in a traditional Northern greeting. Ani was surprised by the dry softness of their finely scaled skin. She thought about the amphibious lizards on Teramar and her reluctance to touch them. Perhaps they felt similarly.

After the pair of lizard aliens had concluded their brief congratulatory comments, they politely excused themselves and left. It had something to do with the chill of the late autumn night and the need to be in warmer conditions to function fully. Ani told Taryn that the very image of a lizard wearing a fur-lined coat was almost unimaginable. They both covered their laughs.

Then the Ishan-Druneeaabe made its way in their direction. The individual approached with a wide smile, its long yellow hair braided and pinned together in an intricate weave. Ani considered asking about the method of constructing such a hairdo. All sorts of bangles and tiny bells were draped across the weave, and each step the creature took caused them to jangle pleasantly. The lilting sound of the bells and obvious smile were in sharp contrast to the marked forehead ridges arching above the opaque, singularly-colored eyes and seemed to pull the skin in pucker-and-tuck fashion to a knot of cartilage that protruded between those pupil-less eyes. She paused in her own memorized greeting. Now that she could see what this species actually looked like, she hardly noticed the yellow hair and colorless skin. She shook her head at the preconceived notions Renloret's descriptions had created.

Were the people of Northern ready to accept the concept of aliens? She wondered how a song would inform the inhabitants of Teramar. How would they react? Too many questions to be asked this late. Without answers, Ani bid the others a good eve and headed for her room. Renloret offered to escort her.

# CHAPTER SIX

The morn sun seemed to be a slightly different color than Taryn remembered. He'd spent several minutes after waking adding the observation to the notebook someone had created just for him the previous day. He had not realized how much he relied on the physical contrivance. During the preparations for the introductory meal, he'd complained to Layson and Diani about the lack of writing materials and explained that he needed them to keep the flood of information straight and in reviewable form. He had appreciated Layson's loan of a recording device, but it was not a suitable substitute for the notebook he was so accustomed to.

He didn't know who to thank, but when he arrived at his room the previous eve, there'd been a dozen palm-sized pads and several writing implements in a box outside his room door. Before he'd gone to bed, he had filled one of the pads, unable to sleep in his excitement until he'd gotten down all that had happened. Now returning to his room after a short run around the guest complex for long needed exercise, he paused and paged through his distilled notes, which he had laid out in the second pad.

A hand on his shoulder startled him, and he almost dropped the pad where he had stopped, which was in the middle of the hall, several paces away from Yenne's door. Taryn turned and smiled at Renloret. The pilot's skin was shiny cinnamon and his shirt was dark with sweat. It looked as if he'd also been exercising.

"Good morn. You're out early," Taryn said.

"As are you, Taryn. Is there news of the Stone?" Renloret mopped his brow and neck with his shirtsleeve.

"No, not yet. But that is to be expected I guess. Another day of talking with Diani and Layson would be nice. I've already filled a notepad." He raised it up and waved it, a triumphant smile on his face.

Renloret chuckled. "I'm sure you can get more just by asking. Our expedition supplies group loves creating those types of items. Were you headed to Yenne's room?"

"Yes. We're scheduled to break fast with Diani and Layson. Would you like to join us?"

"I'd be delighted—if you can wait about ten chimes while I shower off and change clothes."

Taryn noticed that though he'd spoken in Northern, the pilot had used the Lrakiran time term. How many languages did the pilot know? Not for the first time, he considered asking about the bio-teachers. Taryn took the last steps to Yenne's assigned room and rapped on the door. While he waited, he flipped to the next page. It was titled "Ani."

In his observations of Ani, he'd gotten the sense that she was beginning to accept herself as a Stone Singer. It wasn't really a new identity for her. Rather, it was something added, something that made her feel whole. He was aware of a similar feeling of having found a missing *something* in his life.

He glanced down the hall at Renloret's door. Taryn had not had the chance to quiz either the pilot or his sister on the progress of their relationship, though he had noticed they held hands often and Ani was comfortable with Renloret putting his arm across her shoulders in public. And occasionally they sat so close, their legs touched. He wondered if they had moved forward to more than kissing or snuggling and chuckled knowing she would hit him hard if he asked. Perhaps he could ask Renloret without getting bruised or otherwise damaged.

He knocked on Yenne's door again. "Yenne? Are you up yet or did that stuff you forced down our throats last eve leave you with an aching head? Did you forget we are to break fast with the Singers?"

A grumbling noise, not unlike Kela when he was miffed about something, could be heard. The door opened a crack. Taryn saluted the bleary-eyed, sleep-heavy face that peeked out. "What about food?" Yenne rumbled.

"We have an appointment to break fast with Diani and Layson, sir."

"I told you not to call me that."

"Yes, sir. I will try to remember . . . Yenne."

"Give me a few minutes." His father swung the door further open, allowing Taryn to enter.

Taryn stepped in, closed the door, and made his way to a

seat near the fireplace. Water started to run in the washroom. Taryn returned to his notes. He hoped to clarify the assumption that the Time Song had somehow prevented communications between the Teramar research team and Lrakira. It was still not clear why neither the Singers nor the Stones knew that Ani's mother—S'Hendale according to the Lrakiran language and Shendahl as she was known on Teramar—had successfully gotten pregnant and given birth to the prophesied twins until Yenne's return to Lrakira after the attack on the research center. Why had the information not been passed on by Yenne's communication officer?

According to the two Singers, Ani's blood would not have the necessary hormones to produce the vaccine until she reached her menses. The Stones had planned to twist time forward to take her from five to fifteen. The problem had arisen when Selabec, Ani's grandmother and now former Singer for the Anyala Stone, blamed the Stone for the rift between her and her daughter and that her daughter had left Lrakira instead of staying to join with the Stone. The mentally unstable Singer had allowed her perception of rejection by both the Stone and her daughter to fester so deep that she attacked the Stone near the conclusion of the Time Song, which caused time to swing wide of its target, thus lengthening the time twist an additional decade before the shattered song let loose of time and ended. That additional swing of time had caught Renloret's arriving ship in its grip causing it to crash.

Now there was evidence of three more Stones hidden on Teramar, and it had been they who had kept Renloret from dying in the crash until Ani and Kela had found him. The other hitch was that Yenne had not been on Teramar during the Time Song. He had been on Lrakira and therefore had not experienced the forward twist of time with the rest of his family.

Taryn closed the notepad and watched his father, barely ten years older than him, come out of the washroom dressed and grudgingly awake, based on his expression. Taryn agreed with Ani's observation that Yenne was having difficulty with the age difference because he had *not* experienced the twenty-year time twist. During the eve dinner, Taryn had caught Yenne looking at him several times, a wistful expression on his face, and there was a hint of sadness at the loss of something he'd never known until a few weeks ago. Taryn had no doubt it would be a struggle at times for Yenne and him to come to terms with the reality of their relationship. Time would tell. He chuckled. Yes, time would tell because time had caused this dilemma.

Closing the notepad, he stood. "Ready?"

Yenne pulled on his boots. "Yes. Famished too. How about you? Is Renloret in his room or is he with Ani?"

"I met him in the hall as he returned from an early morn workout of some kind. I invited him to join us." He laughed. "If you're asking if they've been together, I don't think they have. I still have a bruise from when I asked if they had kissed yet, so I'm not going to ask."

Yenne clapped him on the shoulder after closing the door. "Not used to having a sister yet are you?"

"No, sir. I mean, Yenne."

"I have two sisters and, of course, a brother. I might be a sounding board if you want advice on how to be a brother. You do remind me of Reslo." The commander's voice was soft, wistful. "How was he the last time you spoke?"

"Concerned about Ani's welfare and finding it difficult to leave her so soon after Shendahl's death. There was an urgency about him then, a desperation to do something that no one seemed to understand at the time. My parents . . ." Taryn hesitated, glancing toward the man who walked by his side. He continued when Yenne did not flinch. "My parents gladly offered to watch over her and provide a family environment. I'm now realizing how close your relationship was . . . is . . . with them." Taryn knocked on Renloret's door. "It will help when we tell them. You'll have to remember that everyone on Teramar is twenty years older than you remember them."

Yenne nodded, frowning. Taryn knocked again.

Renloret emerged and closed the door behind him. Taryn did not get even a peek into the room.

"You're not going to let us in?" Yenne asked, voicing Taryn's thought.

"Why should I?" Renloret replied, a befuddled look on his face.

Taryn and Yenne looked at each other and then at the pilot, their stares speculative.

A sigh of exasperation escaped from Renloret's lips. "Oh, for blades sake. No, she is not hiding in my room. We are not—"

"Fine. I'll take your blade oath on that," Yenne interrupted, his tone firm, more like a father than a friend. "Now, let's get some food in our bellies." He gently pushed the pilot ahead of them toward the exit.

Taryn chuckled. Now he wouldn't have to dodge another hit from Ani. He was relieved Ani was taking her time and that Renloret was cooperating. Even so, he expected it would not be too far in the future that the pair would succumb.

When they reached the dining room, Diani, Layson, and Ani were all present and in avid conversation, mugs of tea cradled in their hands. Kela lay contentedly at Ani's feet. His tail swished in welcome as the three men entered the hall.

Layson waved them over to the table of steaming pots of tea. "The black one is a brisk dark concoction that will wake the dead." She glanced at Yenne and seemed to stifle a grin. "The blue contains the most common teas, and the red one has more of my blend from the introduction dinner. Once you get your mugs, we'll have the meal brought out." She turned back to the conversation between Diani and Ani.

As the son of a master tea maker, Taryn chose three smaller cups and poured a sample of each. He placed the three on a tray and sat off to the side to test each the way Melli had taught him. Ani caught his eye and gave him a wink. He raised the cup already in his hand in salute and finished the test. Then he returned to the table and filled two mugs, one with the dark waking tea and the other with Layson's creation, and placed them at the table already set with plates and utensils.

"Good morn, Singer Taryn." The voice came from a doorway to his right. Diani's granddaughter stood in the half-opened space. He nodded to her, and she curtsied.

"Good morn to you, Juleen."

Her smile widened at his personal greeting. "Are you ready?" she asked.

"Yes, I believe so."

"Very good. I will bring out the fruit." She stepped back and the door swung shut.

Taryn sat and announced to the others, "The fruit is on its way. Come join me."

By the time all were seated, Juleen had placed bowls of sliced fruit and two platters of bread in the center of the table. She paused at Ani's side and said something, her voice so soft Taryn couldn't hear. Ani smiled and reached out to ruffle the fur on Kela's back. The girl held her hand out for Kela to scrutinize and giggled when his tongue washed the back of her hand. She patted his back and then skipped off through the door to the kitchen. A moment later, she returned with a large bowl, which she set on the floor. Taryn watch Kela raise a forepaw for the girl to grasp and then gave her a quick lick of his tongue on her cheek. She giggled again and disappeared back into the kitchen.

"What did she bring out?" Taryn asked, wondering if the Lrakirans also had canines, though he'd not seen any evidence of them. He was curious what they thought Kela would eat.

Ani looked down at the bowl. "Looks like meat and vegetables. Kela says it is a tasty meal." She stroked Kela's back as he continued to eat. "I think we should follow his example." She took the platter of bread, placed two slices on her plate, and passed it on to Yenne.

Juleen brought out bowls of hot seasoned grain and a basket

of meat rolls. Then the girl checked with each person as to which tea they were drinking and refilled each mug before returning to her station next to the kitchen door. The conversation quieted until most of the plates were empty.

The first full day of waiting for the Stone to heal was filled with research through a myriad of books delivered from the library. Taryn wanted to know everything the Lrakirans knew about the Stones, especially if there were other mentions of more than three at any time in the past. Renloret had agreed, saying that in recent decades, many of the older Songs and Singer writings had been neglected and forgotten. Diani and Layson admitted that they had not known about the First Song or The Prophecy of The Blood and The Balance until Renloret had mentioned it. They both promised to mend their ways and had portions of their personal libraries shipped to Awarna. Renloret asked Ani to assist Yenne and him while Diani snagged Taryn to take notes on the items she and Layson found. Every so often, one of the Singers would start singing as they perused the tomes. Taryn even heard Ani humming tunes with Renloret joining in using soft Lrakiran words. And when someone brought attention to a paragraph or verse they thought to be of particular importance, everyone put their work aside to listen and discuss the passage.

Taryn was pleased to see his notebooks fill up. Juleen somehow slipped in and out of the room bringing plates of food for the midday meal before they could request them and kept the teas hot. Taryn wondered if the penchant for tea was a species necessity or social contrivance that had traveled with the people of Lrakira and Teramar, just as the blade culture seemed to have.

Their heads were deep between the pages of various books when Diani shut the book she was working through with a loud bang, startling everyone. She announced that it was past the eve meal and the moons would be rising shortly. Saying that Layson and she would retire to their homes and leave Yenne, Renloret, and Ani to show The Balance around Awarna, she herded Ani, Taryn, Renloret, Yenne, and Kela out the door saying, "May the Stones bless your adventures with music and song." Then the Singers executed Lrakiran blade salutes and marched off toward their quarters.

Standing in the hallway, Ani turned to Renloret. "The hill?"

He grinned. "Perfect. Maybe the meat roll vendor will be in the vicinity."

Kela barked in agreement and trotted down the hall in the opposite direction of the Singers, his tail wagging from side to side. "What time is it?" Ani asked.

Renloret pulled out a small tablet device and glanced at it. "A few chimes past the seventeenth bell. Time enough to find the vendor and eat before observing the moons rise. Taryn, you're in for a treat."

CHAPTER SEVEN

Taryn licked the sauce off his fingers. "That was satisfying."

"Understatement of the day, little brother," Ani said. She still had half of a meat roll pinched between her fingers. She glared at Kela. "No, you may not." She stuck her tongue out at the canine and then slowly took a large bite, closing her eyes and moaning as she chewed. Kela made a disgruntled noise and rolled over in the grass.

"Is he saying three of those rolls did not stuff his belly?" Yenne asked. "Two were plenty for me." The commander patted his own abdomen with a satisfied grin.

Ani peeked through her lashes at Renloret. The pilot had not participated in the banter as expected. Instead, he was staring at her as she swallowed and began licking her fingers one at a time. The pilot was soaking up every movement and sound she was making. She could feel the heat of Renloret's gaze.

Kela whined and stuck his muzzle between Ani's hands, a whisker away from the last bit of roll. Ani shook her head and popped the chunk into her mouth. She opened her eyes to stare daringly at Renloret as she trailed her tongue across her lips. She wondered if he would accept her silent challenge. She had used it often enough on more than one blade ring opponent—ones who quickly fell to her skills.

Renloret slowly rose from the grass, his eyes steady on Ani, and took a step toward her. Their gazes remained locked. Green against blue. Renloret took one more step. The pilot's hand reached toward her. She flexed her hand. Would he see her intent? No.

Before he could take another breath, Renloret was kissing the grass instead of her. With one arm twisted behind his back and Ani straddling him she leaned forward and whispered in his ear. She hoped neither Yenne nor Taryn could hear her words.

Yenne stood and dusted off bits of grass. "Did your mother teach you that? At least she waited until *after* I kissed her to put me in the dirt."

Ani released the arm and stood. Renloret was blushing as he took her offered hand up, a rueful smirk on his face.

The commander smiled and grabbed Ani in a fierce hug. Just as quick, he released her and nodded sharply. "Thank you for showing me that some things live on."

Ani couldn't help but stare at her father. Her mother had never told her that she'd used that move on him. Ani only knew that it could be used to her advantage if a man made unwanted or untimely advances. "It has come in handy on occasion." He gave her a soft smile.

"Shall we?" He pointed to the summit of the hill, ready to change the subject.

Ani listened to the conversation between the men as they climbed toward a group of benches that faced back toward the way they'd come. They took seats while Taryn explained a time when Ani had executed what he termed one of her signature moves. An unsuspecting opponent had underestimated her because she was a woman, and that opponent had made fatal mistakes. Taryn warned Renloret to expect her to fight as dirty as any man. Ani laughed when he added that even if she wasn't an expert blade fighter, she would be unpredictable and dangerous, simply by virtue of the fact that she was a woman.

"Blades, Taryn you sound just like my brother Reslo," Yenne said. Then he frowned. "Ani, do you think he's received any of your messages?"

Ani shrugged. "I'm not sure. The communication networks on Southern are different than on Northern, and Southern has experienced more direct interference from sunspot activity the last couple of months. I certainly have not received any from him during that time. We'll have to try to contact him on our way back to Teramar."

The mention of her uncle and all he had missed brought up her own worries about how much had changed in the last couple of months. Would he be happy she was a Stone Singer? Was she?

Kela sauntered up and lay at Ani's feet, and Ani reached down to pat the fur over his ribcage. She wondered if there would ever be a time in the future when she could be herself again. Who was she anyway? Everything had changed. Her father, long understood to be dead, was alive. She now had a brother, and she was the chosen Singer of a large green intelligent crystal, a real alien creature. Plus, she had traveled on a spaceship to another planet populated by people just like her. Everything had changed . . . except that her mother was still dead. Guiltily, she wondered why her mother, with whom she had been very close, was dead instead of her father, whom she hardly knew at all.

Kela sent her a shushing comment.

*I know,* she sent back. *But why can't I want Mom instead of Yenne?*

*You had her for twenty more years than Yenne. You are further along in the grief process than he is. Remember, he was informed of her passing just a few weeks ago. Do you remember how you felt a few months after her passing?*

*Oh, I remember, Kela. I still berate myself for not putting her in the stasis bag as she suggested. I was the one who let her die because I couldn't stand the thought of—*

*Whoa, don't go there, little one. The past is past. And your future is full of exciting and new things that your mother and uncle trained you for. Look at your father.*

Ani did as Kela asked. Even though he laughed with Renloret and Taryn, she noticed the undercurrent of sadness, and the laughter was short-lived. All this talk of Reslo had brought up the decades of experiences Yenne had missed.

Kela continued his remonstrations. *He has also lost the first twenty-five years of knowing his son.*

*But he said he was okay with how things turned out. Gelwood and Melli are Taryn's parents. He said—*

*We all know what your father says and what he is trying so hard to believe. But none of us can share his guilt for not staying.*

Rising anger toward Kela and his comment brought an edge to her mental voice. *If he hadn't escaped and let the Stones know about Taryn and me, then there is every chance the people of Lrakira would not be here right now. There have not been any children born in years! For blades' sake, Kela, Renloret would not have come and . . .* She stopped her rant with an exasperated sigh. *Curses on you for making me defend him. Well played, Kela. I think I begin to see all the nicks in my blade and all the parts I will play in the true healing of Lrakira. I need to look forward, to learn who I am to be. And I need to help Taryn, Yenne, and the people of Lrakira and Teramar do the same. We are not who we thought. We are so much more.*

A green-tinged hum entered her mind. The Anyala Stone's voice soothed the fire that had risen. *You are The Blood—the most powerful healer. You are needed, with The Balance and the others, to build bridges of understanding and knowledge. You are the conduit between Teramar and Lrakira. No single entity is at fault. We Stones cannot even fault the asteroid for the need to divide our charges to survive. Perhaps the ones who brought you to us knew what would be needed to move your people forward and beyond what you are now. Use this time of discovery to strengthen and ready the people to embrace the changes that will come to the children's children.* The connection faded.

"Ani!" Taryn's exclamation interrupted her contemplation of the Stone's song. She slapped at his waving hand.

"A moment, Taryn." She raised a palm to his face, silencing him. Ani looked at Kela. *Did you hear any of that?*

*No. Was it the Stone? Did it hear us? What did it say?*

*Before I forget, this is what it said.* She repeated the song telepathically. Kela barked affirmation of receiving it and cataloging it for future interpretation. Ani smiled. A sense of acceptance warmed her. She was more at peace than she could ever remember. Maybe the Stone was almost healed. She patted Kela on the head and stepped closer to the bench.

Kela rolled onto his side, offering his stomach for rubbing. Yenne obliged. "You had the look of a Singer. Was it the Anyala Stone?" He did not look at her but kept rubbing while Kela made satisfied grunting sounds.

"Yes." She was not ready to discuss everything the Anyala Stone had said or what it had evoked in her. "I think we may hear soon that the Anyala Stone is healed. It said there is more to our peoples than we know. And we," she circled her hand, "are at the center."

Three sets of eyes looked at her under raised eyebrows. "Us?" the three men said in unison.

She chuckled. "Yes. Us. But the Stone also hinted that whatever *it* is won't happen for several generations. There is time."

Yenne grunted. "Damnable time again."

With new understanding, Ani turned to him. "Yenne, if you had not left Star Valley, the people of Lrakira probably would not have survived. You are the one to be celebrated—not me."

Yenne stopped stroking Kela's fur and faced her. "I *am* sorry I was not there."

She managed a gentle smile. "You were where you were supposed to be when you were needed. There is no fault to be found. We all did what we had to do. Even the Stones understand this." She looked up at Renloret, who had been silent for several minutes. A smile crept into his lips. Blades, she suddenly wanted to taste those lips again. Her heart started to beat faster, and she felt the warmth of a blush start. Taryn coughed.

"Well!" She clapped her hands to her knees and stood. "Aren't we here to show Taryn evidence of alien life, as if the Stones were not enough?" She pulled on Yenne's hand, bringing him off the bench.

Kela ran ahead to the crest of the hill and barked.

"He says shuttles are landing and he thinks the little moon will rise shortly after the full sunset," Ani said, catching Renloret's hand and leading the three men to join Kela.

A few minutes later, they sat at the crest of the hill. Renloret had pointed out several of the buildings, including the historical stone and glass cathedral that was next to the university library where he'd found the First Book of Songs and The Prophecy of The Blood and The Balance. The sun had set behind them providing a graduated blue, purple, and black backdrop that showed the blinking shuttle lights, which brightened and grew larger as the shuttles began their landings at the spaceport.

"Those are shuttles from one of the moons?" Taryn asked.

Renloret shook his head. "No, those aren't from one of the moons. Daily work shuttles usually come from the transfer station that is in synchronic orbit above Awarna. It's easier to fly the smaller transports from the moons to one of the stations and then combine workers on the various shuttles for their home city landings."

Ani watched the small lights flicker against the darkening sky. A ship of some kind launched upward streaming behind flames of bright orange, yellow, and white. Its roar of gravity defiance reached them, and her stomach moved in rebellion. She balled her hand into a fist and pressed it against her abdomen. She refused to throw up again, as she had when she saw the three moons and the shuttles for the first time. An arm crossed her shoulders, and Renloret pulled her closer. Shifting her position slightly, she pressed her head into his chest and felt his lips caress her hair as he murmured something comforting.

Kela moved closer to her other side, and she was bracketed by warm caring. She loosened her fist and massaged the fur at the base of Kela's ears. A rumble of contentment vibrated through her hand as he sent her comfort.

An orb of brightness lit the horizon. Ani heard Taryn's sharp intake of breath as Denert, the smallest of Lrakira's three moons, seemed to leap into sight. The waxing three quarters was at an angle neither Ani nor Taryn had seen before.

"No rings?" Taryn whispered. His voice was filled with awe, not the terror Ani remembered feeling at her first sight of the alien moons.

"Teramar's Viken was the first moon I've seen with rings. You have a stunning orbiter," Renloret replied.

"Ani said there are three."

"The other two will be up shortly but farther to the right. Cranite first then Erid, the largest. There are stations on both. With luck, we may be able to see some of the lights from those buildings. There is usually too much haze for them to be seen clearly most of the sun-cycle. But since this is early winter, we might see those of the two largest communities. By midwinter, the atmosphere is clear of humidity enough that six or seven of the smaller population centers are often visible."

They were all quiet for several minutes.

Taryn looked away from Denert and pointed toward a lightening area on the horizon. "Cranite?"

"Yes," Yenne replied. "It's the middle-sized moon. Over one hundred communities are in operation on its surface."

Ani began breathing slowly. A supportive squeeze from Renloret signaled that he noticed.

Another ship rocketed away from the spaceport.

Taryn stared at them. "Why don't we hear the shuttles landing or launching like that one?"

"Different propulsion system," Yenne said. "The two large launches we've seen are mechanized shipping containers. There are ships in orbit beyond the moons waiting for them. Their supplies will be off-loaded, and the containers will return to be filled again for the next ship."

Taryn shook his head. In the brightening light of Cranite, Ani could see his half-smile.

"Do you need a jacket?" Renloret whispered in her ear.

She shivered as his warm breath crossed her neck. "No, I'm warm enough." She inhaled his woodsy, masculine scent. Did she dare invite him to join her at the practice facility? She wondered how private the private room she'd requested would be and wondered if she could speed up the rising of Erid.

Seemingly in answer to her thought, Yenne pointed. "Here is Erid."

"How long do you want to stay, Taryn?" Renloret asked.

Ani bit her lip as his hand stroked her upper arm, sending little shivers over her skin. She hoped Taryn did not want to stay all night.

Kela tapped in to her thoughts. *Don't you have a blade session scheduled in one hour? You could work off some of the tension you're feeling then go "talk" to Renloret afterward. It wouldn't be so obvious later.*

Ani cuffed the top of his head.

A few minutes later, Erid was a finger-width above the horizon. Taryn sighed as he unfolded his legs and stood.

"Ready to go back?" Yenne asked.

His voice stirred almost forgotten memories of sitting on the deck outside her parents' room cuddled on his lap while he pointed out constellations and told her stories she thought he made up about people who lived on planets that circled some of the stars. She remembered his gentle remonstrations not to tell anyone about his stories because they were just make-believe and not real. That caution had come after one story in particular had fired her imagination and she'd retold it to Taryn.

Ani sat up, separating herself from Renloret's embrace. "Yenne?"

Her father turned to her. The lights from the city were reflected in his dark eyes. "Yes?"

"You stopped telling me stories about the star people about a year before you left. Why?"

Yenne cleared his throat. Ani realized that the memory was not that long ago for him and might have brought up others that were still too fresh or sad to think about.

She started to apologize, but he waved her off. "It's all right. Your mother overheard me and told me to stop. She didn't ask, she told me. She didn't want our four-year-old child, the savior of Lrakira, to be ridiculed for believing in aliens. She said there was plenty of time before you would have to know. I was firmly reminded of our directive to not interfere with the basic belief systems of our surrounding environment and that we should be grateful we had been accepted into the Star Valley community as immigrants from Southern."

"So when you pointed out that star and said it was home, you really meant it was Lrakira's star, your sun, and not the home of a . . . a . . . I'm sorry but I've forgotten the name of the creature. It was a long time ago." She covered her mouth as Yenne bowed his head and brushed at his eyes.

He shook his head. "I'll be fine, little one. I called them swarks."

Renloret laughed. "Swarks? You told a four-year-old stories of swarks? Ani, they're the largest, most vicious land predator on Lrakira, and they have no compunction about having a person for dinner. They don't survive in captivity and need a huge amount of territory. Even so, we have dedicated our largest island to their preservation."

Ani frowned and looked at Yenne. "I thought they were household pets and wanted one of my own. I remember you telling me that they deserved to live their lives without our intervention. But the story you told was how caring they were to their children—like you and mother were to me! I remember crying about the kit that nearly drowned until its father jumped into the river to pull it to safety."

Yenne nodded. "That's a true story. I saw it."

"Can you tell us, Commander?" Renloret asked. He had wrapped his arms around his knees, apparently eager to hear the story.

"Well," Yenne began, "it was on a training mission while I was in flight school. We had flown over the island to practice recon maneuvers while we counted the swarks from the air. A storm had dropped a lot of rain, and one of the rivers was heavily flooded. We watched a mated pair work together to get their kits out of a steep gully before the water washed them away. The female pushed each kit up the embankment as far as she could. Then the male leaned over and grabbed it by the scruff and deposited it behind him. Then the male grabbed his mate and pulled her up. Just as she got her hind paws on safe ground, one of the kits ran to her so fast it couldn't stop, and it fell into the river. We watched the male run along the edge of the gully almost a mile before catching up and jumping in. He managed to keep the kit's head above water until the gully widened enough that he was able to get out."

"And it was a great reunion of the family. All the children were safe," Ani finished, clapping her hands.

Yenne smiled. "Yes, all the kits were safe. It turns out that swarks mate for life and take extremely good care of their offspring. I guess I used what I saw as a metaphor for how much your mother and I cared for you." He was silent a moment. "I wish your mother knew that all of Lrakira's children are safe and that I did not fail in my mission to get you home."

Taryn walked the few steps between them and hugged his father. "I think she knows."

"She certainly always believed you would return," Ani added. "The doctors told me her last words: 'My daughter can save them. Tell her he's coming. She must go home.' So she knew you would return, father." The word slipped out. Ani knew it was important to Yenne—and her. "She never believed otherwise." Ani joined Taryn in hugging their father.

Kela wormed his way between all the legs and announced to Ani, *Shouldn't we be getting back? You do have an appointment.*

Ani sighed. *Yes, I do. But there is time yet.*

*True. But it is getting cold, and I want to sleep by the fire.*

"Oh, Kela, you have such a way." She released her arms and straightened her jacket. Yes, the air had cooled considerably since sunset. She jammed her hands into her pockets and suppressed a shiver. "Well, Kela is getting cold, so we best head back unless Taryn wants to stay longer."

He shook his head. "No, there will be at least one more moonrise before we set off for Teramar, right?"

"Right," Renloret said. "We could run back if you're chilled. This is about as cold as it gets in Awarna. Winters here rarely have snow, unlike my home mountains, but the humidity can make it seem colder." He placed a hand on Taryn's back and gave him a push.

Taryn began to jog away. Yenne waved at Kela, and the two followed, leaving Renloret and Ani.

Lifting her chin and giving him a smile, she said, "At least this time I didn't throw up."

"No, you didn't." He patted her on the shoulder. "And you didn't hit me."

Renloret checked the time again. Almost three hours earlier, Ani had left the men and Kela at the guest quarters and gone to the practice facility. He'd lingered with Yenne and Taryn in the common room for an hour before leaving to distract himself with his own workout in his room. An hour ago he'd crossed the courtyard to the women's dorms, stopping by Ani's room. When she had not answered his knock, he slipped a note under the door. Once back in his room he had paced for over an hour trying to decide whether he should go to the practice facility and offer to accompany her to the guest residences. He wondered if she was in her room by now. He got out of bed and checked that he had not locked the door for the umpteenth time. Would she find the note? Was it too forward of him to invite her to join him in his room?

He padded back to his bed and sat on the edge, his chin in his hands, reviewing the takedown maneuver Ani had used on him. Yes, he could admit that the attempt had been a mistake, but the way she had teased Kela with the meat roll had set his heart on fire. He had only wanted to kiss her again. But her whispered words to him while she sat on his back twisting his arm told him that he was not alone in that desire. "Later, pilot. I know what you want, but not now and not in front of an audience."

Then she had run her tongue along his ear, teasing his desire higher, and said, "If Taryn or Yenne ask you what I just said, you will keep your mouth shut, or I will damage you. Understood?" He had managed to grunt agreement, and she had released him. Perhaps the note had been a mistake.

The bell tower in the cathedral courtyard rang out. He turned to look out of the window, wondering how long Ani would normally work out. Maybe she had found the note and decided not to accept the invitation. At least he had shown his blade and his intentions. He shuffled the covers and settled into the pillows. He would try to get her alone in the morn to discuss her idea of *later*. He could wait. He pulled the blanket up, content to imagine, and drifted off.

He came fully awake and tried not to move. A hand moved to the outside of his hip, to his waist, and round to his front, inching its way to rest over his now pounding heart. His skin seemed to be on fire, and he swallowed a moan, not wanting the sensation to end.

A dusky feminine chuckle accompanied featherlight nibbles at the base of his neck. "Did I wake you?"

He wanted to say no. "Sort of," he admitted. "I was thinking about you."

"Same." She snugged her body along his back and nibbled on his earlobe. He sucked in a breath. "It's later." Her hand slowly moved down his chest, his abdomen, and further. She pressed her hips tight against his buttocks.

"Oh, Stones and blades," he whispered, as he gave in to her invitation.

# CHAPTER EIGHT

"Quiet!" Taryn yelled, his head throbbing. Kela's bark had awakened him.

Kela barked again. The animal was standing at the door. He probably needed to go out. Taryn crawled from under the covers and stumbled barefoot across the stone tiles to open the door. Kela turned and winked at him, then trotted down the hall.

Taryn padded back to the bed. He felt like he'd lost a full-contact combat session with multiple opponents. What kind of alcohol had Yenne served him last eve? He searched the room for a glass or cup, wanting to rinse the stale alcohol and sleep from his mouth. On the writing desk near the window was a pitcher and four mugs. Taryn filled and drained one of the mugs twice. Satisfied for the moment, he scrubbed a hand over his scalp. The hair felt like a soft bristle though it was still not long enough to need a brush.

The heavy curtains kept all but a sliver of light out of the room. He grabbed an edge, shut his eyes, and yanked it to the side. Even with his eyes shut, he could see the brightness on the inside of his lids. He turned his back to the window and gradually opened one eye at a time. Once he adjusted to that amount, he turned back to the window and gazed down on the courtyard.

A door opened on the opposite side of the yard. Ani came through and entered the courtyard. She balanced a tray with two mugs and several plates loaded with food. Her hair swung loose and bounced from side to side as she walked jauntily. Taryn smiled at how happy she seemed to be.

She was coming directly toward the men's wing of the guest quarters. His first thought was that she was bringing him the food. But as he studied her expression, he decided that it was probably Renloret who would be breaking the fast with her. "Lucky man," he muttered. He turned away from the window and moved toward the shower room when a knock on the door stopped him.

"Taryn?" It was Yenne.

"Yes, sir. Coming."

Yenne was leaning against the doorjamb, a grin on his face. He raised a hand. "I don't think they were together last eve after he left us. I saw and talked to the pilot as he came in from a workout. He seems to be able to hold his liquor better than either of us." He pushed off the jamb and entered the room.

Taryn flicked his head toward the window. "Maybe not last eve, but she's bringing him food right now."

"Really?" Yenne turned back to look down the hall. Taryn pulled him into the room and they both tipped their heads just beyond the doorjamb to see Ani enter the hallway and stride to the pilot's door. She set the tray on the floor, pulled her hair to her back and knocked. After a short pause she knocked a second time.

"Renloret? Open up. I have food."

The door opened and Renloret leaned over the threshold and picked up the tray. As he straightened, Ani leaned close, and they shared a quick kiss before she followed him into the room and closed the door.

Taryn grinned and pulled his father back into his room. "Did you see that? Ani would not have brought food to share if she wasn't happy with her choice. Be assured he is her choice."

"I'm not sure how I feel about this. Less than half a sun-cycle ago, she was just five, and now my little girl is entering a man's room. I feel old."

"She's an adult, not a child, Yenne. And thanks to the Stones, you are not an old man. Not yet that is." He winked.

"I guess life has a way of going in unexpected directions. I would never have considered being merely ten or eleven years older than my children, but it has happened, and I understand that the Stones cannot unmake the past once they have moved time forward. But I want it all back."

Tears began to form in Yenne's eyes. "I miss her so much." The commander's voice broke, and then he caught a breath. "You two will need to tell me about her."

Taryn understood that Yenne was talking about his wife, Shendahl or S'Hendale depending on who was speaking or what language they were using. "Yes, I will." He patted his father's back.

There was silence between them for several breaths.

Yenne straightened up with a sigh. "Taryn, you are correct. It's time to move forward and stop wishing for a past I never had. You and I need to discuss how and what to tell your parents when we return to Star Valley. Perhaps we could begin that discussion over a meal." He waved a hand to the door.

Renloret carried the tray to the table while Ani shut the door. Her giggle made him turn to see her waving a piece of paper.

"This was sweet of you." Her smile was seductive. "I found it when I went to my room to change and gather our meal."

"You just now found it?"

She nodded. "Last eve was my idea. I came straight from the practice facility. I didn't stop at my room. I was slightly surprised that your room was unlocked. I thought you might still be awake, but you were already in bed, and I couldn't help but join you. You didn't complain."

She approached the table and ran a hand up his arm and across the top of his shoulders, turning him to fully face her. Clasping his face in her hands, she pulled him to her. "I accept your invitation."

They kissed. Her skin and hair smelled of scented soap and her lips tasted lightly of whirjerata. She had sampled the fruit on the tray. A moan came from her throat, and without breaking the kiss, he carried her to the bed he had just made. He would not be able to eat until he had thoroughly sampled her one more time.

The tea was probably too hot to drink as it was and could cool just a bit longer.

A while later, he stroked her silteene-smooth back, amazed at his response to her. She snuggled closer and teased his senses with the patterns her fingers drew on his abdomen, causing the muscles to tighten. He sucked in a breath and moved slightly so he could press his lips to her forehead. "I am where I have longed to be since I woke in the cabin." Her lips nibbled along his chin line to the base of his ear.

She sighed. "And I too am where I belong."

Renloret rolled to his side and began to explore her face with his lips and tongue. When he reached the base of her throat, she giggled and squirmed, pressing her hands against his chest and tucking her chin down to protect what he now knew was one of her ticklish areas.

"Stop. The tea is probably cold by now," she chided.

He ignored her plea. "There is a warming plate in the cupboard."

"Then we should use it. Kela says we have dallied enough, and Taryn and Yenne are halfway through their meal."

He allowed her to escape his embrace. A rumbling noise came from his stomach. Ah, yes. He was hungry. She giggled again, slapped his bare hip, and slipped out from the covers.

Ani waved her brother and father back into their seats with a smile as she and Renloret joined them. She poured tea and after giving Renloret both cups, she added a little push toward the table. She grabbed the top books from the stacks on the credenza where they'd been left the previous eve, thumped one in front of each of the men, and sat with her own. "Start reading."

The soft whisper of turning pages was interrupted with the arrival of Diani and Layson. Ani looked up from her translated copy of some old Singer's journal to acknowledge their presence. Chairs were shuffled about, and soon everyone was deep into reading.

Sometime later, a joyous lilting mental song began in Ani's head. She closed her eyes to listen. The trio of Stones announced that the Anyala Stone was healed and they wanted the Singers, including Taryn, along with Renloret and Kela, to come to the Stone Chamber. She peeked at Layson and Diani.

Diani closed her book and stood. "Singer Taryn, I suspect you can hear the song."

He jumped a little in surprise and appeared to consider her statement. "I thought it was my own, but now that I listen to the words, I know what they are saying. We should go." He stood as well.

Diani looked at Yenne and Renloret. "Your presence is requested." Both men closed their books and stood. "Do we have everything we need, or does anyone need to return to their room?"

"I have my notes so we can get answers to some of our questions." Taryn waved the pad above his head. Ani, Renloret, and Yenne all chuckled.

"And I." Layson was quick to pull out her electronic recorder and waved it back at Taryn.

Diani raised a satchel for them to see. "And I have the First Book of Songs."

"Let's go," Ani said as she joined Diani in herding the rest out of the conference room.

# CHAPTER NINE

Humming vibrated the air in the chamber. Taryn heard it through his ears as well as in his mind. The Stones were resplendent. Color flashed off the walls and tapestries in a joyful dance.

*We greet you.*

Yenne bowed to the trio of Stones. Even he heard them?

*Yes. A non-Singer will hear us after a touching. We sang together when he was needed to locate the pilot.* The voice Taryn heard was tinged green. Anyala had answered his question. *We also sang with the pilot before he traveled to Teramar.*

"But I heard you before I touched you," Renloret said.

*The pilot was introduced to us by Singer Tivi at the prescribed time.*

Taryn saw an astonished look on Renloret's face. The pilot quickly related the encounter when he was a youngster and his great grandmother, Tivi, allowed him to touch the Kita Stone and hold its blue crystal blade, which he remembered as being as long as he was tall. It was also the first time he'd heard the tune matching the First Song in the book. "My part of this was planned that long ago?"

*From the beginning, pilot.* This tune was the bright cool color of the sky. Taryn looked at the Kita Stone flashing shades of iridescent blue.

*You were and are still needed.* Layson stroked her Stone as a slight smile curved her lips.

Confusion showed on Ani's face. "What about me? I wasn't even on Lrakira until a few months ago, and I heard all three of you before I touched one of you. And my mother said nothing about Stones except when cursing." She blushed at her words, which sounded blasphemous to Taryn now that they were standing in front of the Stones. He remembered hearing Shendahl curse on occasion.

The Anyala Stone brightened. *My blade and Singer did their work well. Singer S'Hendale birthed and raised you in the ways of a Singer while keeping your identity secret until you returned to save our charges. Now here on Lrakira, the blade has sung your accomplishments within the Teramaran blade ring. Most recently, the healing of your injuries and poisoning provided two things. First was the introduction to The Balance. Second for a full blade bonding after S'Hendale's death. Then you, The Blood, healed The Balance so I might be saved.* Taryn was mesmerized again by the flickering brightness accompanying the song of his sister's Stone. So much had occurred without notice or explanation.

Pericha's warm, honey voice entered Taryn's mind. *Much that was prophesied has come to fruition. It was not known which of us would be compromised or by whom.* Diani stroked the amber crystal, tears in her eyes.

*Time was a factor we were unable to control as we were taught. We sorrow for the loss of Singer S'Hendale, just as we are saddened by the twisting of a known instability within Singer Selabec. It was fortuitous the Anyala's blade was passed to S'Hendale before her journey and not delayed as was first prescribed. We assumed there would be time after The Blood's return to ready ourselves and The Balance for his role. I grieve it was my blade Selabec chose.*

Blue and green light surrounded the amber crystal. Taryn felt a musical hug within his mind. It was a curious and intense feeling. Arms around his shoulders brought the mental feeling to the physical. Ani had moved to his side and pulled him into an embrace.

He released the embrace to walk around the three Stones. "Marvelous beings, if we can communicate with you here, can we when we are on Teramar?"

*Not fully until Reunion and when the pathways have been opened. There is a needed connection during the Song of Teaching, which my Singer and blade will provide.* The cool green song of the Anyala Stone sounded in Taryn's head.

"So how do we find the other three Stones? Are they like you in size? Can you tell us where they are? Why haven't they been found yet?" He had his notepad ready.

There was hesitancy in the response. Words crossed from color to color, Stone to Stone. *They awoke with the Time Song, as was designed. They joined together to save the pilot from the ruination of Time. After Selabec's attack we did not have the strength to connect.*

*We do not know their precise locations, though we assume their searches have begun.*

Renloret raised a hand and asked how the Teramaran Stones expected to contact the new Singers before they were found.

*Searching songs touch all, but only those few desirable hear, and they will find ways to answer the call.*

"So not everyone will be scrambling across the continents and digging at the earth to find three very large crystals that glow and sing in their heads?" Of course, that was a worry. He did not relish fighting off hundreds of searchers.

*Each Stone's search song is modified so a small percentage of population would be encouraged to reciprocate in the search. Fewer mistakes will be made.*

Ani shared surprised looks with the others. "Mistakes?"

Taryn could almost feel the Stones shrug. *In the beginning, when we were asked to be guardians, the choosing of Singers created errors. The tunes were corrected.*

"And?" Layson asked.

Again, Taryn felt the shrugs. The colors dimmed and the song softened. *Errors in choice are infrequent. Only one such in one thousand of your years since we migrated to Lrakira.*

"Selabec?" Ani whispered. Her expression was a heartbreaking mix of curiosity and horror because her grandmother had tried to murder the Anyala Stone.

*Not in the beginning. Her genetic line was needed, and she executed her position more than adequately. However, when the plague appeared, an inherent instability sang within her. She did not want to listen, and I could no longer sing the right song. The*

Anyala Stone's minor-keyed tone held incredible sadness. *I could protect S'Hendale by choosing her before Selabec destroyed our only chance for a cure.*

"Is there a song that could cure my grandmother?"

*She must want, in her soul, to be healed. She does not.*

Yenne stepped up beside Ani and ran his hand across the Stone. "I did not know. S'Hendale thought news of a healthy grandchild would bring her mother back from where she had gone. We sent numerous messages to Selabec. They were never answered."

He shared his thoughts on that lack of response, mentioning a woman by the name of Sarinne and explained that she had been the research team's communications officer. All communications between Teramar and Lrakira had gone through her. "For five years we never questioned Sarinne's attention to her duties. Yet, now I wonder. She may well have caused Selabec's break from reality, which ultimately caused the attack on the Anyala Stone."

*At one time, Sarinne was a Singer candidate. She had excellent skills but lacked the proper temperament. Her true skills lay in the science of interstellar communications, and we hoped she would be at peace with the direction she was given. Perhaps she has yet to fully embrace her true self,* the Kita Stone sang.

"I will keep that observation under advisement," Yenne replied.

Kita's bright, cool voice hummed a need to get on to the questions that were filtering through the thoughts of several in the room.

"Yes, well, because Taryn has the most experience in interrogating suspects, perhaps he should go first," Renloret said.

Taryn chuckled and flipped the pages of his notepad to the beginning. He began by suggesting use of the First Song as a frame to understand what had or would happen and asked Singer Diani to read the first and second stanzas.

Diani pulled the book out of the satchel, turned to a flagged page, and recited the words.

> *Circle of Seven sing safe passage.*
> *Divide by two and send in deep sleep.*
> *The Blood and Balance shall each save one,*
> *Awakening three to rejoice with time's message.*
> *Time will soon come for reunion's leap.*
> *Six will Sing, joining three homes and suns.*
>
> *Plague and sickness spur Stones to send*
> *Singer and blade to chosen star unknown.*
> *The Blood and Balance, in one birth two.*
> *She, The Blood, to be aged by Time Song's end.*
> *He, The Balance, in time to heal first a Stone*
> *Then home to awakened three to join anew.*

Taryn tapped the notepad twice. "Okay, the second stanza is almost explanatory. Let's look back at the first. Can we agree that the third line about The Blood and The Balance has occurred, and the fourth explains that the Time Song has awakened the Stones on Teramar?" He studied each of their faces, saw consensus, and made two marks on the page. "Let's look at the first two lines. Why was safe passage needed and what was being divided and sent away?" Taryn looked up from his notepad and saw that Layson, Diani, and Ani were all looking at their Stones while Renloret and Yenne were alternating looking at the Singers and the Stones.

Pericha answered, its mellow tone soothing against the words Taryn heard. *We may be able to twist time with our songs, though only forward, and we cannot control the cosmos. There are other beings that can do that.* The tone rueful. *A comet was seen, and its message to us foretold that an asteroid would intersect with our home, and we had promised to safeguard our charges. We sang a search and found two. Another song prepared them for safe passage to those worlds.*

Kita continued the tune. *Too late we became aware of a missing feature on Lrakira, and there was no longer time enough to search for another sanctuary. The First Song, or Prophecy of The Blood and The Balance, was written to remind our charges of the need to send a Singer to Teramar to birth and raise The Blood and The Balance. Upon their return, the people would be saved and the twins would be accustomed to their new home. Only then would one of us be endangered, and The Balance would save a Stone, signaling the need for male Singers once again. Those portions of the prophecy have all come to fruition, though not quite as designed.*

Taryn smiled at the humorous tone of the last phrase. Did the Stone laugh?

Yenne raised his hand to gain Taryn's attention. "So just how were the people moved from their home planet to Lrakira and Teramar? I assume they did not have space travel at the time."

Pericha answered. *The people were sung into a deep sleep, and the Song of Saving transported them. And then we followed. The explanation of how transcends your science at this time. It is within the power of the song. It took all seven Stones to create the Song of Saving, which is not written in your history. Once safely on Lrakira and Teramar, the people awakened and dispersed according to their own tunes. Our Singers carried us with them so that each Stone could care for those assigned.*

"I can accept that there are things out there we are not yet able to understand," Taryn said. "How about you, Ani? You've been quiet. Are you doing okay?" She was sitting at the base of the Anyala Stone's pedestal, her chin in her hands, her eyes closed.

"I'm fine, and I will have to accept that there are things out there beyond our understanding. Who has the right to know how any of us got to where we are? We know *why*. The Stones saved us from an asteroid strike. Do we have to know *how*? It is what it is. We are here now. I'd rather deal with the now and the future."

"Uhm, okay," Taryn said. "Let's continue to the second stanza. Do we all agree that it has already happened?"

Even Kela nodded his head.

"Now the third stanza, Diani, please."

The Singer provided the third stanza.


*One Stone healed, now three to find.*
*One southern, one northern, and one an island home.*
*Three to teach three then with their worlds to share*
*The Song of Teaching to join separated kind.*
*Writings on walls and cloth the star path for the pilot are shown*
*A course to origin now ready and no longer bare.*

"So I understand this to mean that the three Stones of Teramar are scattered across the two largest continents and The Necklace Islands," Taryn said. "I'm assuming that, once found, the Stones will teach the new Singers, and then the Singers will spread the news that we are all aliens on Teramar. Actually, it sounds like we are all refugees from a natural disaster . . . on another planet. Perhaps the songs the Stones will sing will touch every soul and will ease the naysayers toward reality—no matter how unbelievable it is."

"It's possible," Layson said. "The Stones just said that an entire planet full of people were sung to sleep and transported to new worlds, so I can understand that a Song of Teaching could be sung to inform all of Teramar and Lrakira."

There was a humming in Taryn's head, and he smiled at Layson. "The Stones support your statement."

"What about the last two lines?" Renloret asked. "Those seem to involve me specifically if I understand the moniker the Stones often use when they speak of or to me."

Taryn looked up at the banners that hung above the Stones. "Well, I think you can find a few stars on at least one of the tapestries right here."

All three of the Stones brightened, and shades of their colors danced about the chamber.

"I believe you are correct," Renloret said, chuckling at the display. "But where would walls with star patterns be?"

"Kela says they have to be on Teramar, maybe in a cave," Ani said as she rubbed the base of Kela's ears.

Again, the Stones threw color, and the humming in Taryn's head echoed the joyful scene.

"Sheriff, what do you think this last line means?" Diani asked, pointing to it at the bottom of the page. She read it aloud again. "A course to origin now ready and no longer bare."

"Well, perhaps . . . ," Taryn stumbled over a flood of ideas. He would have to think about that.

"It's healed." The whispered statement drew all eyes to Ani. "The damage done by the asteroid has had one thousand years to mend, depending on when the original planet was struck. And now it's able to support our kind of life-forms again. I think we have an invitation to visit our peoples' original home."

Renloret pointed at the ancient weaving. "And I presume that the stars on the tapestry show what the stars looked like from the surface of that planet a thousand years ago." His smile stretched to its limits. "Ani's correct. The *wall* has to be on Teramar. I'll need to see it so I can triangulate, and then there is the thousand years of stellar movement to account for." He reached for Taryn's notepad.

"Hey! Slow down, pilot." Taryn swung the notepad out of reach and glared at the pilot. "Get your own notebook. And let's not jump to conclusions. Are you even sure those stars are real? I mean, they could be just the weaver's design couldn't they?"

Renloret frowned. "I'll have to study it, and that will take some time." He turned to Diani and Layson. "Can we get a detailed image of the tapestry that I can use while we travel to Teramar?"

"Of course. How soon do you need it?" Layson asked.

"By this eve? Oh, and it might be helpful to have a full-size paper version as well as an electronic image, especially if we might need to compare it to the wall once we find it on Teramar."

"I'll make the arrangements and have it delivered to your quarters." The Singer moved off to stand behind her Stone while tapping rapidly on her tablet.

Yenne cleared his throat to gain everyone else's attention. "I dislike bending the blade here, but science says one thousand years may not be long enough for a planet to recover from a large asteroid strike, depending on its composition and how it impacted the surface of the planet."

Flipping to another page in the notepad, Taryn added a note to ask Lrakiran scientists if they could speculate the length of time needed for a recovery that would allow the people to return. He tapped the paper surface with the marker, trying to wrap his thoughts around even one thousand years. His tapping slowed as an idea evolved, and he underlined a word in his notes. "Time."

"What about time?" Ani asked.

"Three Stones sang a Time Song to age us forward about twenty years, right?"

"Yes. So?" Renloret said.

"I think they only planned to age you forward ten sun-cycles," Diani said a bit defensively.

Taryn ignored her. "Listen. If it took three Stones a couple of hours to sing a song to age one planet forward ten to twenty years, how long do you think it would take one Stone to sing time forward many thousands of years?" He raised his eyebrows and looked at Diani.

Diani sighed. "I have no idea."

"I can't even begin to calculate it," Layson whispered, awe coloring her voice.

Taryn turned to the pilot. "Renloret? Got a guess?"

Renloret did not answer. He took the book of songs from Diani's hands. "Something about the fourth stanza," he muttered as he turned the page. Then he began to sing.

> *With their charges, six of seven sent to distant stars,*
> *new homes to protect and guide.*
> *Await the One left behind its world-healing song*
> *near complete, the plague a sign.*
> *In time to welcome reunion and blending of those*
> *sent safely away,*
> *Traditions of song and blade kept side by side,*
> *though three must hide*
> *Until Stone and Pilot join with six to open star*
> *paths in triangular line.*
> *Each world its people a choice to go or stay.*

The Stones of Lrakira remained silent until the last note ended. Taryn sucked in a breath as brilliant-colored ribbons seemed to wrap around the pilot and the Stones began to sing. Taryn felt the entire song deep inside. It actually made sense. Not that he understood everything about the First Song, but he knew it made sense. The Lrakiran and Teramaran peoples were not native to their current planets, and they were related. That was why they were physically identical. And it was why the customs of blade work, song, and dance were so important to their cultures. The Stones had somehow managed to maintain the cultures, even though three had been in seclusion for a thousand years. It was overwhelming.

And now that the signs that their original home was safe to return to had appeared, the Stones of Teramar needed Singers so they could inform the people of their origin and they could go there if desired. The pilot would find the location of that original home and would join with that solitary Stone to open some sort of pathway between the planets. The pilot was important—as important, if not more so—than The Blood and The Balance. The pilot.

Taryn looked at Renloret, who stood alone in the center of the chamber, eyes closed, the book of songs clutched to his chest, tears visible on his cheeks. He was nodding, unaware of the swirls of color that embraced him. As Taryn walked over to him, he could hear Renloret muttering.

"Yes, I will. I will find the first home, and then we will open the pathways. Yes, I will."

Taryn reached through the bands of waving colors to touch the pilot on the arm. He briefly wondered if he would feel the colors again like he had after pulling the blade from the Anyala Stone. There was no sensation. Ah, well, this was not as intense a situation as saving the life of a talking rock. He gave Renloret's arm a squeeze. "I have no doubt you will, Renloret."

"We need the other Stones. We have to go to Teramar and find them," Ani said.

"And Singers too. You will need two more," Layson added.

"Three Singers. We need three, one for each Stone on Teramar." Taryn jotted more notes on his pad.

"No, just two more, Taryn." Yenne wiped tears from his cheeks. "The song says you're the Singer of one of the Teramaran Stones.

We'll need two more. Shendahl would be so proud. Both of our children are Singers. Barely six years ago, the Lrakiran people were in danger of extinction, and the prospect of ever being a father was nonexistent. Now I am a parent of two, and they are both destined to be Singers."

Ani grasped Yenne's hand and pulled him into an embrace.

Taryn walked over and wrapped his arms around his sister and father. It felt like family. "How soon can we leave? My Stone has waited a thousand years. That is long enough."

# CHAPTER TEN

**"I** have a few more questions of the Stones," Yenne said. "I've been thinking about the Time Song."

"What about it?" Diani asked.

"Well, Ani mentioned several times that she overheard Reslo and S'Hendale discussing a lack of communications with *home*, though Ani would have associated home with Southern rather than another planet." He turned to her. "Can you remember any specifics?"

"Well, they usually stopped talking about it if I entered the room. But now that you mention it, there was one time when a woman burst into the laboratory demanding to be forgiven for not being able to fix a communications array. I don't remember her name, but she might be Yenne's communications officer, Sarinne Flaymatov. She said she'd done everything possible and that after almost a decade, she was still unable to send or receive anything. She requested to be relieved of duty and allowed to try to blend in because the situation was hopeless. Everyone back home would be dead by then, and there was not going to be a rescue ship.

"She stopped shouting at that point because she saw me in the corner of the room. I was doing some schoolwork while Mother finished an experiment. The woman looked frightened and ran out of the room. Mother ran after her. I remember wondering why she didn't just buy a ticket and go back to Southern if she didn't want to stay in Star Valley. I mean, I was only about fourteen, and no one had ever said anything about us needing to be rescued.

"Reslo came in a few minutes later and told me that the woman was overwrought about her family on Southern because she hadn't heard from them in a long time and that she would be leaving us." Ani shrugged. "I dismissed the whole incident. I was too involved with school and blade training at the time to be bothered by one of my mother's employees having family problems. That woman had always bothered me, and I was glad to know she was leaving."

"You didn't like her?" Taryn asked. "Did she ever threaten you?"

"Oh, it was nothing like that. On the rare occasions I saw her, she just stared at me with a creepy smile on her face. And once she said that if anything happened to Mother or Uncle Reslo, she'd be there for me. I thought it was a weird statement because she was never involved with my family. She was just an employee." But now Ani found herself wondering if there was something more to it than that, and the frowns on the faces of everyone else let her know that they were wondering the same thing.

Yenne began pacing around the chamber. "Well, her statement of not being able to send or receive signals for almost ten years supports my thinking that the Time Song created a barrier of some sort. At least around Teramar, and perhaps even around the entire Olbers solar system. Our signals couldn't get out, and Lrakira's couldn't get in. Diani, was there ever a break in the signals from Teramar here on Lrakira?"

Diani shook her head. "I didn't hear of any, but I can find out." She left the room to use the com unit in the hall. A few minutes went by before she returned, appearing annoyed. She confirmed a loss of contact for about five bells—the approximate length of the Time Song. There was also a record of a warning signal indicating that there was an equipment malfunction necessitating the need for repair immediately following the loss of contact. As was always the case when this happened, the system had shut itself down. The system apparently was repaired and restored shortly after Renloret was scheduled to land on Teramar.

"We Singers were not advised of these problems because the communications team did not believe we needed to know or would be interested in being informed of it," Diani said, finishing with a harrumph. It was clear to Ani that Diani would make sure that this oversight was not repeated in the future.

A rueful comment from Renloret suggested that the timing of the warning signal and subsequent shutdown coincided with the end of the Time Song and the suspected blocking of signals between the planets.

Taryn turned to the Stones. "How long was the Time Song

*supposed* to be?" Pericha's warm amber lights flickered, and he sighed deeply.

"Well? How long?" Ani asked. It was obvious that the Stone had aimed the answer at only Taryn.

"It's not as precise as I expected. The Pericha Stone says that the song was to last only as long as needed, but the attack on the Anyala Stone veered time off. The Stones don't seem to think of time in as small increments as we do. All Pericha and Kita know is that the Stones of Teramar awoke and were able to ensure that the pilot was saved. Pericha and Kita could only hope he would bring home The Blood and The Balance. Which he did. The Pericha Stone admits that our limited interstellar communications would have been blocked by the Time Song. But once the barrier dissolved after the shattering of the Time Song, all signals and communications should have been restored." Taryn looked to Renloret.

"Well, when I needed to pull the last star runner from its storage to get Ani to Lrakira, all I had to do was flip the power switch back on. I didn't think to check the communications array. I just wanted access to the star runner so I could get Ani to Lrakira. The equipment was covered in dust, and I had to bang my fist on one piece of it, but the power came up and everything seemed to work just fine."

Yenne cleared his throat. "So . . . after trying unsuccessfully to communicate with Lrakira for about ten years, Reslo may have approved a communications system shutdown because he thought the system was irreparable.

"Yes!" Ani shouted. "That's why he went to Southern! Uncle

Reslo said going there was his only choice." She went on to explain that her uncle had told her he was going because he might be able to use Southern's advanced technology to fix *the problem*, though he never explained what the problem was. And it never occurred to her to question what he meant because she was in the depths of grieving her mother's death. At first, he had contacted her almost daily. Then, about two months later, there were only intermittent communications between them. She remembered Reslo saying it had to do with increasing sunspot activity and that he expected it to decrease over the next year or so.

"Okay, that makes sense, and I will add checking on the communications array when we return to Star Valley to my list," Taryn said as he turned to a fresh page in his notepad. "Now, what about Treyder and his plans for mass deployment of the coma device on a battlefield?"

Renloret raised his hand. "Wait. Before we get too far into Treyder, does anyone have other questions for the Stones? The Treyder discussion can happen on the trip back to Teramar. Taryn, you should write down all you can remember about what Treyder said."

"I guess we can't really do anything about him until we get there and find out if my office has made progress in finding him." Taryn turned to Ani and took her hands in his. "As for finding these three new Stones, can you leave Lrakira? I want you with me."

Ani looked at the green crystal, its life light pulsing to some internal rhythm not unlike a heartbeat, and directed the question to it. She felt the cool, refreshing touch of the Stone.

"Yes, I can leave." She squeezed her brother's hands. "In fact, Anyala says I need to be on Teramar when the Song of Teaching is sung, which it will explain later. It also says that Singers who are off-world can maintain a minimal amount of communication with their Stones if they have their blade nearby. And as we have already noted, the blade retains its ability to heal physical injuries when the proper song is sung." She looked at Renloret. "My thanks for remembering the Song of Healing."

He bowed. "I almost didn't."

She frowned. "But I remember you and Taryn singing for me."

"A tale for another time, dear heart."

A blush of pleasure warmed her face at the endearment, and both Taryn and Yenne smiled.

Clapping her hands several times to get everyone's attention, Diani said, "All right, that will be enough. You can share that tale while traveling to Teramar." She tucked Yenne's arm against hers and moved toward the chamber door.

Kela rubbed against Ani's leg. *I'm not sure I want to hear it. I was there, and I lost you then.*

Squatting at his side, Ani wrapped her arms around his neck. *I'm back now. Forever.* She stood and beckoned to Taryn and Renloret. Offering each man an arm, she stepped between them, and the trio, trailed by Kela and Layson, followed Diani and Yenne out.

△ △ ⵣ 𝔸

Treyder leaned over the balcony and dropped the yellow flag. Fourteen soldiers rushed into the practice battle site from various portals. Each had been supplied with a dozen modified sliver blades sheathed in cross-body sashes. Having been told they were the first to use the unique weapons, the soldiers were eager to earn points by marking opponents with blotches of ink to test the accuracy of the explosive-powered hollow blades.

During their introduction to this deep secret program, they had witnessed the small explosions that would occur when ignition buttons on the hilts were pressed. They had practiced for several hours the previous day, learning how to draw and fire the weapons—without ammunition—from various positions. This morn they were given sashes of loaded blades and brought to the blade practice rings, which had temporary walls, stairs, and other obstacles installed to create a large maze. Every hit would be counted by the observers stationed evenly about the balcony. And when a soldier was hit, he was required to sit and wait until a group of assistants arrived to move them to a special wing in the next building, which Treyder had set up as his new laboratory.

Treyder watched in fascination as the soldiers maneuvered through the maze. Only he, the observers, and the servants assisting knew that along with packages of ink, the blades carried capsules the size of manthra grains that held the first mass-produced coma devices. Not only would this exercise show the accuracy of the soldiers and weapons, it would test the newly designed dissolvable capsules aimed at protecting the tiny devices from damage should the soldier miss and hit a wall or other hard surface. The capsules were easier to locate than the coma device, which was the size of coarse sand. Treyder had been impressed by the mechanic's suggestion to protect the device while still allowing the capsule to dissolve once it entered a body. Once free from the capsule, the device would burrow its way to a blood vessel and travel to the brain, where it would sever or deaden the desired brain functions according to the programming installed.

The training session lasted until the final two soldiers fired simultaneously. Observers noted the length of time from hit to unconsciousness related to where on the body the hit occurred. Servants who moved soldiers before they were completely unconscious reported hearing comments that the hits felt like getting sprayed with gravel, stinging hard but not necessarily bleeding enough to cause concern. Several of the soldiers also endured burns to their faces and hands from the explosives. Every word spoken by the soldiers was dutifully noted for inclusion on the soldiers' records that would stay with the soldier throughout the experiment until death.

After the first few mini-explosions, Treyder ceased flinching but made notes to explore other ways to propel the capsules a greater distance with less noise and no burns. He really did not want to decimate Northern's soldiers with injuries. At the meeting following the training exercise, one of the mining experts suggested replacing the chemical explosive with handheld hydraulic power. He'd even provided Treyder with a sketch of a sliver blade with an attached pump and pressure gauge. Treyder saw that it might satisfy both his and the senator's desires, and he assigned the man several technicians to begin working on the new modification. Pleased with the unique thinking, he gave the group one month to come up with two designs, one for individual use and the other for a machine that would fire up to one hundred encapsulated coma devices with a single powerful blast.

While they were properly distracted from what was to happen to the soldiers, Treyder ensconced himself in the laboratory with its two rows of seven metal platforms. Each platform displayed the naked, freshly shaved body of a comatose soldier. Trusting only himself to apply the electrodes and sensors, Treyder took meticulous notes on what experiments he planned for each soldier. Once hooked into the computers, also provided by Senator Nelham through the soldiers' commanding officer, Treyder made sure each specimen was fully unresponsive by taking baseline readings for two days before starting the experiments.

Now that he had so many test subjects, Treyder was able to do so much more than he would have with only Ani Chenak or the upstart sheriff, Taryn Avere. He now saw the first two as preliminary experiments, which were bound to fail, and he knew he had learned from them. But over the course of the first eight days, Treyder found he was curious about whether the sheriff would make an appearance and if he had also been cured of the coma like the Chenak girl. He tried to remember how many weeks had passed from the fight in the cavern to the girl's surprising appearance at his office. It was about two months. He decided to not worry about it until then and put a note on his calendar two months hence.

⊓ △ ⚸ 五

During the trip to Teramar, Ani and Taryn were introduced to a variety of aliens onboard the large, fast star traveler. Ani was slightly miffed at Kela's particular interest in the telepathic feline-like Slerdonian technician, Grarr. Ani found the alien a thoroughly curious mix of a feline body, an almost human-like torso with a pair of arms, and a Kreline-like head.

Ani had caught herself lamenting over how much time Kela spent with the fur-covered, tail-and-whisker bearing quadruped, even though Kela told her everything he learned about the individual. Secretly embarrassed, Ani frequently caught herself wanting to call Grarr a creature instead of using his name, perhaps because he was now a rival for Kela's attention.

Kela seemed patient with her petulance about the technician, which helped, especially since they'd only known him for barely a week, and he was evidently related to the Slerdonian ambassador to Lrakira. The Slerdonian was the most visually alien individual on the ship Ani had seen. Of course, Kela kept reminding her that the Stones were also alien beings and that at least Grarr had two arms, which Kela did not.

Taryn had also been intrigued by Grarr and spent much of his free time shadowing the creature, peppering him with questions. Having another telepath on board had shocked Ani, though the Slerdonian's telepathy was said to be one-way—from him to a specific person—and he could not read minds or thoughts.

It had surprised Ani that the ship's personnel had received bio-teacher implants loaded with Teramar's Northern language. It made her uncomfortable knowing everyone but Taryn, Kela, and her had an implant. Ani was still resisting the idea, and instead of an implant, Ani used her spare time to study educational vids and listen to the vast collection of cultural songs she had found. She participated in impromptu entertainment sessions, sharing some of her favorite songs from Teramar as well as some of the Lrakiran songs she had learned.

When Renloret showed up at the second gathering, Ani sidestepped performing, though she was entranced when he sang with his fellow Lrakirans. Afterward, she surreptitiously asked other crew members for the titles of the songs and had been practicing a few of the alto parts from several she had particularly enjoyed. She wanted to surprise him.

Kela had made numerous friends over the past five or six days and was treated as if he were, well, Ani could only describe it as *human*. But even though that was how she felt about him, she was surprised at the ease of acceptance by the ship's personnel after so many years of having to hide their telepathic connection and Kela's intelligence. To everyone on the ship, Kela was just another alien. More often than not, when he was included in conversations, Ani was assigned the role of translator. Ani quickly realized that she enjoyed the lack of worry that came along with the acceptance. She found that she hoped the people of Northern would come to accept the reality of alien life-forms so she and Kela wouldn't have to hide their "alienness." She wanted to be accepted as who she was.

By the time there were two or three days left of the trip from Lrakira to Teramar, Ani and Taryn had logged in more story-telling hours than usually occurred in a year. They each shared memories with both Yenne and Renloret. Likewise, her father had filled them in on his pre-Teramaran history and the six years he'd been on Teramar. There had been a few tears and much laughter. Ani had finally admitted that the relationship between Taryn and Yenne was more like cousins than father and son. The two men had latched on to that and were developing a plausible story line to present to the residents of Star Valley, with a few exceptions: Melli and Gelwood, Mroz, and Reslo.

During one of these discussions they were all surprised when an interstellar message came through from Reslo. There had been a desperate tone to Reslo's voice in the automated message, which seemed to be serving a purpose much like an emergency beacon. They guessed that he had somehow managed to get the message attached to the general outreach beacon without the Southern scientists discovering it.

Yenne said that he would write an official response to Reslo with the approximate date of the ship's arrival. He suspected that Reslo had programmed the signal to make any response to the beacon something only he would notice. Yenne had confidence that Reslo would return to Star Valley as soon as he received their response. He asked Taryn to create appropriate messages to be sent to the Star Valley sheriff's office and to Taryn's parents, saying that he was well enough to come home and would contact them in a couple of days.

Taryn nodded and left the room. Yenne sighed and rubbed his forehead before dismissing the rest. Ani realized the strain of the situation was wearing on him, just as it was on her. Perhaps she could be more understanding.

Ani waited with Kela until the conference room had been emptied before heading to the training room she had scheduled. She would be a few minutes late, but the slot was for two hours. She stopped outside the exercise room. Kela was wagging his tail. *What?*

*Renloret waits for you. I shall go in search of Grarr to pass my time.* He gave her a canine grin and dodged out of reach as her hand moved to swat him. His privacy wall slid into place as he trotted away, tail flagging his happiness.

Ani contemplated the door. Over the days that had passed since the ship had set coordinates for Teramar, there was little opportunity for Renloret and Ani to be alone. Either Taryn or Yenne had always accompanied the pilot or her, and she felt it unbecoming to interrupt or ask them to leave so she could have the pilot to herself. She had wondered if he'd noticed how often her name appeared on the training room schedule. Evidently, he had intended to surprise her. But thanks to Kela, *she* could surprise *him*. She touched the entry pad and it slid open.

Steadying her breathing, she slowly raised her foot. A blade nosed out. She smashed the blade from his grip with stinging force, and he stumbled into the hall. She laughed as he cursed Kela for warning her. He turned to face a grinning opponent.

"I thought you'd gone back to your room," she said.

"Obviously, I didn't," he countered, rubbing his wrist. "Perhaps I should have."

She slid a foot beneath the blade and with a kick, tossed it to him. He caught it and playfully brandished it. Instead of shifting into a guard position as he probably expected, she smiled and licked her lips slowly. Brushing his blade aside with her forearm, she stepped close and walked her fingers up his chest and round to the back of his neck.

"My time slot is valid for the next two hours, and it's been too long since we've had time for each other. Let's not waste this opportunity. It may be the last one we get for a while." Her voice was soft with yearning. With a slight tug on his neck, she flicked her head toward the exercise room. "Join me?"

Electronic communications with the sheriff's office had been frequent over the previous two days, so groundwork had been laid for their arrival, with specifics to be given the day before their actual arrival in the valley. Yenne and Renloret had even managed to allow a short connection between Taryn and his parents just prior to landing.

Yenne was careful to stay out of the visual and left the room shortly after the connection was made. Ani noticed him wiping his forearm across his eyes before the door swished shut and made a move to follow him, but Renloret stopped her. "He must figure out how he feels about the plan now that its execution is imminent. Allow him the privacy and respect to grieve over what he did not know he had lost. He needs time. You lost your mother more than a year ago, but he lost her only two months ago. Plus, he knows he is the only one of the original team not to have been aged forward. Even his little brother is seventeen years older than Yenne is now, not three years younger. I think that will be harder on him than what is happening now."

Renloret shook his head when she still tried to follow and pulled her into the chair next to him, clasping her hands in his. "Think, Ani. Can you imagine being in his place?"

She shook her head. "Nor can I imagine being in Melli's, Gelwood's, or Reslo's. It's difficult enough for me, and even though we've talked about it and planned what to say, I know none of us are prepared for what Taryn and his family will go through."

They held hands in silence as they listened to Taryn assuaging his parents' concerns about his health. Ani heard him tactfully talk around the edges of the story they had concocted until they could be face-to-face. He kept repeating that there was much more to tell but he wanted to wait—that it would be better for all if he could explain in private. When Gelwood pressed for those details, Ani was surprised to hear the sheriff voice come through in Taryn's tone. Evidently, Gelwood heard and understood because he abruptly dropped the questioning. Taryn followed up by assuring them that all their questions would be answered when he was with them in the morn. He clicked off the connection and remained in the chair, staring out the observation window, the rotating planet with its ringed moon hanging like a painting against the blackness of space.

He held out a hand to her, his chin trembling. "Ani?"

She moved quickly to his side and embraced him. Ani felt Renloret leave the conference room, giving the siblings some privacy. She relaxed her grip on her emotions, and they cried together.

Once they had voiced their shared sorrow and concerns about how the unchangeable past would impact the future of their families, Ani persuaded Taryn to join her in a lengthy blade workout. They both needed the physical and emotional release a good workout would provide. Taryn had been less predictable than expected and it had distracted them both, wringing out their worries. Now she rubbed her sore muscles as she and Taryn watched the ship settle on the pad, deep in the launch tower.

Taryn had been excited throughout the landing, which had been masked like the earlier ones so it would be undetected by those on the planet's surface. Ani realized Taryn was not as overwhelmed with the experience of returning to Teramar as she had been, and she found herself a bit envious of his self-control. The view had been similarly spectacular as they had approached the planet's surface—though, instead of summer green, the foliage was in its autumnal glory. Shades of gold, red, and purple appeared in a scattered patchwork from the mountains to the fields in mid-harvest.

When the exit ramp lowered, the siblings gathered all their baggage and scurried out of the way as Renloret and Yenne stored the star runner. They all allowed Yenne a few minutes to gaze around the launch tower and controls, which had seen very little activity over the last twenty years. Most of it was still covered in dust from disuse. Yenne had laughingly exclaimed that several Lrakiran scientists would be interested in studying the equipment to see how it had held up for those twenty years. He and Renloret shook their heads at the oddness of time caused by the Stones' song.

Ani held Taryn's hand as they walked through the tunnel that connected the launch tower to the lake house. Before landing, Renloret had hovered the star runner above the house to see if anyone was on the property or making their way up the rutted dirt road to it. They had planned a quiet eve at the lake house reviewing the next day's planned activities as well as where each was going to sleep. Ani was only a little surprised when Yenne refused the use of the master bedroom, deciding to stay in the smallest of the guest rooms.

The simple eve meal was eaten in near silence. After the dishes had been cleared, cleaned, and put away, Ani watched as Taryn fidgeted with his glass of saltren gin. She also found it difficult to be still. Taryn sighed deeply and excused himself from the room. She heard the back door close.

"Is he going to be all right?" her father asked.

"I don't know. And I don't know how to help him," she said

while swirling the cinnamon-laced alcohol in her glass. The ripples looked like one of the very distant galaxies she'd seen from the star ship viewing deck before they'd slowed to enter the star system that was home to Teramar.

*I can go if he needs someone to talk to,* Kela offered as he stood up from where he'd been curled in front of the fireplace.

*That would be good,* she sent back to him. Ani placed her glass on the side table and led the way to the back door.

Her brother was squatting on the far side of the pool, swishing his hand back and forth in the water. Someone, Mroz probably, had come up recently and skimmed leaves and debris from the water surface. The skim nets were leaning against the tool shed alongside a bucket with work gloves lopped over the edge. She'd have to figure out a way to thank the bartender. He would be informed of their return in the morn. Kela reached Taryn and snuffled at his neck. Taryn settled cross-legged and put his arm around the canine.

"He's a good listener," Ani said.

Taryn waved, acknowledging her words. Ani went back inside, confident that Kela would be what her brother needed. In the living room, Yenne and Renloret had not moved. Each stared at the flames and swirled their drinks.

# CHAPTER THIRTEEN

"Are you sure you want to do this alone?" Ani couldn't help asking for the hundredth time. Taryn smiled and nodded.

"It'll be fine. I have the journal and its translation if they want to read it." He patted the bundle he had tucked under his arm. Then he handed over a sheaf of papers. "Can you turn in the notes of my interview with Treyder? I've also made notes of what I can recall him saying about his plans for the coma device before I lost consciousness. And tell them I will see my crew soon. Be sure to use the word *crew*. They'll be more open with you. Then I think we can meet you at Mroz's bar in a couple of hours." He leaned close, kissed her on the cheek, and gave her a one-armed hug. "Now go."

It was all so brotherly, she couldn't help giving him a tremulous smile. Ani watched him take two steps at a time up to his parents' porch. The curtain had moved.

"Nahnah! Dah! I'm home."

The door opened, and arms pulled him inside.

She slipped back into the driver's seat of the wheeler to see Renloret give her a sidelong look and a wink. In the backseat, Yenne reached up and patted her on the back. Last eve they had talked repeatedly about how to share what had to be world-shattering news with Melli and Gelwood. Taryn had resisted having anyone else in the room with him while he explained. She supposed he was correct, but she couldn't help wanting to be there. With a sigh, she pulled her bottom lip between her teeth and pressed her foot on the fuel pedal and eased the vehicle onto the paved road toward the sheriff's office.

A few minutes later, Ani and Renloret were greeted with a squeal of delight as Daneeha scrambled down from her chair and ran to them. After the first rush of greetings, Ani introduced Yenne as a relative of her father who had asked to accompany them back to Northern. Even with his mustache and jawline beard, Ani had prepared him for the possibility that Daneeha would see through the ruse, but they had decided not to complicate things more than necessary. Ani watched the diminutive secretary carefully throughout the first few minutes. She had accepted Yenne's perfunctory salute—done in what she would have recognized as Southern style rather than the usual Northern—without comment or a second glance. Ani breathed a sigh of relief. They might get away with it for a while longer.

Even so, Ani noticed a certain amount of tension in how each person in the office held themselves, and furtive looks passed between the deputies and Daneeha. Ani wondered if Yenne still looked too much like himself, though Daneeha was the only one old enough to have known him twenty years ago.

Yantel asked why Taryn was not present, and Ani explained that he had felt it important to see his parents before doing anything else. He had asked them to go ahead of him to the sheriff's office and promised that he would *see his crew soon.* Immediately, everyone in the office visibly relaxed, and she realized the phrase was a code. The entire atmosphere changed from closed and questioning to acceptance.

Without another word, Yantel ushered them into a conference room where the walls were covered with notes, an occasional photo, and a large map of Northern with several colored flag pins that had dates written on them. Yantel shut the door, took a place at the head of the table, and motioned for everyone else to take seats of their own. The interim sheriff explained that the conference room was sound-sealed, so anyone stopping by unannounced would not overhear their conversation. Yenne grunted his approval, which caused Daneeha to frown and glance at the *relative* from Southern.

Yantel asked Daneeha to read the latest information on the investigation in Saedi City, and Daneeha traced a finger down her notes. Traces of Taryn's blood in the drain at the Saedi City laboratory had been confirmed and his uniform jacket with a torn pocket was discovered in a trash bin in the basement of the building. The tear matched the scrap of cloth Ani and Renloret found in Treyder's research center office. With those two pieces of information, a continent-wide alert had been sent out for Treyder's arrest two days ago. An award for information leading to the doctor's arrest was being offered, and several leads were being followed up on. Then she confirmed receipt, four days ago, of an electronic message from an unknown source. It had been in the special code only Taryn would have known and stated that the coma device had been removed and injuries received through torture had healed enough for Taryn to return to Northern. The office had expected personal contact from Taryn at any time. She looked up from her notes and smiled. "Right on time."

"Now, are there any questions?" Yantel asked.

Ani handed over Taryn's notes. "Sheriff Avere said you might be able to use these in your investigation. They're his recollection of the interview he conducted with Treyder the eve of his abduction and what he recalls Treyder saying and doing before he lost consciousness. We all have read it, so if you have any immediate questions, we can answer for Sheriff Avere. He will be available for further discussion tomorrow. He is spending the day with his parents."

Yantel gave a nod of approval. "As I expected. Daneeha, I'd like you to inform the deputy in Saedi City of the sheriff's safe and healthy return from Southern. Now, let's hear what the sheriff has to say."

The acting sheriff gave a long sigh as he settled into his chair and began reading Taryn's notes aloud. The secretary had a notepad out and wrote comments and questions down as they were voiced.

Four arms encircled him, and Taryn gratefully accepted the

crushing embrace. They were all crying. Yes, this was home. These were his parents. Biology had nothing to do with it. Biology had only expanded his family.

He had no idea how long they stood just inside the doorway hugging and crying. Pats on his back from his father, Gelwood, were a comfortable signal that the first overwhelming reactions were nearing manageability.

"Welcome home, son," Gelwood said in a trembling voice.

Taryn realized he'd never seen his father cry before, and the word *son* spiked through his heart. Would he still be Gelwood's son at the end of the conversation? The next few hours might be more difficult than he had thought.

"I'm glad to be home, Dah." He deliberately used the term he hadn't used in many years. Taryn wanted to affirm, however subtly, his connection to his parents. He turned his head and spoke softly in his mother's ear. "Nahnah, would you make some tea. We have much to talk about."

She used one hand to brush dampness off her cheeks. "Tea. Yes, of course." She patted his cheek, also damp with tears. "Come and sit. The water is ready, as are we." Her hand lingered on his arm as if she dared not let him go. She reached for Gelwood's hand and pulled the two men into the living room.

Taryn doubted they were truly ready for what he was going to tell them, and he was not ready to do the telling.

Gelwood settled into his chair, placing the crutch within reach, and motioned Taryn to take a seat. Melli scurried into the kitchen, returning with a tray of warm cheese muffins and a large pot of her cinnamon tea.

"Now, you said we have much to talk about," Gelwood said. "Our vid call assured us of your full recovery, and you look none the worse for your travails, outside of your hair." Gelwood grinned and reached out to scrub his hand across the bristly growth.

Taryn ducked away. "Dah, it's growing back."

"Yes, it is. I assume you'll be joining in the efforts to find Treyder as soon as we are done here."

Taryn pointed out that he could not conduct the kidnapping investigation himself because he was the victim. He added that the interim sheriff was doing an exemplary job and would keep Taryn informed.

"I've sent Renloret, Ani, and another ahead to turn in my recollections of the interview with Treyder before I was rendered unconscious. However, we have other topics to discuss, which may take some time."

His parents shared surprised glances. "From your tone of voice and reluctance to talk on the tel-com yesterday, we assumed there was more. What else have you discovered?" Melli asked.

He cleared his throat, took a third and fourth gulp of tea, and began.

With an apologetic tone, Taryn startled them by turning the topic of discussion to aliens and what their thoughts were on the rumored involvement of Ani's family with beings from other planets. Gelwood admitted discussing the possibility with Melli after witnessing the bizarre attempt by Stubin Dalkey to break open Shendahl's casket to prove there was no body because the aliens had taken her away. Though they had never seen evidence of such over the almost twenty-five years since the Southerners had arrived in Star Valley, they had accepted the possibility of aliens, what with all the other celestial bodies in the night sky. They could imagine other worlds, other intelligences. But they were not afraid of such.

They surprised Taryn by being more accepting of the idea than he thought they would be. Gelwood mentioned having numerous conversations with the Southerners on the topic and that he enjoyed the speculation. His father had hesitated at that point then asked outright if Taryn had discovered proof of aliens.

Taryn studied their rapt, solemn faces. "You are not far from reality, Dah." Whether or not they were ready, he had to get it all out as quickly as possible. Now was the time.

He hurried on so neither could interrupt. He told them all he'd learned about Ani and her Lrakiran birthright, the reason the "Southerners" had come, and Renloret's stunning realization that Ani was the child whose blood would save his and her parents' people and that she was a Stone Singer. Taryn told them about singing the healing song in the cavern with Renloret, the discovery of the launch tower and its star runner hidden in the mountain behind the old research center, and how he hadn't known if they would ever see Ani again after Renloret left for a planet called Lrakira.

Astonishment registered on their faces. Gelwood was stone still, his tea cup half raised to his lips. Taryn wondered if he was breathing.

Melli had covered her mouth with both hands. Her words were muffled. "Aliens? You're telling me our dearest and closest friends, Shendahl and Yenne, were aliens? And their daughter is now a performer of some type?" She shook her head in disbelief.

"A Singer, Nahnah. She's the Anyala Stone's Singer. It's an interpreter of sorts who passes messages between the guardian Stones and the Lrakiran people." He pushed on.

Another pot of tea had been drunk by the time Taryn had told them all he could about what had happened to Ani before her return from "Southern" and how and why she'd come back to find the twin.

Waving her hand at this point, Melli interrupted. "The twin died, Taryn. She died. I saw her in the wood box just before Shendahl placed you in my arms. I told Ani her sister had died. Gelwood, I told you everything before Taryn was kidnapped, didn't I?" Her voice was soft in shock.

Gelwood nodded. "Yes, you told me." He stood and limped over to Melli's side and draped his arm over her shoulder. Then he cocked his head at Taryn, his eyes pleading for explanation.

"The twin didn't die, Nahnah." He felt his heart crack.

"Did the Stone die?" Melli asked, as if she hadn't heard his words.

Taryn shook his head. "No. It lives. The Balance—the twin— saved it. *I* saved it."

Gelwood bit his lip.

Melli stood. Her hands were twisting and turning, her eyes shifting between the door to the hallway and the door to the kitchen as if looking for an escape. "Shendahl said she had everything she needed or wanted in her daughter, and being able to lay my son in my arms would help her through her grief at losing the twin. She said you were a gift . . ." Her voice buckled as tears streamed down her cheeks.

Taryn would not ever be able to describe the look on Melli's face. His heart wrenched at the pain and confusion, and then the understanding. Finally, an expression of knowing crossed her face.

With tears running freely down his cheeks, he explained that the girl was *their* child. And when Shendahl had been unable to save the baby's life, she had made the impossible choice. Taryn picked up the mother's journal and presented it as evidence. Shendahl had misunderstood the directive and absolutely believed Ani was both The Blood and The Balance, that her daughter's blood would save the people of Lrakira from extinction, *and* she would save one of the guardians.

Taryn paged through the journal, reading snippets. She wrote how Taryn could be the child they might never have and how much she loved Gelwood and Melli Avere. Taryn closed the journal saying, "We may not understand her motives completely, but she was positive it was the correct and right thing to do. And I, your son, would not have it any other way." He handed the journal to Melli. "It's all in there. I had it translated so you and I could read it. Her thoughts. Her feelings. Her resolution to cherish the opportunity she'd been given to share her family with you."

Once again, he wondered if he still had a family. His parents stared at each other for a long time. Their hands were entwined and white-knuckled as they rested atop the journal. Were they breathing? Should he say something? What?

Melli turned to face Gelwood. "Oh, Gelwood. Shendahl

handed me *our* son. I don't care who his mother was, he's ours
. . . our son." She bent her head, tears splashing across the clasped
hands and the journal.

Taryn felt the piercing blue-eyed stare from his father. He
returned the stare. "Dah?" The tears started to fall as Gelwood
held out a hand and pulled Taryn to his chest in a crushing
embrace. "My son." It was a statement of fact.

Taryn sucked in a sob of relief and joy.

A few moments later, Gelwood eased his grip on Taryn. He
gently brought his wife's hands to his lips. "Come. Come with
me to the garden."

Taryn passed the crutch to him, gathered the journal and its
translation from his mother's lap, and followed his parents to
the back door. They walked to the bench and fountain. Melli
sat in the middle and patted the space on either side of her.
They nestled close, Taryn and his father each grasping one of her
hands. A tremulous smile worked its way across her lips as tears
threatened again.

"You know, the fountain was a gift from Shendahl on your
first birthday. I don't think Yenne knew about it."

A trickle of water splashed its way over the various levels into
a small pool. Taryn studied it, seeing it for what seemed to be
the first time. What was the story behind it? In his memory, it
had always been in the garden. He had never really taken notice
of it before. It was just a fountain with statues of three children
playing in the water.

Melli pointed at the engraving at its base. "Do you know what
that says? Shendahl said it was in Southern and that someday

I might want to know what it said. I suspect it's really in this Lrakiran language. Is it in the journal?" There was hope in her voice.

Taryn focused on the tiny symbols of Lrakiran script. Finally, he recognized it. "Yes. Wait a moment." He paged through the translation to about a year after the birth. "Something like it is here. It's a bit longer in the journal than on the inscription." He recited the inscription:

> *He is a freely given gift, mother to mother.*
> *Given with great joy and love.*
> *Our children will forever connect us.*
> *I could not do otherwise.*

Then he read what she had added in the journal. "'I have had the lines engraved and will deliver it to Melli and Gelwood on Taryn's birthday. I have the hope of my world in Ani. Though I will have to leave my dearest friends at some point, we will always be connected through our children. It is my hope that our friendships will outlast the stars. I hope to return to Teramar and explain once my people are safe. My heart is full, and I would do it again without hesitation. What we share is incomparable. May the Stones bless them as they have blessed me.'"

Only the sound of splashing water disturbed the after-morn quiet.

Melli shifted in her position. "To be honest, I'm trying desperately not to be angry, to understand why and how she did what she did. How could she not tell me? Not tell us?" She shook her head. "Did she not trust us with the knowledge?"

"It was her secret, Nahnah. She told no one. Even Yenne did not until he . . ." He stopped. "According to the journal. And I did not know until after the coma device had been removed."

"Who told you?" Melli managed to ask.

"Ani."

"When did she find out?" Gelwood asked.

"The night I was kidnapped by Treyder." He filled them in on what Renloret had read to Ani from the journal. "They were prepared for anything—except that I was her twin."

Melli turned her head into Gelwood's shoulder, and he rubbed her back.

After several moments of silence, Gelwood commented that biology was not the only way to be a family. Melli and he had often talked about adopting, even after Taryn had filled their world with love and laughter. Melli concurred and followed up with a statement that the friendship between the two couples had been strengthened by the birth trials of their children. Even back then, she had felt as though her own family had been expanded because of her bond with Shendahl. She pulled the two men into her arms, affirming to Taryn that their relationship had not changed, even though the history of it had.

They were making their way back toward the house when Melli stopped. "Taryn, wait. According to the journal, Shendahl didn't tell anyone, even Yenne, about the twin. But you also said something about Yenne not finding out exactly who the twin was until he . . . what? You didn't finish the sentence. How would he have found out at all if he was dead?" Her voice was so soft, the question roared in his ears.

He rubbed the stubble on his scalp, suddenly wishing he had all his hair back and he didn't look like a child who'd picked up a croshin infestation.

Melli frowned at him. "He didn't die in the attack, did he?"

Sighing, Taryn shook his head. He had to tell the truth. "No. He escaped in one of the star runners stored in the launch tower during the attack that destroyed the research center. He took copies of most of the research they had completed, verifying Ani was The Blood. He was planning to return within a few months to pick up everyone, but . . . some things happened . . . and time . . . well, time was altered and—"

"And what?" Gelwood asked. Though there was only encouragement and curiosity in his tone, Taryn silently cursed the Stones and the Time Song.

He sighed. "There's more." Taryn explained the ruined Time Song and how Yenne was alive and had not aged forward because he'd not been on Teramar during the song. He added that when Renloret arrived on Lrakira with Ani, Yenne was stunned to find that his daughter was not five years old but twenty-five, his wife was dead a year, and his brother was down in Southern continuing his efforts to get a message to Lrakira by using Southern's satellites. "It's been a stressful couple of months for him, for all of them."

Melli started to say something, but he waved her quiet. "I know this is a lot. Believe me. I know. If I get it all out, we can handle it. Trust me, we'll be all right."

She closed her eyes, squeezing tears out under her lashes. Gelwood reached out and brushed the tears from her cheek.

Taryn felt the lump in his throat threaten to stop his words. He started again. "And yes, I've met him. And we've talked—a lot. We're coming to terms with our shared circumstances—probably better than Ani and him. She's been spending a lot of time in the workout rooms."

That brought a softening to his parent's faces.

"You need to know that without question, Yenne understands you are my parents—not Shendahl and him. He is struggling more with Shendahl's death and the number of years he has missed with his family, with Ani . . . and me."

"He was in the backseat of Ani's wheeler." Melli's voice was calmer than he thought it would be. "How is he handling all of this?"

"Sometimes better than others. Ani and he had a rough introduction from the stories I've heard. And it's taken them a couple of months to start coming to terms with their relationship. Ani thinks he treats her as if she were still five. And even though he's known all his life that time can be twisted in various ways, he's struggling with missing all those years with Shendahl, Reslo, Mroz, and you two. At least I've had both parents for all that time."

Melli tsked several times then wove her arm around Taryn's. "Well, how are you about him?" Sometimes she could strike the target without throwing a blade.

Taryn tilted his head. "He feels more like a young uncle or older cousin than a biological father. He wanted to stay out of the way until you were ready to see him." Taryn looked at Gelwood, who was frowning. "Dah, he has no intention of replacing you as my father. He has said numerous times that you two are my parents. Besides, he has Ani to deal with, and that's more than enough." He couldn't resist chuckling. His father joined him.

Melli sighed and patted his arm. "All right, that's enough for now. My head and heart need some time, and I need to make dinner plans and more tea. I'm not sure how it will be to meet someone who's been dead for twenty years." She turned to Gelwood. "Your thoughts?"

"I've always wished he hadn't died in the attack. I've wanted him to know that Shendahl saved my life and my leg. Life is a series of adjustments. This is larger and more complicated than most, so we'd best get on with it."

# CHAPTER FOURTEEN

Taryn studied their faces over the edge of his mug. The earthy pine scent helped calm his thoughts. He'd just finished telling them about revealing his identity to his parents.

"Mother is all excited about hosting 'aliens,' even though she knows you. She said that it would be more fun to eat with aliens than be eaten by them. She wanted to know how many to plan for." He grimaced. "I told them I'd have to discuss it with all of you."

Kela snugged underneath Taryn's arm and placed his forepaws on the middle rungs of the stool to get his head above the counter. The animal seemed to stare at Ani. Taryn waited to see if she would translate.

"Kela asks if the invitation includes Yenne. Are they ready to meet an unaged alien? And is he ready to see them face-to-face?"

Neither Taryn nor Yenne answered immediately. Taryn studied Yenne, who sat silently with both hands wrapped around his mug. It looked like he was hiding behind it. Taryn understood that Yenne would graciously acquiesce to whatever decision was made. And even though his parents had opened the invitation, Taryn knew the decision was really up to him.

A screech of chair legs on the ceramic tile shattered the mood. Taryn stood, placing both hands on his hips. He glanced at Ani, giving her a lopsided grin and then turned his gaze on Yenne, who lifted his head to meet it. "Fortunately, Mother saw you in the wheeler and guessed your identity. They've been informed of the time circumstances. The invitation includes you. Also, I want to show them more proof about Lrakira and the Stones. I watched several vids on the star traveler that I'd like to share with them if that is allowed."

Yenne placed his mug on the counter and reached across to grasp Taryn's forearm firmly. "I don't see any problems with that. Renloret can get what you need from the star runner mobile translator and . . . thank you."

Taryn and Renloret went out to the camouflaged star runner and returned with a tabletop translator and several three-dimensional vids used to inform new interstellar contacts about the Stones and Singers. Ani trooped them out to the wheeler and headed into the village. Weighty silence filled the air around them as Ani drove toward the Averes' home.

Taryn looked sideways at Yenne then closed his eyes, tipped his head back on the headrest, and practiced blade ring competition breathing, occasionally drumming his fingers on his thighs. In spite of all he had told them, he worried how Gelwood and Melli would react when faced with the reality that Yenne was still alive.

The wheeler maneuvered two more turns. Kela had stuck his

head between the seats and was resting his muzzle on Yenne's arm. Even without a telepathic connection between them, Kela seemed to understand. Whispered encouragement from Renloret seemed to help Yenne steady himself. Taryn heard him exhale as the wheeler slowed, rolling to a stop in front of the house. The engine noise ceased, but no one moved.

"The house looks the same except the trees are taller," Yenne said.

Taryn turned to look out the vehicle window, trying to remember what it had looked like when he was five. There was no specific memory that included the size of the trees. Hadn't they always been tall?

"Ready?" Ani asked.

"Yes," Yenne said as he got out.

Renloret and Taryn were followed by Kela, who galloped up the porch steps to bark at the door. Ani joined the men, and Taryn was able to maneuver Ani past him to stand next to Yenne directly in front of the door. Taryn was pleased to see her take Yenne's hand and give it a squeeze. Yenne reciprocated and added a tentative smile to his daughter. The door opened.

Melli came out, holding the screened door open for Gelwood. They stood side-by-side and seemed to study the still young living image of their friend. After several breaths, Gelwood stepped forward and offered his arm in greeting. Yenne took it and was pulled into a back-pounding shoulder hug. Gelwood's crutch clattered to the porch. Smiling, Melli remained in her spot, allowing her husband time.

As soon as the two men released each other, Melli moved in

and captured Yenne in a chest-crushing hug. Taryn winced at the surprised expression on Yenne's face as he looked over Melli's shoulder. Taryn knew he could hardly draw a breath. His parents might be twenty years older, but their hugs were just as firm as the day they'd thought Yenne had died.

Melli planted a kiss on both Yenne's cheeks before letting go and moving over to hug Ani and Renloret. She knelt, calling Kela to her, and wrapped her arms about his neck before patting his head and standing.

Melli faced Yenne. "Welcome back and welcome home. We've missed you, Yenne."

"With the exception of the beard and mustache, you haven't changed a bit since we last saw you," Gelwood added with a grin. Everyone chuckled. He indicated the doorway. "Please, come in. We have plenty of time to get reacquainted before we eat. As Melli said, we've missed you, and there is much to share on both sides."

Taryn raised the folders and boxes in his arms indicating the materials he'd told them he would bring.

Once inside, Taryn laid out the photos and diagrams, a tabletop translator, and the three-dimensional viewer on the living room table. Taryn waited until both parents pulled chairs closer to the items and appeared engrossed in the photos of Lrakira and its three moons. After a few moments, he cleared his throat. "Do you have any questions?"

Gelwood pointed at the viewer. "What's this contraption?"

"It displays three-dimensional images while a narrator explains what is being shown. Here, I'll show you." He turned on the switch.

With the help of the translator, they watched the official Lrakiran promotional introduction of the Stones and their place as guardians and mentors in the Lrakiran social structure. Taryn was relieved at his parents' relative openness to the unexpected realization that the large crystals could communicate with people. Melli was particularly intrigued by the music base of the telepathic connection, as if by being musical they posed less of a threat.

Taryn said that when he pulled Diani's amber blade from the Anyala Stone, it had felt as if he were seeing the music and hearing the colors. He managed to slip in the fact that Ani was experienced with telepathic communications before her introduction to the Stones because of the unique connection with Kela, which would need to be explained by Reslo. Hiding his surprise at their calm and knowing expressions, he asked why they weren't surprised.

Melli delighted in telling him that they had read a few more sections of the mother's journal while he'd gone to talk to the others, and they'd found an entry about the telepathic connection. She agreed that it explained a lot about the behavior they often noticed between Ani and Kela. Then Gelwood teased Taryn about not reading the entire journal while on the trip from Lrakira to Teramar. He added that they hadn't read it all either, but would do so over the coming days. They had enjoyed skipping around in it.

They asked which of the Stones would come to Teramar and sing with Taryn. He demurred, saying that all three of the Lrakiran Stones had Singers on Lrakira and that three more Stones were supposedly on Teramar, hibernating until the Time

Song woke them. From what he knew, his Stone was somewhere on Teramar's Northern continent, and he was to be ready to find it when he heard its Song of Finding.

Melli and Gelwood accepted the information with rapt attention and few questions until Gelwood raised his hand to stop the discussion. "I think we've heard enough life-altering alien things for one day. Correct, Melli?"

She agreed and said that she would like to move on to more personal topics. "As Gelwood said, we have read portions of Shendahl's journal, and we have discussed how we'd like to proceed. First, this family," moving her arms to show a circle and looking directly into each person's eyes, "is sharing a profound experience. I'm sure we will all have our moments and we will be respectful of each other. Shendahl gave us the opportunity to add a child to our family, and now we have added the rest of you—including you, Renloret. And that will hopefully also include Reslo whenever he returns from Southern. It is good to have a large family to work through the consequences of Shendahl's gift. We may be confused, hurt, and at times angry, but we are not sad. *We* are a family. Do you understand?"

There were murmurs of acceptance, and Melli sat back in her seat, a satisfied smile on her lips. "Now, I think it best that when we have an opportunity to introduce Yenne to others, we introduce him as the son of a cousin of Ani's father who was named after Yenne Chenak. With the exception of Mroz, who evidently knows that Yenne is alive, the fact that Yenne Chenak lives will go no further. There is no need for explanation other than that there is a familial connection."

Ani, Yenne, Renloret, and Taryn looked at one another and nodded. Gelwood followed suit. Taryn realized that while they had developed something of a plan on how to introduce Yenne while on the trip to Teramar, they hadn't filled in the details. His mother had swiftly assessed the situation and come up with a plan that should work until the truth was able to be told. As usual, her blade was sharp.

"On another topic," Gelwood said, "the journal mentions our daughter's grave site. She's near the cabin. We'd like to find it. Is that all right with you two?" He looked at Yenne and Ani, who shared glances.

Taryn was relieved when Ani echoed Yenne's agreement.

Melli added, "We'd like to do so in the morn."

"Are you considering moving her to the cemetery?" Yenne asked.

"We'll decide later. After our meal, we have Shendahl's Remembrance Ceremony to plan," Gelwood said. "Melli and I have the announcement ready for posting when we return from the cabin." He looked at Yenne. Taryn could see the tears building in Yenne's eyes. His father could not claim his true relationship with Shendahl at the ceremony but would only be able to introduce himself as a representative of her "Southern" family. Gelwood whispered an apology and gripped Yenne's shoulder in understanding. Yenne looked a bit grim but seemed to accept the part he would have to play.

There was a moment of respectful silence. Yenne heaved a loud sigh, slapped both thighs with his hands, and stood. "If I can believe my nose, I smell a wonderful repast. May I escort our hosts to the dining room and help serve?"

The dinner conversation concentrated on Gelwood's grocery and Melli's tea and jam experimentation. There were occasional speculations on how the valley residents would react to the reality of aliens when it was revealed, but no one really knew when that would be, apart from the fact that it would surely be after the Stones were found. Then the Song of Teaching could be sung.

Once the dishes were cleared, they assembled in the living room again. Melli produced a pad of paper, and they added specific ideas about the Remembrance Ceremony to her list. Melli and Gelwood planned to allow personal stories interspersed with songs and dances before the closing candle lighting and spirit blade dance. Melli showed them the mockup of the announcement, and, with Yenne's permission, a short speech by the "Southern" representative of the Chenak family was added to the program. They all agreed that two days hence would be just enough time for musicians, dancers, and residents to prepare.

That done, the topic of where the search for the Northern Stone should begin was bantered about.

"Do you have any idea where to start looking for a hibernating crystal?" Gelwood asked.

Taryn shook his head, realizing how much they had not thought through before leaving Lrakira. "The Stones of Lrakira admitted not knowing the exact locations, but even if they did, I suspect they would not tell us because part of becoming a Singer is being able to follow the Song of Finding. The prophecy only states that one is on Southern, one is on Northern, and one is on one of the thousands of islands around the equator. I guess we need to study a few maps. Where are crystals found?"

Ani turned to Renloret. "Where were the Stones of Lrakira found?"

"To my knowledge, they've always been in the Stone chambers on their pedestals. No one has ever asked or written about the topic. For these three new ones, I suppose they would be in remote, unpopulated regions, so not just anyone could find them."

Gelwood mentioned having a stack of maps somewhere in the house and said he would find them and have them ready for study the next eve. As the evening progressed, the topic swung back to the location of the Averes' daughter's grave. That conversation was interrupted by a tel-com buzz. Melli answered and then called Taryn into the kitchen to talk with the sheriff's office.

"Dah, Nahnah," he said when he returned, "could we delay the search for your daughter's grave? Some new information has come up concerning Treyder, and Deputy Yantel wants me to come in tomorrow morn."

Taryn watched his parents take deep breaths in unison. Their hands clasped, his father patted Melli's reassuringly. "Whenever you are ready, son," Gelwood said. "She can wait a few more days."

Yantel finished reporting that several independent security teams in the employ of a medical equipment company that had a Doctor Isul Treyder on their board of directors were now under investigation. Yantel added that the capital investigators were still reviewing information taken from the raided facility where Taryn's blood had been found.

"The main reason we asked for this conference is that we have an eyewitness report that Treyder was seen entering Senator Nelham's office three days ago."

Questions spilled from those around the table. They all wanted to know who had seen Treyder and whether the senator had been interviewed.

Yantel rapped on the table to get everyone's attention. Ani and Renloret quieted. Taryn nodded approvingly to his deputy, pleased with the progress of the investigation while he'd been unavailable.

Yantel stood a bit taller and pointed at one of the charts. "The sighting was in Saedi City inside the senate building. The informant turns out to be a former employee at the Star Valley research center by the name of Sarinne Flaymatov. She used to work here a number of years ago and arrived yesterday to find out if the center still had some openings."

"Sarinne? She's here?" Ani's voice was filled with astonishment. In a softer voice, she muttered, "How did she know you were looking for him?"

Yantel shrugged. "I don't believe she actually knew we were looking for him when she arrived yesterday to reapply for a position on the medical research team. She stated that she overheard the other deputies interviewing some of the past employees who had also recently returned to work here."

"Was she hired?"

"We're still checking her background since she left over ten years ago," Daneeha said. "She seemed a bit too interested in letting us know she knew where he was and whom he had been with. And there are inconsistencies within her story."

Yantel nodded and explained how the former employee had pulled both deputies to one side and given the information in a peculiar tone of voice. She had given far more details than expected, including Treyder's exact attire and a description of the vehicle he'd arrived in. She claimed she'd only just seen the newsline report and was surprised to see him in the covered garage. She said she followed him until he entered Nelham's office and then waited in the hallway to confront him. When he never exited, she entered the office and questioned the senator's secretary, who denied seeing him. She then supposedly returned to the garage and discovered the vehicle was gone.

She bypassed the capital police and came to Star Valley to apply for reinstatement at the research center because she'd also seen an advertisement that former employees would be rehired ahead of others in the rebuilding of the center. It was only after the open group interview in the lobby that she approached the deputies with the information. They felt the sequence of events was odd enough to warrant a thorough and discreet investigation of her more recent past.

"I am expecting a report from the capital in the next day or so," Yantel added.

"Is she still here?" Taryn asked.

Daneeha shook her head. "No. No one has seen her since she gave us the report."

Frowning, Taryn tapped his lips. "I want to go forward based on her information anyway. Yantel, please pass the information on to the capital police and your liaison deputy. Did she get far enough into the application process to be photographed?"

Daneeha smiled and pushed a file across the table. Taryn opened and paged through it. His secretary had added the new application to Sarinne's old employee file. He passed it to Renloret and Ani and then looked at his crew. "I've read the reports on your discovery work at Treyder's lab and domicile here in Star Valley. Well done."

The deputies smiled at the praise.

"Share it with Saedi City, as well, if you have not already done so. Let them know I have returned in good health, thanks to the doctors on Southern.

The deputies rose from their seats and moved toward the door. Taryn stopped them. "Please keep all discussions about suspects, informants, and everything else about this case inside this room, except where noted. Understood?"

They saluted and left, closing the door behind them. Daneeha stayed. Taryn raised his eyebrows in a silent question.

"I honestly don't know what the woman has been up to these past years," Daneeha admitted. "She certainly did not come to visit until the funeral last year. I'm not sure anyone else recognized her then. She was wearing a lot of makeup and dressed quite differently. I recognized her walk and that nervous way she moved her left hand when she was upset. Dalkey's attack scattered most of the crowd, and she just disappeared. I didn't see her again until she entered this office to give a follow-up on her report. The look in her eyes when she saw I was still here could have melted a blade. I don't know her true motivations for coming back, and I don't trust her. I just feel like she's a whole lot of trouble."

Ani frowned. Taryn wondered what she was worried about.

"All right. We'll keep eyes out for and on her," Taryn said. "My thanks for your intuition and forthright comments. Any other comments or thoughts?"

She smiled. "None at the moment. Sheriff, I'm glad you're back."

Once Daneeha had left the room and shut the door behind her, Ani shoved the employee file back to Taryn. "It's a good thing we left Yenne with your parents."

"Why?" Taryn asked.

"Compare the two photos and then I'll tell you."

Taryn opened the file. The two photos were side by side. He had not really looked at them before passing the file. There were more than a few hints of grey in the woman's hair, and creases and wrinkles had aged her more than a typical woman in her late forties. Though still striking, she could have passed for almost sixty. The stress of not being able to repair the communications array and then leaving her people to try to blend in had been hard on her. "Okay. She's older now. What do you expect? What do these photos have to do with leaving Yenne at my parents?"

She leaned across the table, her expression earnest. "Daneeha recognized her at the funeral with a lot of makeup and a different style of attire. Do you think a beard and mustache would keep her from recognizing Yenne?"

Stunned, Taryn glanced out the conference room window at

Daneeha's back. She was on the tel-com and taking notes. "I guess we'd better find a way to bring her up to date before she sees him, even from a distance, and starts asking a lot of uncomfortable questions. I did not understand just how observant my secretary is."

"Maybe we can fill her in at the same time we tell Mroz. They both need to know before the Remembrance Ceremony. Maybe we can do that tonight, after we find the baby's grave."

Taryn motioned to the door. "Agreed. One thing is for certain. They both are too clever to hide the truth from for long. And I'm thinking it's time to fill in Daneeha about more than Yenne."

"She's here. Our daughter is here," Gelwood whispered.

A written description of the location in Shendahl's journal had made the search like hunting for a treasure—buried treasure. Ani found it odd that after all these years of hiking and just being on the mountain, she'd never stumbled across the baby's headstone. Ani led the group, and the others followed at a respectful distance.

Gelwood saw the small stone first. He turned and hugged Melli, and the couple stood with their arms wrapped tightly around each other. Their heads were bent toward the knee-high stone, and Ani did not know if they were crying. After several minutes, they parted and knelt on either side of the headstone and began clearing away weeds and such. Taryn approached his parents and began to help, but there was only a couple of years of growth obscuring the stone, giving the impression that Shendahl had kept it clear until her own death.

Ani observed the tiny clearing. Near the stone was a wooden bench with vines creeping around the legs. The seat was smooth with wear. Ani felt tears building. She tugged on Yenne's sleeve and pointed.

It took a moment before he reacted. Quietly, he stepped over to the bench and pulled the vines away before sitting where his wife had sat many times. Ani felt Renloret's hand on hers, and she leaned into his chest, letting the tears fall.

Kela sidled close as well. His thoughts were clear and supportive. For quite some time, the only sounds were the soft mumbles between the Averes while they finished cleaning around the stone. Then they, too, were silent, their hands joined and stacked on the gravestone top, as flitters returned to their chirping, trilling songs.

Melli's soft voice interrupted the forest sounds. "Shendahl followed her heart by giving us a family. We accept her gifts. She carried this burden for twenty-five years." She held out her hands to Yenne, and he stepped into her embrace. She kissed him on a cheek. "She no longer bears this burden alone." Melli tucked Yenne's hand into the crook of her arm and turned him to face the gravestone. "Let us sing the Remembrance Song. We will need the practice before the ceremony."

Ani reached for Renloret to pull him close, and they began to sing. With each phrase, Ani could feel the healing. Her own guilt at leaving Teramar without telling Melli and Gelwood about the baby paled in comparison to the twenty-five years of secrets her mother had held. Understanding combined with acceptance as Ani sang the song she would lead in a few days at the full Remembrance Ceremony. She would not forget her mother's strength and determination to do right by her people and her friends.

# CHAPTER FIFTEEN

Folding his arms behind his head, Isul Treyder stared at the ceiling as he reviewed the results from his latest tests on the coma devices, particularly the report that one had failed to keep a specimen in the deep coma. Fortunately, Treyder had been in the laboratory when the soldier sat up and began shouting and tearing the electrodes off his body.

Treyder had barely managed to quiet him by explaining that he was suffering from a ravaging fever as the result of a biological weapon of some kind that had been dispersed by an intruder from Southern through the air ducts in the arena during the weapons test. The tasteless, odorless gas had knocked the Northern volunteers unconscious within minutes.

Assuming the attitude of a concerned physician, Treyder had convinced the soldier that his wounds, which included a broken leg and some internal damage, were the result of a fall when he'd lost consciousness. He had gone on to explain that he needed to examine the man and get tissue samples to see if his body was successfully battling the infection. He had gained permission from the man to use his tissue to create a vaccine to test as a possible cure, therefore giving Northern a way to stop further encroachment of the Southern army on Northern territory.

When the soldier asked, Treyder informed him that the perpetrator had been caught leaving the building shortly after the soldiers had started to react to the airborne concoction but had refused to give any information about its purpose or contents. That was why Treyder needed to draw blood and excise some skin tissue. Mollified, the soldier had relented and endured the drawing of several vials of blood by a silent attendant. Treyder reassured the soldier that the electrodes were only used to track body functions and was allowed to reattach them. He had then rubbed a gritty salve over one of the cuts while murmuring comforting words about how the soldier would begin to feel sleepy and the pain would diminish. As the coma devices within the salve took effect, the soldier had been again rendered unconscious.

Treyder was pleased with the detailed notes about the length of time from administration of two additional coma devices to a comatose state that the incident had allowed. Now that he knew at least one of the devices had failed, he had to face the slim possibility that the first two devices had also failed instead of having been removed by the Southern surgeons.

With that in mind, Treyder took out more paper and began writing reactivation code that could be transmitted through the electrodes. He would have to get his hands on Ani Chenak, the sheriff, or both to determine whether the devices had been removed or ceased to work. In the meantime, he now had one specimen in his laboratory to experiment on.

Treyder speculated that if he was successful, he might be able to place inactive devices in selected persons and activate them from a distance. The incident had opened a whole new procedure that would bring him even more money and recognition. There were so many ways he could use that kind of power. He would need to work on remote activation as well as reactivation.

He labored until well after dawn the next day.

# CHAPTER SIXTEEN

After arriving back in the village, Melli and Gelwood quickly spread the news about the Remembrance Ceremony planned for the next day. The announcement was met with uncharacteristic celebration by the Star Valley residents. They were pleased to finally be able to share their stories about how Shendahl Chenak had impacted their lives. A large crowd had gathered at the community hall to sign up for speaking slots. Ani received many hugs and words of encouragement, as was appropriate.

Ani settled next to Melli with a sigh. She was looking forward to the ceremony because it would not be a maudlin one. It would be joyful. Resting her head on Melli's shoulder, she realized it was good to be home. And even with all the changes that had occurred, she was calm and at peace with her new family.

Melli turned to Ani. "Now, I want you to know that Gelwood and I decided to name our daughter Makoshan. Is it all right if we put her name on the gravestone near the cabin? Gelwood wants to do the engraving himself, so no one else need know. We spoke with Yenne this morn before he and Renloret went to the launch tower to test the communications array or whatever it is. Your father approves and wanted me to check with you."

"Well, I guess it's . . . no, that's not correct, I *know* it's appropriate, and mother would be pleased she has a name of her parents' choosing." Her tone added conviction to her words, and she hugged Melli tight, reaching beyond her to pull Taryn into her grasp.

"What do you think of their decision?" Ani asked Taryn.

He shrugged. "It is how they have decided to handle the situation. As the son of both sides, it seems fitting. And the name they chose fits as well. Do you know what it means?"

"I'm not sure I've ever heard it before," Ani admitted.

"Dah told me it's an old name, dating back almost one thousand years, and they found it in a child's story from Dah's childhood. It means 'gift of the heart.'"

"That's what mother wrote in the journal—that you were the gift of her heart to Melli and Gelwood." Ani felt tears welling up. She brushed them away, determined not to cry yet again. She heard a sniffling sound from Taryn and noticed he, too, was wiping away tears.

She laughed. "Aren't we a pair?"

"Yes, we are."

They all met at the lake house for a late midday meal. Yenne and Renloret had arrived through the trapdoor in the living room with exciting news that the communications array was working. They had passed on as much news as possible to the ship hiding behind the giant planet, Kriswen, and the ship had in turn passed it all on to Lrakira. Diani and Layson had responded with news that the Stones of Lrakira had verified that the Teramaran Stones were awake. According to the Lrakiran Stones, now was the time for the Teramaran Stones to be found, and they had begun transmitting the Song of Finding. The new Singers would apparently prove themselves worthy in part through their ability to find the Stones through the Song of Finding. And only the chosen Singers would hear it.

Ani glanced at her twin and saw that he was in thought, his expression both pensive and a bit troubled. "No songs in your head yet?" she asked.

Taryn shook his head.

"Well, if the Lrakiran Stones have only just informed the Stones here that Anyala is okay, I suspect you'll hear something shortly."

"Did you hear anything before you saw your Stone?" Melli asked.

This time it was Ani's turn to shake her head. "Before I saw the Stone, the only thing I heard was Mother humming the healing song while she wrapped me in a warm, green blanket. I heard Renloret and Taryn singing too. I think that was just before the coma device cut me off."

Renloret straightened in his chair and faced Ani. "You hadn't mentioned hearing your mother before, though you'd whispered Nahnah once before we started to sing. Hearing the last Singer is a sign of a full blade bonding after a Passing has occurred. We know there was a Passing of Shendahl's spirit to the blade because

Dalkey said he had seen green smoke moving from her remains to the blade box when he broke into her grave. Remember, there were no bones in the casket when Taryn and I went back to search the grave."

Melli and Gelwood shifted nervously in their seats. "There's no body in the casket?" Melli asked quietly.

Renloret explained that after death, a Singer's spirit passed from the physical body to the blade in preparation for the blade bonding with the new Singer. And once the spirit had transferred to the blade, the body was no longer needed, and it simply disintegrated. Renloret had not found any explanation other than that on why the bodies disappeared. It was an accepted part of the Passing. It was how the new Singer connected with the Stones. He'd read that a new Singer often had conversations with the most recent Passed Singer. He speculated that the telepathic conversation might only be temporary, ending when the new Singer had adjusted to the telepathic communication of the Stone.

Ani pointed out that she had not been in communication with her Stone before arriving on Lrakira. And she had not known certain things about the Stones she would have been expected to know. Diani and Layson had been surprised and confused by it. They now guessed it was related to the circumstances surrounding her artificial coma, which first affected the blade bonding. The removal of the coma device was one step in the process, and when Taryn removed the Pericha Stone Blade from the Anyala Stone, that was another step. Ani felt a faint song from the Anyala Stone confirming that full communication and knowledge sharing between the Stone, the crystal blade, and Ani was now as expected. It was the coma device that had cut Ani off from not only her mother's spirit and Kela, but also from the Stone. Ani relayed the Stone's words about the consequences of the coma device.

Several seconds of silence followed her revelation. Ani was not surprised that the conversation shifted with the mention of the coma device, and Taryn shifted into sheriff mode. "Daneeha, Yantel, and the other deputies are working with the capital police on the investigation and how the senator may be involved. Yenne, I think it's time to shake out a blade by the name of Sarinne Flaymatov and hear what she has to say. Are you up to seeing your communications officer after twenty years?"

Ani watched the emotions play across her father's face. Confusion seemed to struggle against anger. It was several breaths before he answered.

"I suppose so. Does she know I'm here?"

Taryn shook his head. "Nope. In fact, no one has seen her since she reported seeing Treyder at the senator's office. She may have decided to abandon the application and return to Saedi City. But the word is out in Star Valley and if anyone does see her, the sheriff's office will be told.

"Oh, that brings up another point. We need to get you together with Daneeha. She's an observant woman and won't be fooled by the beard and mustache. We need to tell Mroz about Yenne too, so I've invited Daneeha to meet with us at Mroz's bar. That way, we can sharpen two blades at the same time. Mroz is back in town now from his supply run to Saedi City. I contacted him after we left the cabin. He's expecting a visit from us later, and I told Daneeha that the office could do without her late this afternoon and that I'd like her to join us. I also told her to invite her husband if he could get away. She peppered me with questions I declined to answer, so I know she'll be there, and I'm going to guess she will manage to get her husband there too."

Ani ran her finger along her father's jaw outlining the beard. "She recognized Sarinne at mother's funeral with a lot of makeup and different clothes. This won't be enough of a disguise to keep Daneeha from figuring out who you are, so it's a good thing we're telling her. But don't go shaving it off. I like it because it makes you look older."

Yenne gave her a bemused smile. "Since you put it that way, I'll keep it. Thank you. Taryn, just let me know when you find Sarinne. As her commander, I can handle her. No doubt she'll be surprised, but time shifts are not unheard of. And unless she has completely rejected her training, she will follow the rules. If she doesn't, she'll be returned to Lrakira to answer for her dereliction of duties, which led to the near extinction of our people and the possible death of one of the Stones. She could be incarcerated for quite some time if found guilty."

Ani recalled the tune the Pericha Stone had sung about Sarinne not having the correct temperament to become a Singer. She was sure the Stones would not forgive the communication officer's apparent omissions about Ani's birth and first five years of good health in messages sent by both Shendahl and Yenne to Lrakira. The lack of that information about Shendahl was now, in Ani's mind, the basis for Selabec's loss of control and subsequent attack on the Anyala Stone.

But for the time being, they all needed to turn their attention to letting Mroz and Daneeha know what was going on. For Mroz, finding out that Yenne was on Teramar would no doubt be a surprise, but Daneeha was about to learn that several people she knew were aliens. Ani couldn't wait to see her reaction.

Taryn peeked through the tavern door. "He's wiping down the bar. I can't see any other patrons. You can set up the sign."

Taryn was feeling a bit silly about the stakeout-like behavior, but he did not want any interruptions for at least a couple of hours, and they had already waited over an hour for the last hover-car to leave the parking lot. Melli was helping Ani and Renloret set a triangular board a few feet in front of the door so the hastily drawn announcement that the bar was closed until further notice due to a plumbing problem was visible to all walking or driving by.

Taryn placed three fingers on his lips. "Shush. All of you get out of sight and wait out here until I let you in." He pushed the door fully open and closed it behind him.

"Hey! Bartender, set me up a drink. It's cold outside, and I'm in need of some interior heat!" He removed his jacket and tossed it on one of the wall hooks.

Mroz looked up and a large smile crossed his face. "Sheriff Taryn! I'd heard you were back in the valley. What took so long for you to stop by? I've been busy getting supplies for the winter solstice coming up, so I haven't been able to break away."

He came out from behind the bar, pulled Taryn into a tight hug, and pounded Taryn's back several times before pushing him to arm's length and taking a good look at him. When he released him, he rubbed the two-month-old stubble on Taryn's scalp. "So good to see you, youngster. By the blades, you look better than the last time I saw you. Looks as if they healed you up right, those docs on that planet. What did Renloret call it, Rakiri or something?"

"Lrakira," Taryn replied, correcting the pronunciation. "Yes, they removed a coma device, and they were delighted to have another subject to study. Nasty things if you ask me."

Mroz dragged him over to the closest table and pushed him into a chair.

"So, I heard Ani and Renloret came back with you? Did any others? I'd love to meet a few more aliens." Mroz scurried to retrieve a bottle from the shelf and two small glasses from behind the bar. There was a soft puff of air escaping as Mroz uncorked the bottle and poured a small amount of cream-colored liquid into each of the glasses. Then he took the chair opposite Taryn.

"Yes, Kela and one other," Taryn said, giving a wink to the bar owner as he picked up the closest glass. He raised it with a nod. "My unending thanks for helping Ani and Renloret rescue me. They both vouched they would have failed without your assistance. I heard you did not come away unscathed. Have you healed?"

Mroz lifted his hair a bit and leaned forward. Taryn saw the light tan line of the scar and winced. "Looks like it hurt."

"Not more than seeing the condition Treyder had you in. It

was worth every minute." He raised the other glass. "To friends and family."

Taryn heard the emphasis on the last word and smiled. "To friends and family." They both tossed the liquor to the back of their mouths. Taryn struggled to avoid coughing. He'd not had Mroz's special distillation in quite some time—not since the blade ring championships almost three years past. Though not as strong a drink as vaquin, Mroz's special always set off a fit of coughing on Taryn's part.

Mroz brought him a glass of water. "My apologies, Taryn. I forgot."

"It's a fitting salute, Mroz. I really don't mind. I don't know why I cough every time." Another cough threatened. He took several swallows of water and waved his hand above the small glass. "This should wait, Mroz. We need to talk about what you know and who is involved."

He almost laughed at Mroz's confused expression and reached across the table to pat the older man's hand. "For starters, I know you know about my sister and me. All that is okay. My parents know now too. They will want to talk to you, and we've decided that only a few people will know the truth. Please continue to keep it to this small group." He waited for Mroz to acknowledge his acceptance of the warning before continuing. "I want to add one more person to the inner circle. I think you might remember him."

Taryn got up and opened the door.

His parents, Ani, Renloret, and Yenne entered. They shed their coats, hung them on the hooks, and turned in unison to face Mroz, all grinning.

Taryn watched as Mroz stepped closer to look the five over. He smiled and nodded a welcome to Melli and Gelwood, then gave a quick hug to Ani and grasped Renloret's forearm firmly. He started to reach out to the fifth person in line and stopped. A frown crossed his face, then he covered his face with his hands, rubbed them around, and looked again. He turned to Taryn, his mouth open in shocked surprise. "Really? This is who I think it is?"

Taryn nodded. They all nodded.

Mroz reached out to grasp Yenne's forearm and yanked his friend into a fierce embrace, laughing joyfully as he lifted Yenne off the floor and swung him around. "All the hells of Teramar! You're not really dead?"

"No, not yet, but I might be soon if you don't let me down," Yenne said breathlessly.

Mroz lowered Yenne's feet to the floor and danced around him. "Oh, my blades. You have no idea how much I have missed you. So many years, so very many years."

"It doesn't seem that long ago for me, my friend—thanks to a time shift. These time shifts can create havoc. We're so sorry this happened, but it seems while it was planned by some, we did not know the plan. It's been a struggle, even for those of us who know about the possibility of a time shift."

Mroz seemed to shrug off the attempt at explanation. "Oh, there's so much to tell. Come. Come, all of you. Let me get more glasses." Mroz waved them all to the table and dashed into the back storage area, returning shortly with three large bottles and mugs for them all.

Daneeha's reaction when she and her husband Prakwel arrived at Mroz's bar was priceless. The diminutive secretary recognized Yenne despite the crude—as she put it—attempt at a disguise. Without fanfare, the couple was informed that Yenne, Ani, and Renloret were aliens. They accepted that information with great composure, as if the knowledge that some of their friends were aliens was something they heard on a regular basis. They were also told about the time bubble that had created the odd age difference between father and daughter. There was a slight waiver in their poise with that information.

But when Taryn revealed that he was also an alien, Daneeha's face lit up and she squealed, "I always suspected there was more to you than anyone guessed!"

Daneeha and Prakwel then turned as one to look at Melli and Gelwood, their question apparent.

"No," Taryn said in answer to their unspoken query. "My parents are not aliens. And no, I'm not explaining further. That is a story for another time."

Daneeha opened her mouth to speak then closed it. Taryn guessed that his expression had made it clear that he'd already revealed as much as he intended. No mention was made of the Stones or the twins.

Prakwel brought up the disease that he remembered had brought the "Southerners" to the valley and asked about whether a cure had been found. Yenne explained briefly that a vaccine had been created with a derivative of Ani's blood.

Daneeha and Prakwel were honored to be included in the secret of real aliens until official contact was made between leaders at some point in the near future. The rest of the evening was a wonderful reunion of old friends. Stories and an abundance of alcohol were shared.

By the end of the reunion, they somehow all managed to get safely to places where they could sleep. Any thought of dinner was long forgotten.

# CHAPTER SEVENTEEN

Ani opened her eyes. A narrow slit of light from between the curtains caused her to blink rapidly. The room was as blurry as her thoughts. Where exactly was she? The bed was warm, but it did not feel quite like hers at either the lake house or cabin. She pulled the covers over her head to block the light and moaned slightly as the movement sent little sparks of pain from her shoulders to her head. By the blades, she should not have drunk so much and eaten so little.

When she tried to adjust her position, she felt a warm hand slide up her back. Where had it been? Her waist. Alcohol-blurred memories shifted through her thoughts. The hand began kneading the knotted muscles of her neck and shoulders. It felt good, but there were things that needed to be done. There was a list somewhere. She reached from under the covers toward the small table. She vaguely remembered the folded piece of paper she placed there before crawling into bed sometime before dawn. The hand stopped massaging and held her shoulder back.

"Shh, too early to get up," a deep warm-breathed whisper said. "Don't move. Let me do this."

She opened her eyes. The hand worked its way to the base of her skull, through her hair, and around to her temple. The circular movements of the fingertips eased the ache of the hangover better than more drink would have. Beginning to relax, she decided the list could wait. Ani exhaled slowly, willing the massage to continue. At the moment, she didn't care who was providing relief. A warm leg slid over hers, and she felt the heat of another body—a naked male body if she identified certain parts of a body's anatomy correctly. A concerned frown wrinkled her brow. Who was she in bed with?

"Ren?" she said hopefully.

"Yes. Who were you expecting?"

She let out the breath she'd been holding. His fingers had reached the bridge of her nose and now pushed the wrinkles upward, smoothing them away. The headache eased and was replaced by a growing urgency to move. She tried to roll over to face him, but his hands gently resisted, keeping her on her side, her back to him.

"It's my turn to pleasure you."

His whisper rippled across her skin. While one hand continued to cradle her head, the other traveled tantalizingly from her forehead to her jaw, neck, and shoulder, gradually moving downward until it cupped a breast, his fingers circling and teasing the nipple until it was hard. Each breath came faster. She tried to lie still, absorbing his exploring touch, but her body moved toward its own desires. She squirmed against his body as her heart rate increased and her skin tingled.

He chuckled. "Don't help me yet. I'm learning you as you have learned me."

As Renloret's hand moved from the breast to her abdomen, Ani felt the quiet closure of Kela's mental privacy barrier. She had not even realized he had been awake on the edge of her thoughts. He was respectfully leaving her to the experience, and she didn't need to worry about him listening or sharing. She would express her gratitude later. With a purring sigh, she gave in to Renloret's caresses.

A long while later, they continued to snuggle, keeping as much skin-to-skin contact as possible. Renloret's lips were nibbling her neck, creating small waves of lingering excitement. Her entire body wanted him, but there were things that needed doing. She kissed his chest, then his chin. "The list. We should get started."

She felt his lips on her forehead. "Yes. I know. I just wanted you all to myself for a bit longer."

She moved to sit on the edge of the mattress, looked around the room, and realized that they were in Melli's guest room. She was not sure if she had been quiet during their lovemaking and wondered what Gelwood and Melli might have heard. What would they say? Would they say anything? There was only one way to find out.

"I'll shower while you make the bed," she said.

She began to stand, but Renloret had taken her wrist and pulled her back into his arms. "We could save water and take it together."

"Stop it, Ren." She slapped at his attempt to further delay her efforts to get on with the day. "Do you realize whose home we're in?" The smile he gave her was endearing, and she considered surrendering.

"Yes, they invited us so we wouldn't have to drive to the lake house. They were the ones who said we could use this room. Don't you remember?"

She shook her head and sat up again. "No, I don't." A sudden thought that her father might be in the next room brought her eyes wide open. "Is Yenne here too?"

Renloret chuckled. "No, he stayed with Taryn." He glanced at the timepiece on the dresser. "They will be here in about half a bell."

"Blades, why didn't you say so?" She jumped off the bed and marched into the necessary room. When she heard the soft whistle of the tune they had danced to months ago, she wondered how he had remembered it and turned around, putting her hands on her hips.

He was smiling at her. "You are making it very difficult to think about anything else."

Turning with a huff she growled, "Make the bed!" He was incorrigible. She turned the water on to drown out his laughter. But as she stepped into the shower, she found herself smiling. He remembered the tune, and so did she.

Taryn woke abruptly. A tune lilted through the hangover fog. He wondered if he could remember it long enough to play it on his cyralist, and he wondered if there were words. None came. It felt like a flitter's awaking call—a questing. It was not urgent, just . . . an introduction. He smiled. At least one of the Stones of Teramar was searching. Was it his? Would he hear all of the Stones' calls? How many other candidates would hear the call? Were there only two others?

The First Song had stated that one of the three Stones was on Northern, one on Southern, and the third presumably on one of the thousands of islands that circled the equator like a necklace. There was a lot of territory to cover to find the hidden crystals. Didn't the Lrakiran Stones say that often, there were multiple candidates when a Singer retired or died? That multiple choices for Kita and Pericha were the norm? The tune drifted away, and he checked the time. It was early enough that he could linger in the shower before heading to his parents' home for a morn meal.

On his way to the necessary room, he knocked on the spare room door. "Yenne? Wake up. We need to be at my parents' house in an hour." He heard a muffled response and continued to the shower.

A little more than an hour later, they were at the house helping the others set the table.

Halved gedniums edged each plate and Melli was spooning a sauté of sausage and tacara roots over fried bread slices. Renloret took each plate as it was filled and placed it on the table in front of a chair. Gelwood poured tea while everyone else chose a seat. Once everyone was seated, there was a moment of silence as they all shared glances and smiles.

"I'm finally home. My thanks, Melli and Gelwood," Yenne said, his voice a soft rumble of gratitude.

"Welcome, friend," Gelwood replied. "We will discuss plans for Treyder and the search for the Stones after we eat, and then we will meet at the dance hall for the mid-day Remembrance Ceremony. Does that suit?" He didn't wait for responses. "Now pass me the bowl of plantains."

And with that, the conversation flowed around subjects other than the two he'd mentioned.

After the dishes had been handled, they all moved into the living room, which they were using as a conference area. There were two easels, each with large paper pads. One was titled "Treyder" and the other was titled "Stones." Each chair had a pad of paper and writing implement waiting. Not long into the discussion, Taryn recognized he had underestimated the combined force his parents offered in ideas and strategies. Every time one of them spoke, he felt Ani's eyes on him. She would give him tight-lipped smirks every time he acquiesced to their methodology. She had even leaned close once and whispered that with parents like his, she now fully understood why he was the sheriff of Star Valley at such a young age. He had nudged her away but acknowledged her comment with a smile.

The discussion on Treyder was brief because Taryn had emphasized that any clues or ideas were to be reported directly to the sheriff's office. When Gelwood said he would offer to help the investigation, Taryn squashed it saying that this matter needed to be left to the law enforcement professionals. Acting sheriff Yantel, the deputies, and the Saedi City police were doing an exemplary job and should not be interfered with. Both Gelwood and Melli had quietly desisted and turned their attentions to the other easel.

Once again, Taryn watched as his path was outlined. He decided to add new information for them to contemplate. He held up his hands and told them about the music he'd woken to that morn. He explained that though he often woke with ditties and melodies rambling through his head, this felt different. And while it felt neither urgent nor demanding, it was compelling in a way he could not describe. He hummed parts of it and looked at Renloret. "Is it familiar to you? I didn't hear words, so I don't know if it truly came from a Stone or was just my usual creativity with music."

Renloret asked him to hum the bars again and shook his head. "I've not heard that tune before, but it does have the feel of Lrakiran music rather than that of Northern influence. And it hints that there is more to come, so it may be an introduction. That is good, Taryn. I think the Stone knows you are on Teramar."

Taryn nodded. He looked at Ani. "Has the blade reacted or said anything to you?"

She pulled the green crystal blade from her boot sheath while shaking her head and turned the blade over in her palm. Taryn saw a spark of light near the pommel, and the blade began to glow. He heard gasps from his parents as the room was bathed in a green wash. It was not as brilliant a green as from the Anyala Stone, but he felt a tingle of mental touch from the blade. It was calming, reassuring. Ani smiled at him.

"It knows only that the Stones of Teramar have awakened," Ani said.

"Can it tell us where they are?" Melli asked.

A shake of her head gave Taryn the disappointing answer.

Ani shrugged. "I get the feeling that the new Singers must prove their acceptability by searching out the Stones on their own. It's like the blade ring test I was required to pass when I became Anyala's Singer." The blade's glow brightened and then disappeared, and Ani slipped it back into the boot sheath. "A sense of great height is the only other thing I get from it."

Gelwood got up. "I'll get a map of Northern for you to study, Taryn." Tucking the crutch under his arm, he moved through the maze of chairs to the hall.

He returned quickly and tacked the topographical map across both easels then pointed at several mountainous areas. "Most of the high peaks are found here and here. But the highest point on Northern is clear over here." Gelwood's finger tapped at a spot halfway around the globe.

"Where would you like to start?" Renloret asked.

"When do you want to go?" Ani added.

Taryn mulled over the questions. "Let's discuss it with Mroz after the Remembrance Ceremony. I think he served some military time in two of those areas. He'll have a better idea of the equipment we should take." He glanced at the timepiece on the wall and shook his head. "Too many important things to get done today. We best head to the hall. The band members will be there in about a quarter of an hour."

# CHAPTER EIGHTEEN

The hall was quiet as Ani made her way back to her seat. She had been the last to speak and was relieved she'd made it through her remembrances without too many tears. She wanted the people to remember the happy times.

Yenne leaned across and grasped her hand. He was rolling his lip between his teeth again, probably trying not to look more aggrieved than a distant relative would, though she could see the tears welling up. He blinked them away as the drummers began.

Young boys and girls slowly filed in balancing the trays of lit candles, pausing briefly as onlookers selected and passed candles to those seated or standing in the rows behind them. Once all the candles were handed out, one of the band members began to rhythmically shake the little memory bells, and the drummers moved into a quicker pattern to match.

A line of dancers wound their way into the center, their thin, flexible swords raised above their heads. The colorful flags attached to the pommels flowed as if in a breeze as their steps became ever faster, and they twirled their swords about in intricate patterns. When the drums and bells reached a crescendo, the thin blades were woven under and over each until a gleaming star was created. All but one of the dancers released their blades and the lead dancer raised the woven sword star high in celebration at the last beat of the drums.

Ani stood and began to sing. Her voice was soft on the first two phrases of the Remembrance Song. Then everyone joined in. She reached out her hands, and the lead dancer lowered the star onto them. The flags attached to the sword pommels draped together like a skirt and brushed the floor. Slowly, she embraced the star, taking care to avoid the blade edges. As she raised her eyes to the ceiling, she thought of the Anyala Stone and her mother's blade promise to it and to the people of Lrakira. The promise had been fulfilled. S'Hendale could rest in peace.

The next day, with search plans well underway for the Northern Stone, Taryn laughed and motioned Mroz to top off the frosty glass mug. Mroz's tavern was closed to the public for the private gathering, so the conversations were relaxed and laughter was easy.

It was good to be home. His parents were in the back room of the bar setting up a full dinner celebration. He could hear them talking about the brief star runner flight Renloret had taken them on the previous eve after the Remembrance Ceremony.

Thus far, the morn's conversation had included showing Mroz the three-dimensional video of the Stones and images of Lrakira, including a few clips of other alien races—which even Taryn's parents had admitted were not as terrible as they imagined. When asked for help in pinpointing possible hiding places, Mroz had jumped at the chance to assist in any way he could, with the caveat that he be allowed to accompany Taryn on his search. Part of the current conversation was planning what else might be needed to find the Northern Stone.

Voices drifted out of the back room. Taryn couldn't hide his grin as his parents laughed about the possibility of visiting other planets. This was a topic he'd never considered hearing prior to a couple of months ago, let alone that his parents would be so positive about their son becoming a translator for aliens. He blew out a breath. At least it seemed to have overshadowed the altered family makeup.

Now they were all waiting on the arrival of Ani and Renloret. Those two had gone up to the cabin and lake house to see if Reslo had sent any messages to the tel-coms at those locations and to send yet another message to Southern requesting that Reslo return to Star Valley as soon as possible. Taryn glanced at the timepiece above the bar and then at Yenne on the stool next to him. The two lovers were at least an hour late. Yenne didn't say anything, just shrugged one shoulder and winked at Mroz, who joined in on the unspoken assumptions with a laugh.

Mroz moved the jug to fill Yenne's glass, and Taryn sucked a mouthful of froth from his. Yenne pushed the bowl of fried tacara slices to Taryn and leaned close to Mroz to say something. The bartender was nodding his head and grinning at Yenne's whispered words when the jangle of bells caused him to glance toward the door. "About time you two got here! What can I pour . . ."

Taryn turned his attention to the man whose entry had silenced the gregarious Mroz to frozen astonishment.

"Hey, hey, Mroz, watch it!" Yenne grabbed the jug from the bartender as the drink glugged over the mug and splashed onto the counter. Mroz didn't move.

Taryn felt Yenne's glance but could not take his own eyes off the man standing just inside. "Hold," he whispered to Yenne, forestalling his turn in the chair. Taryn slowly set his drink on the bar.

The commander stopped moving, his forehead creasing with frown lines. "What is it?" Yenne whispered back.

"*Who* is the question you should ask. Stay put. Don't turn around—yet." Taryn stood and pasted on a smile. "Reslo! Did you just arrive? Have you checked your messages lately? We've been trying to contact you. Much has happened in the last few months."

Taryn noticed the sudden paleness of Yenne's face and slapped a hand companionably on his shoulder, squeezing hard to keep the man from turning around. Bending toward Yenne's ear Taryn added, "Let's see how long it takes him." He squeezed the shoulder again and pushed off to greet Ani's uncle. His smile widened as he realized that Reslo was also his uncle.

The forearm grip was firm from the older man and his smile was relaxed. "I just floated in and saw the lights on. Thought I would stop in and listen to some rumors before I head up to the lake house. Unless Ani is in town."

Taryn chuckled. "Oh, she'll be here soon."

Reslo looked at him quizzically but said nothing in reply.

Mroz coughed heavily. Taryn glared at the bartender. "Set up a stiff one. He's going to need it in a . . . *chime*." He grinned as he pulled Reslo to the bar stool to Yenne's right.

Yenne kept his back turned from Reslo but started to cough at Taryn's use of the Lrakiran time term. Patting him on the back, Taryn laughed.

Mroz seemed to have come to his senses as he finished mopping up the spilled brew. "What are you drinking now, Reslo? Anything new from Southern?" Mroz set a tall narrow straight-sided tumbler in front of Reslo. "Or should I just start pouring?"

Reslo's eyebrows arched in surprise. "The rumors are that good?"

"You have no idea," Mroz muttered as he poured three fingers of vaquin in Reslo's glass.

Taryn doubled over Yenne's back almost knocking the commander off the stool, and they both started to laugh. Taryn could tell that Yenne was working hard at keeping his back to his brother. "Nothing on Southern is going to prepare you for this," Taryn managed to say. Tears were threatening to roll down his cheeks.

Reslo stared at him in bewilderment.

Mroz stayed Reslo's hand before he could take a sip. "Perhaps now would be a good time to introduce your *friend*, Taryn." Mroz nodded at Yenne, who had resettled on his stool and downed about half of the brew in his mug.

Taryn straightened and cleared his throat. "Please don't hit me, Reslo." He tapped Yenne on the shoulder to turn around. "Reslo Chenak, it is my honor to introduce you to my friend Commander Yenne Chenakainet, your brother." He stepped out of the way and glanced at Mroz who sealed the expensive liquor and placed it behind his back without taking his eyes off the brothers.

The two men stared at each other in the silence that followed.

Taryn watched tears begin to fall unheeded down Reslo's cheeks. The man's mouth opened and closed several times. Then he put the tumbler of vaquin to his lips and knocked the entire contents into his mouth, swallowed, and shivered. "Stones and blades be damned to all the hells of Teramar. Yenne?" Taryn realized the curse was a mix of Lrakiran and Northern.

Mroz brought the vaquin around, uncorked it, and poured another three fingers. He raised it at Yenne who shook his head and pointed to his half-full mug. The bartender poured a short two fingers of vaquin into a smaller glass and downed it himself before exchanging the bottle for the jug of brew, topping off Yenne's mug—this time not spilling a drop.

Gelwood limped through the doorway separating the private dining room from the main bar area. "Hey ho, the eve meal is ready." A shocked expression crossed his face.

Taryn waved Gelwood over. "Mroz, better set up two more. Even my mother may want one when she sees him."

Gelwood looked over his shoulder. "My dearest? Please join us at the bar. The gentleman we were worried about is here."

Melli strode through the doorway, stopped abruptly when she saw Reslo set down his glass, and covered her mouth with her hands.

Taryn was stunned to hear her mumble curse words he still got in trouble for saying and raised his eyebrows at her. She ignored him as she took a few more steps toward the nearest table, grabbed a chair, and sat.

Mroz poured the two glasses, handed one to Gelwood, and made his way over to Melli. Gelwood leaned the crutch against the bar and pulled himself onto a stool. He raised the glass to Reslo and took a sip. Melli accepted her glass and took a good-sized swallow, grimaced, and then set the glass on the table hard.

"Reslo, did you receive my thanks note for the dried fruits?" Melli asked, her voice barely over a whisper.

"Yes. I tried several times to respond, but until five or six months ago, I assumed the sun flare activity was the culprit. I was wrong." He looked at Yenne.

Yenne nodded, adding a smile. "They know."

Reslo gave his brother a short nod of understanding. "Seeing Yenne now confirms my suspicions. A few months ago, something happened—something even I didn't suspect. The satellite base where I work experienced a massive flood of signals, and I was needed to catalog and analyze those signals. Some other surprising things have happened, and I must speak with Ani and my brother privately."

"Reslo, they really do know," Yenne said. "They know more than our superiors probably would like, but it was the only way. They know about The Blood and The Balance." He placed a hand on Reslo's shoulder. "Yes, and you need to know that Lrakira is cured. There is much to tell you."

"Wait," Melli said. "Not yet. There is time. Taryn said it was not urgent." She went over to Reslo and pulled him into a hug. "First, welcome home, my friend. My apologies for my reaction. We are truly happy to see you. The last few days have brought many changes, and it's a struggle to keep up and keep them all under control. How long was the trip from Southern? Weeks I suspect. And no communications at all during that time."

She pushed him to arms-length and then pulled him close, giving him a light kiss on both his cheeks. "It's been frustrating for all of us. But now you are here, and we can stop all the worrying. As Yenne said, there is much to tell, and we'd like to hear all about Southern. But that can wait until after the eve meal. It's getting cold. Ani and a friend will be here shortly. Come, join us." She tucked her arm around his and escorted Reslo into the back room.

As they passed him, Taryn heard Reslo ask if cinnamon tea was part of the menu. His mother laughed and said, "Of course."

Taryn looked back at the door. Still no Ani. He could guess what had delayed them and grinned as he handed his father's crutch to him and followed the others into the back room.

While platters of food were passed from person to person, Reslo was caught up on the happenings during the most recent months. He seemed a bit unnerved when Yenne mentioned that he was now seventeen years younger than Reslo instead of three years older. There were a few tears, mostly of relief, when he was again assured that Lrakira's people were truly cured, and he stared long and hard at Taryn when his identity was revealed. Taryn took it upon himself to waylay the unspoken concerns by reiterating that nothing more than kissing had ever occurred between Ani and him. There was an audible sigh, and Taryn returned the nod of acceptance from Reslo.

While at first seeming shocked that Shendahl managed to keep the information about the twin birth totally secret, Reslo mentioned several discussions during which she had expressed concern about how close Ani and Taryn appeared to be getting while in their mid-to-late teens. But it had eventually become apparent that the two teens were basically extremely close friends and that a true romance would most likely not occur. Reslo mentioned only seeing them kiss a couple of times and that Ani had seemed uneasy with each exchange.

"Well, I understand Shendahl's concern now," Melli said. "Until a few months ago, my Gelwood always hoped they would marry. Then we would finally get a daughter." That sobered the conversation considerably, and while Melli reacted to her own words with tears and Gelwood put his arm around her to console her, Taryn whispered a quick explanation about the couple's infant daughter.

Reslo reached out and patted Gelwood's hand, which rested on Melli's shoulder. "It would not have happened even if the truth had never been discovered. When Ani returned from the Continental Blade Championships, she told me every female of reasonable age had eyes on Taryn, and she was happy that he might find a true love outside of Star Valley. She said she was not interested in him romantically and was content with being his best friend."

Taryn added that she had declined his proposal, and he had realized at the spring dance that the newcomer Renloret was the man who made her heart beat faster.

"Who is this Renloret?" Reslo asked. "The name sounds Lrakiran."

"It is," Renloret said. "I was the pilot of the rescue ship that took Ani to Lrakira to save our people."

Everyone at the table turned to see Renloret and Ani standing in the doorway.

Taryn stood. "You're late."

Ani stepped into the room, putting her hands on her hips. "We were reading all the messages. Uncle Reslo's last message said he was coming home, but he didn't say when. You always told me details like that should not be left out." She ran around the table and embraced Reslo. "You almost beat your message!"

"The only problem is, I sent it almost three weeks ago. But my guess is that you had the excuse that you were on Lrakira at the time."

Yenne coughed and said, "And I'm guessing you were on a sailing ship and did not have access to a personal messaging system when we picked up your hidden message from the Southern space probe. I'm not surprised you figured out how to do that."

"So, someone did receive it?" Reslo asked excitedly.

"Yes, we did. We were already on our way here. We replied as the message requested. Seeing you here makes me hope that will not create a problem for you at the Southern space center."

Reslo waved his hand and explained exactly how hidden the coding was that executed his desperate message and that only he would recognize a response. Reslo paused. "That means the anomaly is truly gone." He sat and put his head in his hands for a moment before looking up. "But you already knew that. And Ani has been to Lrakira. And the future of our people is assured." He shook his head. "I wish S'Hendale were here."

Ani touched his hands. "She knows."

"How?"

"Because the Anyala Stone told me shortly after Taryn pulled the Pericha blade from it. It was all in its song. Mother fulfilled her promise to the Stones, as did I. Now we have four searches to commence."

Reslo looked confused. "Four?"

Feeling a bit sorry for the man, Taryn jumped in and explained that three of the searches were for the Stones located somewhere on Teramar.

Reslo stopped shaking his head and became energized. "That's why I'm back! I mean, I was planning to return months ago for S'Hendale's Remembrance, but the flood of information we received kept me there longer than anticipated and . . . it's just that I think I know where one of the Stones is. I'm pretty sure the people of Teramar were originally from Lrakira, and they brought at least one Stone with them. It's near Southern's Tianet Mountains in an archeological dig recently discovered by Professors Jaikeer Bricka and Camfel Tondon."

Stunned silence answered him.

Reslo held their attention as he related his visit with the two Southern archeologists after seeing a newsline article about their discovery of a possible alien landing a thousand years ago. The article had been published almost two months after the space probe had overwhelmed the aerospace facility where Reslo worked. Enough information had bombarded the facility that it would take decades to work through and thoroughly categorize. He had guessed that the probe had been sending signals for many weeks but had somehow been blocked from being received on Southern until about three months ago.

Renloret raised his hand. "That was about the time I arrived here and the Time Song was destroyed."

"Time Song?" Reslo asked.

After another brief explanation, Reslo nodded. "I considered the possibility but dismissed it as too coincidental and rare. I thought the solar flares from Olbers were more likely the culprit. They crop up cyclically, but it has only been in the last twenty or so years that they've been recognized because the invention and growth of electronic communications is very new on Teramar. We are coming to the end of a flare cycle, so we should have improved communications for at least a decade. I had planned to return to Star Valley much sooner because we assumed the probe had failed—that it was lost. My superiors on Southern are building a second probe to be launched in two months. It is carrying a second hidden message aimed at Lrakira.

"Anyway, now that the flood of information has diminished and is coming in at the manageable rate I was expecting, and now that the backlog has been at least minimally categorized for further study by the Southern scientists, I was able to return to my usual schedule. That was when I found the article announcing the evidence of alien life on Southern."

"How long ago was that?" Taryn asked. He touched his pocket and frowned when he realized that he'd forgotten to bring his notebook. Ani's smirk resulted in a glare from him.

"About a month ago. It took me almost a week to get the time off and travel to meet Jaikeer in person." He shook his head. "I think he's a bit of a daredevil. Almost got us killed by racing a train to a crossing."

"How close?" Taryn was thinking he might like this archeologist if he could shake up Reslo.

"Too close if you ask me, but we made it to the dig site." Reslo leaned across the table, looking at Ani. "You've got to come back with me. There might be technology there I can use to get you . . . no, you've already been to Lrakira. I forgot." He covered his face with his hands. "This is hard."

Yenne clapped a hand on his little brother's back. "Yes, it is, but we will get through it together."

"We've spent twenty years trying to find a way to get Ani home. We never gave up, Yenne. Oh, blades, we thought you dead when you didn't return within the three months we expected. And then there were no ships, no messages, nothing, for twenty years! S'Hendale was so determined to see her promise fulfilled. I only went to Southern because we thought it would be our singular chance to get a message through. I didn't want to go. Before she died, she made me promise to do everything I could imagine to . . ." He stopped as he choked on the emotions.

Gelwood and Melli moved their chairs closer to Reslo. When Melli whispered something in Reslo's ear, a brief grin flashed across his lips and he nodded his head.

"Yes, thank you," Reslo said. "I will try." He brushed the dampness from his cheeks, straightened in his chair, and cleared his throat. "Listen, it is still important for Ani to go to this dig. It may be one thousand years old, but the glyphs discovered on a door talk about The Blood and The Balance."

"Fascinating," Renloret said. "The first book of Songs is also a thousand years old, and that is the first mention of The Blood and The Balance on Lrakira. The song is supposedly prophetic in nature. We believe the Stones knew Lrakira's people would be in trouble in the future and would need Teramar."

"Was there anything else besides the glyphs?" Taryn asked, thinking Reslo might have seen a Stone.

Reslo told of a painted chamber discovered behind the door with the glyphs. He described vivid paintings covering the walls, floor to ceiling. One area of the painted walls depicted people sliding down a purple, red, and yellow rainbow from one large circle to another slightly smaller circle with an even smaller circle surrounded by rings. There was also a second tri-colored rainbow arching away from the large circle to an indistinct smudge. He thought it was incomplete, as if the painters were uncertain where the other rainbow ended or where the people had gone.

Reslo paused in his narrative and then whispered that because the second rainbow was green, amber, and blue, he thought they might represent the guardian Stones of Lrakira. Perhaps the painting depicted the arrival of the Stones on Lrakira and that the people of Teramar had come from Lrakira. He suggested that the large circle in the middle was a stopping or refueling point.

Reslo reasoned there might be one or more Stones on Teramar

near the painted chamber. He stared at Ani for a few breaths before continuing. "After you won the blade championship, your mother used the crystal blade to set marks on your forearms. It was the first time I knew she had the Anyala Stone blade with her. Do you remember her telling us the markings declared your championship in the way of our people, but that I could not read them? She told me later the markings were in ancient Lrakiran and only Singers received marks in that language." He reached toward her. "May I see them again?"

Ani rolled up her sleeves. Reslo studied the light-colored scar patterns and shook his head. "I still can't read them, though they are similar to the glyphs on the door. I thought they might be related to Southern script, which I have learned to read this past year, but I don't think so now." He patted her arms and smiled sadly at her. "Perhaps my hypothesis is incorrect. But among her last words, S'Hendale said the Singer title had been passed on as she had been directed. Ani was now the Anyala Stone's Singer, and the Stone would be patient and wait until she arrived to complete the bond. I was not to tell Ani until I had found a way to get her back to Lrakira."

Reslo conjectured that if he brought Ani to the painted chamber, she might be able to find one of the Teramaran Stones and then might be able to communicate with it and get a message to the Lrakiran Stones.

An excited discussion ensued, and Taryn informed Reslo that there were three Stones on Teramar, not one, and they had supposedly begun their searches for their male Singers. Reslo was surprised by that but was quick to understand the implications of having both male and female Singers to achieve a sense of balance. He heartily congratulated Taryn on being one of those new Singers and asked if the Northern Stone's location had been discovered. Taryn replied that he'd only heard what he assumed was a questing song very recently and they were mapping out mountainous parts of Northern to begin searching. There seemed to be no urgency in the song, so Taryn felt there was time to go to Southern and help find the Southern Stone if it hadn't already been found during Reslo's trek to Star Valley. Then he would return to Northern to find his Stone.

A portion of the rest of the eve was spent in planning their trip to Southern. With Reslo's news, Taryn realized that it was all coming together, but he also found himself wondering who—and where—the Southern Stone's Singer was.

CHAPTER NINETEEN

More than five thousand miles away, a tel-com interrupted Treyder's work. His pen wobbled and the ink line curved when it should have been straight on the meticulous drawing. He cursed. Nothing had gone right since the sheriff had been rescued from the laboratory and a large percentage of the notes had been destroyed or stolen. His anger burned deeper, seething and eating away at his usual calm. It was all the senator's fault for hiring a handful of sloppy, ill-trained guards. Treyder crumpled the drawing and threw it across the room in a fit of frustration. The tel-com buzzed again. Why had he given the senator his private number?

He inhaled, trying to use the breathing technique his former blade trainer had insisted he learn, and exhaled as the buzz sounded again. The breathing wouldn't do any good. He punched the button. "No, Nelham, it is not done because you keep interrupting."

"My apologies, Doctor. I thought you would like to know that funding for your projects has been cut off and Nelham is under investigation." The voice on the other end was that of a woman, not Nelham.

Treyder scrambled away from the design table in his surprise. It was the woman in the shadows. He was sure of it. How could he forget the Southern accent that reminded him of his beautiful Fairaden? But why would she be calling him? And why was she using the senator's private number? What had she said? What was cut off? Who was being investigated?

"Who is this?" Treyder demanded.

"I'm calling to warn you, Doctor Treyder."

"Warn me of what?"

"The senator will spill out his plans for your marvelous little device. The police have enough of your notes to imply a connection with the sheriff's kidnapping and subsequent torture. There was blood in the drain, Doctor. It was a match. They are looking for you, and they will find you unless you let me help you."

"Who is this?" Treyder repeated. Had the senator ever called her by a name? No. She was just the woman in the shadows. Treyder tried to remember the last time he'd seen her. Ah, yes. The night he'd dropped that pup of a sheriff at the laboratory the senator had constructed for a backup facility in case the Star Valley lab was compromised. He calmed down. She couldn't possibly know where he was. The village at the base of Mount Piffital, Wharton, was too remote. If he was careful, he could find out everything she knew and still be safe.

She ignored his request for her to identify herself. No matter.

He would let her talk and then decide what to do. "How do you think you can help me?"

"I know the identity of the laboratory guest taken from you. I just haven't figured out why you chose him." Her tone was a curious mix of confusion and confidence. "You should also know that he is all better now and back in Star Valley, just like his blade ring partner, Ani Chenak. And they're not the only ones coming after you."

Treyder touched a button on the tel-com in an attempt to bring up the caller vid. It was blocked somehow. He frowned. She shouldn't be able to tell if she was on vid and she shouldn't be able to block his coding. He knew it had worked two days ago with the last call from the senator. What was different?

He wanted to test her knowledge. She might be a spy for the police. "Why is he after me?"

Her laughter was mirthless. "Well, if rumors around the research center are correct, you are responsible for his injuries and his coma, though the Southern surgeons seem to have figured out how to remove that intriguing little machine of yours. It took less time than it did with Miss Chenak. Out of curiosity, did *you* shave his head or did *they*?"

"The sensors don't adhere well to body hair, and the readings are not as accurate." He gritted his teeth. He had admitted to being responsible.

"Ah, well, in a couple of months, no one will suspect he's been ill or injured."

He knew that details about the condition of the kidnap victim had not been revealed in the newslines, so how did she know?

When she'd been in the lab, he'd just arrived with the inert sheriff. And unless the senator had tried to impress her with his project, she should not have known of any injuries, though she had been there and witnessed the comatose state. But that was all. Then her words came flaring back. The research center. The sheriff was back.

"They told you about his injuries?"

Again, her laughter screeched along a blade edge. "Oh, yes. The senator was most enthusiastic when I told him I could volunteer to *replace* you at the center after you disappeared, and I could keep him informed of possible repercussions of the sheriff's return if it happened. You had left, without a word, and the senator wanted someone he trusted there. Plus, it suited me as well."

"Why?"

"I used to work there, Isul. Don't you remember me? I was Fairaden's best friend. I left years ago because I couldn't stand being there after she died. They didn't care about her, you know. They talked about not wanting to help her or you. That you were just in the way. They wouldn't let you work on your amazing machines. And when she lost the baby and went into a coma, they were just glad she was gone."

What was Fairaden's friend's name? He racked his brain. Sarin? No, Sarinne. Now he could place a face with the voice, though they did not quite match with the appearance of the woman he'd seen with the senator. That woman had struck him as bitter and dangerous. Sarinne had been his wife's ally when the Chenaks had discouraged their marriage and most especially, their attempts to have a child.

He had thought that he might be able to find and fix the cause of his wife's coma if he could manufacture a machine small enough to go inside a person. Reslo had not agreed with him. Had outright said it was not possible. So Treyder had left Star Valley to care for Fairaden.

He had built a small workshop and hired some help with Fairaden's care so he could continue researching a cure for her coma. And when Fairaden had succumbed to the coma, Treyder vowed he would demonstrate to Reslo that it was possible to build the machine, and he had demonstrated it, twice now. But Reslo had not been a witness to either.

"Are you there, Treyder?"

"Yes, I was thinking about Fairaden. You say you can help me. I have two questions. Why do you want to help, and how would you?"

"The senator asked me to help. And since I also have a history with the Chenaks, I was compelled to see how I might help. He gave me his tel-com so I could contact you after my initial foray back to Star Valley.

"Fairaden said you were a genius, and I remember some of the machines you developed while you were in Star Valley. Before you left the research center to care for Fairaden, I overheard Reslo Chenak say you were working to build a very small machine to fix your wife's coma. He said it was impossible."

Treyder didn't answer.

"I think you succeeded, but the machine you succeeded with does not *cure* a coma, it *causes* one." She paused.

Treyder held his breath. What was she up to?

She went on to explain that she'd been hired by Senator Nelham to assist him in some manner and her knowledge of the Star Valley research center would come in handy.

"He told me about your marvelous coma device, and when he shared his plans for it, I insisted on seeing for myself. If you remember, I was with the senator when you brought the sheriff to the Saedi City laboratory as proof that your invention worked."

He grunted a noncommittal response.

"It evidently worked until the sheriff was rescued because of the senator's ineptness at hiring the right kind of security. And then you left, again, Isul. And you've refused to tell the senator where you are. I know you met with him and he gave you things the police don't know about."

Treyder wondered if she had been the emissary waiting to see the senator at the end of the last face-to-face meeting before Treyder had left for the mining district.

"I was sent to Star Valley to search your office and laboratory for signs of where'd you gone. But when I arrived, the deputies were interviewing the staff at the research center about you. And the staff hadn't seen you since the day before the sheriff was rescued. According to your coworkers, you left with boxes of notes and equipment. I waited until the deputies were leaving to tell them I'd seen you entering Senator Nelham's office a couple of weeks ago."

Treyder sat down and paid closer attention to her words. She had connected him to the senator with the authorities, which was one of the things he had worked hard to prevent.

She continued. "The sheriff's office has passed on my bit of information, and I believe that led to this morn's announcement of the investigation of the senator and the cessation of funding to all military related projects he has sponsored."

Treyder was unsure of how to react to this news.

"How does the investigation of Senator Nelham affect me? Many people go in and out of the senator's office. Even you."

"Ah, but don't forget that I also saw you with the sheriff's body in the laboratory."

Blades be damned. "So why do you wish to help me?" There was a pause, and he could hear her breathing. "Why?" he repeated.

"If we help you, then you can help us."

"What for what?"

First, she and the senator needed to know how close he was to achieving a mass deployment system and how many of the coma devices he had available. The senator wanted to schedule a demonstration of the devices for the military leaders. Nelham was certain that they would support use of the device to stop any aggressive actions by Southern. Once he had the military's support, a second demonstration would be planned for the full senate. That would strengthen Nelham's position in the senate, and Nelham would use that influence to see to it that any kidnapping charges against Treyder were dropped. And he would not only receive all the funding he desired, but also the accolades he had long deserved.

Treyder hesitated only briefly because he really did want to tell someone who understood how marvelous his invention was. Plus, the first boxes of coma devices had rolled off the conveyer belt just hours ago, and he was within a few days of testing them.

Sarinne repeated her request for his location. When he told her, the surprise in her response was obvious. Evidently, she had never considered that he would be in such an isolated area. He refused to answer her questions about how he had managed to manufacture cases of the device in such a short period of time. The facility had been under construction for more than a year, but he did not divulge that information.

It was only after ending the conversation that Treyder wondered if telling her his location had been a poor choice. She could just as well reveal his location to the police, and he would be caught—his works destroyed. What was done was done. He might have to find a new hideout. He glanced at the global map on the wall. Perhaps he should reconsider some of his previous options. He looked at the number of pins scattered along The Necklace Islands. Yes, he had options.

# CHAPTER TWENTY

Southern's Tianet Mountains were snow-covered as was the meadow in which the camouflaged star runner landed. Ani sat in front of the forward view screen studying the new vista. The mountains felt younger with their sharper edges and abrupt cliffs jutting exuberantly into the sky in defiance of time, which had not yet begun to age them. According to the geological history they had all read on their way to Southern, this particular mountain range was tens of thousands of years younger than her beloved peaks surrounding Star Valley, and though not quite as tall as the Northern ranges, she acknowledged their majesty. They were stunning and threatening, especially cloaked in the deep snow.

She idly wondered how different the view would be in summer. Would she be on Teramar then? She pushed aside the question. There was much to accomplish in the coming months. First, there were Stones to find.

An hour ago, Reslo had pointed out the village where they were to meet the archeologist, Professor Jaikeer Bricka. Renloret had circled the rendezvous location several times before choosing a landing site. Ani checked the time and turned an ear to the sounds coming from farther back in the star runner. She could not make out words, only the quiet hum of conversation among her brother, her uncle, and her . . . Renloret. Kela's mental voice chuckled, but he did not comment.

Even at half a globe away, their telepathic connection seemed as strong as ever. They had wondered at what distance it ceased. They already knew they could be several hundred miles apart on Northern and still communicate. That had been tested years ago. This was yet another test at over nine thousand miles. The next would take place with one of them in a star runner as it flew away from Teramar. Until then, she was delighted with his cheeky comments, only some of which she passed on to the others. He kept her informed of the happenings in Star Valley since they'd left.

Yenne, Gelwood, Melli, and Mroz were continuing to renew their friendship while planning strategies for when Taryn returned and started his own Stone search. Ani knew there would be long conversations that Kela would allow her to hear in the coming days. And Reslo was hopeful that the sun flare activity had lessened enough to provide more consistency in communications between the continents. Everyone aboard the star runner was more relaxed about being so far away from Star Valley with the knowledge that Kela and she had the telepathic connection. Reslo had been somewhat reluctant about leaving his brother so soon, but he had also been urgent about returning to Southern to find the Stone he *knew* was there.

A dark blob of movement appeared at the edge of the trees. Ani straightened and toggled the magnifying lens. The antlered beast stepped carefully through the drifts of snow. Puffs of breath rhythmically fogged its features. Easily three times the size of the tri-pronged sueders that populated the central mountains of Northern, this creature moved as though it was at the top of its food chain. Ani wondered what sized predator would be able to take it down. The antlers were wide and the palmation between the points would protect vulnerable parts of its body at the turn of its head.

As it lifted and placed each splayed hoof with careful precision, Ani understood that it knew exactly where each of its limbs were and would probably deliver maiming and killing kicks with the same precision. She watched as it turned its head sideways and with deft twists of the head scooped or swept the snow into piles until it had cleared a circle of dried grasses on which to graze. Ani grinned at this additional advantage of palmation. But how was it able to walk among the tightly growing trees from which it had emerged? Surely the antlers were an impediment.

Would Renloret's bio-teacher know what it was called, or was it only programmed for Northern? *Kela? Can you see this?* There was a chance that he might know since he had been with Renloret when his bio-teacher was downloaded with the updated language nuances of Northern.

*Oh my, that's a big one. What is it?* Ani heard the surprise in Kela's comment.

*I don't know yet. Do you think Renloret might have it in his bio-teacher?*

*You can only ask. I'm not sure how much, if any, of Southern's language is part of it.* Then he gave a mental laugh. *If you want my opinion, that looks delicious!* The feeling of hunger accompanied his pronouncement.

Ani turned in her chair and hollered down the passageway. "Ren? Can you come up? You should see this creature. Bring Reslo and Taryn too."

The muted conversation was replaced by footsteps, then all three men joined her. Ani glanced at each of them in turn. Even Uncle Reslo was staring at the massive animal. "You ever seen one before?" she asked him.

He shook his head.

The animal raised its head and brandished its antlers. Stretching its neck forward and tipping its muzzle upward, it bellowed, and a large cloud of exhaled air momentarily hid it. The star runner's audio system picked up the sound, and they all winced at the volume of the ululation.

Ani subconsciously counted the seconds as the call continued to rise to a painful pitch before falling dramatically to a rumbling growl. After a second or two of silence, the air around the creature was again engulfed by a frosty cloud as it issued another bellow that lasted six to seven seconds longer and ended with lung clearing coughs.

Just after the second call started, Renloret snapped switches that simultaneously opened other view screens and began recording.

"Look, there's another one!" Taryn said as he pointed at a screen that showed an equally large ungulate approaching from the rear right side of the camouflaged star runner.

The newcomer twisted and lowered his rack to scoop up snow with one of his antlers. With a grunt, he whipped his head sharply to the side, bringing his muzzle almost to his flank and successfully throwing the snow in a wide swath.

All eyes in the star runner turned to the forward screen to see what the first animal would do.

Reslo put a hand on Renloret's shoulder. "Are all screens recording?" Renloret nodded. "Good."

Ani glanced between the screens, a frown on her face. Was the star runner between the animals? Could they actually see through it? She voiced the questions.

Renloret cocked his head and frowned as well. He bent over the console and studied some of the readouts. "Well, it is close. Should we move or should we decloak so they don't run into us and damage the ship or each other?"

The first animal had stepped out of his grazing circle and begun to toss snow from side to side. A low rumbling sound punctuated the end of each threatening movement. The second animal was pawing up the snow with all four legs, each spewing high arching plumes.

"Decloak," Reslo ordered.

Renloret reached to his left across Ani's chest to get to the switch. "My pardon, love."

She suppressed a giggle at the unconscious endearment and leaned forward slightly, letting his arm brush against her chest. Her peripheral vision caught the grin on his lips and she grinned back.

"Whoa!" Taryn laughed and pointed at the screens.

Both animals had abruptly stopped their threatening behaviors and were standing stone still, heads as high as possible, forelegs straight and stiff, hind haunches almost touching the snow, legs bent like springs. Ani joined Taryn in laughing at the mirrored expressions of shock as the animals were suddenly separated by the towering star runner.

"I sort of feel sorry for them," Ani said. "Perhaps they'll just go away."

The first beast snorted and stomped the snow aggressively as if to challenge the hulking metallic thing that had appeared in its meadow without warning or sound. He coughed defiantly and shook the thin covering of tossed snow off his back before wagging his head back and forth.

Ani checked the smaller screen to see what the second animal was up to. It bellowed a call, raked its antlers through the snow, and jumped twice toward the star runner. When his threat went unanswered, he turned the antlers to face the star runner and took several long steps. With no movement from his perceived antagonist, he backed up a step, tossed his head back, and gave an eardrum-splitting high-pitched call as he continued to step back until his hindquarters contacted the trunk of a tree. A startled look crossed his face at the contact, and after giving one more insulting call, he turned abruptly and disappeared into the dark shadows of the trees.

The first animal was voicing threatening grunts as it turned in circles while keeping the broadest part of its antlers facing the star runner. After several minutes of nonreaction from the silent thing in the middle of the meadow, the animal gave a gravelly snort of disgust and lowered its head, returning to grazing for a few minutes. And then it too slipped back into the forest.

"So how long should we stay uncloaked?" Renloret asked. "I don't want to take a chance of being seen by people, but I hadn't expected we would need to reveal the ship to a pair of rutting behemoths so they wouldn't be damaged by running into it." A grin accompanied the question and complaint.

"You could probably safely engage the camouflage now. Just have the sensors listening and watching for a return appearance of either animal," Reslo said. He patted the pilot on the shoulder and turned to head back to the staging area.

Ani asked if the camouflage could be rigged to show something solid so other animals would avoid it. Renloret muttered to himself for a few minutes and then announced that the ship was now a pile of rocks.

Ani pulled on her jacket, shouldered her pack, and exited the ship down the ramp. She was between the ramp and the trees before turning around in the knee-deep snow. Yes, it looked like a huge pile of rocks had been dumped in the middle of the meadow. Renloret had even added touches of snow to make it more realistic. Startled by the appearance of Taryn and Reslo, followed closely by Renloret, she memorized the part of the rock formation they had walked through so she could get closer to the ramp area when they returned, even though she knew that once beyond the edge of the image, she would be able to see the star runner perfectly.

It wasn't too long before they had trudged over the hills and found the road leading to the village. With the tree-lined road well plowed, they began to jog. Reslo was familiar with the road and had told them they were just a curve or two away from the rendezvous point he had arranged at the gate of the small power plant. He pointed above the trees at the steam cloud as proof.

Ani unzipped her jacket once they arrived at the gate. The exercise had been a good remedy for the hours of sitting in the star runner. The others also opened their jackets to cool off. Studying what buildings she could see, she marveled at how well they blended with the terrain. "Is the entire village like this?" she asked, waving her hands at the thick forest that still blocked some of the view.

Reslo shook his head and explained that the other side opened to a wide plain that ran into the base of the mountain range where the dig site was located. He reminded them that Jaikeer had taken him to the dig site on the road that ran from the village to the mountains, crossing the train tracks. He added that the road they were on was a tertiary road and not traveled as much as the others. It led to a couple of farms on the other side of the hills they had just left. Their path from the star runner had come out halfway between the village and the farms. They all turned toward the village when a musical blast sounded. A supply vehicle skidded to a stop, the tune sounding again.

"Hey ho, good to see you again, Sir Reslo!" the driver shouted through the side window, his heavily accented Northern reminding Ani of Renloret's early words. "It is a good thing I brought a vehicle with more seats than mine, as you suggested."

Ani smiled as she remembered her uncle's description of his

heart-stopping trip from the village to the archeological dig and the race with the train. The driver leapt out and waved a hand above his head before circling it down and to his chest in a blade salute. He added a deep bow.

"Greetings my Northern friends." Ani was surprised at the wink he aimed at her. "I, Professor Jaikeer Bricka, am honored to meet the prophesied Blood and Balance. You don't look too poorly for being one thousand years old." The driver winked at her again.

Ani realized that they were all staring openmouthed at him. How much had Uncle Reslo told them? A glance at her uncle showed that he was also stunned to silence.

"We have much to show you and many questions. Please, get in. Professor Tondon is anxious to meet you." He opened the rear door and held out a hand to Ani. She took it, and he pulled her close enough to whisper in her ear as she stepped past him and in to the vehicle. "Your uncle told us you are The Blood and he needs to find a way to get you to your people. If what we've found so far is fact, there may be alien technology hidden further into the caves that will help you and your uncle. We don't know yet, but we are hopeful."

Before she could think of anything to say in response, Professor Bricka had practically pushed her uncle, Taryn, and Renloret into their seats and shut the door. He was chuckling as he slid into the driver's seat.

Ani leaned toward her uncle. "Is he sane?"

Reslo was staring at the back of the archeologist's head. "I thought he was."

Renloret stuck his head between theirs. "Exactly how much did you tell them?"

"Do not berate him." Professor Bricka's words were loud enough to carry over the sound of the engine. "We are scientists and have come to terms with the reality of aliens. As I said, we have much to show and tell. More evidence has been found in the weeks since Sir Chenak left to get his niece, and you may provide insight and answers to our questions. Only one article was released, and that brought us Sir Chenak. We are grateful for his honesty, though at first, we thought he was just another interested scientist—until he vomited all over the tunnel."

Reslo gave an embarrassed groan and cradled his head in his hands.

"You threw up?" Ani laughed, remembering how she had reacted and done the same thing at the top of the hill overlooking Awarna on Lrakira as two of the three moons rose. At least she wasn't alone in the manner of reaction to life altering experiences.

Renloret patted the older man's shoulder. "Did you hit anyone?" His blue eyes flicked to Ani, and she realized he was remembering what she had done to him after she'd emptied her stomach. She reached back and swatted at him. He chuckled as he avoided the halfhearted gesture.

Reslo raised his head, which was flushed with embarrassment. "You didn't have to tell them that."

Professor Bricka laughed. "Perhaps not, but it was what convinced us you were telling the truth." He looked over his shoulder at the four Northerners. "Strap in. I have a train to race." His grin was contagious, and his passengers laughed nervously.

The interior of the vehicle was suddenly filled with raucous music, and the professor began to sing along in Southern as he accelerated while turning the steering wheel sharply around, throwing the passengers to one side. Ani heard her uncle mutter several Lrakiran curses. His eyes were tightly closed, accentuating the creases at the outside corners. From his behavior, it was apparent he was not sure they would survive the trip.

# CHAPTER TWENTY-ONE

The bone-jarring ride finally slowed to a stop and the professor slapped off the music. Ani thought she could still hear echoes of the music bouncing off the walls of the vehicle.

"Well, that wasn't as bad as I expected," Reslo said, his voice a mere whisper.

Ani stared at him. "You mean that there wasn't really a train this time?"

He nodded. "I think he was teasing, and the last couple of miles were smoother in this vehicle than the one he drove then. At least we had full safety belts for everyone."

Professor Bricka laughed as he slid the side door open and bowed to each as they exited. Ani wondered again at his sanity. Could he hear anything after listening to the high volume music all the way to the site? The trip had taken almost two hours. She still could feel the beat of the last piece inside her head. It had been almost hypnotic, and her feet had tapped with the rhythm. In spite of the intriguing music tastes of this professor, she wondered if they were safe so far from the village.

She executed a circle, taking in the stunning view. They were atop a frigid, windblown mesa that rose at least a half mile above the valley floor. The last bit of road had zigzagged and spiraled along the sides of the mesa, alternating an open view of the valley and what seemed like a blade-width distance to the sheer rock wall. When the vehicle had lurched to the top, bounced, and grumbled to a stop, Ani had taken a deep breath. Renloret and Taryn had done the same. Seeing a blue tent-like structure tethered tightly against the elements a short walk away, she conjectured that it must be the headquarters of the archeological dig. She hoped it would be warmer inside.

Hadn't Uncle Reslo said something about guards? Where were they? She turned to circle again more slowly. The mesa top was not completely flat. There were ripples in the stony surface and large piles of rocks seemingly randomly placed. A flicker of color between two spire-shaped stones above them got her attention. Guard number one. His scarf had come untucked. Now that she knew where he was, Ani watched him hurriedly tuck the offending flag of fabric back under the collar of his dust-colored outfit. She smiled as she recognized the shape of a camouflaged crossbow leaning against one of the spires. The guard waved. Was he signaling another guard? Then she heard a whistle from her left. She turned her head in time to see one of the piles of rocks change shape. Guard number two.

Taryn and Renloret had stepped close to her, turning their backs to the wind so they could hear each other.

"So, how many do you see?" Taryn asked, almost shouting.

Ani nodded toward the twin spires and then heard another soft whistle from the pile of rocks.

Renloret's eyes flicked to the spires and he frowned. He had not seen that one. "I've also seen two. One is behind the building and the other is the whistler."

Ani felt a blush bring a warmth to her skin as she realized she had missed the one behind the building. She glanced at it. A flash of light announced an unsheathed sword.

"And that makes at least four then," Taryn said. He pushed his chin forward, indicating some larger rock formations on the other side of the vehicle. Another flash of light showed her where the fourth guard was.

Ani was glad that she, Renloret, and Taryn had been attentive and observant. Together they were safer and more informed than if any of them had been alone. Studying the bank of rocks Taryn had indicated, Ani saw a slight movement of tan against tan and nodded. "Well trained. Professional and very expensive." She elbowed Renloret. "I'm betting we would not have been able to rescue Taryn if this group had been guarding him. Good thing the senator wanted to keep expenses low."

Renloret grunted in agreement.

"Come, I will introduce you to my compatriot," Professor Bricka said, interrupting their conversation. He slung an arm over Reslo's shoulders and without checking to see if they followed, led the way to the blue tent-like building.

Once inside, Ani studied the wood lattice interior frame over which insulating fabric had been stretched. The front space held two desks, both stacked high with papers and books. There was a large rectangular table in the center with what looked like maps scattered across the surface, and an iron stove gave off waves of heat near one corner. Professor Bricka had shrugged out of his jacket and draped it over the back of a chair at one of the desks. On his way to the stove, Reslo took his off and tossed it to the professor's outstretched arms. Standing in front of the stove, Reslo rubbed his hands together and held them out to capture the rising heat. Then he turned his backside to the heat and grinned as he rubbed his buttocks. Ani laughed and went to join him.

"Camfel?" the professor shouted as he pointed out the row of hooks for them to place their coats. He jabbered on in Southern, though Ani heard her name as well as Reslo's.

Scuffling noises came from behind an accordioned screen that backed a pair of head-tall bookcases. A female voice answered. The woman sounded tired and there was a complaining edge to her words. Ani watched as three stacked boxes with legs came from behind the screen and shuffled their way to the central table. The box carrier bumped into the table and the top box slid off and broke open on landing. An assortment of things bounced and rolled, and some just fell to the dirt floor.

Words came in a rush. From the tone and harshness of the syllables, Ani assumed the woman was cursing her clumsiness. Taryn bent down and began picking up the scattered items that had tumbled from the box. Ani took a couple of steps toward the two remaining boxes and steadied the one that teetered in a threatening manner. The woman shoved her hips forward, scooting the stack fully onto the table with an unhappy harrumph.

Scolding words came forth as the woman straightened, but she quickly covered her mouth with her hands as she came face-to-face with Ani. Close-cropped black hair accentuated high cheekbones, and her wide grey eyes were framed with thick lashes. She dropped her hands and gave Ani an impish grin. With a short nod to Ani, the woman turned to Professor Bricka and said something that sounded slightly accusatory. Then she flicked her head sideways, sending her bangs to one side and out of her vision. Turning back to Ani, she gave a Southern blade salute and outstretched her forearm in greeting. Ani grasped the woman's arm briefly, noticing the stronger than expected grip. She took a step back, gave a Northern salute, and added an honorific bow for good measure.

The petite archeologist smiled politely at Renloret and bowed to Reslo, with whom she was already acquainted. Then the grey eyes flicked questioningly at her coworker. "Jaikeer?" Her voice was smooth and carried a lilt that hinted at a possible soprano singing voice, though Ani knew that sort of assumption could often be incorrect.

Professor Bricka stepped forward. "I present Professor Camfel Tondon to our new Northern visitors." He introduced Renloret and Ani and then looked around. Ani followed suit, and wondered where Taryn was before noticing a pair of boots sticking out from under the table.

What was he doing on the floor? "Taryn, you're being introduced." She nudged her boot along his ribs.

"Oh, a moment." He backed out but not far enough, and he

rapped the back of his head on the edge of the table as he tried to rise. "Blades be damned." A hand popped up, put something metallic on the top of the table, and then braced itself against the table surface. Taryn eased his head from under the table and stood sharply, taking a moment to brush the dust from his pants. With a grimace, he rubbed at his scalp. "You really could use a few rugs in here. It would cut down on the dirt." He had nodded in Professor Bricka's direction before looking attentively at the only person he had yet to meet.

"Taryn Avere, Star Valley Sheriff, Professor Camfel Tondon," Bricka announced.

Taryn's mouth dropped open as if to speak, but nothing came out. Ani glanced at her uncle. He was grinning, not at either her or Professor Tondon but at Taryn. It seemed even Renloret was aware of the uncharacteristic speechlessness because he looked from Taryn to Ani with his eyebrows raised. The female scientist appeared equally stunned.

Ani began to count her breaths, timing the pause. This would be something she could tease Taryn about in the future.

Reslo spoiled it all by clapping his hands together. "Well, now that the introductions are done, what have you dug up since I left?"

Turning to hide her smile at how both Taryn and Camfel Tondon had jumped at the claps, Ani caught Renloret's wink. Was this how she had looked and behaved when she first met Renloret? Probably, she admitted to herself.

"Professor Bricka?" Renloret subtly moved attention from the still flustered pair to the head archeologist.

"Let us not be so formal. Only our students and employees address us so. Call me Jaikeer."

Professor Tondon seemed to have recovered her composure. "And I wish to be called Camfel."

Ani noticed that she looked directly at Taryn as she made her statement. Taryn gave her a brilliant smile and softly repeated her name. She blushed charmingly as she tried out his name.

Renloret coughed to cover what sounded almost like a laugh and cleared his throat. "Jaikeer, Reslo said you have found a door with an inscription that mentions The Blood and The Balance. May we see it?"

"Oh, yes. Come," he replied. "We have completed the cleaning, and all is readable."

Camfel reached out her hand to Taryn and pulled him toward the door.

"Won't you need your jackets?" Reslo asked with a slight smile to his lips.

Everyone grabbed their jackets and made their way out into the wintery air. Ani stuffed her hands in her pockets and positioned herself between Renloret and her uncle. They followed Jaikeer and the bemused couple.

"Wow, I didn't expect that to happen," Reslo said. "I'd always thought Taryn would end up with a local gal."

Ani laughed at the look he gave her.

Renloret draped an arm around her shoulders. "This local gal is mine."

The confidence in his voice warmed her more than the jacket. She felt his lips touch the top of her head and leaned into him.

"It looks like we won't have to worry about Taryn, now that you are solidly out of contention, Ani," Reslo said. "It will be interesting to watch these two, for sure."

"I like her already," Ani replied.

The blustery wind pushed them from side to side as they trudged along a well beaten path in the snow. It led them around the large pile of rocks that had partially hidden the two guards.

Jaikeer waved off the guards as they approached a long, downward-sloping ramp. Ani peered into the depths and began to speculate on how high the walls would get before her claustrophobia unsheathed itself. How had she managed to put herself in this previously unbearable situation? As the ramp dipped below ground level, she began counting her steps while trying to think of something to say to distract herself from the space that was closing in. Why wasn't she sweating and having trouble breathing? She could reach her hand overhead and touch the smooth, slightly curved ceiling. And the lighting was dim, making the tunnel look even narrower than she knew it was. Despite its length, the tunnel was smaller than the cramped little lift in the building where Taryn had been tortured. She should be running back outside. Why wasn't she? Why wasn't her heart racing?

"Are you all right?" Renloret asked, taking one of her hands in his and giving it a squeeze.

She knew he'd seen only a small example of how she reacted in confined spaces. "Yes, I am. Surprisingly."

"Do you want to go back to the top?"

She shook her head. "No. Really, Renloret, I'm okay. I don't feel any panic."

In the dim light she could see his concerned expression change to skepticism, and she squeezed his hand. A thought occurred to her. "Is it possible that the healing songs heal more than broken bones and torn muscles?"

"That would be an interesting side effect," he replied. "Can you ask the blade?"

She reached down to her boot sheath where the crystal blade now resided. There was no voice, no song, only a feeling of belonging, of knowing it was where it should be. "It doesn't think or sing like the Anyala Stone."

"Well, then we can ask the Stone the next time we're on Lrakira. Or maybe one of the Teramaran Stones will have the answer." His voice was hopeful.

"We have to find them first."

"Come on, we're falling behind." Renloret pulled her to almost a jog toward the brighter lighting ahead.

# CHAPTER TWENTY-TWO

A ni ran her hands over the engravings. The symbols were at once familiar and foreign. She pulled back the sleeves of her coat to bare part of her forearms and held them up next to the intricate designs that covered the thick stone door. "What do you think?" she asked the silent group standing in a crescent behind her.

She heard dual gasps from Camfel and Renloret. The similarity was startling even with the variances of a curve and the addition or lack of a line here and there. She had seen it right away, having studied and memorized the championship markings her mother had carved on her skin with the crystal blade.

When she and Renloret arrived at the door bathed in the bright-powered lights, Renloret had dropped her hand and stood in shocked silence, turning his head to the right and left, a frown on his face. She imagined he was trying to figure out why it looked familiar, but it was out of context for him. Instead of telling them what she saw, she showed them. "It's ancient Lrakiran, isn't it?" She turned to look at Renloret.

He stepped forward, traced a symbol on the door, and then pointed to a similar one on her arm. "It's like a written dialect. It has its own 'accent,' as it were."

The pilot turned to Camfel. "Jaikeer says you translated this first stanza to Southern and he translated that to Northern after Reslo arrived."

The petite woman nodded, her short hair bobbing. "Yes, Reslo became sick when he heard it in his language." She gave Reslo a motherly smile. "He was very upset and did not understand how a thousand-year-old artifact had the name of his niece. I did not understand either. He explained that he came to Teramar from another planet far away to save his people. He did not look like we expected someone from another planet to look, so Jaikeer and I had trouble believing it."

Jaikeer smiled and pointed to the carved glyphs. "We know this language only in its written form and have only surmised how it is pronounced because of the similarities with our written Southern. Professor Tondon is the leading researcher on what we know as Old Southern. We have only a few actual documents in storage at regional universities. Camfel has copies of them here to help her decipher the doorway." He studied Renloret. "You know this written language?"

"I know what it says, if that is what you are asking. It is the written language of our guardian Stones. We call it ancient Lrakiran, and it is really a song."

"A song?" both Southern scientists exclaimed in unison.

Renloret smiled. "Yes." He ran his hands over the lines of carved script. "This is the first stanza of the First Song. It's also known as The Prophecy of The Blood and The Balance."

Ani touched his arm. "Sing it for them."

Halfway through the second line, to the amazement of all, Jaikeer joined him, his bass vibrating the walls of the tunnel. His eyes were closed, and his face shone with joy. At the end of the stanza, Renloret stopped singing, though Ani knew he could have gone on.

Renloret was staring at the archeologist. "Wait, how and when did you hear that song?"

Jaikeer blushed. "The tune is one of several in my head for many weeks. I hum them while we dig. Until now, I did not know it has words." He turned to a smiling Camfel. "The pronunciation is different than we thought but close enough, yes?"

Camfel began bouncing from foot to foot. She grabbed Renloret's hand and pulled him to the narrow opening at one side of the door. "There are more words inside and a painting you should see. Come."

Ani watched as they disappeared into the blackness. She could hear scuffling noises as boots rubbed against gravel and fine sand. Light filled the slot, and she heard a muttered Lrakiran curse from Renloret.

Jaikeer tugged at her jacket and flicked his head toward the slot, smiling. Taryn was already entering with Reslo close behind. The cursing was repeated by Taryn, this time in Northern. Ani followed Jaikeer.

The powered lights Camfel had switched on illuminated the interior of a large chamber. Ani recognized the smooth machine excavation that had also been present in the tunnels that ran between the lake house, cabin, and research center. She wondered at their age. Had the Lrakirans had that technology for a thousand years? Most of the wall surface appeared to be painted, which accounted for it being named the painted chamber. The only areas unpainted contained carved script like that on the entrance door.

Renloret was standing in front of one of three carved sections murmuring as he touched each of the glyphs, his hand moving from right to left. Reslo and Camfel were standing just behind his shoulder, the petite grey-eyed woman rapidly scribbling on a tablet. Ani didn't remember seeing her carrying the tablet before. Perhaps it had already been in the chamber.

Turning about, Ani discovered a small desk piled with books and sheaves of paper. Yes, Camfel had been working in this chamber for some time. Ani moved closer to the desk and shuffled through several pages of double-columned writings that were spread out across the center part of it. While she could not read half of the text, the right-hand column had the look of what she knew was ancient Lrakiran. Ani held up one sheet and matched it with the section of glyphs on her left. This was Professor Tondon's translation.

"Ani?" Taryn's voice redirected her attention. Ani replaced the paper in its original position and walked over to her brother.

"Should this be familiar?" He had crossed his arms, possibly to keep from touching the painted surface, but he was tipping his head toward a large central circle with two sets of rainbow-like images arching away from it.

She studied it. Recognition made her shut her eyes. The tapestry in the Anyala Stone's chamber had a similar image. But those tricolored rainbows had been arching away from a circle of seven robed people holding blades up to join their points. Ani stepped close and examined the large white circle. Near the base of the rainbows she saw a tiny golden circle with seven lines drawn to the white center. Each line was a different color. She saw red, blue, green, amber, yellow, purple, and a brighter shade of white. Each rainbow contained three of the colors. One arched away in amber, blue, and green. The other was yellow, purple, and red. She distinctly remembered the two rainbows in the tapestry as being the same color combinations and briefly wondered about the seventh line. Did it represent the Stone left behind on the origin planet? Was it white?

"Well?" Taryn's whisper brought her back to the Teramaran chamber. "It's like the tapestry, isn't it? With the rainbows?"

She pointed at the tiny gold circle. "Do you see that? I think it represents the circle of people holding up their blades."

He murmured assent and leaned close to whisper in her ear. "What about all the dead people?"

Ani realized they had not talked much about the tapestries that had hung around the edges of the Anyala Stone's chamber. She had not even asked Layson or Diani about them when she had the opportunity to ask questions during her interview prior to the blade proving. Didn't Renloret have photographs of the oldest tapestry? She whispered back, "I didn't think they were dead, Taryn. I thought they might be asleep."

"Hmm. I hadn't thought of that."

"Remember that the second line of the first stanza says they were divided and sent away in deep sleep."

"Oh, yes. Well, that's a more comforting way to see the bodies all stacked up in the corner."

Ani backed up a couple of steps and pointed to one of the rainbows above them. "Do those markings look like people to you?"

Taryn stood on tiptoe to get closer to the painting. "Not exactly. If they are, they don't have clothes on." He smirked at her, and she stuck out her tongue, making him chuckle.

"I think they represent people," Uncle Reslo interrupted, moving to stand next to Ani to study the painting. He pointed to the rainbow on their right, which arched in blue, amber, and green. "See where it stops?" He traced the rainbow's path to a smaller disc. "If you look close enough, you can see three other smaller circles around it."

"So?" The single syllable word was full of the sheriff's inquisitiveness.

Reslo looked askance at Taryn. "This is Lrakira."

Ani realized that Renloret and the two archeologists were no longer holding their own conversation. They appeared to have finished with the transcription of Renloret's translation from ancient Lrakiran to Northern and Jaikeer's help in translating that to Southern for Camfel. Now they were paying rapt attention to the image Ani, Reslo, and Taryn were studying.

Camfel smiled and tapped Jaikeer's shoulder. She pointed to the endpoint of the red, yellow, and purple rainbow. "And this is Teramar. See the little moon with its own set of rings?"

No one spoke as they all studied the full painting. Awe and understanding filled Ani. The Stones were powerful enough to move people safely across the billions of miles between star systems—even galaxies if she understood the basics Renloret had been teaching her. She needed to hear the First Song again.

"Ren, say the words again."

He seemed to know exactly why she needed them because he didn't hesitate. He spoke the words instead of singing them. "Circle of seven sing safe passage. Divide by two and send in deep sleep. The Blood and The Balance shall each save one. Awakening three to rejoice with time's message. Time will soon come for reunion's leap. Six will sing joining three homes and suns."

Ani's mouth dropped open. She was sure she understood it now. "There's a circle of seven people with blades on the tapestry in the Anyala Stone chamber. Two rainbows in those colors arch away from the apex of their blades." She pointed at the two painted rainbows. "And there is a very bright star in the sky with a tail—a comet. I think it was a forewarning sign of the asteroid that was on collision course with the planet of origin. Which means the Stones and their Singers were saving all the people from the asteroid by sending them to two different planets. That's why there are two piles of people on the tapestry! Taryn thought they were dead, but the song says they were in a deep sleep."

Taryn started to interrupt, and she waved him off. "Shush. Let me continue, please." She glared at him, and he placed three fingers against his lips. She ignored the frustration in his expression.

"We know about The Blood and The Balance saving the people of Lrakira and the Anyala Stone, so the second line is complete. Then the Time Song—even though it got ruined and there wasn't much to rejoice about—woke up the three Stones of Teramar, and they've started their search for their new Singers. As for Reunion's leap, maybe it will happen in a couple of years or even a couple of generations when all six of the Stones have Singers and the people of both Teramar and Lrakira know about each other. The six Stones will sing a reunion song to join Lrakira and Teramar with our planet of origin." She stabbed a finger at the large white disc high on the wall. "See? Three suns and three homes."

She stopped on those words because of the expressions on Jaikeer's and Camfel's faces. "Right. You haven't been flown on a star runner or been to Lrakira and seen the triple moonrise. You've only just discovered that aliens *might* have been here one thousand years ago."

She looked at Reslo, Renloret, and Taryn. "You could help me here, couldn't you?"

Reslo was grinning. "You're doing a fine job of overwhelming them on your own."

"But you said you told them everything," she retorted.

"But I didn't know about the First Song, more Stones, and male Singers until a few days ago, little one. And I didn't tell them about the Stones at all. I only told them I needed to get you to Lrakira so you could save the people. I didn't even know one of the Stones was going to get injured. So I couldn't have told them everything."

Ani felt very small and just a bit silly at her information dump. She was sure their expressions were something close to what hers had been when she realized she was no longer on Teramar. "My apologies if I scared you. Really, the people of Lrakira are just like us, and the Stones . . . the Stones are huge intelligent crystals that are alive. And because they don't have mouths like us, they communicate telepathically with music, songs, and color. And they're so beautiful, you can't imagine until you actually see one."

The two Southerners gave each other sidelong glances before turning back to her. She wondered if she'd just made it worse.

A wide smile lit up Jaikeer's face, and Camfel began speaking rapidly in Southern. Her hands gestured from one side of the painted chamber to the other. Then she pointed at the sections of glyphs she and Renloret had been examining and translating. When she stopped, she was staring at Renloret, hands on hips.

"What's she saying?" Taryn asked.

Jaikeer turned to him. "She wants to know where he has seen the glyphs before. He is too familiar with them, and the translation was too easy. Additionally, all of you are talking about rocks being alive. She says that there are other very old writings she has found that tell of singing stones, but she thought they were mere tales. Now she is sure they fit with these. She thinks the singing Stones are the true alien visitors." He paused.

Camfel was still staring at Renloret as if daring him to lie.

"She wants to see the book of songs he mentioned," Jaikeer added.

Reslo frowned. "You were able to bring one of the ancient books here?"

Renloret shook his head. "Not the actual book. Images of the text. They're on the star runner." Renloret waved his hand in the general direction of the village. "It's camouflaged in a valley beyond the village."

Jaikeer stared at him for a breath and then said something quietly to Camfel, whose eyebrows rose in surprise.

"Star runner? Here?" she asked. "Can we see it?"

"Not at the moment. It is disguised so no one will find it," Renloret replied.

"We should go now," Camfel said. "I need to see proof of this." Her tone brooked no argument.

Ani exchanged looks with everyone else.

"Well, it may help if she knows the truth." Taryn said.

Ani shook her head. "But what about the Southern Stone? Shouldn't we wait to show them the ship. Jaikeer has been hearing the Stone in his sleep. He knew the song, didn't he?"

Even Jaikeer nodded affirmatively.

Camfel sighed in resignation. "Okay, we will find the singing rock then see the star runner." She slipped a frown at Ani. She apparently didn't like not getting her way, but she had given in quickly when the prospect of finding one of the fabled Stones was put directly in front of her.

Then she turned the frown on Taryn. He took a step back and held up his hands in defense. Camfel gave a sharp jerk of her head. Ani wondered what Taryn had done to deserve the glare.

"How do we find this rock?" Camfel asked, aiming the question at Taryn.

"Camfel," Ani said, drawing the Southerner's attention, "Jaikeer said you have found other writings that tell of singing stones. Do you have them here?"

Camfel's entire demeanor changed as she grinned and held up her hand to signal that they should stay in the chamber. She left at a run and was back with several sheets of paper. "The stories or fables tell of time waking a stone. I brought copies because I recognized the same line on the door," she said as she shoved them at Renloret.

Renloret glanced over the writings. Without looking up he asked, "Where did you find these?"

She shrugged. "On an island."

His head snapped up. "An island? Which one?"

Ani knew there were hundreds if not thousands of islands at the edges of the two large continents as well as along the equatorial Necklace Island chain. She turned to the nearest glyphs on the walls and pointed. "Doesn't one of these say something about an island?"

"Yes, an island is one of the three homes of the Teramaran Stones. The other two are on Northern and Southern," Renloret replied. His eyes were back on the paper in his hands, and he started mumbling the words.

Ani stepped closer, drawn by the half-intelligible feel of the words. She realized he was searching for a tune that fit. "Start from the beginning, Renloret."

# CHAPTER TWENTY-THREE

J aikeer had moved closer as well. Taryn studied the Southern scientist. His eyes were intense and his lips were moving along with Renloret's.

The pilot began again, speaking rhythmically, discovering the cadence of the words. A buzzing began in Taryn's head. Was it music? Jaikeer had started to hum, and it matched what was in Taryn's head. Recognition brought sleepy, half-remembered thoughts alive. It was one of the dream songs he'd been having since arriving back on Teramar. He harmonized with Jaikeer's bass, and the foreign words became pronounceable. Jaikeer tugged on his sleeve to get his attention and pointed toward one of the piles of rubble that had yet to be removed from the chamber. There were cracks in the painting above the rubble that glowed with reddish light and appeared to outline a small door. Still singing, both men moved toward the pile and began flinging the rocks and clods of dirt to the side.

Taryn waved for Reslo and Ani to help.

The debris was cleared quickly, and they all stood looking at what had to be a door. Taryn felt the song disappear, leaving him with a sense of satisfaction and yearning. He needed to get to the other side of the stone door.

"What do you feel, Jaikeer?" Taryn asked. He hoped the answer would validate his own impression.

"I . . . I must go through the door. It is pulling me. It needs me to find it?" His voice was full of astonishment.

"Is the song gone?"

"Yes, but I must answer the summons. Camfel, get the tools."

She left and returned carrying several small picks and axes, two shovels, and a length of rope. She handed them out and immediately went to work scraping at what Taryn now saw as mortar in one section of the glowing red line.

With all of them working on various sections, the line was soon two finger widths wide. Jaikeer and Camfel took the rope and stuffed it around one of the upper corners, leaving two long tails sticking out. Taryn backed away and indicated the others should as well, giving the archeologists room to do what they probably had done to open the first large stone door to the tunnel to gain access to the painted chamber. Taryn noticed that the red light had disappeared, evidently no longer needed to show them the way.

A few minutes of tugging and the archeologists had rocked the stone slab far enough out that the four men could grasp the inner edge of it and pull. Their combined strength managed to swing it outward to reveal yet another tunnel. This one was barely wide enough for two people standing shoulder to shoulder. Camfel handed both Jaikeer and Taryn hand-lights and made shooing motions with her hands. Taryn returned her excited smile before following Jaikeer into the tunnel. The roof of the tunnel tickled the half-inch of hair on the top of his head. He tucked his chin and jogged after Jaikeer. After a couple of steps, he realized the tunnel was not only sloping downward but was also curving to the left.

An exclamation by Jaikeer stopped Taryn.

Light from Jaikeer's hand-light bounced off the machine-smooth walls. This tunnel was a smaller version of the tunnels between the research center and the lake house. But how could they have been constructed one thousand years ago? Had the early settlers brought machinery with them on their escape from the asteroid?

"Are you all right?" Taryn called.

"Yes. Get Camfel and the others. They need to see this."

Ani and Camfel entered the tunnel first when he told them Jaikeer had found something they should all see. Reslo was close behind the women. Taryn lagged, allowing his hand-light to play against the walls, which were so smooth that the surface was mirror-like and almost as reflective, successfully lighting their way.

Softer exclamations echoed through the tunnel and Taryn slowed up so he would not run into anyone. A sharp turn in the path ended abruptly in a squarish room. Camfel and Jaikeer were squatting on the ground next to a pile of golden cloth and whispering to one another. The words were coming too fast and were too foreign for Taryn to make out much, but he caught several phrases or words similar to those he was now familiar with from hearing Renloret talk in what he termed ancient Lrakiran. Reslo, Renloret, and Ani were leaning over the archeologists, their expressions ranging from surprise to concern.

"What'd you find?" he asked as he took a step closer. Reslo and Renloret backed away as Camfel stood, allowing him to see the rest of the cloth pile.

Gold robes, eerily resembling those worn by Singers Layson and Diani, rested against the wall as if laid out for wearing. Large boots with laced up fronts protruded from the bottom of the robes. The whole scene looked as if the person wearing the clothing had fallen asleep and then managed to escape from the clothes without disturbing them. He thought back to the cemetery and finding the empty burial robes in Shendahl's casket. What had Renloret said about the lack of a body? A Passing? Yes, the spirit left the physical body in the form of a smoke-like substance and disappeared into the blade until the new Singer was chosen and a blade bonding occurred. Unneeded after the spirit left, the physical body then disappeared, leaving no evidence.

Taryn squatted in front of the robe. "Male?" He pointed at the boots and the empty short blade scabbard buckled about the limp waist.

"No touch, please," Camfel said as he reached toward the scabbard. "I want to record the findings as they are, undisturbed."

"Okay. How long will that take?"

"Only a short time. I'm quick." She brushed dirt off her knees and without further word, left.

He considered following her, just to be alone with her for a few minutes. The Stones could wait a bit longer, couldn't they?

This Southern sprite of a woman did something to his breathing and heart rate, and he wanted to feel it again.

A chuckle from Ani brought him back to the underground room with the long empty robes. He glared at her, and she smirked back.

"She said she'd be back, Taryn," his sister said.

Now he understood Ani's behavior when she was around the pilot, especially those first couple of days. Would Professor Camfel Tondon feel the same about him? He shook his head. They'd only just met. Why did he feel like he'd always known this Southerner? It was very different from how he'd ever felt about Ani. Ever. Would Camfel come to Northern with him? Realistically, maybe not right away, but at some time?

"Taryn? Did you hear me?"

"What?"

Ani pointed to the robes. "How do you know it's male? Are you guessing from the size of the clothes and boots?"

"Yes. A woman did not wear this robe."

"Do you think he was a Singer?" Reslo ventured.

Taryn shrugged. "The song says the people were divided into two groups and three would be awakened by time's message. My guess is that 'time's message' is the Time Song. We know there are three Stones on Lrakira, so there should be three Stones on Teramar. The Singers on Lrakira wear gold robes why not the Singers who came here to Teramar with the other half of the people? Plus, there's a history of female Singers on Lrakira, and the Stones gave me the impression that three men would be Singers here on Teramar. I'm thinking that female balances male, and the Stones need that balance to achieve the reunion of the two peoples divided a thousand years ago." He'd finally been able to put his thoughts into words.

Ani was peering at him, her expression quizzical. "I've considered that as well. There is strength in the balance. My guess is that Layson, Diani, and the Stones of Lrakira are having many conversations with their people, preparing them for male Singers, and that there are more Stones. I hope they're reading the whole book of songs and communicating with their Stones better than they have in the last couple of decades." She looked down at the limp clothing. "It looks as though he died alone." She touched the hem of a sleeve, then she gave the empty robe a Northern salute. "May the blades honor and protect him."

Directing her question to Renloret, she asked, "Is there a death blessing in ancient Lrakiran?"

"It is very similar. I think you have honored him."

"I wonder what his name was," Jaikeer said. "Perhaps it is written somewhere on the walls of the tunnels or in this chamber." He stood, brushed at his knees, and began to slowly examine the walls, his fingers brushing away layers of dust on every crack, looking for carved glyphs.

Rapid steps announced the arrival of Camfel. This time, her arms cradled two cameras and at least two notebooks. Jaikeer helped her unload and set up a tripod stand. After eight or so chimes—Taryn laughed to himself as he said the time in his head in Lrakiran terms—the petite archeologist announced that the scabbard could be removed and more closely examined.

Low whistles of appreciation filled the small space as the

dust was gently wiped away and jewels and intricate metalwork sparkled and gleamed in the lights as Camfel continued to film. Camfel spoke in Southern, and Jaikeer turned the scabbard so she could record different angles.

"Hold there. More glyphs, I think," Camfel said. "Will you read it, Renloret?"

Renloret looked at the tiny markings on the edge. "Bayleden. That's all. It is a rare term meaning something like 'red warrior.'"

Camfel grunted softly. "We have a similar word in Southern. Belladine carries a similar meaning. It is the color of warrior blood. Could that be the name of the blade?"

Jaikeer pronounced it. "Bayleden."

Taryn turned to Ani. "Does your blade have its own name?"

She shook her head. "Only the Stone has a name as far as I know."

"Bayleden," Jaikeer repeated, his voice deep and full of longing.

An internal hum rose in Taryn's head, and he felt his lips move of their own accord. "Bayleden."

"Are you all right?" Camfel asked, touching his arm, her grey eyes concerned under a frown. He patted her hand and nodded toward Jaikeer. The archeologist stood facing the warrior-Singer's empty robe, the empty scabbard held in both his hands above his head, saying the word over and over. It was more question than song. Taryn could feel the tension in the little chamber tighten. He was waiting for an answer—wanting an answer.

Jaikeer gasped, and Taryn looked up to see red light outlining a long brick in the wall above the dead warrior's robe. The light pulsed with each syllable of the word when Jaikeer voiced it.

Glyphs on the surface of the brick glowed pale red, the color of watered wine.

Jaikeer stepped toward it and stretched out a hand.

Renloret held up his hand. "Wait. The inscription—it's a warning."

"Read it," Jaikeer said through gritted teeth, his hand trembling as he held it in check.

"'I will burn any not a worthy Stone Singer. He who is mine next will sing with Bayleden, and together, they will teach the people of their origin and their choice to go or stay.'"

"Isn't that last part in the First Song, Ren?" Ani asked.

"Yes, or something along those lines. A Song of Teaching is certainly mentioned, and there is also a choice to go or stay at the end of the last stanza of the First Song." Renloret turned and backed away from the brick.

"I believe Jaikeer is the next Singer," Taryn said. "He was the one drawn here by the Stone's song." He felt a longing building up inside him. When would he hear the call from *his* Stone? Where was *his* Stone and blade? Was he too far from the Stone to hear its song? Perhaps he shouldn't have come. Perhaps he should have stayed on Northern and begun his search.

With a solemn expression, Jaikeer stepped around the robe and began to scrape away the cracked mortar that sealed the arm-long brick in place. When he pulled the brick out, there were more exclamations as an iridescent red crystal blade was revealed. Its fire-hot glow spilled out from its place of hiding.

Jaikeer's reach stopped just above the hilt of the short blade. "You're sure I won't get burned?"

"You were the one who heard the Stone's call." Renloret gestured toward the shelf. "It's yours, or rather, you are its Singer. Take it. Listen to what it says. Ani says her blade talks to her."

"It acts as a conduit to the Anyala Stone," Ani added, "and the Stone doesn't talk so much as sing. It's mostly emotion from the blade. The Stones have a much larger vocabulary than we do."

Jaikeer reached again into the space above the hilt but did not touch it. "Positive, Renloret?"

The pilot nodded. Quickly then, Jaikeer grasped the hilt and brought the blade out. The blade's glow expanded, washing the tunnel in shades of red light. Jaikeer moved the blade through a series of training moves, and what had been a frown on his face changed to a smile. "It is well balanced, and my hand fits the hilt. It has been almost a year since I last held a short blade."

"So you have some skill at blades?" Ani asked, smiling. Taryn knew she had been concerned about the blade skills of the new Singers—or lack thereof—after having to demonstrate her skills against Layson on Lrakira.

"Everyone on Southern has had some training," Jaikeer replied. "I have placed well enough in regional competitions, but my interest in the past slowly took over, and though I have not held a true blade in more than a year, I still practice with wooden facsimiles to retain my fitness. It is wondrous to hold such a fine weapon."

"It's my understanding that you'll need practice to prove you're capable of protecting the Stone," Renloret said. "And you'll probably have to go against Ani to demonstrate your skills."

The smile disappeared and Jaikeer turned to Ani, bringing the shimmering red blade up in a salute. "My pleasure. When must this proving happen?"

Shrugging, Ani replied, "Evidently, I was the Singer of the Anyala Stone for over a year before I was introduced to the Stone and informed I had to prove my skills. But that is a tale for another time."

Camfel, who had been leaning against the carved walls, took a step toward Jaikeer. "What is that?" she asked, pointing at Jaikeer. "Is it burning?"

A thin red wisp of smoke was rising from the blade in Jaikeer's grasp. He held the blade in front of him, turning it side to side, trying to see what was happening. The haze curled and twisted hypnotically, seeming to dance in front of the new Singer. Jaikeer made a motion as if to throw the blade out of reach.

"No. It won't hurt you," Taryn and Renloret said in unison.

"A similar thing occurred in the cavern after Ani was injured," Taryn said, vividly recalling the green ribbons traveling from the crystal blade to cover Ani's inert body.

"It is the second half of a Passing," Renloret added, his voice carrying a reverent quality. "That's when the spirit or consciousness of the last Singer, which has waited within the blade, is passed on to the next Singer. The Lrakiran Singer histories are not clear about it all. And in Lrakira's more recent history, there have been few true Passings because the Stones and blades have been passed on from living Singers. I thought I'd never see this even once, but now I've seen it twice."

Jaikeer pointed to his head. "There is singing here." His voice was filled with wonder.

Taryn shared an understanding smile with Ani and Renloret. "We three have heard the Stones of Lrakira sing. A Stone can direct its songs to an individual or multiple people. Since I am not hearing it, I assume you are the sole recipient of its song." He glanced at Ani and Renloret to be sure they, too, were not hearing the red Stone. They concurred. "Listen and tell us if it allows."

Jaikeer stood still and let the smoky red tendril wrap around him until he was fully embraced. Tears began to fall down his cheeks and he whispered, "It asks if I willingly take on the responsibility of Singer of the Bayleden Stone. To lead my people from their past to their future. To protect the Stone as it will protect the people."

"Do you?" Ani asked.

Nodding acceptance and whispering the Stone's name, Jaikeer knelt as the ribbon seemed to soak into his body. Hugging the red blade to his chest, he began to speak in strongly accented Northern so Taryn and Ani would understand. "It's the . . . spirit . . . of the warrior. Mahzali was his name. He was Bayleden's last Singer. He . . . he says that his assistant would finish the hiding of the blade after his passing and then oversee the collapsing of the tunnels to protect both the blade and the Stone from being discovered too soon. He says the Stones would call for a new Singer after the Time Song awakened them, after The Blood and The Balance had been taken home.

"Once his people arrived on Teramar, Mahzali dedicated his remaining years to ensuring the blade culture of his people was continued so it would not be lost. This was so the next Singer would be able to protect his beloved Stone, to protect his beloved people.

He had carved the warning in the stone covering his blade during the hours before he died. He died a very old man, he says. He senses that I am young and curious about the history of this Teramar, his second world. He hopes I will be among those to see his first home world and . . ." Jaikeer paused in his retelling as if he was trying to figure out how to translate the Southern he was undoubtedly hearing to Northern. "And something else. Mahzali hopes I will be the grandfather or great-grandfather of one who will return to origin home to become *more*. We are not to fear our destiny." He went limp, as if being released from an invisible restraint, and turned questioning eyes to them. "Any ideas on the meaning?"

Ani, Renloret, and Taryn shook their heads.

"We are all still learning," Renloret said. "We need to keep our minds open to the future and listen to the Stones. They are the guardians and guides of the Lrakiran people. And they will be helping the people and the Singers of Lrakira rediscover their past. According to the First Song, once the three Teramaran Stones are found, they and their new Singers will teach the people your true history. You will be learning much, I have no doubt."

Jaikeer's face was suffused with a mixture of joy and wonder, as well as a bit of fear.

"Did he say anything else?" Taryn asked.

"Only that he and his two cohorts had worried the prophecy would be forgotten and the people of Lrakira would not find Teramar in time. Mahzali is glad the planned prophecy has come true and *all* are safe. He may rest now."

"Okay, what's the next question? If the blade is here, where's the Stone? I assumed they'd be together," Ani said.

They all looked around them. Camfel and Taryn began running their fingers along any crack they could see.

Jaikeer nodded his head. "Yes, it pulls me like a magnet." He had taken a few steps back into the tunnel. "Come, it leads me."

They followed Jaikeer, who held the blade in front of him as if letting a compass needle guide the way. Not quite halfway back to the opening of the tunnel, the blade brightened to an intense hue as they passed a slight indentation in the tunnel wall. Almost immediately, the blade's glow dimmed.

Camfel pointed to the mortared edges of another doorway, and after telling them to wait, she dashed the rest of the way back to the painted chamber where they had left the tools. By taking turns scraping and digging at the mortar, the outline of a door, almost the same size as that which hid the painted chamber, was revealed. Camfel asked Taryn to help her with the ropes to repeat the process used earlier to wedge and wiggle the slab outward. When they had worked it loose, they peered into the cool, lightless space beyond the body-width opening.

Camfel pulled Jaikeer close and handed him a small hand light. "You go." She gave him a gentle shove. Taryn heard her whisper what sounded like a prayer.

The tone of Jaikeer's quiet exclamation in Southern rooted Taryn and the others in place. All but Camfel grinned, knowing he was seeing quite possibly the largest crystal in Teramaran written history. Taryn assumed it would be red to match the blade Jaikeer carried and that the crystal was probably beginning to glow.

Camfel stepped through the narrow opening. With her intake

of breath and exclamation, Taryn pushed forward, wanting to see for himself what might be destined for him. And he wondered which color his Northern Stone would be—yellow or purple. The chamber barely held them all as they sidestepped to space themselves around the simple pedestal topped with a red crystal. The life light within the Stone flexed like a heartbeat.

With a look of awe, Jaikeer touched the Stone. The life light filled the crystal and splashed the small stone room with stunning blood-red brightness. Jaikeer's smile brightened with it.

The new Singer's lips moved as his head began to nod, and a humming tune vibrated through Taryn. He was hearing the Song of Welcome. He recognized the words Renloret had pronounced when helping Camfel read the song from the paper etchings she had brought from the island. Taryn looked at Ani. Her face shone with joy, and her lips moved in time with Jaikeer's. She could hear the Stone. Her alto voice gave the song a verbal life. Taryn added his tenor, and within a few measures, Renloret's baritone blended in. They turned to look at Jaikeer, encouraging him to sing aloud. He nodded and closed his eyes. His booming bass issued forth to complete the four-note chord. Camfel appeared to relax and began clapping her hands. Taryn wondered if she, too, heard the Stone's song or was just enjoying the quartet on its own.

The song ended softly, and the chamber became silent.

"Bayleden says it will soon begin teaching me how to teach my people," Jaikeer said humbly. "However, it knows I need time to adjust to my new role, and it has felt the presence of the Anyala Stone's Singer and others who can help me. It says it will sing to me in my sleep so I can begin to understand. I need not cease my interests or vocation because I am now its Singer, and while it longs to share our bonding with the others, there is time to acquaint me with knowledge beyond the atmosphere of Teramar. It agrees with the pilot that there is much time to learn and teach both worlds of their pasts before the Song of Reunion is sung."

Jaikeer reverently slid the red crystal short blade into its bejeweled scabbard and buckled it snugly about his waist.

Taryn shook his head in amazement as he pondered what had just taken place. He had witnessed a Passing. A Stone had called its Singer. Awe mingled with envy in him. How long would it be before he was called?

# CHAPTER TWENTY-FOUR

Ani stared at the blade's scabbard and frowned. Did her blade have a sheath or a scabbard? She had rarely seen the green crystal blade outside its plain, black, silteene-lined storage box. She could not remember ever seeing her mother wear a scabbard. Indeed, Ani had rarely seen the blade prior to the championship ceremony almost five years ago when her mother had, in the privacy of her personal practice room, laid the crystal blade on Ani's forearms to mark her accomplishments. Even in the mother's journal, which Shendahl had continued to write in as a diary until her death, there had been no mention of the blade.

Ani looked down at the boot sheath from which the plain hilt of her crystal blade protruded. Should she have Diani and Layson search her grandmother's quarters for a scabbard? Did she even know if her mother had brought the scabbard with the blade on her trek to Teramar twenty-six years ago? She should search every possible nook in the lake house, cabin, and research center. Maybe the blade knew where the scabbard was. Could she contact the Anyala Stone through the blade and ask?

She glanced at Reslo. He had known about the crystal blade. Perhaps he had seen the scabbard. She should ask him first, but not now. Jaikeer, Bayleden, and the red blade were far more important than the issue of a scabbard for her blade. She leaned down to touch the hilt. It was comfortable and at rest in the simple boot sheath. It was a part of her. It did not need adornment.

With a smile to herself and a pat on the hilt, she listened to the now quiet conversation. It had been a long day, and it was obvious all were wrung out from the excitement of their discoveries. They gathered up the cameras and tools and moved back to the painted chamber, leaving the Stone on its pedestal. As they walked, Jaikeer kept one hand on his blade's hilt, fingers caressing it, and it seemed he might even sleep with it. He had grumbled at the teasing, though with a smile and self-deprecating laugh.

At some point, Camfel had glanced at a timepiece and exclaimed that it was past time for the eve meal and they should eat. Ani's stomach rumbled in agreement, and they all laughed. Camfel requested that Taryn assist her, and they left, smiling. Ani was glad Taryn did not hear the teasing comments from Reslo.

During and after the meal, they all talked long into the night, sharing their stories. Jaikeer and Camfel quizzed the others about other planets. They were open about their thoughts and curiosities, and they were not fearful about the reality of alien life-forms. Jaikeer mentioned that he'd discovered some very alien-like creatures in some of his digs and shared some of the drawings of what he thought the creatures would look like from their skeletons.

Ani's thoughts went to the scaled lizard-like alien from the Caason Sector who had attended the meal on Lrakira when Taryn had finally met Yenne. She wondered if the creatures in Jaikeer's drawings had governments. Could or would they have built structures, created art, studied the stars, or done any of a myriad of other things she thought of as signs of intelligence?

She asked Jaikeer if he knew why they were not roaming around Teramar now. He answered that the planet had changed in ways that they were not suited for and they had died out, leaving only fossilized bones and extinct plants as evidence. And he had chuckled at the possibility that they had built buildings or held meetings. But Reslo and Renloret happily cautioned that it might have happened, if not on Teramar, then on some other planet. Ani had expected a little skepticism from the Southern scientists, but they seemed to understand how much they did not know.

On occasion, Jaikeer would look toward the tunnel that led to the small chamber where the Bayleden Stone resided, a bemused look on his face. He finally fessed up that the Stone was listening and enjoying the first human conversation in a thousand years. It had remarked at one point that those thousand years were not really that long when compared to its own life span and that it had seen magnificent creatures develop and recede on its home world, over and over again. It hinted at the fact that an imminent asteroid strike, with its warning comet in the lead, had caused the Stones to transplant their charges to safety on Lrakira and

Teramar, the two closest planets to the home world that had suitable environments and a lack of competing species.

When the Bayleden Stone expressed gratitude that portions of The Prophecy of The Blood and The Balance had been successful, the discussion then wandered in and about the First Song and what it might portend.

Camfel had situated herself next to Taryn, and when he spoke, he had looked directly at her as if she were the only person in the room. Ani again wondered if that was how she had looked at Renloret when they'd first met. Long after the glasses of Southern wine had been emptied, the conversation finally died down. The Northern visitors were escorted to a group sleeping room, and they had settled on what was to be done the next day, including a tour of the star runner for Jaikeer and Camfel.

An hour or so after dawn had crept through the window and roused her, Ani finished lacing up her boots and was beginning to braid her hair when Taryn sat up abruptly, flinging off his blankets. Ani watched with concern as he dressed without a word. As he reached for his jacket, she called his name, but he didn't seem to hear. Was he sleepwalking? To her knowledge, he'd never behaved in such a manner. Something was very wrong.

She flipped the half-done braid to her back and moved to intercept her brother before he could leave the room. "Taryn?" She kept her voice soft to avoid jolting him out of whatever state he was in and put her hand on his arm, gently restraining him. He tried to shake her off. She didn't understand his mumbled words. They sounded like ancient Lrakiran, which she knew he did not speak. As she called out to Renloret and Reslo, rousing them to assist, Taryn kept up a running stream of the ancient language and tried again to get into his jacket. She waved her hand in front of him, but he didn't blink. He was deep within an active dream.

Renloret joined them, placed both hands on Taryn's shoulders, and called out his name. Taryn stopped moving but continued in the ancient language. Ani felt the questioning tone of his words.

Taryn stopped speaking for a moment, blinked, and spoke again as if answering someone. This time, Ani noticed he was looking at Renloret, but there was no recognition in his eyes. She frowned. Reslo had worked his way around their huddle and stood in front of the door with folded arms, barring Taryn's possible exit. She shared worried looks with her uncle.

Without taking his eyes off Taryn, Renloret whispered, "I think the Northern Stone has communicated with him. He says it calls for him. There is something wrong about where the Stone is, and it fears discovery by the wrong people. Taryn has to leave—now."

Taryn's shoulders drooped, and he let the jacket slide off to the floor. "Chandaron." Each syllable was heavy with worry. His eyes rolled up and he fainted. Renloret caught his body and eased him to the floor. Ani rolled up the jacket and put it under her brother's head.

"Was it ancient Lrakiran?" she asked.

Renloret nodded. "Hopefully, he will remember when he wakes. It was a little fast for me. Get a glass of water."

Ani quickly complied, and after a few gentle shakes and words, Taryn groaned and turned to his side on his own. His eyes fluttered open and he frowned. "Why am I on the floor?"

"A waking dream had you leaving the room," Ani said.

"Did I fall?"

"Fainted more likely," Renloret replied.

Taryn grunted as he moved to a sitting position. "Water?"

Ani handed him the glass.

He drained it and handed it back. "I fainted? I've never done that before."

"Have you ever had a waking dream before?" Ani asked.

Shaking his head, he reached for Renloret, who took his hand and pulled him onto his feet. Together, they moved to the nearest bed. Ani, Renloret, and Reslo hovered in front of him. He held his head in his hands and began to mumble again in ancient Lrakiran.

Alarmed, Ani whispered, "Is he still in the dream?"

"No, I'm not," Taryn answered. Brushing his fingers through the finger-width-long hair on his scalp, he sighed. "No. Not a dream." He looked up at Renloret. "What did I just say?" A guarded look settled on his face. His hands went to his pockets and he patted them all.

Clearly, he wanted a notebook. Ani left the huddle and searched Taryn's backpack and returned with one, along with a pen.

"Well? What did I say, and what does it mean?" he asked Renloret again.

"You said, 'High north, three rivers. I await.'"

"Who awaits?"

Renloret shrugged. "We think your Stone has contacted you and told you where it is."

Taryn scrubbed at his scalp again. "Why did it sing in ancient Lrakiran rather than Northern?"

"I don't know."

Taryn had opened the notebook and begun writing in it. "Did I say anything else?"

Renloret repeated the comments he'd made to Ani before he fainted.

Taryn stared ahead without comment or writing for several breaths. "Will Camfel be all right without us here?"

"And Jaikeer?" There was a teasing note in Reslo's voice.

"Oh, yeah. Him too." Taryn gave them a quick grin before turning somber.

"I don't see why not," Renloret replied. "We don't need to be around for the Stone to explain things to Jaikeer. They can keep us on the same blade while we go find Chandaron."

Taryn frowned. "Who?"

"Chandaron. I think that is your Stone's name."

"That makes sense. I keep hearing the word in my dreams."

Ani gave his shoulder a push. "How long have you had these dreams?"

"Three nights." He reached for his jacket. "I need to tell Camfel I'll be leaving. There is something very wrong happening near the Stone, and I need to go as soon as possible." He pulled the jacket on and brushed by Renloret and Ani on his way to the door. "Are you coming?"

The door swung open, forcing Taryn to jump backward to keep from getting hit.

"The Island Stone has been found!" Jaikeer announced.

Camfel crowded in behind him. "On the island where I found glyphs two years ago! I was close to it but didn't see it. It was hidden well." Though she was frowning in concentration to speak in Northern, she didn't look as if she were totally unhappy about not finding it. "I have been asked to come. They want to see my translations, so we go now!" She took Taryn's hand and pulled him toward the door. "Will you take us in the star runner?"

The questions flew back and forth so fast no one was able to answer. Reslo finally shouted them all down until they contritely found seats at his command.

Reslo cut through the chatter to piece together the essence of the announcement about the Island Stone. Before they had gone to bed, Camfel and Jaikeer had published their findings of the crystal as a follow-up on the original article that had brought Reslo to them. The discovery supported their supposition that aliens had landed on Teramar. Within hours of The Necklace Island newslines picking up the story, Camfel had received a private inquiry from a group of fishermen hinting of a similar discovery. The fishermen wanted their discovery to be kept secret until they could decipher the writings carved on the inside of the watery cave. And for that, they needed scientists—specifically, Camfel Tondon. The elders of their village urged the fishermen to contact Professor Tondon because she had done some research on the island in the past. Now they wanted to know if she would come and help them.

Camfel had recognized the coordinates of the island as those of the island she had visited several years ago where she'd found the Song of Finding. She was all packed to go. She was insisting that a flight in the star runner would get them to the island much quicker than any other form of travel. The fishermen wanted verification that their find held archeological significance, so the site could be protected from possible looters. Camfel commented on how logical their request was, and the sooner she was able to get there, the less likely vandals would destroy what they had discovered.

Renloret gave a small shrug and smiled. "Of course we can take the star runner, Professor Tondon. We were planning to show it to you today anyway. No need to keep it hidden from the Stone Singers and their entourage. Everyone will soon know about the Stones. But I caution you that the fishermen will probably question the speed at which you arrive."

Camfel clapped her hands with glee. "I thought of that. I told them luck was present and I was close by. I could be there soon. They didn't ask where I was." Camfel looked at Taryn. "No need to waste time." She pointed at the bag she had placed just inside the doorway. "Get yours and we'll go. Jaikeer should stay here and learn to sing with Bayleden."

Jaikeer grinned. "Yes, my night dreams were full of songs. I woke knowing Bayleden says more time is needed for me to learn the right words before the Song of Teaching can be sung. Bayleden now sings to me in Southern. It said I needed the Mahzali bond to hear in my language." He bowed to Renloret.

"Well, from what I hear of Southern, its root language is ancient Lrakiran. Few beyond the Singers of Lrakira are fluent in it, and even the populace on Lrakira does not speak it, though they know it exists. It is the 'language of the Stones' to the

Lrakiran people. You will have less difficulty learning it than you have had learning Northern, which is very different."

Reslo laughed. "Perhaps that is one reason I did not need a bio-teacher."

"Perhaps."

"So can we go now?" Camfel asked insistently. She kept bouncing side to side on her feet, looking between Taryn and Renloret as if trying to decide which one would give her permission to go with them.

"Well? What's keeping you youngsters here? Grab your stuff. Time is wasting," Reslo said as he clapped his hands together.

After some minutes of hurried gathering, Jaikeer drove them to where they had come out of the woods to the road. The group retraced the trail they had made in the snow to the flat meadow where the ship was hidden.

As they broke through the trees, Camfel exclaimed in disappointed surprise that the star runner was not there.

"If it is as big as you say, where is it?"

Ani struggled to stifle her laugh and sobered up only after Taryn thumped her shoulder. He pointed out the trail in the snow that seemed to start out of the pile of rocks. "You will be beyond the visual camouflage one step past that spot, and you will see it." Her brother urged both Camfel and Jaikeer to lead.

When Ani stepped past the star runner's camouflage barrier, she bumped into both Southerners as they stood gape-mouthed, staring at the ship. Jaikeer was the first to venture toward the ship, his eyes wide with a mix of wonder and envy. There was no fear on either face. Ani realized she'd been holding her breath at their reaction to seeing their first alien conveyance.

"Can I see inside before you go?" Jaikeer asked as he stroked the metallic underside.

Taryn had taken Camfel's hand and approached the side of the ship where the ramp was located. He pointed where she should place her hand, and the ramp slid out. She laughed and clapped her hands.

"Come, Jai, come!" she shouted as she skipped up into the star runner. After giving Ani a broad grin, Taryn jogged up the ramp behind her. Jaikeer laughed and jumped on the ramp midway up to join Taryn.

A little disgusted with the memories of her first look at the star ships on Lrakira, Ani turned to Renloret. "Have people always behaved like this when they see the ship for the first time?"

The twinkle disappeared from his eyes. "Sadly, no. Even now, after careful planning, showing new contacts one of our ships is done with caution. Often in the past, they were angry or so fearful that the first contact teams felt it best to leave and try again later or not at all. There are several planets on the schedule to visit in a generation or two after the rumors have died down. Sometimes we leave small observation teams hiding on the ground or among other planets or on moons to keep an eye on them. We have learned to be patient and choose carefully."

"We were fortunate to look almost identical in appearance to the people of Teramar, so we were able to blend in better than most," Uncle Reslo added. "Imagine our surprise when we discovered that the blade culture was eerily similar as well."

"Why wasn't this made note of in any of the communications with Lrakira?" Renloret asked. "I've gone back over almost five years of files, and there is not one word that they might be the same."

Reslo cleared his throat. "We were, perhaps, too focused on saving our people to allow the similarities to distract us. However, we did use them to our advantage. It was several years after Yenne escaped that S'Hendale and I speculated about the infinitesimal odds of such a thing happening. By then, I had lost hope of a rescue and assumed the Lrakiran people would die out unless I could find a way to build a ship or reconstruct the communications array to contact them about Ani."

"But the Stones had other plans, which they had not divulged even to their Singers. The Singers had forgotten the first book of songs," Renloret added. He sighed as he placed a hand on Reslo's shoulder. "The blade has turned out well, even though the annealing process was faulty. And soon, Teramar will know of Lrakira."

"Yes. I am only sorry Ani's mother is not here to share the news," Reslo added.

Ani laced her arm through her uncle's and pulled him gently up the ramp. "Her spirit knows, Uncle. Come, let us share the truth of our connections and the joys of awakening for two more Stones."

# CHAPTER TWENTY-FIVE

Barely two hours later, Renloret switched the star runner from atmospheric flying to landing mode as the island's central valley, which Camfel had described, came into view. The steep cliffs that ringed the valley were remnants of ancient volcanic eruptions and were softened by luxurious tropical growth. The long-silent volcano that had built the island left behind a mineral-rich surface, which weather had ground down to black sand. That mixed with the wind-carried dust, seeds, and the droppings from multitudes of sky and seafaring wildlife had supplied the island with a verdant green-blue foliage speckled with brilliant splashes of colorful blooms.

As the star runner settled in the largest clearing, Renloret heard Camfel quietly sharing her knowledge of the island's geography. Her voice, in careful Northern, carried an excited undertone as she recounted her last excursion to the caves where she'd found the mysterious glyphs and drawings the sparse local population had asked her to study. Though that trip had been two years ago, she had kept in touch with the elders of the nearest village, Cabithayin, and shortly after taking off, she had contacted them through the star runner's communication devices, alerting them of her impending arrival. The elders were aware of the new discovery. They added that their island society held secret tales of singing rocks, and they wanted Camfel to verify, if possible, the existence of such entities.

In the equatorial heat and humidity, they shed the winter clothing required while at the Southern dig site, and they exited the still camouflaged ship in what Renloret considered was closer to underclothing than what he thought appropriate. He couldn't keep his eyes off Ani as she walked ahead of him, her head bent near that of the shorter Southern woman. Mesmerized by the swaying of her hips, he stumbled on the tangled roots of the massive trees shading the path Camfel said led directly to the village. Reslo caught him by the elbow and gave him a knowing grin. Renloret grinned back and tried not to be so distracted by the amount of cinnamon-brown skin showing between Ani's tied up blouse and the large scarf she'd used as a skirt. He tripped again and was brought upright by Taryn.

"You all right?"

"Yes." He shook off Taryn's support. "It's just hard to watch where I step with those two in front of us."

Taryn chuckled. "I understand. I'd like to get to know the little professor better, myself."

"Ha! I thought so," Reslo commented as he passed them. "Good thing I'm too old for her and related to the other. Quite a sight they make."

He caught up with the women and said something too quiet for Renloret to hear. But he couldn't keep the blush from darkening his neck and face as Ani and Camfel looked over their shoulders simultaneously with alluring smiles.

"Blades be damned," Taryn whispered. "I knew Reslo would be trouble. He thinks himself a chaperone on this trip. I'll probably never get time alone with her."

"It's more likely he is concerned about Ani and me than you and any woman you're interested in," Renloret replied. "I could run interference if you need, though. I may have more alone time than I want. Besides, you should make a connection now with the 'little professor' before your Stone commands all of your energy."

Taryn grunted in apparent agreement and gave a shove to Renloret's back to hurry after the three.

Having landed in the center of the long dormant volcano, the path to the seacoast and village was steep and winding. Along the way, they encountered several rope-and-plank bridges that swayed rhythmically at their crossing. Soon Renloret's skin was shining with perspiration, more from the humidity than from exertion. He almost envied Taryn's lack of hair as he tucked stray strands of his own behind his ears. He wondered if he should shave his head to match but remembered Ani's approval when he allowed it to lengthen to brush his shoulders. Plus, he liked how it felt to have her comb through it with her fingers, especially when she kissed him. Perhaps he could find a merchant in the village who would have headbands he could purchase to keep the hair out of his eyes. A few more inches and he would look like his brother,

Theyech, who believed a man wearing his hair long telegraphed a higher than average level of sexual prowess. Renloret shook his head. Hair length had nothing to do with that.

"Hey, hey!"

The shout from Camfel brought the group to a stop at the edge of the trees.

Renloret made his way to the front. The village of Cabithayin sprawled about the gentle slope, each building surrounded by waist-high fencing draped with a profusion of flowering plants. A slight breeze brought the scent of the blooms with a hint of ocean. The buildings were close enough to block the view of the shoreline.

He heard bells pealing out a tune. Were they striking the hour or were they a call to gather for some ceremony? He tried to remember the location of this village from the reconnaissance flyover he'd done before landing. Yes, he had noted the large cathedral with several bell towers in the center of the largest village. The aerial view had reminded him of Awarna with its stone cathedral, though on a much smaller scale. The island village had been separated from the shoreline by a couple of miles of regimented crops. There had been vehicles roving the roads and streets, and people moved in and about without noticing the camouflaged star runner that had hovered briefly overhead.

"Hey, hey, Professor Tondon!" A small group of people emerged from one of the buildings and bustled through a gate. A tall man with greying braids and skin nearly as dark as Yenne's spread his arms and bowed until his back was horizontal. Behind him, the others in his entourage echoed the salutation.

Camfel turned and said in Northern, "Please bow the same."

The five visitors executed similar motions. Renloret judged that their actions met with approval when the man smiled and clapped his hands together twice before stepping forward to take Camfel's forearm in his grip. Though not a linguist, Renloret recognized that their words were like Southern with a decided slurring of specific consonants. It was closer yet to ancient Lrakiran. He smiled as he picked up enough words to get the gist of the conversation and tucked away a question about the vast difference between the Northern continent's singular language and those of the Islands, Southern, and ancient Lrakira.

These were the village elders Camfel had told them about on the way to the island. They were excited to host such an esteemed scientist as Professor Tondon for a second time. The fishermen who had found the new cave filled with glyphs and drawings were waiting for her and her entourage. It was evidently not far from the cave she'd investigated during her first trip. They asked if she'd brought her translations of the cave writings she'd discovered then. She had nodded and indicated the four people behind her, saying something like "I've brought other specialists to assist in deciphering and understanding your discovery."

A brief introduction of Reslo, Ani, Taryn, and Renloret followed, and they were quickly surrounded by the elders and ushered into a building where a long table and chairs awaited. Once seated with an elder between each of the five visitors, wait staff appeared and plates piled high with a variety of fruits were placed before them. Renloret noticed that two of the matronly elders had bracketed Reslo, and they were in deep conversation in Southern. Ani's uncle did not seem to be having any trouble, making it apparent that his year of speaking only Southern had served him well.

But Ani and Taryn seemed quiet, though they smiled and nodded politely as they busied themselves tasting the food on their plates. The elders on either side of them used hand motions and single words or short phrases in Southern while pointing at each fruit and demonstrating how to peel or deseed it.

A tap on Renloret's shoulder brought his attention to the youngest elder, a man approximately ten to fifteen years older than him. The man pointed at his own chest and uttered, "Dowhe Nou." He then pointed at Renloret and raised an eyebrow, a galaxy-wide gesture requesting that Renloret provide his name too. Bringing his hand to his chest Renloret stated his name and added the ancient Lrakiran word for pilot.

The elder clapped his hands and rushed into a long sentence, almost too fast for Renloret to follow. Renloret waved his hand to stop the onslaught and explained in ancient Lrakiran that he'd learned the language from reading script and singing very old songs. He appealed to the older man to slow down. Hearing the language spoken so fluidly was delightful, but it was difficult to follow because the cadence and pronunciation were different from what he had been taught.

Dowhe Nou smiled and slowed down. "You are one of the translators?"

"Yes. I recently assisted Professor Tondon in transcribing the song she located on your island two years ago. Your script has changed dramatically from the ancient words carved on the walls, though the spoken words seem to have retained close similarity. She had difficulty transcribing the carved phrases." He hesitated, wondering why the script had changed but not necessarily the spoken language. And not for the first time, he wondered why Northern was so different.

The elder interrupted his wonderings. "Yes, the cave we asked her to decipher is near the cave Mihalas was drawn to."

"Who is Mihalas?"

"The fisherman who found it. He waits at the new cave for Professor Tondon."

"You said he was *drawn* to it?"

"He said he woke from a dream needing to take his boat to the cove and climb to the cave. That is where he found the wall of glyphs. He said he heard music when he went far back into the cave. When the cave lit up without any fire or lamp, he became frightened and returned here requesting help."

"Did the elders go to the cave to see it?"

"No. We did not. Mihalas said it was farther back in the cave the professor explored when she was here. And when he returned to the village, the newsline was speaking about the large glowing crystal she and another archeologist found in a cave on Southern. Because we knew of Professor Tondon through her work here a couple of years ago, we sent a private message asking her to come. Mihalas fears he is crazy. He says the music fills his head, and no one else hears it. We hope she will be able to tell him what the glowing marks in the cave say. He thinks he is to say them aloud, but he does not know the words—or even if they *are* words."

Renloret leaned back in his chair. "Well, I'm sure Professor

Tondon can do just that. She already translated one of the sections. The one she photographed helped us find the Southern crystal. We are planning to use it to find something very special."

"A treasure?"

He nodded. "A treasure indeed." It was then he realized no one had mentioned a blade, let alone a crystal, though the wording of the messages had hinted at *similar* findings to the crystal found on Southern. Had they found either the blade or a Stone and were afraid to divulge more information? He didn't want to ask straight out, but at the thought of the blade, he leaned forward. "Did Mihalas find a short sword with a scabbard or maybe even a skeleton or old piece of clothing?"

The elder's eyes showed how shocked he was. "No. Why would he find a skeleton with a sword? You think the glyphs lead to a treasure of a long dead criminal?"

"Not exactly. A treasure perhaps, but if there is a skeleton or empty robes, he is not a criminal. He was protecting the . . ."

Renloret suddenly realized everyone else was quiet, all listening to his conversation with the elder.

Camfel stood. "If Mihalas is waiting for me, then we should go. Now." She spoke in accented ancient Lrakiran, just as the island elder. For Renloret, it was more evidence that the spoken language had not changed as much as the written language in the last thousand years—at least on The Necklace Islands. With his knowledge of the written forms of ancient Lrakiran, Renloret could again assist Camfel decipher the glyphs in the cave faster— almost immediately if they were the same as she'd shown him on her transcription of the Song of Finding.

All the elders stood and bowed with their arms outstretched. "To the pier," one of them said.

Renloret and the others were escorted out of the building and down the main thoroughfare to where two small boats were tied up.

Small alcohol-powered motors propelled the boats along the coast for about an hour before turning into a steep walled inlet that ended in a black sand beach. Renloret craned his neck to study the sides of the cliffs.

"Hey, hey!"

The shout echoed, making it difficult to locate the origin.

Camfel pointed to the right side of the little beach and up almost halfway to the top where a young man stood waving a bright yellow piece of cloth. She leaned close to Renloret. "Sorry, I did not explore that one." She shrugged, her expression chagrined. "I went where other markings were found. The Song of Finding is there." She pointed more at the center of the wall. The cave opening there would have been noticeable because of its size, even without the numerous flags that delineated the pathway to it.

Rapid, slurred, and skewed ancient Lrakiran was being exchanged between one of the elders and the man on the cliff, and Mihalas started to run down what Renloret hoped was a well cleared trail, clapping as he came. He met them at the base of the trail and immediately hugged Camfel. Then he took her hand and began to pull her up after him. "Come, you can tell me what to say and how to say it. Something is wrong. The music is getting louder in my head. It wants me to find something called

Geth." Renloret translated for the rest of the Northern visitors.

Everyone began to run.

The cave entrance was low and narrow, and it ended about five body lengths from the opening. All but Camfel had to hunch over or tuck their heads a bit to keep from scraping the ceiling. Mihalas had placed hand-lights facing upward to light the tunnel. The elders allowed their Northern visitors and Camfel to go ahead of them.

Once at the dead end, Mihalas pointed at a series of markings carved into the black stone. "Tell me what they say."

The carvings were in ancient Lrakiran script. Camfel turned to Renloret. "You know better how to read this." She backed away, allowing Renloret to come forward.

It didn't take long to understand that the glyphs were directions to unlock the Stone's chamber. Renloret studied the glyphs while he half listened to Mihalas explain how he had been drawn first to the cave itself and then to this seeming dead end. Renloret recited the instructions, pointing to the glyphs that Mihalas would have to press. The young fisherman nodded. He pressed five of the glyphs, waved for everyone to stand back, and rubbed his hands along his thighs in excitement. Everyone exchanged looks. Renloret wondered if Mihalas was ready to meet his Stone.

There was a grating sound and Mihalas fell to his knees, hands over his ears. Whatever he was hearing, it was loud. Then Taryn and Ani covered their ears too and cried out, twisting away from the slowly opening door. The wall of glyphs moved to the side and a brilliant yellow light flooded the tunnel.

Renloret knelt beside Ani. "What's wrong?"

She let her hands drop but shook her head. "The Stone is singing, but I don't exactly understand it. It is very loud, almost as loud as the Lrakiran Stones right after Taryn pulled the blade out of the Anyala Stone. It . . . it is searching." Though she covered her ears again, Renloret got the impression that doing so did nothing to muffle the Stone's powerful song. He did not hear anything other than the ocean scrubbing the black sand in the bay and the muffled whimpers of pain from Taryn, Ani, and Mihalas.

Taryn was trembling. "The blade. He has to find the blade first. This is the Stone." His voice was tight with pain and he was blinking in the brightness. He yanked Camfel's shoulder bag from her. "The song is in here, right?"

She knelt on the ground, helped him pull out the papers, and paged through them. "Ha! Here. Tell him to sing these words, the ones Renloret helped Jaikeer sing before he found the warrior and blade. He should read the translation on the bottom."

Taryn shoved the paper into Mihalas's hand, pointing to the second grouping of words as he began to sing. Ani immediately added her voice. Mihalas looked at the paper and mouthed the words.

"You have to sing it, Mihalas," Renloret said in ancient Lrakiran. He pointed at Taryn and Ani. "They sang it with Jaikeer. The song will direct you to the blade that you need to complete a type of bonding so you can communicate fully with your Stone." The fisherman frowned but haltingly added his voice. He was a baritone like Renloret.

Within a few phrases, the haunting tune coalesced. Renloret

felt the vibration along his skin and began to study the tunnel walls. "There!"

A fine yellow line had appeared in the shape of an arched doorway. Camfel pulled out several hand tools from her pouch and passed them around.

"Keep singing, Mihalas. We will open the door." Taryn left off his part, as did Ani.

It was quick work—easier than it had been at the Southern dig site, especially when Mihalas stepped between them after they had broken away most of the mortar and began to push. He continued to sing throughout his efforts, his voice now full of joy. The door slid backward until there was enough room for a person to pass. A pale-yellow glow pulsed in the darkness beyond the door, thrumming in time to the song.

"Go on. The blade calls you," Ani said.

Mihalas stopped singing and pointed to his head. "The music is quiet when I sing the words. It is listening—waiting for me to find Geth." He bowed to Ani, Taryn, and Renloret.

"Yes, we know," Taryn said. "As she said, go in and meet the last Singer of your Stone. Don't be afraid. Neither he nor the sword will hurt you."

While the fisherman edged warily into the room beyond, Renloret spoke in Northern. "I think I know why Jaikeer found the blade first and then the Stone. A Singer needs to be bonded with the blade before the Stone's singing can be interpreted by the new Singer's mind. Ani was connected to her blade weeks before she encountered the Anyala Stone. And I remember a piece of the Ceremony of Transition that stated the new Singer had to carry the blade to the Stone. Only then would the Stone accept the new Singer."

Renloret turned around to face the huddled elders, but he spoke to Reslo. "Reslo, you are far more fluent in Southern than me. Explain to Camfel that Mihalas was supposed to find the blade first and then the Stone. He needs to take the blade to the Stone. All should be fine after that."

An exclamation came from the room. Camfel translated in halting Northern. "He says there are robes of a dead man inside. Mihalas has the blade." She looked a little concerned. "Can we go in? I want to see."

Taryn gave her a Northern salute and waved her toward the opening. They followed her, and the elders crowded in behind them. There were gasps of surprise.

Mihalas stood in the middle of the room holding the pulsing yellow blade overhead. His body was wrapped in wraithlike swirls of yellow smoke. One of the elders called his name in alarm. Camfel explained that Mihalas was not being burned and it was the spirit of the last warrior talking to him.

Though her tone was calming, the elders wore shocked expressions when she confirmed their suspicions of an alien life-form. She teased them about a children's folktale that mentioned the island was the resting place of a Singing Stone that had been brought from the sky by a tri-colored rainbow. The tale also said that the Stone had sung to the people of The Necklace Islands, promising a great future when the *others* would need them. Only then would the Stone sing once more.

The elders nodded their heads. Yes, they remembered hearing

the story from their grandparents, but science had never provided an adequate explanation and it was considered a mere tale. A few smiles softened the frowns, and there were murmurs of more recent tales about several of the island's young men who had awakened from dreams of music. The elder who had called out Mihalas's name said that the young fisherman was one of them, but his dreams had been more vibrant and insistent.

The others in the room ceased talking as the fisherman sank to his knees. "He asks if I willingly take on the responsibility of Singer of the Ellashin Stone. To lead my people from their past to their future. To protect the Stone as it will protect the people." The fisherman paused before dipping his chin twice in agreement.

"Geth!" Mihalas whispered. The yellow smoke-like spirit seemed to soak into his body. As Jaikeer had, he was crying at the impact of the last Singer's message.

"Geth was his name." Still on his knees, Mihalas wiped the tears from his cheeks and pointed a damp hand toward the golden robe that lay on a stone platform along one wall. "Geth is not a thing as I thought, but a man, a warrior, a Stone Singer. He taught many about the importance of the blades in our societies. He says he was old when he built this room to protect the blade of Ellashin from being discovered too soon. Geth says his family promised to hide the blade and block the entrances to these caves after his Passing. He says his Ellashin Stone will sing to selected men after the Time Song is sung by the Stones of Lrakira?" He phrased the last as a question. "What is this Time Song? Do you know?"

"Yes," Renloret said. "It can be explained later. You should follow Geth's suggestions."

Mihalas nodded. "Geth wishes me to use the blade to find the Ellashin Stone. Then the Stone will teach me to teach the people of The Necklace Islands." Mihalas bowed his head. "He does not know I found the Stone first. I think I was supposed to find this first to receive Geth's message."

Renloret walked over to him and placed a hand on an elbow, steadying the fisherman as he stood. Slowly, Mihalas began to move the blade in a training pattern that Renloret recognized. Jaikeer had used similar movements. The fisherman sped up his actions, spinning the blade faster and in more intricate patterns than the archeologist, expertise and recent familiarity showing with each move. A smile of appreciation brightened his expression. "A finer blade I have never held." The crystal blade flashed and sparkled in the light of the many hand-lights that now illuminated the room.

Renloret went over to the stone pallet upon which the robe of Geth lay, the sleeves wrapped protectively about a scabbard. Even with the film of blackish dust that covered both robe and scabbard, he could see the jewels glinting. In Northern, he said, "Like Jaikeer's, this one is also highly decorated. Professor Tondon, do you want to photograph any of this before it is disturbed further?"

She arrived at his side, camera in hand. "Yes. My thanks. Mihalas says he pulled the blade from its sheath with care. Do not move it before I have photographed it, please."

A few minutes later, Camfel had Mihalas unbuckle the

scabbard belt and slip it from under the robe. Ani stepped forward and carefully folded the robe. During all of this, the elders had remained respectfully quiet, though several had crowded close and one reached toward the hilt of the blade, which Mihalas had placed next to the scabbard.

Renloret waved at Ani to get her attention and flicked his head toward the elder whose eyes were only on the pale-yellow blade. She gave a small shrug. Perhaps Ani wanted to see if the sword would protect itself as they knew her blade had done when Dalkey had touched it. Renloret remembered the blisters the demented man's hands had received even *through* the storage box that the blade had rested in. Later, the general had worn heavy gloves just to be able to hold the box, and even then, he had not kept it in his grasp for long, complaining of the extreme heat. Neither Taryn nor Ani had ever experienced a burning sensation when they held the box.

Ani positioned herself just behind the inquisitive elder and motioned to Renloret that she would pull him from harm's way. The elder's hand was barely a finger's width from the hilt when the blade began to glow. Ani grabbed a fist full of fabric and yanked the man away. His shout of surprise stopped all conversation in the group huddled around the dais and robe. They all turned to see the elder shaking off Ani's grasp, and he was demanding to know why she'd done such a thing.

Camfel's voice cut through his tirade, first in ancient Lrakiran, then in Northern. "We were warned at the Southern site that only the next Singer could safely touch the blade. All others would be burned. Miss Chenak saved you from serious damage." The glow from the blade diminished as she spoke.

Mihalas picked up the blade and gave the offending elder a scowl before turning his gaze to the blade and humming a soothing tune.

Instead of calming the blade as Renloret expected, the fisherman's humming seemed to cause the glow to increase. Remembering how Jaikeer's blade had brightened and led them to the Bayleden Stone chamber, Renloret said in ancient Lrakiran, "Wield it as a compass. It will lead you to your Stone. We will follow."

The fisherman-turned-Stone Singer smiled. "It pulls at me," he said in ancient Lrakiran, which was beginning to sound more like what Renloret expected to hear.

Renloret grinned as he realized he was already getting accustomed to hearing multiple people speak the language he'd thought only old academicians and Lrakiran Singers spoke at ceremonies. The elders formed two lines, and Mihalas walked between them. The elders honored him by bowing low, their arms outstretched, some touching the floor with their fingers. Renloret and the others followed Mihalas out of the small cave and along the path back to the first cave where the Ellashin Stone waited for its blade-bonded Singer.

Hours later, back in Cabithayin, Renloret and all but Camfel bowed and saluted their good-byes before hiking back to the star runner. Camfel had elected to stay behind to translate more of the glyphs and search the caves for drawings that might match with those found on Southern. There was still much work to be done at the Southern site, as well as here, and she was eager to get started. She had cheerfully waved good-bye, shouting that she hoped to see Taryn again and wishing them all well on the hunt for Taryn's Stone.

Throughout the return hike, Taryn was quiet, and when Renloret asked him about it, he reported that during the short search for The Necklace Islands Stone and blade, he had experienced an easing of the beckoning song from his own Stone. Now the feeling of urgency and even dread was increasing at an alarming rate. Renloret had never seen Taryn this fidgety, and during the entire flight to Star Valley, the sheriff paced the length of the ship, occasionally stopping to practice hand-to-hand moves or fight imagined opponents. Renloret mentioned the unusual behavior to Reslo and Ani. When Ani tried to get him to sit down, he waved her off, uncharacteristically muttering about wanting to be prepared in case a fight was needed.

Shortly before they landed at the lake house, Taryn stomped onto the star runner bridge. "Why am I the last to hear from a Stone? Why is it a cry for help and not the joyous Song of Finding? Why is it harder for me than Mihalas or Jaikeer?"

Renloret slapped the control console with both hands before swiveling his seat to face the agitated man. "Stop it, Taryn! We don't know why the Stone needs help. And we're getting there as fast as we can. Feeling sorry for yourself won't get you there any faster. You don't have to do this on your own. You can't. Allow us to help. We're all in this. All of us are responsible for the safety of the Stone and *you*. Your family and friends will get you to the Chandaron Stone in time. Then we can work on everything else. Now sit down." He pointed at a seat and hoped his outburst would cut through the worry that paled Taryn's face.

Taryn closed his mouth and slumped into the indicated chair. Releasing a sigh, Renloret turned back to the controls to set the landing coordinates. "Ani, call Melli and tell her to brew up a batch of calming tea. Her son needs it so he can focus on the right things."

# CHAPTER TWENTY-SIX

Yenne pinned the map to the easel and tapped a finger at the western-most mountain range. "Here's where Mroz and I think the Stone is hidden."

"Why there? It's so far away from Star Valley? And what if it's not there." Taryn could feel his voice edging toward a childish whine and cleared his throat. He looked at the empty teapot. The calming brew was not working. He just wanted to find the blade-damned Stone and stop the panic that had built up during the flight from The Necklace Islands. He stood and began pacing again. He couldn't sit still. He needed to go—*now*.

"Son, sit down," Gelwood gently urged.

Taryn turned on his father. "It's calling me, Dah. It needs *me* to protect it!" He covered his mouth in surprise. He'd never shouted at his father before. The room was silent and everyone was staring at him. He looked at each shocked expression. Renloret didn't appear shocked, but he was leaning against the fireplace mantel with his arms crossed, a frown on his face. And Yenne? He had the stone-still face of a rock—no emotion at all. How could Taryn explain the feeling of the song in his head?

"Something is terribly wrong," Taryn whispered. "I'm the only one who can fix or prevent it."

Gelwood rose from his chair and hobbled the few steps to reach him. "Let us explain why we think it's there before you go off on any of us."

Taryn glanced at Yenne. The commander was rolling his bottom lip between his teeth. What was he trying not to say? Even Kela looked disappointed in his behavior.

"Taryn." Gelwood put a hand on his shoulder and squeezed hard.

"Yes, Dah?"

"There are numerous caves and mines in that region. The villages are sparse and have small populations. There are no histories or tales here in Star Valley about talking rocks." Gelwood paused as Yenne pointed again at the map. "But there are in the village of Wharton."

Yenne took up the explanation. "It's a mining village near the base of the second tallest peak. It is at the source of one of three rivers that join near the base of the mountain range to flow to the western coast. And your mother," he nodded at Melli who was now moving about the room with a fresh teapot, topping off everyone's cup, "discovered an older than old rumor in that village about a hidden jewel protected by a giant with a glowing sword."

Melli smiled as she stopped in front of him to top off his cup, which sat on the end table. She set down the teapot and handed him the cup. "Your fathers and Mroz weren't getting anywhere on their overly logical search for possible locations, so I decided to find out if there were any tales or rumors about treasures."

Taryn picked up on the plural she had added to *father*. Clearly, the three of them had come to some sort of agreement on what relationships they would be most comfortable with, at least between them. While good to know, it was not what he needed at the moment. He needed to find the Chandaron Stone and its blade.

Melli raised three fingers to his lips to stop his words. "Now, drink." She tapped the cup.

After giving a long sigh, he obediently sipped and let the bright sting of cinnamon burn away at the panic. She had changed the tea from the calming one to one of energy. Then she pulled him over to sit on the couch and nestled close to his side, just as she had done when he was small and she was telling him little stories.

She told him the mining village of Wharton was founded hundreds of years ago by a treasure hunter of the same name. He discovered that the western mountains were full of high-grade mineral ore needed for the growing industrialization of the Northern continent. A few years after starting his mining operations, he claimed to have seen an immense gemstone in a cave his excavating had opened. And when he tried to pick it up, he'd been attacked by a giant with a glowing sword. He also claimed that during the attack, the giant warrior spoke in what he knew as Southern, his grandparents being from there. The warrior warned him away from the gemstone, saying time had not been sung to nor had balance returned to the stones.

She patted Taryn's knee and continued. Wharton was told to re-hide the chamber so all the people of Teramar would flourish until time was ready. He had apparently done as instructed because there had been no other mention of such treasure since. Only the fable of a giant's treasure remained.

Ani, Renloret, and Reslo gasped with the telling of the tale. When it seemed that Melli had finished, Ani leaned from her chair and touched Taryn's other knee. Kela's tail thumped a happy rhythm against the wall, announcing his feelings about the story. Stunned, Taryn could think of nothing to say. He gulped the rest of his tea and methodically placed the cup back on the saucer. Could it be that easy? No. Not that easy. It was, however, the very best place to start. He hugged his mother.

"There's more to the story, Taryn," Gelwood said. "Continue, my dear."

After all were settled into seats and Kela had crawled under the low table, poking his head up between Taryn's knees to have his ears rubbed, Melli continued with the story of Wharton's treasure. Melli mentioned that there were several later versions of the story that included piles of jewels and a multitude of sword-wielding criminals, but she had focused on the oldest and simplest of them because, to her, it seemed more likely true than the more fanciful tales. And more importantly, it was the only one that mentioned a Time Song and the word *balance*.

In this, the earliest version Melli had found, Wharton had been threatened with death if he or anyone else found the gemstone or blade before time had been *sung forward*. Purportedly, though Wharton had promised to hide the entrance to the carved-out room that held the glorious Stone, he had continued to mine the mountains surrounding his namesake village and became quite wealthy. He never repeated the story, remaining silent after the first publication. The story was soon regarded as folktale.

While they studied the map, Taryn connected the physical location of Wharton near three rivers with his waking dream speech about the Stone being near three rivers and at a high altitude. A bit more at ease with the choice, he helped make lists of supplies needed, and decided how many would take the trip to the village of Wharton. Gelwood noted that the village was experiencing another boom time in recent months with the discovery of a huge deposit of craudlin, a mineral used in the production of some new-fangled device that would ease the pain of surgery. Melli said that was suspicious enough on its own merits. She blurted out that it sounded like Isul Treyder's work, and combined with Taryn's continued unease about who would find the Chandaron Stone, she urged all who were going to go to pack every weapon they had. She declined to go with them, saying she had to keep an eye on Gelwood and that the grocery store had to be open for the Star Valley residents.

It took two days before they were ready to leave. After deciding that the news of the other Stone discoveries would soon be widely talked about, Taryn decided to reveal to the rest of his staff what he had already told Daneeha. He was a bit taken aback by the relative calm with which they took the news. When he admitted as much to them, more than one said that they wanted to believe there were other forms of intelligent life beyond the scope of their miniscule planet.

But Yantel was the first to admit his relief that his "alien" boss did not have scales, multiple arms ending in pinchers, or some other alarming physical feature. And while there was laughing about that confession, the others disclosed their own relief about that.

When Taryn explained that he'd been chosen to become one of the Singers, there was a round of applause coupled with looks of uncertainty when he said he would be out of the office while he searched for the Stone. He explained that the Singers could continue whatever occupation they had and that he was expecting to remain sheriff. He felt duty-bound to protect the people of Star Valley, and once he found the Stone, he would be able to expand that to the other people of Northern. Turning to Yantel, he formally assigned him to continue his acting sheriff duties until the Northern Stone was found.

Then he asked about the investigation on Treyder. All their faces had clouded up. The trail they thought had been clear had vanished. No one had heard anything from or about the missing doctor for over a month. There was a continent-wide warrant for his arrest in Taryn's kidnapping and torture, and the capital police were keeping the Star Valley sheriff's office informed of the evidence piling up against Senator Nelham, who was now claiming that Doctor Isul Treyder had manipulated and blackmailed him to provide needed funding for his experiments. Nelham claimed he'd had no idea whatsoever of the terrible things of which Treyder was capable.

Yenne had asked Taryn to inquire on the whereabouts of Sarinne, who had returned briefly to Star Valley, given a firsthand account of her last encounter with Treyder, and then vanished before she could be questioned again. The deputies promised to continue looking for her and to investigate her connection to the senator and Treyder when they found her.

They all wished him well and hoped to meet the crystal alien when he returned. He just hoped he wouldn't have to move to the western edge of Northern. Could he bring the Chandaron Stone home to Star Valley? Hadn't Layson and Diani brought their Stones to where the Anyala Stone was to sing the Time Song? Then they had stayed there after Selabec stabbed the Stone. Now that the people had been saved and the Anyala Stone was healed, would Layson and Diani return to their home areas with their Stones? He pulled the notepad from his pocket and added those questions to a lengthening list.

Momentarily, he wondered how the Anyala Stone was faring while Ani was on Teramar. She had not spoken about the Stone for almost a week. Could she feel it at this distance? Yet another question. So many questions. He stuffed the notepad back into his pocket. This being an alien was much more difficult than being a sheriff.

"Lots of activity for a small mining village," Renloret said. The pilot toggled the view lens to magnify the image while keeping the star runner high above Wharton.

Ani pointed out the new metallic buildings, which almost glowed in contrast to the dirt-encrusted log buildings built many generations earlier. People were bustling in and out of the new buildings. "What do you suppose they are constructing?" she asked. "More of those blade-damned coma devices?"

"Let's hope not," Taryn replied. "We're not even sure Treyder is here."

Before leaving Star Valley, Melli had shown them several newsline articles from the western mining village touting the increase in employment opportunities after winning a military defense contract to produce several types of experimental weaponry, along with a groundbreaking device that allowed surgery to be conducted without anesthesia. Though Treyder's name was not mentioned specifically, Melli's supposition that the doctor was involved seemed logical.

Wharton was supposedly the only place on Teramar with the needed minable resources requested by the military, and they had a ready and willing supply of workers. The village had gratefully accepted the influx of soldiers who now guarded the facilities. The articles had said that the craudlin mineral was also only one of several vital ingredients necessary for the new non-blade weaponry the military was experimenting with. With all the news about secret Southern attacks against Northern, Wharton was pleased to be of service. Melli had snorted derisively at that, offering a steep wager that the people had not been told *exactly* what they were constructing because if they knew, they would have refused.

Taryn had felt the pull of the Stone to the spot on the map when Yenne had first pointed it out. While he was nervous about finding the blade and Stone, he was downright alarmed about the possible presence of Isul Treyder so close to the hidden artifacts.

"It's nearby." The low-level hum that had been with him since Jaikeer had connected with Bayleden had increased exponentially since the star runner had arrived above the village. He was sure everyone could see him vibrating with the telepathic song of questing.

He placed a hand on Renloret's shoulder. "Can we go to the mountain? We've wasted enough time here. I must get to Chandaron's blade before someone else discovers either it or the Stone. I suggest that Yenne, Mroz, and Reslo go to the village and find out who is at the head of this factory. If it is Treyder, the authorities need to be informed."

"Agreed," said Yenne. "We'll also purchase additional food supplies. We may be here a while during your search. Renloret can let us off on the other side of that hillock." He pointed at the view screen. Renloret nodded, and the view changed as he maneuvered the star runner into place and settled. The commander clapped his now older brother on the shoulder and nodded to Mroz. The three left the bridge to gather packs, remote communication gear, and extra apparel in case they had to stay in Wharton overnight.

Kela sidled up against Taryn's thigh and stared up at him with icy blue eyes. Taryn looked at Ani with raised eyebrows. "What's he saying?"

"He's concerned about your physical state."

"My physical state?"

She nodded. "He senses that you have not slept. Your scent tells him you are beyond the usual levels of stress. He wants you to rest before you begin your search."

Taryn knelt to get eye-to-eye with the canine, placed his hands on either side of the animal's head, and kneaded his fingers through the deep fur. "My thanks for your attention, but I am in control. I . . . it is the Stone's song that has me on edge. Chandaron is pulling or pushing me toward the blade. I can't rest until it is in my hands. Then I can protect the Stone. It fears it will have to do an unthinkable act to keep a person from within the Stones' guardianship from attacking it as the Anyala Stone was."

"It knows about that?" Ani asked, her voice almost a whisper.

He nodded and rubbed his hands through the black inch-long hair on his scalp. "It is singing to me now that the wrong people are too near its location, and it fears being found before I can be there. I must locate the blade soon and stand between them and the Stone so it will not do what is forbidden—what it nearly did to a miner who inadvertently broke through the disguised tunnel. It managed to create a mental image of its last Singer in the miner's mind and warned him away. I guess that confirms the story of Wharton and the giant's treasure. It also knows the Anyala Stone was attacked and the Time Song ruined, thus bringing all of us to the very edge of extinction. It desires to hold to the tenets of guardianship laid before them when the people were given into the Stones' care. No Stone shall kill one of their charges, even if it means the Stone ceases.

"Chandaron sings that there was a need to protect their charges in the face of the asteroid, and that was the only reason the people were divided and sent away. *All* the Stones and Singers will be needed to open the pathways across the stars in Reunion, and the future will be accessible for those desiring to return home. It calls to me, Ani. Constantly. Whether awake or sleeping, I hear its song. It must live so that we, their charges, can move forward. It is the Stones' destiny to provide guardianship until our people are ready for the next steps." He sat heavily, releasing Kela from his grip, and rubbed his forehead.

"Kela is correct. I have not slept because of the songs. They have changed from a call to find the blade and Stone to a cry for assistance. Chandaron knows the other two have been found by their Singers. They are safe. Chandaron is not. It sings that though the blade can protect itself, it cannot. I, its human blade, must protect it. If a Stone is damaged beyond healing, Reunion will likely not happen, and the Stones will have failed in their duty. Also, if Chandaron commits the sin of protecting itself from an attack, it believes all the Stones will die before the people have attained their intended future." He shook his head in confusion.

Ani was now sitting beside him on the star runner bridge floor, and her hand was warm where it rubbed his neck and shoulder. Renloret had swiveled his command chair to watch.

"How can you be hearing so much from your Stone before you are bonded to its blade?" Ani asked. "Jaikeer and Mihalas heard or understood only the Song of Finding until they took up their Stone's blades and the last Singers passed into them. Only then were Bayleden and Ellashin able to sing fully to them. You have yet to grasp the blade of Chandaron. You don't even know its last Singer."

"Ask it, Taryn," Renloret said. "If you can hear it, then it can hear you."

"Of course. Thank you, Renloret. I had not thought to try to speak with it directly." Taryn inhaled, slowly forming the question, and exhaled, mentally humming the words. The Stone's constant song of explanation ceased as it listened and then it answered.

*You are The Balance. You saved one of us, for you an unimagined life. You have restored our combined destiny. The future is possible because balance is almost complete. You have been touched by a Stone's blade so we, the Stones, would know The Blood and The Balance when the Time Song was sung. You have grown worthy of my blade. All Stones sing to all Singers as needed. I, Chandaron, can sing to The Balance without the blade bonding or a passing of a Singer because you are known to us. Did you not question why the Anyala Stone's blade did not burn you when you sang the Song of Healing? And did you not question the lack of burning when you removed the blade from the soul of the Anyala Stone?*

*No*, Taryn answered, carefully wording his answer in silence. *It never occurred to me that the blades would burn me. The green crystal blade never harmed me.* Did Chandaron laugh?

*No blade will burn a prophesied Singer.*

Taryn glanced at Renloret, speculating as to why the pilot had not burned any of the times he had held a crystal blade. For which Stone was he destined to be the Singer? Wasn't there something in the First Song about it?

*Yes. The pilot has been touched by a Stone's blade, and he will have the opportunity to accept his place as the others have. His search for our home of origin has begun. There is time.* The rich cool song from Chandaron sang in Taryn's head.

*Listen, my Singer. You are near. Follow the song to the blade.*

*Accept the passing, then come to me. The others are too close.*

The song in his head changed back to the melody of the Song of Finding, which Taryn had now sung twice. The urgency lessened to a manageable level, and he was able to push it to the background.

Taryn quietly related to Ani, Kela, and Renloret most of what Chandaron had sung. At the end of the recitation, his gaze had rested briefly on Renloret, who frowned at him but did not ask. Taryn hoped that after the third blade and Stone of Teramar had been found, there might be time to ask and answer many new questions. Now it was his duty to find the blade, meet the spirit of the last Singer, and then, finally, meet the Chandaron Stone.

# CHAPTER TWENTY-SEVEN

"**D**octor Treyder!"

The call stopped Isul in his walk to the next chamber. He was surprised to see an employee from the dining room jogging toward him, her brown food service coat fluttering like wings in her haste. The youngster, not quite out of her teen years, was all one color with dirt-brown eyes and skin blending into the coat. Even her leggings were brown. The only break in the drab coloring was a triangle of green peeking above the wrap point of the coat.

Isul also noticed the short cut of her hair as typical of a village native. All the villagers seemed to prefer nape-length hair or even partially shaven scalps, presumably because the dust from the mines was easier to remove when bathing when they had little or no hair. Not that he cared a whit about the length of hair a person had, but he silently wished the women in the village wore theirs to their shoulders. He could then identify their gender better at a distance. It was exactly that little difference that marked possible intruders or spies. Still, there were far more important things to occupy his time. He glanced over his shoulder at the blue door now behind him. He needed to check on the specimens.

He stopped, allowing the girl to catch up to him. "How may I assist you?" He studied the teen, who was still breathing a bit quickly. When had he sanctioned the hiring of employees not yet in their twenties? And female? Men were notably more capable of handling the duties he needed accomplished. Why was she here?

She straightened up and jerked the brown coat back into place before dipping into a curtsy. "Sir, I was sent to find you. Your presence may be required. There are strangers in the village."

"Really? How many?" He drew the words out, surprised and dismayed by how quickly his location might have been discovered.

"Three. Two old men, and I think the third is son to one of the older men. They arrived in time for the eve meal at the dining center. My fa . . . the chef decided to allow them to eat while I came to get you."

"Did they ask about me?" Had the last newsline revealed his location? He thought he'd done everything possible to keep his name from being spoken. He had verified every interview, written or vid, before allowing its release.

She shook her head. "Not when I served them. They've been hikin' round the near peaks for a week or more and came down to taste civilized food. They're a scruffy bunch, having been in the mountains for so many days. I don't think they mean to stay long, but the chef wanted you to know."

Isul's thoughts ran down the list of managerial positions. Ah, Grundel was the chef and evidently, the girl's father. She was trying very hard to execute her father's orders. "Did they say anything else?" It could be a ruse by an opposing senator to get a spy inside his operations.

"No, sir, less'n you mean them asking about a market. Seems they're runnin' low on food supplies."

"Do you know if they have coin to pay for the meal?"

She bobbed her head up and down. "Yes, sir. They paid in advance, saying that way, they would be sure to get big portions for their empty bellies."

That would not have been how he imagined any spy would try to get in. If they had been spies, they might have come seeking jobs, just as he and the imbecile Stubin Dalkey had done more than twenty years ago. Certainly, that was not enough time for any government or even a private agency to set up one spy, let alone three.

He glanced over his shoulder again at the door. His specimens were awaiting their next trial. Hungry mountain hikers were of no consequence. Treyder turned back to the girl saying that he did not need to see them yet. And perhaps Grundel should warn them away from trying to climb Mount Piffital, where all the mine tunnels were located. For safety reasons. The girl bobbed another curtsy before rushing back the way she'd come to convey his response to Grundel. Treyder would talk with the chef later.

Isul hurried to his lab and smiled at the rows of cold metal tables with their tubing and wires that wove above the specimens to the mobile screens and keyboards placed at the end of each table. He walked slowly by each, studying the results, pausing to type a note or two and set a timer here and there for the next round.

This was so much better than the single specimen he'd had to work with only a few months ago until the senator's guards had let three unknown assailants carry off the sheriff. Being out from under the senator's control had freed up his imagination on what experiments he could run, and the money he had wrangled from the politician had gone further than expected in this village. The villagers were delighted to be receiving double their usual annual pay, and those working in the assembly plant gladly kept their jobs secret. He kept them away from this room. It was where he could test the results of the changes he was making to the miniscule device implanted in each specimen.

The villagers mined the minerals he needed, followed his construction plans exactly, and didn't ask any questions about what it was all for. They'd even improved on his mass delivery system based on one of their compressed air hammers. There was now no smoke or flames when the tiny hollow sliver blades were expelled from the massive tubes. Only a thunderclap-like sound was heard, and in this mining area, it was not unexpected— especially when firing tests were accomplished during the almost daily rainsqualls. A few more weeks of testing a variety of the devices and Isul would be ready to show off his magnificent tiny machines. He would single-handedly win the war against Southern.

His laugh echoed about the room, unheard by the comatose specimens who were waiting for the next round of cuts, breaks, acids, and poisons. He decided to leave his specimens in favor of observing the newcomers in the dining room. If they were of the right age range, Treyder could add them to his collection.

From the dining room balcony, Isul watched the youngest of the three strangers push his plate aside, indicating the fullness of his stomach. He must be in his mid-thirties, Isul thought. A good age for Treyder's experiments. The younger man glanced around the large dining facility until he found a sign for the public necessary room. He pointed at it and then apparently excused himself to use the facility. He stood and the two older men looked up from their plates of dessert. Their faces were plain to see. Isul gasped, and his heart jumped irregularly in his chest. Mroz and the year-gone Reslo Chenak! Both were in Wharton, so far away from Star Valley that Isul had trouble believing his eyes.

"Are you all right, sir?" the chef's daughter asked. She had discretely brought him up the stairs to this vantage point and directed his gaze to the trio.

"Yes. Fine. Thank you," he replied, managing to control the shakiness of his voice. "You may return to your duties." The girl bobbed a curtsy and left, leaving him alone on the balcony. He moved to stand behind a pillar to better conceal himself.

Mroz and Reslo stood and pulled on their jackets when the younger man returned. The young man seemed rather agitated and had leaned close, speaking quickly. Mroz had turned his head toward the public necessary, his eyebrows raised in surprise. Isul wondered what the excitement was about. Surely, they did not know he was here.

Isul sifted through his memory. Had his real name been on any document related to the enterprise he had created? No. He'd been careful to remain in the background, allowing others to speak for him. The Wharton populace had embraced the new technologies he had brought to them in the past few months, and he had been astounded at the speed of building and development that had occurred in such a brief amount of time—faster than he'd seen during his years in Star Valley. Of course, his ideas had been patently ignored by the Southern scientists and the Chenak family in particular. They had thought to make Star Valley the center of their own success. Isul had found the freedom to be creative in this isolated village he had lacked under the constant limitations placed on him while in the employ of the Chenaks.

The men were hurrying out of the dining room. Isul looked around. Where was the chef's daughter? Could he have her follow them? Perhaps she could get close enough to overhear their conversation and relay information to him. He took the back stairs and returned to the kitchen to find her.

Several hours later, a knock on his door startled him. Who would disturb him in his personal quarters? He closed the notebook and toggled off the computer screen before unlocking the door.

Grundel's daughter, still dressed in her brown food service attire, stood before him. "I did what you asked, sir."

"And?"

"I followed them to the market. They purchased more than enough produce and meat to feed the three of them for a week or more."

"So?" He wondered why she thought he would care about the amount of food they had bought.

"T'was odd because they said they're done climbing here and would be out of the district in a few days. I think there are more than three of them."

"Why do you think that?"

She glanced up and down the hallway as if making sure no one else was present to hear. "After they left the market, they huddled behind the miners' quarters and spoke into a little box the younger of them had in his pocket." Her expression told him she didn't understand exactly what she'd seen, but she was reporting it anyway.

"Did you hear what they said?"

She nodded. "The younger one said, 'He's here. His photo was on a bulletin board notice.' And a voice came out of the box." Her eyes were wide with excitement. "It said, 'I'll pass it on to the authorities right away. We're getting ready to head up the mountain to find the crystal. We'll let you know when we find it.'" Her expression had changed to one of confusion. "So I think at least two more are up there. That makes five or more, and they're not hikers, Doctor Treyder, they're after the giant's treasure!" Her voice ended in a squeak.

He frowned in disbelief. "Giant's treasure?"

"Yes, sir. My nah heard about it from her gran when she was little. There's an old story about a giant with a sword that protects a pile of crystals and jewels. It's hidden somewhere 'round here, but no one's found it yet, if'n it exists at all."

Isul nodded. There were always tales of lost treasures. In his opinion, the older they were, the less likely they were true. And if this child's great-gran had passed it on, it was probably some mine owner's imagination to keep the miners digging. It could have provided a powerful incentive if the owner had offered a finder's fee or an ownership percentage.

Isul gave the girl a practiced smile. "Ah, yes. Well, if they find it, then they are welcome to it. What I've built here will provide for the entire village, not just a few individuals. But my thanks for the information." He paused. He had planned to reprimand Grundel for putting his daughter to work, but she'd proven of some value this day. "Tell your dah I said you could continue to work in the kitchen and dining room."

She curtsied, and he closed the door, twisting the lock before returning to his notes. He added the girl's information to his daily report and remembered the faces of Mroz and Reslo. So the coward had finally returned from Southern, and they had tracked him to Wharton. Those two had evidently brought along some help. He was grateful the girl thought they were only interested in lost treasure. However, the fact they were here was something to worry about. He'd have a word with the head of the guards to keep eyes on them. If they stayed in the village, it would complicate his plans and restrict his movements.

A thought crossed his mind. He could leave. Maybe even check in with the senator. It had been at least a month since the last tel-com communication. And Isul had been very busy setting up this ideal location with the correct materials and a readymade, eager workforce. Yes. He should tell the senator of his progress and have him schedule a more public demonstration for the military since the first had been secret and had given him the specimens currently in the Wharton laboratory. He picked up the tel-com and punched in the senator's private number.

Unfortunately, he reached someone other than the senator. "What do you mean the senator is not available?" He slapped a hand flat against the desktop, making the pile of papers bounce. "And who are you, anyway? This is the senator's private number. No one else has ever answered one of my calls. Where is he? I need to speak with him. Now!"

The voice on the other side did not rise in anger. It held steady. Isul gathered in a breath, struggling to regain a sense of calm. The woman simply repeated that Senator Nelham was unavailable. She offered no explanation. She did, however, ask for his name and from where he was calling. Without another word, Isul disconnected the call and threw the tel-com against the wall. The sound of it shattering brought a grim smile to his lips. He wished the tel-com had been the senator.

It took him a long time to stop pacing. Other items from his desk were scattered across the floor. The crunch of them under his feet allowed the anger to dissipate slowly. By the time the adrenaline had subsided, he had created several optional plans. He finally moved to his chair, picked up a pad of paper from the floor, found a writing implement, and quickly outlined them.

Satisfied and now much calmer, Isul leaned back in his chair and glanced at the large screen on the wall opposite his desk. He hadn't watched a newsline report in weeks. For the first time in a very long time, he thought there might be something pertinent and of interest on the capital newsline frequency. Curious, he toggled the switch on his desk, and the screen lit up. The visual was not as clear as he would have liked, but the audio came through just fine.

A few minutes into the newsline Treyder heard Senator Nelham's name mentioned, and he focused on the blurring screen. Hearing that Senator Nelham was under investigation was bad enough, but when he heard his own name, he stared at the screen with his mouth agape. He was being connected to the kidnapping and torture of the Star Valley sheriff as well as what they were referring to as illegal experimentation. There was a continent-wide search for him.

He was the object of a continent-wide search? It was a good thing he'd asked that his real name not be made public to the residents of Wharton. Very few people knew, and he planned to keep it that way. He would have to call a meeting of the mining consortium and explain how wrong the information being broadcast was.

The newsline program then switched to a weather report, and Isul leaned forward to toggle the program off. Had there been a photo of him? The visual reception had been so poor he did not know. He balled his fists and pounded the desk. Just as he was reaching the pinnacle of his work, all the hells of Teramar had turned against him. What could he do now?

A meeting with the local investors was in order. They were the only ones who knew his true name. Then he remembered that the chef's daughter had called him Doctor Treyder. How had she known his real name? Why hadn't he realized that earlier? A separate plan was in order. He would have a full box of the devices delivered to his office in the morning. A sickly smile stretched his lips. It was time for another demonstration, and the investors were the perfect test audience. Then he could go to Saedi City and meet with Senator Nelham to demonstrate the devices for select members of his committee. Once the committee understood the multitude of potential uses for the coma device—from military to surgeries without anesthesia—Treyder could return to Wharton and focus on expanding production and developing a medical market for the device.

## CHAPTER TWENTY-EIGHT

Ani tossed a backpack at Taryn along with his favorite blade and leg sheath. "As soon as you can."

He gave her a quirky grin. "You've been in my quarters!"

She shrugged as she knelt and laced her boots. "Sisters go where they need to."

He saw the hilt of the green crystal blade peeking above her leg sheath. She stood and pulled up her sleeves and adjusted the wrist blades.

For a moment, Taryn's attention shifted back to the tel-com conversation he'd just had with Yantel. Not only had he given Yantel information on the whereabouts of Treyder, but he had been updated on the latest developments in Saedi City.

According to the Saedi City police, even the senator did not know where Treyder had disappeared to. The acting sheriff filled in Taryn about the current status of the investigation into the senator. Evidently, Senator Nelham was about to be interrogated about crimes against the people of Northern and falsely accusing

Southern of starting a war. Nelham had bribed several Northern military officers to lie about incursions on Northern soil by Southern armies. At least two officers had admitted to bribing some of their soldiers to "accidently kill" members of their own divisions in what was supposed to be mock battle training. Everyone was being rounded up. Interestingly, the fourteen soldiers supposedly killed had literally disappeared.

When asked by an investigator if he knew Doctor Isul Treyder, Nelham admitted acquaintance, saying the doctor had contacted him first about a new type of weaponry. The senator claimed to have had no interest in the device until Treyder approached him again, a couple of months later, saying that this same weapon might have medicinal uses. Because of that, the senator had helped the doctor set up a laboratory. But he had threatened to end the arrangement when he learned that Treyder had abducted the Star Valley sheriff and was using him in experiments. According to Nelham, Treyder had threatened to do the senator's family harm unless he received military backing for his projects. The senator had acquiesced but did not know to where the illusive doctor had gone.

It was a real mess. Yantel admitted that he didn't trust the senator any more than a starving kreline. Taryn instructed Yantel to notify the Saedi City police of Treyder's whereabouts and that they would likely need reinforcements to get the doctor arrested in Wharton.

Renloret arrived grumbling in Lrakiran, and Ani chuckled as she assisted him in tightening the straps to a set of forearm sheaths and guards.

"What do those hold?" Taryn asked. They were a bit thicker than usual.

The pilot grinned, pulled a wicked blade from one of the sheaths, and carefully handed the hilt to Taryn.

A soft whistle sounded through Taryn's lips. The blade's fuller was decorated with barbs. It was masterfully designed.

A chuckle from Reslo announced his arrival. "So you gave them to Renloret, did you?" he said to Ani.

Ani nodded. "He was intrigued when he first saw them and asked if he could practice with them. They're a bit large for me, and he seems to have developed a knack with them. I would not want to be on the receiving end." She stared at the pilot, completing the last knot without looking.

Taryn covered his smile. It was getting less painful seeing them together. Being a brother and friend was turning out to be the best possible relationship—for him. She'd never be able to get rid of him, and he'd always have her, in ways no one else ever would. It was good. Very good.

Renloret took the blade back from Taryn and gave a careful blade salute to Reslo. "It is an ingenious design. You may be sought after to create more of them once warriors and soldiers see what they can do. I would only use them in situations such as we may encounter while on this upcoming foray." He slipped the blade into the sheath, the hilt ending above his wrist.

Reslo stepped close to study how Renloret had strapped them on. "You can throw them with either hand?"

"Yes. I'm more accurate with my left backhanded throw. By

mounting it on the outside of the forearm, I get a smooth, single-motion draw and throw."

Reslo grunted approval. "Well done. I'm honored to have an appreciative user. S'Hendale thought it was too gruesome. She called it a kreline blade because the predator's four largest fangs have barbs. I'd been thinking about the hooks we use for fishing. Either way, I wanted to create a blade that would cause more damage coming out than going in because, honestly, some opponents deserve it."

They finished arming and slung packs to their shoulders. Renloret checked the camouflage settings around the star runner and they left the ship at a jog. Taryn led them up a faint trail—humming the Song of Finding as he followed the music in his head.

Excited voices echoed in the tunnel, but the reverberation made it impossible to understand any of the words. Taryn, Renloret, Ani, and Kela stepped into a side tunnel and extinguished the hand-lights. A few minutes later, the main tunnel showed dimly, and scuffs from several sets of boots could be heard. The voices were quieter now and did not echo so much, though Ani still had trouble distinguishing words.

*Kela?* In the darkness of the smaller tunnel she felt his muzzle nudge her hand.

*Something about how they're going to divide up the treasure. They're headed back to Wharton to find someone named Vradly who might be able to cut up a crystal once they fully open the chamber.* The canine's worry colored each word and chilled Ani.

"Taryn, Kela says they found a large crystal and are going to bring in someone to cut it up," she whispered.

She heard the hiss of surprise from both men.

"Now that I'm so close, Chandaron only sings the Song of Finding," Taryn whispered back. "How can they have found the Stone? It was sealed up."

*They spied it through a hole. They want this Vradly to be there when the chamber is fully accessible. They say the crystal is iridescent and glows. They think they will be wealthy men in a few hours, and if they are careful, the treasure will only have to be split between the three of them.*

Ani relayed Kela's further explanation in hushed tones. She added, "If we take them now, only two will know."

"Shush, they're close," Renloret said.

Mentally humming a preparatory song, Ani slid the crystal blade from her boot and heard the soft whoosh of two more blades being pulled from their sheaths.

*I will stop them. Then you can do as you wish.*

"Kela's going out." She felt the bump of his body against her thigh as he slipped out to the main tunnel.

"Good."

She barely heard Renloret's response.

The bouncing and winking of the miners' hand-lights steadied at the same moment she heard surprised exclamations.

"What's that?"

"How'd it get here?"

*I was hungry and I followed you.*

Ani stifled a chuckle. "Go," she whispered as she moved forward, bumping against one of her companions. They moved as well, and within four or five steps, all three had joined Kela in blocking the exit path. As if they'd planned it, Renloret, Taryn, and Ani switched on their hand-lights, effectively blinding the two miners who stood side by side in stunned silenced. Slowly, they lowered their lights.

"Why are you here?" Renloret asked.

Ani was surprised at the calm authority in his voice. Evidently, so were the miners because they looked at each other to see which one would take responsibility for whatever they might be accused of. She stopped herself from glancing at him, keeping her eyes on the miners. Let Renloret handle this, she told herself.

"Do I need to repeat the question?"

The miners' mouths flapped open and closed. Ani wondered if their supervisor knew where they were. Still no words of explanation came from them.

"One of you best start talking or I'll release the beast here."

*Oh, I like that. Now I'm a beast.* Kela's tone was full of delight. He took two steps forward, bared his teeth, and growled.

The miners backed up. One grabbed the other's shirt to keep him from turning and running. "We was e'plorin', sir. Didn't know this here branch was off'n limits. We saw a light. That was all. We came to investigate."

The other's head bobbed in agreement. His eyes shifted from his coworker to Kela, who had stopped growling but curled his lips higher to show more of his teeth.

Renloret moved up alongside Kela and moved his light from one miner's face to the other. "And what did you find?"

They blinked from the brightness, and one started to raise a hand to block the light.

"I wouldn't do that," Taryn hissed. "The beast might think that's a sign of aggression."

Kela crouched, ready to spring forward, and resumed growling.

Ani kept tight control of her facial muscles. Kela was having way too much fun.

The miner who'd spoken slapped at his coworker's hand. "Be still, you id'jut." Then he offered Renloret a respectful blade salute.

Before he could say anything else, Renloret repeated his last question.

The looks of disappointment were obvious. They both sighed.

With a tremulous voice, one of the miners said, "The giant's treasure, sir."

"The what?" Renloret asked.

"We'd heard the stories, and we decided to look when we were off shift. Didn' think there'd be harm in lookin', seein' as how it's not been found yet."

Renloret guffawed, and its echo through the tunnel accentuated the absurdity of the miner's statement.

The miner stepped forward in his eagerness to explain. "But we found it. Yes'n, sir, we found it."

A growl from Kela made him step back. The man swallowed and stared at Kela.

"You? You found the giant's treasure?"

Ani marveled at the incredulity Renloret was able to put into his voice. Exactly like she thought any other right-minded person would.

"Show us," Taryn ordered.

Ani glanced at him. He was wincing in pain, and his breathing was quick and shallow. "Commander," Ani said, directing her word at Renloret.

He turned his attention to Taryn and studied him briefly before turning back to the miners. "You lead." All seriousness now, he waved the light down the tunnel. "Move!"

Kela jumped at the miners, and they about-faced and began to run. Ani heard Kela's laugh in her head as he trotted after the terrified men.

Renloret reached out and grasped Taryn's arm. "You all right?"

"No. The Stone knows about the miners, but because there were only two and because I'm near the blade, it decided I would be able to protect it before the miners . . ." He rubbed his free hand across his brow, which was gleaming with sweat.

"Ask Chandaron to quiet its song so you can concentrate on finding the blade," Ani suggested. She tugged at her brother. "Come on. You said we're close."

He stumbled forward a few steps. Then his head came up and the frown left his face and he began to run after the miners and Kela.

Renloret and Ani followed close behind. They came to an abrupt stop when they caught up with the others. The miners had stopped at a smaller tunnel that branched off from the main one. There was a fair amount of loose rock shoveled into piles along the edge of the main tunnel.

"This'n here branch ain't on any of the maps. We busted through yesterday and saw that." The miner pointed at a stream of lavender light that pierced the darkness of the smaller tunnel and directed his hand-light on its walls. "An' this ain't normal either." He ran his free hand along the smooth, polished surface.

The walls were engineered like the tunnels and chambers on Southern and The Necklace Islands, as well as the tunnels that connected Ani's lake house to the research center and launch room in Star Valley. She wanted to ask Renloret how long that type of engineering had been in use on Lrakira. Had it been for at least a thousand years?

Renloret cleared his throat. "Where's this giant's treasure?"

"You's kin see it through here," the miner said. He went down the passage and put his eye to the hole in the end wall before backing up a couple of steps to allow Renloret a look.

Renloret sucked a breath in through his teeth and pushed from the wall, turning to Taryn with an affirming nod.

Taryn sheathed his blade and stepped up. "Chandaron," he whispered. Then he backed away, holding both hands to his head, and slid down the wall.

Ani knelt beside him, looked up at Renloret, and tipped her head toward the miners. "Get them out of here. Make sure they can't tell anyone else about this until he's found the blade."

She turned her attention to Taryn, not caring how Renloret would accomplish the assignment. She heard some scuffling of boots and a grunt or two. Kela informed her when the pilot had the two miners far enough away that they would hear nothing and sent a picture of Renloret binding their hands and feet. She thanked him and whispered to Taryn, "They're out of the way. Can I help?"

He shook his head and whispered back, "I have to find it. That's part of the process. But it must be very close. The others weren't that far from the Stones."

"Can you stand?" She offered him a hand, and he took it. He was grimacing in discomfort. "Does your head hurt?"

"Not really, but seeing the Stone is kind of . . . well . . . stunning, and it knows I'm here. The song has changed, and it has increased in volume. I can't concentrate well." He shook his whole body like Kela would after a swim and leaned against the end wall. The violet light shining through the gap in the shielding wall was above and to the left of his shoulder. "Chandaron says . . ."

"Chandaron says what?" Ani prodded.

Taryn chuckled. "Well, well, looky there." He put his hands on her shoulders, turned her around, and then pointed, his arm parallel with the purplish beam.

Ani's eyes traced the beam to where it struck the wall of the main tunnel. A faint blue-purple line glowed in a rough rectangle. "Oh. You are correct, little brother. The Singer and his blade are not far from one another."

Taryn rolled his shoulders back and around. "Did we bring the tools?"

"Of course," she replied as she grabbed one of the packs and pulled out a spade and a hand pick.

"Then let's get to work."

They'd been scraping away at the thin purple line for only a minute or so when Renloret joined them.

"Kela is watching the miners."

Ani nodded. The canine had already told her.

"I told the miners that the dog would be delighted to eat either one of them if they tried to escape," he added.

Ani nodded again. Kela had already passed that on to her too. Once Renloret had disappeared around the slight curve of the tunnel, the miners had begun to talk to each other, unaware of the dog's telepathic abilities. Kela was now allowing Ani to overhear their conversation. They were disgruntled about the turn of events, and they were now discussing how they might convince these three interlopers to at least give them a finder's fee.

Renloret was working to loosen up the sealing compound across the top of the doorway. "Ask Kela if they've said anything about Treyder."

Ani did so and relayed that the only names they'd said so far were Vradly, the stone cutter, and Grundel, who was not only one of the larger investors in the new mining endeavor but also the head cook in the dining facility.

"There!" Taryn dropped the trowel and brushed bits of stony debris from the crack. "Where's the rope?"

"I've got a few more inches, Taryn. Be patient," Renloret said.

Taryn grabbed the trowel and started digging at the other end of the line. Ani finished her line and peeked through. A soft purplish glow illuminated a pair of large boots thickly layered with dust—undoubtedly signs of the last Singer. The boots were larger than Taryn's or Renloret's, so perhaps the "giant" part of the folktale was but an exaggeration of reality.

Renloret allowed Taryn to brush out the crumbled filling while he dug into one of the packs for the length of rope they'd brought in case it was needed to see-saw a stone door open as they had in Southern. The two men prepared the rope, and the three of them yanked and pulled until their arm muscles were sore with the strain. They took a break to drink from the flasks of water, and Ani passed around a bag of nuts and dried meat to augment the fluid.

Ani rubbed her biceps and grinned at Renloret who was doing the same. His skin shone where the hand-light beams reflected off perspiration. "After this I'm going to need a massage," she said.

He stopped rubbing his own arms. "Agreed. Do you think there are any hot springs nearby?"

She could hardly see his expression in the thin light, but she heard the desire in his voice and smiled at the promise.

"That's a good idea," Taryn added. "I wonder if Professor Tondon would want to come to Star Valley and try our hot springs." Taryn's eyes were closed and his head was tilted upward. A smile softened his face, which was smudged with dust and sweat, and he went back to work in earnest.

Ani felt Kela's inquiry about how they were doing and answered him. *The door is almost wide enough for Taryn to get through.*

*I don't like being away from the action. But I know you appreciate my guard duty.*

Ani chuckled. *Okay, I get the hint. We can talk about an appropriate compensation for your talents after Taryn is blade bonded to Chandaron.*

"Kela?" Renloret asked, touching her shoulder to get her attention. "Is there a problem?"

"Nothing a steak or a pat on the head won't fix."

*Steak.* Kela's mental voice was firm.

She openly laughed. "I guess we'll have to buy some steak."

"We'll do that after our current project." Renloret patted Taryn's knee. "Come, old man. A few more inches and you get to meet Chandaron's last Singer." The pilot held out a hand to the sheriff and pulled.

It did not take long for them to wedge the door the final inches and Taryn, followed by Ani and Renloret, entered the chamber.

A soft whistle was sounded by Renloret as he walked the length of the robe that lay on the platform. "He must have been over seven feet tall!"

"And look at the size of his boots!" Ani exclaimed.

Taryn was sure the soles were easily twice the length of hers. He stood in the center of the circular room, slowly rotating, checking every detail. The song had quieted once he'd started prying away the sealant around the door. He stopped to study the Singer's robe and nodded. Here lay evidence for the basis of the giant in the folktale. The robe would have dragged a foot or more on the ground if he had put it on. Could he talk his mother into hemming it?

Taryn frowned as he surveyed the room. Where was the blade? The room was suffused in a violet light that could only be supplied by the crystal blade. A Passing had taken place, just as had occurred with Geth and Mahzali. So where was the light coming from?

Ani and Renloret were slowly making their way around the room, examining every crack and cranny. As sparsely furnished as the chambers of the previous two Singers, there were not many hiding places for the Stone's blade.

"Maybe the blade is under the robe," Renloret said. He bent down, raised the edge of the robe, and slid his arm under it, moving it carefully side to side. "Nothing I can feel." He began to roll up the fabric.

"Should we do that?" Taryn felt a twinge of fear trickle down his spine. He knew Camfel had meticulously recorded placement of everything before she'd allowed the others to be moved. She wasn't there, of course, and he hesitated.

"He's already passed into the blade, Taryn. He doesn't need the robe anymore." Ani walked over and pushed Renloret away from the platform. She whipped the robe off and unceremoniously shook it, scattering dust into the air, which caused all three to sneeze. Then she laid it out again and began folding it.

Shocked by her seeming uncaring treatment of the gold robe, Taryn had to take several breaths before he could think of anything to say. Then he heard her humming. It sounded familiar, though he couldn't place it. It seemed out of context. "What are you singing?"

"It's the farewell song from the Remembrance Ceremony, Taryn. We sang it at Mother's ceremony. Don't you remember?" She returned to her humming as she continued to fold the long golden garment.

Listening closely, he knew where she was in the song, and he felt compelled to add the words. Ani switched from humming to singing, and by the next stanza, Renloret had added his baritone. The trio ended the song only to hear a solemn howl echo through the tunnels. Kela had joined in his own way to respectfully remember the yet unnamed Singer.

Ani patted the folded fabric and turned to survey the space. "Well, neither scabbard nor blade was under the robe." She raised an eyebrow at Taryn. "Now what?"

"Does Chandaron say anything?" Renloret asked.

Taryn realized the Stone had been quite silent since their entry into the room. "No. The blade must be in this room, but it has been hidden very well." He stretched out his arms and turned slowly. Could he use his arms to find the blade as Jaikeer and Mihalas had used the blades to find their Stones? There was no buzzing in his arms. The glow was diffused evenly about the room. No one spot was brighter than the others. He looked down, slowly lowering his arms in defeat and watched the shadows of his arms disappear. He studied Renloret and Ani as they moved about. There were no shadows.

Raising his arms again, the shadows appeared, as if the sun were directly overhead. He looked up. The ceiling of the room seemed a bit brighter. "Renloret, help me move the platform to the center."

"Why?"

"Neither of us is tall enough, but the Singer might have been."

Renloret shrugged and gave Ani a let's-tolerate-the-guy look. Together they shifted the platform and Taryn jumped on top. Stretching, he was able to touch the ceiling. He ran his palms across the surface in search of some sort of straight-line crack that might indicate a mortared brick.

"Ah, yes, there you are," he muttered as his fingers settled into a crease. "Hand me one of those trowels." He lowered a hand to receive it and began digging. The mortar dust fell onto his face, and he had to close his eyes and scrape away by touch. When he felt he had cleared away most of it, he struck the trowel handle against the arm-long brick several times. It moved. He smiled as he pushed up the narrow ends until he could tip the brick. When he had removed the brick, he handed it to Renloret and reached into the hole for the sword or the scabbard. His fingers touched nothing, and he moved to get a better view of the opening.

"Taryn. It's not there," Ani said.

Feeling panic building within him, he replied, "It's got to be." He stood on his toes and tried to find the internal edges of the opening.

"It's not up there anymore. It's here," his sister said. "In the brick." Her voice carried an odd, puzzled sound.

"At least that's what the note says," Renloret added. "And there's light coming through tiny holes on the underside of the brick." He had tipped the brick up, and the purple light was directed at the wall.

Taryn looked down at the two of them. "Interesting. Now, what note?"

Renloret was waving a piece of cloth at him. "Someone wrote you a note, and it wasn't the Singer."

"Show me." Taryn jumped off the platform to stand between them.

The large piece of cloth had been folded, and Renloret spread it out next to the brick. Taryn recognized the script as ancient Lrakiran. It looked to have been freshly created. There was no fading of the ink or paint. He touched the fabric. Lrakiran silteene? Yes, like the blood-red fabric that lined the storage box of Ani's blade, but this was white. The small intricate glyphs were purple and appeared to have been carefully placed. Some of the lines were so thin they resembled strands of hair.

"What does it say?" Taryn asked as he brushed off the dust from his shoulders and arms. He was wishing he'd had a bio-teacher implant so he wouldn't have to keep asking for a translation. He would be able to read whatever it was by himself instead of wasting time. At least Renloret was fluent in ancient Lrakiran.

Renloret's lips were moving as he silently read the note, his fingers tracing each line. He backtracked a few times as if deciphering the exact meaning of a phrase. When he reached the end of the note, he tapped the signature.

"Well?" Taryn demanded. "Is the blade really inside the brick."

Ani harrumphed and mumbled something. Taryn glanced at her. She was running her hands over the brick, pressing the corners with her fingers.

"Ani, do you think the Singer disguised a blade storage case?" he asked. "It is long enough to hold a short blade like your mother's."

Her green eyes flicked in his direction and then returned to examining the brick. Renloret nodded in agreement.

"Yes," the pilot replied. "But before you start trying to open it, you need to listen."

Ani set the brick-like box on one of its long sides and interlaced her fingers behind her back. Her attention was rapt. "Kela says to hurry up. He'd rather be here than down the tunnel guarding the thieves."

Renloret straightened from his examination of the note. "This is from the Singer's attendant. He does not give his own name, just that he is Singer Valik's attendant."

"And?" Taryn could feel the impatience in his own voice.

"I'll read you what he wrote. 'The Chandaron Stone's Singer, Valik, commands me to write this so you, The Balance, will know why you are needed to become the next Singer of Valik's beloved Stone. If all has occurred as the Stones predict, your sister's blood has saved our divided people from extinction, and you will have saved one of the Lrakiran Stones and returned to Teramar, your birth world.

"'While there is much we will not know of the ensuing thousand years, if you have found this chamber and the blade box, the Stone has promised our people will reunite in a great song. Much is dependent on you and your fellow Singers. May the Stones of Teramar guide you as your true heritage is revealed, and may you use the blades to protect your people and the guardian Stones.

"'There may be conflict and confusion when the people of Teramar learn of the grand deception we have perpetrated. We grieve that it was the only way. Though the Stones can twist time with their songs, they cannot change an asteroid's path. Once the planets had been chosen and the people transported by the Song of Saving, there was no time to find an alternative to Lrakira, and so the prophecy was constructed. The people were divided to ensure basic survival of at least one half. The Stones were divided as well, each promising to follow the plan until time and song heals our home and it is safe for the people to return.

"'My master, Singer Valik, has died and passed safely into the blade. I will hide the blade and seal his tomb as he sealed the chamber around Chandaron. I have spread a rumor of a giant wielding a glowing sword who protects these mountains. It is hoped that the small number of locals who hunt in the area will maintain the superstition and thus preserve the safety of the Singer's blade and the Stone. Should it be necessary Chandaron will use the rumor to protect itself and the location of Valik's chamber.

"'One thousand or more sun cycles hence, The Blood and The Balance will be birthed here on Teramar. May the Stones join in song again and the skies be filled with their brilliant light. May the prophecy be followed and our people united once more. It is my privilege to serve Valik, Chandaron, and my divided people. I am glad you will know the spirit of Valik once you have opened the blade box. Press the center of the box three times, matching the beat of your heart, to release the lock. May you discover the joy and knowledge of the blade and Stone. Chandaron awaits.' It is signed simply, Singer Valik's attendant."

# CHAPTER THIRTY

Taryn stared at the disguised blade box. Now that he knew what he was looking at, he saw that the rough surface had been applied on all sides of the box. He scraped away the plaster with his old metal blade, revealing the underlying box. It was identical to the storage box the Anyala Stone's blade was in. A slight discoloration, almost a shadow, showed itself in the middle of one side. He used a quieting breath to listen to his heart then pressed his finger down and released it three times. A brilliant purple line was revealed. Turning the box on its narrow edge, he pried the two sides apart. The box popped open.

He blinked in the brightness of the crystal blade. It was nestled against gold silteene. The hilt was rather plain, without the jewels with which the blades of Southern and The Necklace Islands had been decorated. He leaned close to examine the weapon and smiled as he realized it was actually not plain at all. It was decorated with subtle, intricate lines of gold and silver embedded in the near-black metallic surface.

Renloret's intake of breath caught Taryn's attention. "What?" Taryn asked.

"The hilt is a Liander-metal crystal. It's extremely rare. I have heard of examples from across the stars, and those were much smaller and used as pieces of jewelry. Under certain conditions it can be melted and made into shapes without losing its crystalline properties. It can only be changed once, and when it solidifies, it is unchangeable. It cannot be broken or shattered. The skill it took to create such a piece is unfathomable. The hilt alone is beyond worth." Renloret sucked in a breath and released it with a sigh. "This blade is yours, Singer Taryn."

"Take it," Ani said.

Taryn wondered what it would feel like to have a long dead spirit enter him and reached into the box. As he gripped the crystal hilt, a welcoming warmth spread from his hand up his arm and into the center of his body. He was compelled to lift the point above his head, and when he did, he saw the purple wisps begin to dance and flow from the blade. A question entered his head. *Do you willingly take on the responsibility of Singer of the Chandaron Stone? To lead my people from their past to their future. To protect the Stone as it will protect the people.* He answered firmly. Taryn felt the warmth of Valik's spirit tingle through every fiber. As Valik wandered through his thoughts, Taryn felt bared but unafraid.

*Ah, it is time. Greetings, Singer.* The deep voice chuckled and rumbled inside Taryn's head. *A thousand years is not so long as I imagined.*

*Valik?*

*Yes, and so you know me before I have said my name. And I now know you, Taryn Avere. You will continue to protect your people as you take on protecting Chandaron. You have read the note my attendant scribed for you. I was too weak to finish the hiding of the blade. He did as I bid, laying me on the platform properly and holding the blade box nearby so I could enter my final resting place.*

*I gifted him the scabbard for his decades of service to me. He was protected from the blade by the artificial covering I designed to hide the blade above my body, where only The Balance would think to look. I was too old, having lived well beyond my usefulness as a Singer, but I knew I would be the last. It was sad feeling Mahzali and Geth leave their bodies to enter their blades, though Chandaron kept me company and eased my way. The Stone said I would not know the passage of time, and so it feels I have only slept a short time. A dreamless sleep I have had, Singer. As I was the last to die, so too you are the last to find your way to the blade and Stone destined for you.*

*Chandaron will teach you so much more than I knew. Through you, I will experience reunion with the Stones of Teramar and Lrakira, and perhaps for a second time, I will travel the star paths on the colors of the Stones as we did in the Song of Saving. I am at peace with the evolution of our people. We are destined for great things. You are strong and not of a closed mind. I feel a direct descendant of your line will be among those who decide to go forward to the next stage. Until then, there is much to do, Taryn Avere. Chandaron must be awakened. You must learn of your people's past to lead them to the future. Use the blade to guide you. Chandaron awaits.*

Taryn opened his eyes as the voice echoed to silence. His knees folded, lowering him to the chamber floor, and he brought the purple blade to his lips. Renloret and Ani were watching him, their eyes serious. He coughed and growled to clear what felt like one hundred years of dust from his throat. "Chandaron awaits." His voice sounded faint, distant.

Ani stepped close and tipped a water flask to his lips. The spirit within him relished the moisture. She tipped it again, and he drank as Taryn Avere, Sheriff of Star Valley not as Valik, last Singer of Chandaron.

"My thanks, sister." He remained on his knees as tens of decades of memories were added to his. "Valik was well over one hundred when he died. He gifted the blade's scabbard to his attendant in payment for services that included staying with him until he Passed. Then the attendant completed the tasks of hiding the blade and sealing this room."

The blade's glow fluctuated. Taryn lowered the tip and pointed it at the doorway. It brightened. "Now to officially meet the Chandaron Stone."

Renloret took his elbow, steadying him as he rose to his feet. After a couple of shaky steps, he moved into the tunnel, the blade lighting the way. It pulled him toward the wall behind which the Northern Stone waited. He stood still and studied the wall with the eye-sized hole in it.

*The Balance is welcomed. You may enter.* Chandaron's voice was similar to that of Valik's. Over his shoulder, Taryn whispered, "Ani, can you hear it?"

"No. It speaks only to you, brother."

*Place your hand here.* A shape, radiating violet light appeared on the wall surface.

As directed by the short tune in his head, he covered the shape with his hand, and the surface vibrated and throbbed. The tune changed and filled his body. He pushed, and the wall moved slightly. There was a sensation of immense power from deep inside his body. Valik? Could a spirit help him physically?

Valik's voice carried joy. *It is good to be young and strong again. Do not worry, Singer. I will help only when I am truly needed.*

Leaning against the wall, Taryn planted his feet and used the strength of his legs to push again. This time, it felt as though the door was swinging on a hinge, and Taryn stumbled into the chamber.

The Chandaron Stone was about the same mass as the Anyala Stone, being only slightly larger than Jaikeer's Bayleden and Mihalas' Ellashin. All shades of violet and purple danced through the air and reverberated off the walls of the chamber. Music welled up in his head. A glance at Ani showed that she saw the colors but did not hear the Stone's song. She was twirling about, in and through the colors, as if she could feel them. Renloret was likewise mesmerized by the display. A tendril of rich purple ribboned around the pilot briefly before floating deliberately to do the same to Ani.

Taryn thought back to the moments when Jaikeer and Mihalas had met their Stones. Had the colors also seemed to caress those present. No. They had only surrounded the new Singers. Why was this different?

Words matching the now lilting tune in his head answered his silent question. *We did not want to frighten those not destined to be Singers. All present in this chamber are or will be Singers. Come nearer so I may greet you in person.*

Taryn had the odd impression the Stone was smiling while it sang. He walked forward and brought the iridescent blade flat against his chest in a blade salute when he was within a hand-width of the flashing deep-purple Stone. Kneeling close, he placed both hands, one still holding the hilt of the blade, at either end of the oblong crystal and bowed his head to connect with the surface of the Stone. It was cool against his skin.

*You have done well in holding to your destiny of The Balance, Taryn Avere. You are a trained protector. You will continue to protect your people.* The song hesitated. *We sorrow for the damage done to the Time Song and thereby, the lives of so many. Your families may be stronger for these struggles. We shall weave this into the Song of Teaching. We will begin when you have brought the Stones of Teramar to one place. Bayleden and Ellashin are preparing their Singers for the journey.*

*There is still danger here. You must see to it, for I cannot move against those who wish to harm. With Anyala's Singer and the pilot, you can protect more innocent people from a quietness I cannot reach. Then we shall travel to your home and join with the others to sing to the people of Teramar.*

The cool, calm internal voice faded. Taryn opened his eyes, which he'd not realized he had closed, almost in supplication. The life light of Chandaron pulsed rhythmically—a heartbeat of sorts. He considered what the Stone had told him and relayed its words to Ani and Renloret. They were quiet for more than a few breaths, bathed in the less intense purple aura of the resting Stone.

"'A quietness I cannot reach,'" Ani quoted. "Sounds like it sort of knows what Treyder has been building and needs us to stop him before the Stones can sing either the Song of Teaching or the Song of Reunion."

"Agreed," Renloret replied. "We know the blade and the Song of Healing could not remove the coma devices from either of you, though through both blade and song, your bodies were healed. It took the surgeons on Lrakira to remove the nasty things."

Ani looked toward the main tunnel.

"What? Is that Kela?" Taryn asked.

"Yes. He says we should ask the miners what Treyder is having them build."

"All right, let's go." Taryn handed the blade storage box to Renloret and carefully slid the deep purple crystal blade into his boot sheath, sliding his old metal blade beneath his belt. The crystal blade was longer. Its hilt stuck above the sheath by a hand-width, but it did not hamper his movement. He would have to make a full waist or back scabbard for it. A project for later. He then turned to the Stone. "I can seal you safely inside again if I touch the lock?" He said it out loud, forgetting that he might be able to just *think* his question.

Once again, he felt amusement in the Stone's affirmative answer. He waved Ani and Renloret through the opening to the main tunnel and pressed his hand to the faintly glowing shape on the stony door. Jumping backward and out of the way as the stone door swung closed, he stayed until the section of wall seemed to be secure and nearly invisible. He noticed that the narrow beam of violet light had disappeared. Had the Chandaron Stone gone to sleep? At that thought, he heard an internal lilting chuckle and then, very softly, another short ditty. *I never sleep.*

He chuckled to himself, thinking he might enjoy this new identity, this new and wondrous connection. The smile stayed on his lips as he followed his companions.

The miners were eager to tell the trio everything the benevolent Doctor Jarden had done for the Wharton village community. He'd tripled the miners' pay and provided jobs for anyone above school age in his manufacturing plant. They were a bit confused that none of them had heard about the wondrous device that would allow doctors to perform surgeries without anesthesia. Hadn't they seen the report that was supposed to have been broadcast continent-wide just last week? Even Kela looked askance at them. Ani wondered if this Doctor Jarden was an alias Treyder was using to further hide his whereabouts.

The miners were proud their village would be the providers of this device. No mention was made of using this miracle device as a weapon, and when Taryn stated he had first-hand knowledge of such use, the miners were horrified and assured him that was certainly not the intent of the esteemed Doctor Jarden. Taryn asked for a description of the doctor, and Ani's suspicions were confirmed.

"Why does Doctor Jarden need to have his company here?" Renloret asked.

"'Cause we's got the right combination of minerals all right here. He says craudlin is only found in large enough quantities here, and it's the only stuff that works. Thought it'd be best if'n he located the manufacturing at the source." The miners shared nods of affirmation.

"We was throwin' it in the tailings 'cause we'd no use fer it until Doctor Jarden come," the other miner added. "Now we found the giant's treasure too!"

That earned the speaker a two-footed kick from his compatriot. "Shut yer mouth, id'jut. I ain't had the chance to bargain with 'em yet."

"No bargaining needed," Taryn said, sliding his old blade from his belt and pointing it at the throat of the speaker.

Both miners edged back in wide-eyed fear. Taryn stepped forward and pushed the tip of the blade under the talkative one's chin. The man flinched in pain.

Ani saw the bloody nick in the skin. "Taryn!" She could not let him continue in this vein, though he might be well justified.

He glanced at her and sighed, then he stepped back and returned the sword to his belt.

Renloret expelled a breath. She'd not been the only one to question the act.

Ani put a hand on her brother's shoulder. "We'll handle them, okay?"

He nodded and paced back around the curve in the tunnel, out of sight. She hoped he would calm down.

Renloret took Taryn's place in front of the miners. "He is correct in that there will be no negotiations. We will let you live instead, if that's all right with you?"

The two men nodded enthusiastically.

"But we're going to keep you here until we can settle other matters. If we come back, you'll be free to talk about what you've witnessed. If we don't . . . well, you won't have the chance to tell anyone."

Ani turned a surprised look at him. "Where'd you have in mind to put them?"

"With Valik."

Ani pursed her lips and whistled. "I hadn't thought of that. That's good." She looked at the bound men. "I'll untie their feet." After Renloret gave a sharp affirming nod, she knelt and loosened the ropes.

*Does that mean I'm done with guard duty?* Kela asked.

She felt his desire to be closer to the action than through her eyes and thoughts. *I don't see why not. Besides, I want you closer to me too.*

He gave her a wink.

Ani assisted the miners to their feet and urged them back toward the burial chamber. "They'll be okay for a day or so with water, but one of us will need to come back to release them."

"If we can," Renloret replied.

She stopped the miners, retied them, and drew Renloret aside to chat with him in private.

"You want to change your mind?" She'd be willing to just leave them tied up in the tunnel, maybe a bit closer to the main entrance. "You realize they only know what Treyder told them. They're not responsible for his actions, only their own."

"And if they'd gotten to Chandaron, they might well have killed it when they cut it up." Taryn appeared from the side tunnel that led to the Stone's chamber, his expression dark and brooding. "Then where would Lrakira, Teramar, and all the Stones be?"

"Why don't we move Chandaron right now?" Ani suggested. "We could take it to the star runner where it would be safer than here, and then we could move these guys to a more conspicuous place without endangering them or the Stone." Ani hoped that might be acceptable.

Taryn and Renloret stared at each other. Did they know what the other was thinking without telepathy?

"Chandaron agrees, Ani," Taryn said. "It does not want to harm any of its charges, and if they tried to cut it, it would have difficulty in not choosing to protect itself—especially with the Song of Teaching to be sung and reunion yet to take place." Taryn grinned at them. "It does not necessarily feel that the loss of two undereducated miners would affect the outcome of future events, but it also does not want to chance personal interference in its charges' futures."

"Well, then let's get it," Renloret said.

"I wonder how heavy it is?" Ani asked, as much to herself as to the others. "I guess we'll find out."

Kela agreed to watch the miners a bit longer while the three went back to the chamber.

When Taryn opened the chamber, its Stone's life light pulsed brighter. It didn't take too long to reconfigure two of the backpacks into a sling that could be carried by two people. They draped the sling over the top of the Stone, with Taryn and Renloret holding the straps. Ani slid her fingers under an edge, tipping the Stone on its side, then pushed it over the edge of the pedestal while the men tightened their hold to keep the sling under it and slowly lowered the entire contraption to the ground.

"I wonder if it minds being hauled around upside down?" Ani couldn't help asking with a giggle.

"It says there is no wrong side up," Taryn said. "However, it appreciates not being dropped." Ani and Renloret joined in when Taryn laughed.

"Do you think you can carry it all the way to the star runner?" Ani asked the men.

They worked their way into the shoulder straps and snugged up the buckles, agreeing that they thought they could manage it before carefully setting it down again. The miners had to be attended to.

The three returned to the miners, and Ani untied them while the others stood guard. Then they led them to a point in the tunnel closer to the opening before retying them with their hands in front of them and tossing them canteens of water.

Now released from his guard duty, Kela returned to the chamber with them to retrieve the Stone. With the makeshift sling on, Kela thought the men looked like a sway-backed ovline. After seeing them take a few steps, Ani had to agree, but she kept her comment in telepathic mode.

"Ready?" she asked.

"As ever. Let's go!" Taryn followed Kela's lead back to the mine's hidden entrance.

Ani took her place as a rear guard, her blade ready in case the miners had lied about not telling others of the giant's treasure and more miners showed up to help them retrieve it.

# CHAPTER THIRTY-ONE

A loud knock on his office door startled Isul. His hand squeezed the box and about half of the sample encapsulated coma devices squirted out, tinkling noisily as they struck the desktop and scattered. He cursed softly. "Yes, what is it?" He let all his irritation at the interruption color his voice.

"You have a visitor, sir." The voice was muffled coming through the door.

A visitor? Who knew he was here? Was it Reslo Chenak? Had someone slipped up and revealed his identity before that coward had left the village? Isul forced himself to remember the oft-stated admonishment of his blade instructor to only unsheathe a knife or sword after knowing the identity of his opponent. Best not to worry before he had to, he thought as he finished corralling the manthra-grain-sized capsules containing the devices and put them back in the box.

"Enter."

The door was opened by a young man wearing a green wrap,

signaling he belonged to the security force. The youth saluted and then stood tall, staring ahead. "Sir, I present an emissary from the continental government." He saluted again and took a sideways step, revealing the visitor behind him.

Isul felt his eyebrows rise in surprise before he could stop them. It was Sarinne Flaymatov. She had only recently been in contact to warn him that his funding was being cut off and the senator was under investigation. All sorts of questions flooded Isul's thoughts. Now she was an emissary from the government? Sarinne was not smiling. Her eyes moved from left to right, studying his office. She stepped forward, crossing the threshold into his territory before giving him an appropriate though all too quick salute. Isul was suddenly wary. He responded with a similar action and then pointed at one of the two chairs facing his desk. She took the other one. Isul clenched his teeth.

Once she was seated, Isul looked at the security escort. "My thanks. You are excused." The youth snapped a salute and turned about, closing the door softly behind him. Isul remained standing. Now what?

"Sit down, Doctor *Jarden*," she said.

He swallowed nervously and sat. She smiled, though he noticed her eyes remained flat. "How did Sarinne Flaymatov become a government emissary, and why are you here?" he asked.

She didn't move. "Oh, I used that emissary title to get directly to you. But I do work for Senator Nelham, so government emissary seemed an appropriate title. As I warned you, Senator Nelham is under investigation. The senator instructed me to inform you that three days hence, you are to be in Saedi City with as many of the *devices* as you have ready. You will accompany him to a hearing where you will demonstrate the device. A subject will be provided. If the demonstration is well received," she paused to give him another cold smile, "he will be able to proceed with his plan for you to continue the development of the device, including the exploration of using it for mass deployment."

She leaned forward and placed both hands on his desk. "For your information, though *you* told me where you are, I did not pass it on to the senator. Your factory's location is among other things in an envelope that will be opened if I don't return. Now, how would you like to proceed?"

This time, Isul was able to keep his expression flat. He would replace the demonstration he'd planned for the mining investors with a rousing speech on the news that the government was asking for proof his device would eliminate the need for anesthesia. And if approved, the village of Wharton would become a magnet for medical research much like Star Valley had become twenty-five years ago. He would emphasize the medical uses for the device at the investors meeting even as work on the military aspects the senator wanted continued. Isul pulled at the hem of his jacket and leaned back in his chair, no longer worried. This was going to work out just fine. But he had a few questions.

"If the demonstration is successful, he will be able to continue funding the project?" he asked.

She nodded over steepled fingers. "We have every reason to expect that continued funding will not face opposition."

"And if it is?"

She shrugged. "I suspect you will no longer be in the invention business due to your incarceration."

"It will not fail." He was confident of that.

"So you say."

There were several moments of silence between them. He studied her face. It was the first time he'd seen her clearly. She'd always managed to stay in the shadows when she'd been with the senator, and it had been almost ten years since he'd seen her before that. Had it been just days before Fairaden died? Then she'd been holding his wife's hand, talking to her in their incomprehensible Southern language. Now there were creases around her eyes, and her cheeks sagged a bit, but she was still comely enough to turn a man's head.

"Sarinne." He acknowledged her with a tightlipped smile. "I'm not sure you need to keep the location of my facility a secret. I think they already know."

She sat erect in the chair, suddenly interested. "Really? I was not informed. Who are *they*?"

"I think Reslo Chenak is here."

Her eyes went wide in surprise. "Reslo? Here? In Wharton? Now?" She turned in the chair to look at the door, as if Reslo might be standing there.

"He was with two other men. They claimed to be on a hiking expedition, but I think it was a ruse. One them is the owner of a Star Valley bar. The other could well be a deputy from Star Valley, though I did not recognize him. ."

"So why would they be here?"

"They told an employee of mine they were looking for a

giant's treasure." He smiled. Would she be interested in treasure?

"A . . . a giant's treasure?" Sarinne seemed flabbergasted. She chuckled. "Not likely, Treyder. Reslo Chenak was never a treasure hunter. He was too wrapped up in following the rules and demanding we stick to promises that went too long unanswered."

Isul was struck by the amount of bitterness her words carried, but he could empathize with her characterization of Ani Chenak's rule-bound uncle. Wasn't that one of the reasons he'd been dismissed? He hadn't wanted to follow the rules laid out by Reslo and Shendahl. He was surprised to find that he and Sarinne had something in common.

"Do *you* believe there's a treasure to be found?" she asked in disbelief.

He told her the local folktale about a gold-robed giant who protected a massive pile of priceless jewels with a glowing sword. She sobered up when he expected her to laugh aloud. Was there something to the tale? She quizzed him for details he did not have, and he finally waved off her questions, returning the conversation to the reason Senator Nelham had sent her.

Sarinne accepted the topic change with aplomb and reiterated Nelham's instructions for her to call him with verbal proof that more than one device was functional. She was to accompany Treyder back to Saedi City for the hearing.

Isul pulled the box from a drawer and opened it. Sarinne reached across the desk and carefully picked up several of the miniscule machines. "How do these put a person in a coma?"

"The exact *how* is my secret, but all you have to do is introduce one of these to the bloodstream, even through a scratch, and they travel to the brain and shut off all but the necessities of life, like heart and lung function."

She glanced from the little balls in her hand to him. "You're a genius, Treyder. A real genius."

He smiled a real smile at the compliment.

She put her hand above the box and dribbled the devices back into it. "And these are all working?"

"Yes. We can take the box to Senator Nelham. I don't think he'll need more than a few to get his point across, but I'll take the whole box in case a second demonstration is needed."

Sarinne peered into the box. "There are more than a few in there."

"Yes, there are."

Sitting back in her chair, Sarinne folded her hands. "How soon can you leave?"

"I have a scheduled meeting with the other investors later this afternoon. May I tell them about my summons to the capital to demonstrate what they have built under my direction? Of course, I can exclude any reference to the potential for military use of the devices. I would say we could leave in the morn. Is that timely enough?"

She nodded in agreement. "Now that the important items have been discussed, why don't you tell me more about this supposed treasure a giant is protecting." She stood and began walking to the door.

Isul hurried around the desk, slipping the box of coma devices in his pocket. "I'll take you to the chef's daughter. She will recount the tale with more clarity than I ever could."

# CHAPTER THIRTY-TWO

Taryn was pushed back from rounding the corner by Renloret's arm barring his path.

"What do you see?" Taryn asked.

"I'm sure it's Treyder. He's talking with a woman and the waitress from the dining hall."

"Let's change places," Taryn said. They did so. Taryn felt anger bubbling up at the sight of his kidnapper. He lowered his hand to the hilt of the Chandaron blade. It felt warm. It knew what he wanted to do.

"Patience, little brother." Ani's whispered words spoiled his thoughts. Her hand was light on his shoulder. "Renloret thinks there is a way to get closer without being seen." She pulled on his sleeve to backtrack with the rest of them.

Reluctantly, he backed up and followed. He had to admit Renloret was good at slinking around corners and sliding between buildings.

"Watch it!" The hissed warning from Yenne brought him up short.

The four wires of the fencing were two finger widths from his leg. He quickly studied the nearest post. Small red circular balls were attached to each strand and an antenna wire extended above the top of the post. Another step and he would have gotten an electric shock that might have been fatal, and the antenna would probably signal their presence to the security force. Stepping sideways, he quietly thanked Yenne, and they continued sneaking along the building.

Taryn heard another hiss and stopped again. This time it had been Renloret at the lead position. He was at the corner of the building.

The pilot looked over his shoulder at Ani. "I need Kela to get close enough to hear them talking and tell you what they're saying."

Kela moved forward and looked around the corner then up at Renloret. His tail wagged, then he trotted straight out. Taryn and the others watched him wander about the open space, sniffing here and there, marking territory on taller weeds or bushes. He moved to the right and out of sight beyond the edge of the building. Taryn turned his attention to Ani. She was leaning against the building wall, her eyes closed, breathing softly. He tried to imagine what she was seeing through Kela's eyes, what she was hearing.

A flicker of a smile raised the corners of her mouth and then was gone. "He's pretending to dig for a drigwan. They haven't noticed him."

Taryn glanced at Renloret. The pilot was staring straight ahead. A breath later, Renloret twisted his head to the side and whispered, "He eats them?"

Taryn grinned. Renloret had been checking his bio-teacher for the definition. Taryn whispered back, "Predators in the wild can survive on drigwans, particularly during the winter. Drigwans provide an amazing amount of protein for their size. Canines of all types help people manage pest populations in remote villages."

The pilot shook his head and turned to check on Kela's position.

"Whoa, the woman is Sarinne!" Ani hissed.

"Sarinne?" All the men spoke in unison, equally shocked at the woman's identity. "They're discussing the giant's treasure and if it's real!" Ani's voice was quieter now but still held the remnants of surprise. "Did anyone know she was here?"

They all shook their heads.

"We need to let my office know we've located her," Taryn said. "Neither Yantel nor I had the opportunity to question her further. No one remembered seeing her after she gave her report on Treyder's last whereabouts. She disappeared as quickly as she arrived."

"Shh, wait. The girl just said she overheard a couple of miners talking about actually seeing the treasure mentioned in the tale and how they planned on digging it out soon. She doesn't know where, nor does she know the names of the miners. Too many miners eat at the dining room."

Ani paused in her retelling of the conversation Kela was eavesdropping on. "Geesh, Sarinne is a bit too interested. She's scaring the girl with all the questions about the glowing sword." Ani pushed off the wall and smiled at Taryn. "Well, we know it's true and we know they won't find it." She turned to Yenne and Reslo. "Would Sarinne connect the tale of a glowing sword protecting a crystal with the Stones of Lrakira?"

Reslo was the first to respond. "Perhaps, but we never expected there would be other Stones, so I'm not sure she would connect the two."

Taryn added, "The Stones of Lrakira said she was disqualified as a Singer candidate because of her personality but that there were more important things she was destined to do."

"What if she didn't agree with that assessment?" Ani asked.

"So if she couldn't become a Singer, perhaps a trip to another planet with the chance of saving our people was second choice on her part to gain recognition," Reslo speculated.

"She was a fully qualified communications officer," Yenne said.

"Why are you suddenly defending her?" Ani asked, turning toward her father.

Taryn flinched in surprise at her fiery tone. Her father had just crossed swords with her and didn't know how much trouble he was in. Taryn wondered how long he should wait before interfering.

"I'm stating facts as I know them from experience."

"But the fact is, she *didn't* send all of the information she was asked to, did she?" Ani was sounding petulant, though Taryn knew she was correct.

At first, Yenne seemed reluctant to agree with his daughter, but he finally acquiesced. "I didn't know she hadn't passed on the information until I landed on Lrakira. Right now, I'd like nothing more than to ask her why she didn't do her full sworn duty."

"That'll have to wait," Ani replied. "The girl is leaving, and Treyder and Sarinne are headed this way. Kela says we need to move. Now." She made shooing motions with her hands at Taryn, Reslo, and Yenne. Renloret was already passing them, leading the way to the end of the building. He had not turned back to look around the corner to verify Ani's statement.

Three quick turns later, they found themselves at the edge of the compound. Taryn could hear Reslo's faster breathing, signs of less physical conditioning. He'd been down in Southern for the better part of a year and probably had not had much opportunity to continue his rigorous workouts while sitting in meetings and studying computer screens. Plus, he was the oldest by at least seventeen years, Taryn thought. He visually checked in with each of the others, getting nods. When he caught Ani's eye, he asked, "Kela?"

"He'll be here in a chime."

"Did he follow them?" Taryn asked. "I want to know where Treyder went. We can deal with Sarinne later."

Kela trotted up behind them, his tongue lolling over his teeth. Ani turned and knelt to rub the base of his ears and thanked him out loud for his reconnaissance. Ani relayed Kela's observation that the unlikely pair had returned to the building that housed Treyder's office.

As she filled the men in on the overheard plans, Taryn pulled the notebook from his chest pocket and added lines as he listened.

"It seems Treyder had lost contact with her after Fairaden died, and they hadn't seen each other again until a couple of months ago when Treyder saw her with Senator Nelham at a meeting. It took him a while to recognize her, but they now appear to be on decent terms. She's here delivering a message from the senator."

Taryn bit back a curse. Yenne wasn't so quiet about his reaction, and Mroz had to grab his arm to keep him from retracing their steps. There was a short, hushed conversation between them, and Mroz prevailed. Taryn watched Yenne chew on his bottom lip. He wondered why he had never developed the behavior. Perhaps because he'd never lived in the Chenak household.

Ani continued. "They're going to Treyder's office to prepare for an investor meeting. They're going to bluff about the cutoff of funding with news that Treyder's presence is requested in Saedi City to demonstrate the devices to some sort of committee. And Treyder wants to add to his collection."

"His collection?" Taryn asked.

"She asked about that too. It seems he has fourteen patients in his current collection under observation here in a laboratory," Ani said.

Taryn held up his hand. "Wait. He has a *collection* of patients? Here?"

"Do you remember the supposed Southern attack on the southwest coast a couple of months ago?" Ani asked. "Treyder told Sarinne it was a training accident resulting in the disappearance of fourteen soldiers. The military has refused to comment and has yet to investigate, supporting Nelham's hotheaded rhetoric that it was Southern declaring war, though the Southern government has unequivocally denied anything to do with it.

"Sarinne seems surprised that Nelham bribed several military officers to acquire volunteers to test a new weapon. The volunteers are now patients—or specimens—in the lab where Treyder is continuing the work our rescue of Taryn interrupted."

Taryn frowned. "That can't be right. Treyder showed me his only working example when he injured me. After you rescued me and stole his research, he should not have been able to manufacture even one device in a matter of weeks. The timing is wrong."

"Unless he already had this facility. They might not have had time to produce a working device when you were injured," Mroz said flatly.

They stared at each other in silence.

"Stones and blades."

"All the hells."

The curses were bitterly spoken in two languages.

"Fourteen you say?" Yenne's dark eyes looked between Ani and Kela. Ani nodded and Kela growled. "We've got to stop him—now, before he can add a couple of politicians to his *collection*."

"Can the Stones help us?" Mroz asked.

Taryn flinched when Chandaron answered in the negative. The Stone had been listening. It regretted that the Stones could not directly harm one of their charges, and Treyder was one of their charges.

"I think I know the answer to that," Ani said, "but judging from the look on your face, Taryn, I think Chandaron has answered that question. What exactly did Chandaron say?"

"It can't help us. We must do what is needed on our own. It does not control. It guides." There was a finality in the Stone's words and song. Well, the whole of Teramar had done much without the aid of the Stones in the last thousand years, so he could respect the position, and he was silently glad *he* wouldn't have to adhere to such a confining set of ethics.

"So . . . no magic words or songs can solve this problem," Mroz said.

"No magic. Just us and our blades," Taryn replied. He patted the hilt and noticed a quick warming of the blade in the leg sheath.

# CHAPTER THIRTY-THREE

Treyder sat silently at his desk. The lull in the discussion with Sarinne provided time for him to review the past hour or so. He couldn't quite figure out what was bothering him. It was not the surprise visit by Sarinne, nor was it the senator's demand that he return to Saedi City to demonstrate the devices. It wasn't the change of plans he would need to convey to the local investors. He could leave Wharton enthused about his report to the government on the medicinal power of the devices the villagers were constructing. No, none of these things were bothering him. It was something else, something small that could ruin everything.

Treyder shook his head. It was not even the trio of hikers that worried him. It was something else. Something more recent. Something was out of place. He glanced at Sarinne. Was it her?

He watched the senator's confidant pour a finger-width of local alcohol into two small glasses. She swirled one of them and brought it close to her nose. A slight frown bunched up the creases between her eyes. Treyder let his mind wander. It was one way to filter through impressions and subconscious thoughts.

Sarinne handed him one of the glasses. After he finished the drink, they would hold the meeting with the investors, and then he would show her his collection. He sipped. She could give the senator an eyewitness account of his successes. He smiled again and sipped. Confidence returned as the liquor warmed him from the inside. But he couldn't quite enjoy it as much as he wanted. What had gone wrong in the past couple of hours? He needed to figure it out. He took another pull at the liquor and decided it could wait.

A short two hours later, Treyder pulled the laboratory door closed, saluted the guard, and tucked his arm into the crook of Sarinne's elbow as they walked away. She'd been strangely quiet throughout his tour.

She'd behaved quite differently during the short presentation to the local investors. Jubilant or enthusiastic would have been good descriptions of her then. She had told them Senator Nelham had asked her to come and see for herself the marvelous machines the village was building. She was looking forward to accompanying Doctor Jarden to Saedi City to present the progress reports. She had encouraged the investors to increase their own funding so they would receive well-deserved credit for their support from the government, exclaiming that the senator was fully behind the doctor's plans and inventions. She'd even added that Senator Nelham was hoping to announce additional funds while Treyder was in the capital. He had ended the meeting shortly thereafter and then suggested a personal tour of the laboratory to Sarinne, so she could provide a detailed account to the senator.

"Do you have any questions?" he asked, being careful to make his tone solicitous.

She kept her eyes straight ahead. "You're sure they don't feel any pain?"

He chuckled. "Oh, I'm quite sure. Do you remember the blue line?"

"Yes."

"That indicates the brain's reaction to pain. I tested it against non-comatose patients first to assure that none of the comatose patients would feel or remember any pain. It is quite accurate."

"When will the devices be removed?"

He hesitated. "When the experiments are complete." He did not want her to know that no patient had yet survived the removal of the device, though he'd only tried to remove it on the animals he'd used in the beginning. He did not let slip that the experiment would be complete only when the patient died. He planned to remove the device during autopsies.

He bit back a bitter internal self-admonition. There was evidence the Southern doctors were ahead of him in that part because both Ani and Taryn had obviously either had the devices removed or disabled in some manner without ill effect.

The Southern doctors might be ahead of him, but he was going to catch up quickly. He was working on how to turn the machine off and perhaps restart it without having to remove it. He would have a tremendous amount of control over people if he could work out that last bit of coding. But he didn't let on that there was still a lot of work ahead. He just wanted to be recompensed appropriately for his genius. His invention had multiple advantages. One was the lack of the need for anesthesia in surgeries; another was the devastating effect such a device would have on opponents in a war.

What would happen afterward was still in development. It had not been part of the initial discussions with the senator or the military and therefore was not within the project's scope. He didn't have to answer any questions on those points. It was up to the military to figure out.

Fortunately, his quick answer seemed to mollify her. They continued to walk across the common ground between the laboratory and his office above the dining hall. He paused his steps when they reached the spot they had questioned the girl about the giant's treasure.

"What's wrong?" Sarinne asked, twisting her left hand as if flicking away an insect.

He frowned as he rotated his gaze. His memory flagged a warning. "When we spoke with the girl this after morn, did you see anything unusual?"

"No. Why?"

She scanned the area, as if searching for something new or unexpected, and he pointed to a spot not far outside the commons. "Was there a canine over there?"

Sarinne shook her head. "How should I know? I was facing the girl and the laboratory. What does a canine have to do with anything? Everyone has one. They're a nuisance."

He chuckled at her response. She obviously did not care for pets. He wondered briefly whether she cared for anything other than herself. At least he could admit to knowing she had cared for Fairaden.

"It was a large variety. Familiar in some way." He struggled to bring up the sight of the animal digging in the ground, presumably for drigwans, as many canines were wont to do. It had been a large canine. He'd seen it previously, but not in Wharton. He cursed as he remembered. "They're here!" He pulled on Sarinne's arm, encouraging her to run with him.

"Who's here?"

"Chenak's daughter and probably the blade-damned sheriff. That canine belongs to Ani Chenak. If the canine is close by, so is the blade champion." He yanked open the door and pushed Sarinne ahead of him.

"I've got to call out the guards. They can't get me before you take me to Nelham. He'll protect me, especially after he hears your report of what I've accomplished. Hurry!"

He dropped her arm and ran for the steps, taking them two at a time. Once in his office, he clicked on the internal tel-com, rousted out the entire complement of guards, and motioned Sarinne to lock the office door. She shoved the bolt into place and shrugged off her coat, then sat down as he moved about the office gathering up folders into a satchel. She didn't say a word.

A few moments later, he could hear the pounding of boots outside of his office. Knocking sounds and shouts told him that the guards were checking each room along the hall.

When they reached his door, someone rapped on it and called out. "Doctor Jarden? This is Commander Pren. Are you okay?"

"Yes, at the moment."

"Are you alone?"

"No. Senator Nelham's representative is with me."

"Do you need assistance?"

Treyder went to the door, unlocked it, and invited the commander into the room. "No, I don't need assistance. But I have reason to believe there are a number of intruders within the village limits who plan to disrupt our activities."

"Can you identify the intruders?"

"Not exactly, though there is a large canine and a female blader among them, so you might keep a look out for those first." What else should he tell them? Treyder had not expected a direct attack in Wharton because of its remoteness. At least he'd had the sense to hire itinerant bladers with some military training rather than rely on the incompetent rabble the senator had hired in Saedi City. Commander Pren seemed to take his role seriously, and Treyder was confident the man would find the interlopers and either send them packing or kill them.

Perhaps Commander Pren and his men could distract the Star Valley sheriff long enough for Treyder to escape. Once in Saedi City, Treyder was confident his demonstration would finalize his place in history, and he would receive the reward his years of research and development deserved.

Treyder allowed a smile. The expression on Sarinne's face was not one of confidence, however. He would have to demonstrate his leadership to her before he demanded she accompany him across the little-used pass to the next valley, where they could purchase transportation to Saedi City on the senator's account.

Clearing his throat and lowering his voice, he told Commander Pren to do whatever was needed to keep the intruders from his office, the laboratory, and the factory. When asked if that included lethal actions, Treyder replied in the affirmative. The possibility the sheriff would no longer be a problem was a pleasant consideration. Treyder glanced at Sarinne. Her acquiescent expression gave him more confidence.

A shout in the hallway pulled Commander Pren away to supervise the soldiers, and the room quieted.

After a few moments of consideration, Treyder turned to Sarinne and pointed to the desk. "There's a second box of coma devices in the top drawer. Get it while I open the way to get us out of here." He stepped to the bookcase and slid his hand between the shelf edge and row of books. The wall panel to the left of the bookcase slid open, and an internal light illuminated the stairway. He slipped into a coat and gestured that Sarinne do the same. He knew the coming evening air could be quite chilly.

He shoved the box of devices she handed to him into the pocket of a small satchel along with a stack of reports he'd grabbed from the opposite drawer and added a hand light. Slinging the loop of the satchel diagonally across his body, he moved toward the opening in the wall and gestured to Sarinne to follow him. "I can get us to the next village while Pren's men delay or stop the intruders. There'll be transportation available to rent, and we can be in Saedi City before the senator's deadline."

She followed him through the wall opening to a flat metal landing. He slapped at a switch on the wall and the panel slid smoothly back into place. A thin smile showed her approval. They slipped out to the rear of the building in short order.

After closing the disguised exterior entrance to the stairway with a flourish, Treyder led the way across the narrow opening between the building and the forest.

Sarinne looked back at the building. "Where next?"

Treyder could hear faint shouting. His guards had engaged the Star Valley intruders. He pushed through the thigh-high brush to a narrow path, explaining as he went. "It's about a mile to the top then about two hours downhill to Chignan. It's a good thing Wharton is the highest village in the area. All else is below us."

"So we'll be in Chignan about an hour after dusk?" Sarinne asked as she fell in step slightly behind him.

"If we don't take too many rests," Treyder cautioned.

# CHAPTER THIRTY-FOUR

"Hells of Teramar!" Taryn backed away from the corner of a dormitory-like residence. With his back flattened against the side of the structure, he turned and announced his finding. "Looks like our presence has been noticed. There are troops positioned in front of the laboratory and the dining hall. We can't just walk in and take the stairs to Treyder's office."

"Could this be a training exercise?" Mroz asked.

"It could be, but they're carrying real blades and slings. We're decidedly outnumbered."

"By what ratio?" Yenne whispered.

Taryn peered around the corner again. "More than five to one."

Ani could almost see her father working on a new plan. They had decided to be straightforward and walk directly to Treyder's office above the dining hall. They were all smarting a bit about not taking advantage of the earlier opportunity to just follow the pair into the building after the discussion with the waitress, and now they were stuck. One lapse in judgment by all had put them in a precarious spot.

Reslo, Mroz, and Renloret all let out exasperated breaths. Ani chewed on her bottom lip and rubbed Kela's ears.

"Ideas?" Taryn asked. "Anyone—including Kela?"

Ani conferred with Kela and gave Taryn a wink. "Kela and I will test them. If it is a drill, they won't do much. If not, we'll know our original plan is a broken sword and we'll probably have to fight our way in."

When Ani and Kela moved forward, everyone but Taryn grumbled.

"No, she's correct," Taryn said. "They will not be expecting a woman and her canine to be of importance unless Treyder or someone else somehow recognized her."

Ani glanced around looking for something she could throw. Kela suggested a smallish stick he noticed not far from the building foundation, and Ani told him to get it.

Kela complied with canine exuberance. She side-armed the throw, and the stick rotated parallel to the ground as it flew into the plaza. Kela raced after it, and Ani followed at a trot.

"That's a good boy! Now bring it to me!" Ani stopped and squatted down as Kela dutifully returned the stick and bounced in anticipation of another throw. Ani and Kela repeated the action several more times, slowly working their way across the plaza. Though they did not move from their positions, Ani could feel the attention of the soldiers. Perhaps it was a drill. No alarms had sounded. She tossed the stick again, then turned to wave at them. "Everything all right?"

She imagined the curses from the rest of her group, but wouldn't anyone living in Wharton ask that? She boldly faced them, putting her hands on her hips. "Should I be worried?"

The leaders of both groups exchanged looks. They were probably trying to figure out who in the name of the hells of Teramar she was and then deciding their next steps. Both men unlatched their short swords and drew them. The soldiers behind them followed suit. "Stay where you are," one of them warned as he began walking toward her.

*Dung heaps, it's not a drill, Kela.* She planned to wait until they neared her before pulling the Anyala Stone blade from the boot sheath. All the soldiers were watching her, not Kela. She tried a disarming smile and spread her arms out. Hopefully, they would assume she was weaponless. A warmth along her calf announced that the blade was readying itself. She didn't dare look down to see if it had started to glow.

"Hey, youngster, didn't I tell you the plaza was off-limits?" Reslo said as he stalked across the grounds as if he had every right to be there. "Your father will bloody my ass if you disturb these men in their duty!"

Ani glared at him like a recalcitrant child. "But he's not here, so why should you be concerned, Uncle. I was just exercising your canine. You've kept him inside too long since I came to visit." Kela snickered in her head. He had worked his way off to the side and was observing the behavior of the two groups.

The lead soldier hesitated. Reslo had thrown him off. Maybe he was questioning his orders. Hopefully, there were enough new people in the Wharton area that he wouldn't know them all.

"Sir! Stop!" he called out as he began to advance again. "I need to see identification from both of you."

Ani saw the corners of Reslo's mouth quirk upward. She would follow his lead in this delicate dance.

"And what's it to you? Our cards are in our rooms. She didn't know she had to carry the blade-damned things all the time, and I was in the shower when she left. As soon as I realized she was gone, I dressed and came lookin' for her. I'll clear her and the beast off here, and you can go about your business."

The soldier was about ten feet away, the short sword in a ready position. He'd had some training at least, but Ani didn't think he was ready for two blade ring champions, even if one of them hadn't competed in over ten years.

"Your presence in Wharton is my business, sir. If you will come with me, we can clear this up in no time."

Ani cocked her head at Reslo. "Should we warn him, Uncle?" Kela whispered to her a negative.

"Naw, he'll find out soon enough," Reslo said. "Unless he already knows, in which case, whatever happens will be his undoing." He reached for his blade, ignoring the confused look on the soldier's face. "Oh, and the rest of us decided that we should try not to kill them *all*. Debilitating wounds will be enough. Understood?"

Ani frowned in disappointment. "Really?"

He gave her a curt nod and finished drawing the blade from its sheath.

"You're cramping my style, Uncle."

"Need I remind you who we need to stop?"

She put her hand on the pommel of the crystal blade. A forceful need to protect the innocent villagers and herself flowed from the blade up her arm. She gasped and released it. Perhaps hand-to-hand would be a less aggressive way to start.

Reslo smiled. "I've heard tales of Stone blades in battles. You may be fighting more with the blade than these men. Take care, little one." He turned to the officer. "Sir, we cannot comply with your request. You may make the first move to take us into custody." He gave a Northern blade salute.

Ani bit her lower lip to keep from gawking. Her uncle was goading the man into action. He had always warned her about goading an opponent, and here he was doing just that. She was astonished. She glanced at the officer. He snapped a responding salute and stepped forward, accepting the old champion's invitation.

*They're all moving toward you.* Kela's warning caused her to glance at the soldiers. Both groups were spreading out to encircle Reslo and her. They didn't seem to have thought there might be more than an old man and young woman to deal with. And they certainly had discounted Kela—to their detriment.

As Reslo readied to engage the officer, the second man in charge waved forward two of his men. Having sheathed their blades, they approached Ani as if she were unarmed—as she'd hoped. She would try to handle them without pulling the blade, though it was heating up the outside of her leg.

Both men reached for her arms. She shifted her weight and jabbed with the free leg at the same time she struck out with the opposite arm. Both men went down, one with a broken knee, now bent completely the wrong way. The other, well, he might not survive. He had leaned down at the last second in his reach for her wrist instead of her bicep, and her aim had been just a tad high, striking his throat instead of his solar plexus. There was an audible gasp from the soldiers at the suddenness of her movement. The man with the shattered knee was trying to crawl away from her. She allowed it. Their officer yelled four names and four men advanced with blades drawn. Ani cursed. She'd probably have to use the crystal blade.

A clashing of blades sounded to her right as Reslo and the first officer had ceased dancing around each other. The four soldiers smiled, apparently assuming their leader had done something impressive. Ani shook her head. Their eyes were on the two men and not her. Three steps and a twist followed by a double kick brought their attention back to her, too late for two of them. The third had jumped back enough that her trailing elbow glanced off his chest, only knocking him off balance. He stumbled out of the way as Ani contemplated pulling the now hot blade. Her decision was made for her by the fourth soldier when he thrust his blade. She parried with her bare arm across the flat side of his blade, pushing it up and out of her way, and ducked under his arm as she pulled the crystal sword out of the leg sheath. *Guard—protect*, the emotions from the blade buzzed inside her head.

Sounds of surprise erupted from the twenty-some witnesses. Reslo's opponent yelled in pain as he was distracted by the eerie green light. She shoved the pommel into the fourth man's unprotected lower back as he prepared to execute a twisting downward swing of his blade. He crumbled. Ani mentally counted the number of soldiers out of the fight. At least six of the original thirty-something. If they continued to come in small numbers, she and Reslo would be able to handle them all. A shout to engage told her that would not happen. The remaining soldiers raised their weapons and began running, closing in on Ani, Reslo, and the last of the four who had attacked Ani.

Ani looked over her shoulder toward the residence buildings and smiled. "Reinforcements come."

"About time," Reslo said as he turned his back to hers to face the circle of attackers. "It's a new blade. Introduce yourself to it." His soft reminder sent a surge of excitement through her, fueling the adrenaline already building in her. She began to hum, answering the blade's call to use it as needed to protect herself.

All of the soldiers on her side of the circle had eyes on her glowing green blade and had not yet noticed the arrival of Renloret, Mroz, Taryn, and Yenne, even though they were in direct line of sight. There were advantages to wielding a visually stunning weapon. She slowly moved it through a warm-up series to familiarize herself with its weight, shape, and personality. Then she saluted the opponents and began to sing as her mother had taught her.

As the words flowed out with the tune, she realized the language was ancient Lrakiran. While similar to Southern, there was a decided alien feel to them. And to her surprise, the blade answered.

One of the soldiers elbowed a man next to him and shouted, "All the hells of Teramar, do you know who she is?"

Soldiers on either side of him frowned and shook their heads.

"We're going against Anyala Chenak, the first female short blade champion on Northern!" the soldier exclaimed.

"Why's she here?" someone asked.

Ani took a step forward, continuing the sensual patterns of testing a blade. "Because your Doctor Jarden's true name is Isul Treyder, and he is the object of a continent-wide search for the kidnapping and torture of the sheriff of Star Valley. What do you think he's doing with the fourteen milits he has wired up in the laboratory?"

A few of them lowered their swords in confusion. Their commanding officer shouted at them to ignore her verbal baiting and her pretty bauble of a sword. Reslo laughed and yelled back, "Not just any decorative sword does she wield, sir. You'd best relinquish your own swords and save yourself maiming or death. Her blade is hungry for your blood."

"So you say, old man. Who are you?"

"You would know me by my titles from long ago, youngster, and I know exactly how good Miss Chenak is with a short sword and other weapons because she has exceeded my training. Look upon the manner of your death, commander."

Ani turned her head to speak without the soldiers hearing. "Perhaps you talk too much, Uncle. The fight has only just begun, and we are still outnumbered."

"I can see reinforcements spreading out, and there is a glorious glowing sword among them. However, I take your point. We're wasting time better spent on locating and capturing Treyder." She heard humor in his voice. He moved toward her left. "Turn and see your brother and Chandaron's blade."

Ani glanced over her shoulder. Taryn was calmly walking toward the backs of the soldiers. The purple light emanating from the blade was just as stunning as the cool green light from hers. He, too, was moving through warm-up movements, and he was not smiling. The reflected light from his blade colored his blue eyes purple. He nodded to her and changed his warm-up movements to those of battle. She felt a pulse of power radiate from her sword's pommel up her arm. "Uncle?"

"Yes?"

"We better make this a brief encounter."

"All right. The others are ready?"

"Yes."

"On my mark!" he shouted, and the warmth of his body left her back as he ran toward the soldiers.

Ani kept her place until Renloret, Yenne, and Mroz were solidly in position, then she let out an ululating yell. Several of the men backed up in astonishment. They turned around when Taryn gave a full-throated answer. Two men closest to her brother simply dropped their weapons and ran past him. They would survive. Ani was not sure about the rest. Two others stepped forward and jabbed at her brother. As he made an almost impossibly fast swing of the blade and the purple crystal bit into their flesh, Taryn let out a yell that sounded more a reaction to pain than a battle cry. He jumped over the fallen bodies and motioned for more to come.

A clash of metal told her Reslo had also engaged the enemy. Boots pounded the ground as the soldiers ran to close in. Mroz was next to meet metal with metal, then Yenne and Renloret.

Kela barked a warning aimed at Yenne. Ani turned and saw a soldier maneuvering behind her father, who was focused on his immediate opponent. In her head, Kela told her he'd take care of it. She watched as he launched a four-footed strike into the soldier's back and then managed to keep from getting rolled over on. Kela closed his jaw around the man's sword arm. The man screamed as teeth tore muscles away from bone and the bones were crushed. Ani felt the taste of blood in Kela's mouth, and her crystal blade whined at her in sympathetic reaction. It wanted more of her.

She whipped her blade over her head lasso-like and allowed the blade full access. She spun to meet an approaching soldier who held his sword with both hands and had begun his high backswing, opening his side and chest to her. She brought the Stone's blade down and across his chest diagonally. Subconsciously, she knew the speed of her strike was implausibly fast, the blade fueling and enhancing her skill. Red blood wetted the blade edge then disappeared as it was absorbed into the crystal, keeping the weapon clean. A hot fire of pain and sorrow coursed through her as the blade drank. There was no joy in this work. She screamed as she answered the demand to protect her people from Treyder and his unnatural coma device.

She and the blade merged to protect the future of two worlds.

# CHAPTER THIRTY-FIVE

Renloret checked the bindings on the few soldiers who had relinquished their weapons when it had become apparent they would not win and told them they would be released once Treyder had been found. They had been eager to give him whatever information they had on the fugitive. They had been terrified by the pair of crystal swords and the cries of Ani and Taryn as they mangled and cut down soldiers with unimagined speed and grace. Renloret had recorded names and positions of the five as being helpful and promised leniency once all was under control.

He glanced up as Yenne, Mroz, and Reslo exited the medical wing of the laboratory building after depositing those with survivable wounds into the hands of doctors for care. Renloret knew the medical staff had been warned against interfering, and after seeing the extent of the wounds, they were probably grateful they had not participated in the skirmish on the plaza. He had seen curtains move aside as residents remained in place until they received some type of all-clear announcement.

Renloret glanced at Ani and Taryn, huddled side by side on a bench outside the dining hall. The crystal blades had been returned to their sheaths and no longer glowed. Renloret remembered the close strikes he had barely parried away each time Ani or Taryn had screamed when their blades cut into bodies. It sounded as if the siblings had sustained the wounds they delivered.

Unbidden, a section from one of the old books rose from his memory.

> *A Stone blade bonding commands the Singer*
> *to protect the Stone and its charges, even at the*
> *destruction of those wishing to do harm. While it*
> *is rare for the Singer and blade to be in the thrall*
> *of protecting, it is necessary that the Singer have*
> *the skills, knowledge, and selflessness to do what*
> *is commanded. Grave consequences shall befall a*
> *Singer who forgets their protective promises.*

A hand on his shoulder startled him, breaking his reverie.

"You all right?" Mroz asked. He sported a bandage on one bicep but otherwise appeared unharmed.

"I will be better when we have Treyder and Sarinne." He jerked his head toward the bound soldiers. "These men said Treyder and the woman are hiding in the doctor's office."

Rubbing his chin, Mroz's eyes shifted between Renloret and the pair of Stone Singers. "How long before they are ready to go after them?"

Renloret shrugged. He experienced a weird sense of fear as he stared at the woman he loved and her brother. He had witnessed the incredible enhancement of their already consummate skills while wielding the shining blades. They had been blurs of green and purple as the swords were put through movements Renloret thought impossible. It was no wonder the Singers were warned about using the blades in anger. The blades were designed to assist the Singers in true battle, not to be used even in the blade ring. They were designed to kill if needed—and to heal when called upon. Renloret scanned the plaza. Even Kela accounted for at least two of the ambulatory wounded. Almost to a one, the dead soldiers had been the ones to engage either Ani or Taryn. The length of time from first contact to the last three surrendering was not quite a full quarter of a bell.

He stared at the Singers, loathe to interrupt their conversation. He wondered how this brief and terrible fight would change them.

Mroz harrumphed. "The blades are glowing again."

Indeed, they were. Ani was quickly enveloped in green ribbons, Taryn in purple. Their shoulders dropped and their backs straightened—the tension visually draining from their bodies. Taryn brushed a long lock of Ani's hair off her face and kissed her forehead. Ani wrapped her arms around her brother's shoulders then pushed him away. As they stood, the wraith-like ribbons melted back into the sheathed swords.

Ani left her brother and ran to Renloret, stopping in front of him. Sliding his hands around her waist to her back, he pulled up, lifting her feet off the ground. Her lips nuzzled his neck, sending shivers across his shoulders.

"Are you injured?" Her voice was breathy, the air being squeezed out by the tightening of his embrace.

He loosened his hold, but not much, keeping her full weight in his arms. "I will have some heavy bruising, but I don't think I bleed." He really had not checked. "You?"

A negative movement of her head indicated her answer. She pressed her lips to his jawline. "The Anyala Stone . . ."

He set her down, moving his hands to her shoulders so he could look directly into her eyes. Those green eyes held a curiously faraway look, as if she were puzzling out something.

"The Anyala Stone what?"

"It sang that we did what the Stones could not do. If we had not engaged, our ability to stop Treyder might have been curtailed. Now we have a chance." She paused. "Oh, Diani sends word through Anyala that the surgeon who removed the coma device from both Taryn and me has offered to come to Teramar to perform what surgeries will be needed to remove the devices from the fourteen Northern soldiers. A ship will be leaving Lrakira on their next morn with an estimated arrival in nine of our days. If the Song of Teaching has not been sung yet when they arrive, they can use stasis bags and a camouflaged star runner or two to transport the victims to the ship to avoid frightening the Teramarans with the sight of a real star traveler."

Renloret shut his mouth with a grin and squeezed her shoulders. She had answered a few of his questions. With so many people looking on, he chose to kiss her forehead.

"What about you and Taryn?"

"What about us?" Ani looked at Taryn, who had walked up to them.

"Well . . ." How could Renloret word the question he wasn't sure he wanted to ask or know the answer to?

"We are dealing with what we did, Renloret. We will have time later to discuss it." Taryn's tone carried a hollow sound. "For now, we have more to do before we can sing."

Renloret looked at his friend. A ghost of shock darkened his expression.

"We should get Treyder *now*," Ani said.

A short time later, three shoulders driven by three men broke the lock on Treyder's office door. They spilled through the doorway, blades already drawn, but the room was devoid of people. Reslo, Taryn, Ani, and Kela followed on the heels of Renloret, Yenne, and Mroz.

Ani waved her hand, and Kela walked the perimeter, nose to the base of the walls. He had already told Ani that neither Treyder nor Sarinne had left the building through the main doors or via the central staircase, and no scent trail newer than an hour was found by the canine's sensitive nose as they made their way to the office. Kela passed on to Ani that the scents were fresher here than in the hallway. He completed a full circle and then backtracked to a section of wall.

He rose up on his hind legs and sniffed along the edge of the shelving, then he puffed out a breath.

"Kela says that Treyder's hand was last here," Ani said.

Renloret stepped up and slid his hand between the book and the shelf interior. There was a slight indentation in the surface, and he pressed it. A section of wall slid to one side revealing an internal staircase.

Kela was the first to enter.

"Kela says that Sarinne is with him and that they used this within the last hour," Ani said. "We may be able to catch them."

They followed Kela's lead and were soon on the trail through the trees.

"Hey! Treyder!"

Treyder stopped and turned around. The senator's representative was slowing him down. Didn't she understand they had to get to the next village before the secret staircase was found? Maybe he should just keep going and let her fall behind and be caught. Wouldn't Nelham love that? His personal representative caught in the high western mountains? Treyder started to think of a dozen ways to twist and bend the blade of truth to his advantage. This was the last time he'd stop.

"What now? Another rest?" He was surprised at his own fitness, especially at this altitude. Living in Wharton had improved his lung capacity. After he dealt with the senator and the military leaders, he might make Wharton his permanent headquarters. Once he'd gotten paid, he'd have time to investigate the story of the giant's treasure. That might be fun.

Sarinne was puffing hard. "Yes, please. One last time." She gulped air through her mouth instead of her nostrils.

"Oh, all right. Three minutes." He pulled the timepiece from his pocket. Three minutes would be okay. They were well away from Wharton, and he could see the bottom of the valley that held the transportation hub for the area.

She came close. "Do you intend on using the coma device on the senator?"

He laughed. "Oh, no. He has yet to pay me. If necessary, I'll use them on his committee members. That should be incentive enough. Then if the military balk, a few more higher-ranking soldiers will join my collection in Wharton. That should seal the deal, and I'll . . ."

Her expression of shock stopped his words.

"What? You're surprised I want to see this through? This device will help so many people."

"Have you successfully removed it?" She was no longer breathless.

"Well, that depends on your definition of *successfully*."

She put her hands on her hips. "How about we define success as the patient regains full consciousness and physical functions."

He laughed again. "I have plenty of time and samples to perfect the removal."

"If you didn't remove the devices from the Chenak girl or the sheriff, who did?"

Treyder struggled to shove away the flare of defensiveness as he'd been taught in those first few blade lessons a little more than a year ago. "Some lucky Southern surgeon." He still wondered about that, but it was merely a distraction.

Sarinne cocked her head. Her palm pushed at his shoulder,

knocking him slightly off balance. "You're planning to keep those soldiers in comas until you figure out how the Southern surgeons removed two of them without repercussions?"

Her voice had risen unacceptably in Treyder's opinion. He thought the expression on her face was closer to outrage and wondered why, even after showing her the wonderful work he'd already accomplished, she would be so negative. "Yes. My methods will save the lives of so many, and there will be no more difficulties with residual anesthesia."

"Are you insane? Deliberately putting Ani and the sheriff into comas and then asking the senator to bribe commanding officers to allow you to do the same thing to those soldiers, all so you can perform those horrible experiments—"

"But they can't feel anything, they're not in pain!" he shouted.

"You can break every bone, cut and mangle their extremities and internal organs without hearing them scream! If you ever figure out how to remove the devices, what condition will their bodies be in?" she shouted back.

She hit him again on the shoulder, more forcibly. He stumbled backward, stopping a fall by grabbing a low tree branch. The rough bark scraped the palm of his hand. "You have no authority to question my methods, Sarinne. The senator knows and understands the consequences of the machines. He asked that I test the limits of a soldier's body."

Sputtering in indignation, Sarinne continued her rant. "He *told* you to perform the experiments?"

"Don't forget that you were there when I brought him the sheriff. He demanded more of the devices. He could see how the machines could limit losses in a war, and he wants to leverage that ability if a war with Southern becomes imminent. These tiny machines will end war on Teramar, Sarinne. Aren't fourteen soldiers worth ending all war?"

"Is that what the senator told you?"

Treyder nodded.

"Did you explain to him that you could not remove the machine?"

He nodded again. He knew he would be able to if given enough time and funding.

"What would happen to all the soldiers who received the device on the battlefield?"

"They would go into a comatose state within a few minutes."

"And then what?" Her voice and body language challenged him as she stepped closer.

"What do you mean?"

"What happens to a comatose body if it is left on the battlefield, unattended, forgotten?"

"It would be up to the Southern military and government to care for them."

"But what if even one soldier is not found and moved to a medical facility? What would happen to his body?"

What was she trying to get at? He tried to understand. "I suppose the body would succumb to the elements in time. But what does it matter? They wouldn't feel anything. It would be better than dying on the surgery table or from an allergic reaction to anesthesia." He took a ragged breath. Why couldn't she understand? "It will save lives, and it will end the use of anesthesia." He paused in frustration. Then he decided to tell her. "I've never told anyone, but Fairaden died because of the anesthesia the doctor's used when she miscarried our baby. It was what put her in the coma."

Sarinne shook her head. She didn't believe him.

"The doctors admitted it was the only thing they could account for. It was the anesthesia. I will stop them from using anesthesia ever again. Fairaden and our child will not have died in vain. To my dying day, I will work to stop them from killing people. I will make all surgeries safe. People will not have to experience pain while recovering either." He brushed his hand across his pant leg and winced at the bark scrape on the palm.

The relative quiet of the surroundings was pierced by the hunting call of a faraway kreline.

"It was not the anesthesia, Isul," Sarinne said. "It was something beyond your comprehension and imagination that caused the coma and her death." Her voice carried a soft sadness that hit his core.

"What are you talking about? How can you know? You're not a doctor." He disliked wanting to defend the doctors who had told him they had made a mistake in not testing Fairaden for an allergy.

"I cannot tell you, but I can stop you from proceeding with this madness." She grabbed his scraped and bleeding hand, twisting the wrist until he fell to his knees. "Then you will know what you have put your subjects through, but there will be no one near to find you."

She pulled her other hand from her pocket and rubbed it

across his injured palm. He felt a momentary roughness as if she were rubbing the palm with fine pebbles. She released him. Remaining in a crouch, he examined his palm. Had she poisoned him?

"What did you do?"

"I gave you one of your precious devices. Now you will know what it is like." She backed away. Her lips snarled around her words. "I may not be of this world, but I have lived on Teramar long enough to learn the preciousness of life, even if there is pain—physical, mental, or emotional. Life is not without pain or loss."

Sarinne's image clouded, as if a fog were approaching. He knew he'd fallen to his side because Sarinne was now standing perpendicular to him. He had not felt his body hit the ground. "How did you get one?" He was having trouble forming the words his mind wanted.

She laughed. "You asked me to get the box, remember? It was easy to pinch up a few, in case I needed them. I wanted to be sure at least one entered your bloodstream. If you hadn't cut your hand on the tree, I would have used a blade.

"Before you slip away, I will tell you that I caused Fairaden's death. Neither of us knew the full consequences of what we planned. She wanted to give you a child, and I helped her. We used a vial of Ani's blood to prevent the plague from killing her outright. But I guess it was too early or something. Maybe Ani wasn't old enough yet." She looked toward the north at the kreline's cry.

"Anyway, according to you, it won't be long. You won't be in pain anymore. And you won't be able to cause anyone else pain, whether they can feel it or not." Sarinne yanked the little satchel with his papers and the box of coma devices off his shoulder.

Treyder watched as she cocked her head again. She had caused Fairaden's death by helping her get pregnant by using Ani Chenak's blood? That made no sense at all. He focused on Sarinne's face. What was that about her not being of this world? He tried to shape his tongue and push air from his lungs. "Alien?"

Sarinne laughed again. "Oh, yes, and so was Fairaden. Ah, well. I've redeemed myself in her death by giving you the gift of a painless coma. You'll never know exactly how you will die or what becomes of your body." She turned and began walking away.

He heard the kreline yowl again. Was it louder—closer?

"Wait!" His shout sounded feeble to his ears. He couldn't move. This could not, should not, be happening. He wasn't done. He hadn't been paid for his work. Sarinne's laughter was fading back along the trail they'd come. His ears focused on another sound. There was a woofing sound. Was it a kreline?

Had the sun set? He couldn't see. He couldn't feel. It was silent. Dark.

# CHAPTER THIRTY-SIX

Kela stopped, and his ears pricked forward, straining to hear. *Kreline. Hunting. Ahead.*

Ani waved to the others to halt their jogging. They had just crossed a ridge about a half-mile below the top of the pass. The men joined her.

"What is it?" Taryn asked.

"Do you see them?" Reslo was leaning against Yenne. His breathing was more labored than everyone else's, but it was nothing that concerned her. She was feeling the altitude herself.

"Kela hears a kreline," she said.

All four straightened up and adjusted their positions to provide a protective perimeter around her, and she hid a smile.

"He *hears* one, not smells one. It's far below us but near enough to the trail that he wants us to be aware as we move toward the village. They're not known for attacking people, especially when in a group like ours. We are safe, but I don't know about Treyder and Sarinne."

"Not our problem if they get into trouble with a kreline." The bitter tone of Taryn's words made her look at her brother. "Well, I at least wouldn't mind if one of them, preferably Treyder, met up with the four-fanged critter." There was no humor in his voice.

Mroz and Reslo grinned maliciously. There was no doubt about which side of the blade they were on.

"Okay." Ani accepted that he had a right to feel that way. She certainly didn't care who or what stopped Treyder, though she felt heat on her calf where the crystal blade was nestled. She resisted the urge to pull it out and run down the trail.

Ani reached out to brush Kela's back, smoothing the longer guard hairs. "Hear anything else?"

*Not at the moment. It is more than a mile away and may never cross the trail anyway.* He sat down and wrapped his tail about his paws. His ears swiveled independently. *I will be vigilant.*

"Good. Proceed." Ani waved him forward. Kela took off at a trot, winding his way down the switchbacks. Ani waited until Renloret reached her. Through unspoken agreement, their hands touched and then clasped. They'd had little private time together since leaving Star Valley for Southern and The Necklace Islands. And the intensity of the last few days was wearing on her desire to be alone with him. He raised their entwined hands to his mouth and kissed the back of hers. The adrenaline had left her body, and her muscles were beginning to react to the power of the crystal blade. She considered singing the healing song but thought it would not be considered proper for a few sore muscles.

Renloret kissed her hand again before releasing it. "Later."

Twenty minutes later, they paused again for a short water break.

The trail edged around a large pond with two musky dam weaver mounds. They heard a splash as one of the animals sounded a warning. Concentric ripples in the water surface appeared from behind the farthest mound.

*Not us.* Kela slipped into the trees.

Ani motioned for everyone to back off the trail and retreat into the trees. Within three breaths, they had dispersed, blades drawn. The pommel of the crystal blade was cool in her hand and did not glow. She wondered if it could sense an impending attack. Why was it cool now when it had been fiery hot with the need to protect during the fight? Ani felt Kela stalking toward the far end of the opening. *Kreline or something else?* she silently asked.

She slowed her breathing and focused on listening—with her own ears as well as Kela's. A few more breaths and he answered.

*Someone.* He sat at the base of a large tree and opened the connection further so she could see.

It was Sarinne, leaning against a tree, looking behind her. Ani wondered if she was being chased. Then the woman pushed off the tree and stood straight. Her breathing was calm and her face turned toward Kela without seeing him. She looked down at the timepiece strapped to her wrist. Even Ani could see the smile as the woman glanced first toward the pond at the edge of Kela's sight, then along the trail she'd just come up. Her lips moved. Ani couldn't hear.

*She says we might be close by now. She'll have to be careful.*

Ani watched as Sarinne loosened her hair and mussed her fingers through it. She even grabbed a few twigs from the tree and worked them into the tangles. She knelt in the dirt of the trail, grubbed her hands up, and then swatted at her neck and cheeks. Kela sent his impression that she was disguising herself. The woman brushed her dirt-covered hands against her hips and thighs a few times and began to stride toward the pond.

Ani wondered if she could signal one of the men to step into view. Before she could, Taryn burst out from his hiding place, running several body lengths before stopping as if in surprise at seeing Sarinne.

"Hey, have you seen a man on this trail?" he called to her.

Sarinne had jolted to a stop at the confrontation, and Ani watched her closely. The woman put her hands to her face, rubbing her eyes with her dirty hands. Ani saw the tears of irritation muddy the dirt Sarinne had put on her cheeks. Then Sarinne pointed behind her. The movement was tentative, not like she wanted Taryn to run past her to get Treyder.

"He tried to . . ." She took a breath. "He said I was insurance . . . his ticket to safety." She gulped air as if she'd been running for hours.

Now, suddenly faced with a person before she could complete her disguise, she seemed to be struggling to figure out just how to present herself. She was having to work up her act. Ani suspected she hadn't expected to be met so soon. Plus, she didn't really look upset, just dirty and surprised.

The woman stood still, not looking at Taryn. Ani studied her. Her lips moved as if she were saying something, but even Kela heard nothing. Her left hand twisted several times. Then she took a large breath and straightened. She grabbed both of Taryn's arms and stared at him.

"Listen, he's experimenting on soldiers! Hurting them." Sarinne's tone was different, almost pleading.

Ani felt there was truth at the base of the emotion behind the words. Could she have second thoughts about the path she had been on where it concerned Treyder? Ani grunted, not sure of what she was seeing or hearing.

*Not likely.* Kela added a grunt of disbelief of his own. He had slipped up to Ani's side, still hidden in the trees. Ani stroked the fur between his ears.

Sarinne's gaze remained on Taryn.

"You saw them?" Taryn asked as he pried her hands off his arms. Once free, he took a step backward.

She stepped forward, staying close. "Yes, he has fourteen, I think. They're in comas. He's been experimenting on them. Breaking things. Giving them poisons. He says they can't feel anything so he can do anything he wants." Her voice suggested doubt and her face expressed revulsion.

Ani had to admit that the woman seemed truly bothered by seeing physical evidence of the torture.

"Where is he now?" He glanced down the trail from where Sarinne had come. She rubbed a hand across her face but not before Ani, and presumably Taryn, saw the slight upturn of her lips. Taryn put on his best I'm-concerned-about-you expression. He was in full sheriff mode. He had noticed the conflicting actions, tone of voice, and minute body movements.

"I . . . I tripped him. I had to come back to tell someone how wrong it was." She was still rubbing at her eyes as if she were really crying, but her voice was not husky with any emotion when she spoke of possibly being chased by Treyder.

"How long ago?"

"I don't know. Can we go back to Wharton?" She started to move past him. He barred her way.

Taryn looked toward Ani's position. Ani waved and started to move out to the open. Moving his head to the side, he indicated that she should stay in the trees. She backed away several steps to put more trees between them before turning and taking a circuitous route to the trail—as if she'd been behind Taryn, not ahead of him.

"Psst! Here." Renloret's whisper caught her attention. Kela wagged his tail and pushed through a large patch of shadow willows, and Ani followed.

She whispered, "Kela, where are the others?"

*From the sound of their movements they're also returning to the trail. Follow me.* Kela moved away.

Renloret took her hand and held it until the trail came into sight. She reluctantly allowed their fingers to slip apart when she heard quiet voices. They stepped onto the trail and hurried around a switchback to meet her father, uncle, and Mroz. Then they all moved toward the open glen where Taryn and Sarinne waited.

Sarinne stood up from her seat on a log near the pond edge when they entered the glen. Taryn waved at her to remain where she was and approached them.

"She's telling an interesting story, some of which I believe." Taryn said.

He paged back through his notebook and quickly summarized.

He'd been asked by Senator Nelham to contact Treyder about the cessation of funding for his device unless he appeared before an oversight committee within a specific time period. She claimed to be shocked when Treyder showed her his collection of victims. Sarinne said Treyder seemed confident he was following Nelham's directive. She claimed she didn't know he, Ani, and the others were in Wharton.

Treyder had insisted they leave his office through a hidden passage when some sort of scuffle was reported by his head of security. It all seemed odd and confusing to her, but she felt she had no option except to follow him into the forest on foot.

While on the way to Chignan, the doctor confessed that he was planning on using the devices on several of Nelham's committee members. She had balked, wanting to return to Wharton. He'd gotten angry, and they'd gotten into a scrap. Treyder had tripped as she pushed him away from her, causing him to tumble down the slope.

When she didn't see him get up right away, she left him and started hiking back to Wharton. She said that meeting the sheriff on the trail had been a relief, and she was willing to testify about what the doctor had said and shown her.

Ani had watched the woman while Taryn summarized his notes. Her stance belied concern for personal safety. Sarinne was not afraid Treyder was after her at all. The look on her face said she believed her story would not be questioned.

"Does she know where Treyder is now?" Ani asked. "She doesn't look too concerned."

Taryn glanced over his shoulder at Sarinne. "No. She said she just fled in the opposite direction."

"We should look for him," Mroz said.

They all agreed. Ani glanced at the sun. "We don't have much daylight left. Is there enough tel-com signal to contact Chignan? They could get him before he gets on a train to Saedi City and hold him until we arrive to take him into custody."

"Right." Taryn stepped away and made the call.

While her brother forewarned the authorities in Chignan, Ani and the others approached Sarinne.

"Sarinne, it's nice to see you again," Yenne said. "It's been a while."

A mix of emotions crossed Sarinne's face. Curiosity, worry, and confusion seemed to struggle for dominance until surprise won and the woman sat down hard on the log. "Stones and blades." The Lrakiran curse had tumbled out of her mouth before she could stop herself.

Yenne did not smile. "You look a bit worse for wear. Are you injured?"

Sarinne shook her head, then stood unsteadily and combed her fingers through her hair. She saluted. "Commander Chenakainet." Then she looked from Yenne to Ani, her expression indiscernible. "How?"

Yenne ignored her question and helped her sit back on the log. "I'll be right back." He returned to Ani and the others, and Taryn soon joined the group.

"There's a full watch out for Treyder in Chignan. They're going to send a team up the trail to see if they can intercept him before he gets to the village."

They went over to Sarinne, who remained seated on the log

and was looking both confused and resigned to whatever was going to happen next.

"We have to find Treyder," Yenne said. "Please take us to where you last saw him."

When she hesitated, he raised his eyebrows. "We won't let him hurt you."

"Fine," she replied, clearly upset but now looking determined she set off on a march ahead of them.

The sun was below the treetops and the evening shadows were adding to the high-altitude chill when Kela growled. They all stopped. After a brief discussion, Ani sent Kela out around the perimeter as Renloret and she moved forward through the trees into a wide clearing. In the shadowed gloom near the base of the trees, Ani saw a kreline dragging something into the underbrush and begin to scrape twigs and dirt on top of whatever it had found. She waved Renloret to a stop.

*How close are you, Kela? A kreline just came out into the opening. Be careful. There may be more than one.*

Kela whined in her head. *There is only one. I am downwind. It is not feeding on a tri-pronged sueder, and the carcass is wearing clothing.*

"Hells of Teramar!" she shouted as she moved loudly into the open. "It got Treyder, Ren!" She ran toward the predator waving her arms and shouting curses in Northern and Lrakiran. The animal spun around in surprise before crouching to face Ani. Even in the dimming light, Ani could see the blood about its mouth. Its barbed fangs were bared in a snarl. She tried not to compare them to the throwing blades Renloret carried on his forearms.

Renloret pounded past her, adding a terrible yell of his own. He was swinging his blade in one hand and the other gripped one of those barbed weapons. Kela burst out of the trees, raised hackles almost doubling his size. Under their onslaught, the kreline withdrew, but not before snatching up a piece of the carcass. It wasn't going to leave everything for them.

As Renloret and Kela took off in pursuit of the kreline, Ani reached the body. She'd seen the results of numerous kreline kills before and had only seen them as a natural part of life. But this struck her as unnatural. It didn't matter who the body was. She bent over her knees and fought to avoid vomiting. Even Treyder did not deserve such an end. No human did.

# CHAPTER THIRTY-SEVEN

It was full dark when the Chignan sheriff arrived with his team of deputies. They set up large battery-powered lights around the remains and asked Ani and Sarinne to identify the body. Taryn gave a summarized report that included the attack in Wharton as well as Sarinne's account of the missing soldiers now being held in comas and tortured in Wharton. When the Chignan sheriff offered to send two of his deputies along to escort them back to Wharton, Taryn accepted with the condition that they remain in Wharton until the Saedi City authorities arrived.

Once back in Wharton and free of the Chignan deputies, the group made the brief hike to the hidden star runner with Sarinne in tow. They had managed to convince the Chignan sheriff that Sarinne was needed for questioning in Star Valley and would be made available for subsequent interviewing by the Saedi City authorities, along with the rest of the group if needed. It was clear that the sheriff viewed the entire affair as barely within the realm of belief and almost entirely out of his ability to manage. He seemed happy to see them all go. As for Sarinne, she seemed cautiously relieved to be returning to Star Valley on the star runner.

Sarinne tried to quiz Yenne about the time shift and other details of what had transpired within the last year or more, but Ani watched him skillfully dodge most of her queries, sometimes saying that all would eventually be revealed. He did reveal that the Lrakiran people had been cured with Ani's blood and that the Stones had suggested making diplomatic contact with the governments of Teramar. A meeting of dignitaries was being set up in Star Valley. "They have sent the Anyala Stone's Singer as emissary," he added.

Ani stared at her father, speechless. Sarinne launched off in excited Lrakiran, which Ani could not follow until she heard her grandmother's name. What was Yenne up to? Surely he would not reveal her as the Singer or tell Sarinne that the dignitaries would be there for more than a meeting, that the time had come for the Song of Teaching. She was relieved when he only reiterated that the Stone's Singer was on Teramar waiting for appropriate representatives from Northern, Southern, and The Necklace Islands to arrive.

When Sarinne said that she thought Singers were not allowed to leave Lrakira, Yenne shrugged before responding. "We all assume much about the Stones and their Singers. I think we have much to learn. Perhaps in the coming days we will all know more."

He put a hand on the woman's shoulder and directed her toward the crew quarters. "You can use the fourth cabin on the left to clean up and rest. Renloret?"

The pilot stepped forward and saluted as prescribed. "Yes, Commander."

"We all need some sleep. We'll leave for Star Valley in the morn. Please secure the ship."

"Yes, sir." Without another word, Renloret headed to the bridge.

Yenne stepped close to Ani and whispered, "I don't trust her enough to tell her everything. I don't care that she believes Selabec is here. It suits my purpose. I did not lie that the Anyala Stone's Singer was on Teramar. She is." He gave her hands a squeeze. "Sarinne will be informed about the Teramaran Stones and male Singers during the Song of Teaching. Now, either go be with your pilot or find a bed and rest. It has been a very long day."

Ani headed to the bridge. She slid into the copilot seat and kept quiet while Renloret finished securing the star runner. He sighed deeply and leaned back, one hand covering his eyes and the other reaching out to her. They sat silently for several minutes, and he seemed as glad to have the time alone with Ani as she was to have him to herself while the others slept.

"I think we should contact Lrakira," she said. "The Stones and Singers need to be informed of what has transpired—if they don't already know from the Anyala Stone. Diani and Layson may have suggestions on what to do next."

He gave her hand a squeeze and opened the communications link. Several breaths later, Diani's image appeared on the vid screen. Yes, she was privy to the fight in Wharton and the subsequent actions ending with the finding of Treyder's remains, thanks to the link between the Anyala Stone, its blade, and Ani.

And though she was concerned about the loss of life in the cause of stopping Treyder, she accepted the outcome.

Renloret and Ani shared the telling of the new Stones and their Singers' blade bondings. Diani passed on that the Lrakiran Stones had informed Layson and her that the Song of Teaching could be sung when representatives from the governments of Teramar could be gathered with the Stones and Singers, presumably in Star Valley. Diani suggested that Taryn and the Chandaron Stone schedule a high priority meeting with Northern's chancellor as soon as possible and prior to the Song of Teaching. She smiled at Ani's head shaking and comment that it might be weeks before that occurred.

"Pericha says that Chandaron can be very persuasive. I would not be surprised if the Song of Teaching is sung within the next ten or twelve of your days. Ani, let your Stone know when all is ready, and we will gather here as directed. May the Stones bless our coming adventures." She lifted her fingers to her forehead in a Singer's salute and ended the transmission.

Renloret rotated his chair toward Ani. "How are you doing with all this?"

Ani contemplated his question. "A lot of amazing things have happened the last couple of months. I've discovered I'm not who I thought I was, but at the same time, I realize I am more. So much more." She felt the crystal blade warming her calf through the boot sheath. It seemed to be agreeing with her assessment. She reached down and caressed the hilt. A humming began in her head—the Anyala Stone was aware. She smiled. "I have a larger family and more responsibilities than I ever imagined."

A calmness and confidence settled within her. "I'm ready."

Her blue-eyed pilot returned her smile and pulled her onto his lap. His arms encircled her. She felt safe and loved. She nestled her head against his shoulder, breathing slowly as she considered her next words.

"The Song of Teaching involves more than the Teramaran Stones and their new Singers." She paused as words were sung in her mind. Renloret waited patiently.

"I was allowed to come back because I am needed here on Teramar. I am the Anyala Stone's blade. The crystal blade and I are the conduits through which the Stones of Lrakira will sing their half of the Song of Teaching simultaneously with the Stones of Teramar. Both populations will learn their shared history at the same time." Wonder and awe filled her. Could she contain it? Could she manage it? Chords sang in her mind. "Yes. The crystal blades are only tools. Each Singer is the true blade of their Stones—to protect and serve the people."

Renloret's lips brushed her forehead. "Yes, I know." His words were soft against her skin. She sighed. This eve she would sleep with the blade—not Renloret—to be closer to the Anyala Stone, to begin learning her part.

The Teramaran sun, Olbers, had already lit the sky and caressed the mountain ridges with warming color by the time Renloret and Ani entered the star runner's dining area. Taryn was already there, spooning food into his mouth between animated sentences with his parents on the vid connection. Not wanting to interrupt, they scrounged up food of their own and sat in a corner. After a few minutes of listening, it became apparent that Chandaron had told her brother to contact someone in the upper echelons of the Northern government on the need to communicate with the chancellor about the discovery of the Stones, and now he was waiting for a response. Ani approved of Taryn moving forward with that. Her brother ended the call with a cheery wave.

As the screen went blank, the dining area door slid open and the others entered with Kela skidding in on their heels. He trotted over to Ani, demanding sustenance before complaining about voice-activated doors. Ani was struck by how normal the morn felt after all that had happened in the last few days.

Before they arrived above Star Valley, Sarinne accepted Mroz's suggestion to stay in his guest room until her plans were solidified. Yenne had already told her that she could return to Lrakira if she desired because there was a ship available.

Ani began to get excited about the upcoming events and was engulfed in planning and activities over the next several days. The Northern chancellor had responded quickly to the request for a meeting, and with the Chandaron Stone neatly boxed, Taryn traveled to Saedi City, first to meet directly with the chancellor and then with the senate. He had been a bit circumspect in his request for the meetings, and the chancellor no doubt assumed that the meetings were being requested so that he and the senate could be filled in on what had transpired in Wharton and the demise of Treyder. And while Taryn did provide that update, both the chancellor and the senate found themselves on the receiving end of a great deal more information than they could have possibly anticipated.

Taryn reported to Ani that the Chandaron Stone had been patient and understanding in discussions with the astonished government leaders about the alien Stones and their Singers. In the end, the leaders of Northern were united in their agreement to the plan, no doubt thanks to the Chandaron Stone's ability to align them. With Taryn and the Chandaron Stone at his side, the chancellor contacted the governments of both Southern and The Necklace Islands to request an unprecedented meeting between the three governments. Their acceptance of the proposed meeting was achieved with the same ease as the leadership of Northern had come to accord.

Whatever the Chandaron Stone had done to gain such easy agreement to what would normally be prolonged diplomatic arrangements, Ani suspected it had something to do with the Stones' ability to impart information and understanding through direct transmission. It likely also had something to do with the fact that Southern and The Necklace Islands governments had been contacted by Jaikeer, the Beyleden Stone, Mihalas, and the Ellashin Stone.

Taryn had instructions from the chancellor to prepare Star Valley and its residents for the arrival of the government representatives, as well as the Stones and Singers from Southern and The Necklace Islands. The meeting was to take place in only a few days, so many hands were needed to pull it together.

Ani, Renloret, Taryn, Yenne, Melli, and Gelwood set about to organize an event such as Star Valley had never seen.

Several days later, Star Valley buzzed with activity. The last of the diplomats had finally arrived earlier that morn and were housed in residential homes as honored guests, and the government representatives had congregated at the dance hall in surprising companionability before the planned welcome meal at Gelwood and Melli's home. Taryn had enjoyed getting to know his own quartet of houseguests, Mihalas, the bright yellow Ellashin, the irrepressible Jaikeer, and the blood red Beyleden. Of course, Melli had decided that the three Singers should be in the same location to limit the possibility of the Stones being seen by residents of Star Valley prior to the Song of Teaching. The arrangement allowed the Singers uninterrupted time to learn their parts in the coming ceremony as well as the lengthy Song of Teaching. The last few eves, though enlightening, had been long, and all three Singers were probably in need of undisturbed sleep.

Taryn yawned. He didn't know how long he'd been sitting on the edge of his bed with portions of the Song of Teaching rambling through his mind while staring at the resplendent Stone when a banging on the door roused him.

Ani's call to hurry or they'd be late for the gathering at his parents' home was followed by more banging. Surprised at the length of time he'd been enthralled with the Song and the Stone, he hollered that he was just finishing dressing as he fumbled into the clothes he'd laid out after the morn meal. When he paused to caress the Stone on his way out of the room, encouragement seeped into him along with a jaunty hum. He was reluctant to leave the quiet companionship of Chandaron and muttered a curse as more door banging and yelling by Ani demanded he play his prescribed part.

Ani took his arm and hurried him to her wheeler. Taryn was a little surprised at how jovial Reslo and Yenne were as they scooted aside to make room in the back seat. They declined to comment other than saying that they were looking forward to Melli's party and all the people who would be there. All Taryn could think about was the necessity of listening to a multitude of diplomats trying to impress each other. He yearned to return to the sanctuary of his room and the purple crystal that would sing him to sleep.

As distracted as he'd been all day, he'd not considered the number of people filling his parents' home. All the lights were on and silhouettes moved back and forth behind curtains. Muffled laughter and conversational hubbub leaked out.

A hand clapped Taryn's thigh and Yenne leaned close. "Out, youngster. Friends and food await us."

Ani had turned in the driver's seat. Taryn could see the sparkle of the house lights in her eyes. They studied each other. The connection he'd always felt when he was around her was still there, even at the brink of momentous change. He altered the words in his thoughts. Not change, addition. He was more. She was more. The peoples of Lrakira and Teramar were soon to learn they were more. As if reading his thoughts, Ani gave him a subtle nod.

All the vehicle doors opened at the same time and they piled out. At the top step, Taryn glanced behind him. Renloret had tucked Ani's hand around his elbow in an escort position. Ani blushed as the pilot kissed the top of her head. Taryn thought back to the petite Southern archeologist with the big grey eyes. How would his parents react if he were escorting her into their home? He touched the notebook in his pocket. Her tel-com number was there somewhere. He would contact her after the Song of Teaching and ask her to come to Star Valley. He levered the door open and motioned for the others to precede him.

Hellos and other shouted greetings filled his ears as Taryn closed the door and made his way to the living room. He picked out the two Singers, Jaikeer and Mihalas, and made his way toward them. The visiting Singers introduced their respective governmental representatives, whose names Taryn immediately forgot in all the noise, but he saluted properly. He'd ask his mother later and write them down. The vice chancellor of Northern approached and reintroduced himself, adding a gracious comment about how much he looked forward to working with Northern's guardian Stone and its Singer.

Taryn looked around for his parents and didn't find them, though he could hear Melli explaining to someone about the names of some of her teas. Ah, the kitchen. He worked his way toward the kitchen to offer help with the trays of teacups and whistlepots his mother was probably loading up. He stopped mid-stride as the kitchen doors were pushed open and a girl with short-cropped hair backed into the room. Taryn thought it might be Keci's eldest daughter, but his jaw dropped as she turned around with a wide smile on her face.

"Camfel?" That was all he could say. She was *here*. In Star

Valley. He wouldn't have to call her and ask her to join him. He wouldn't have to ask Renloret or Yenne to take the star runner to Southern to get her.

She was nodding her head. "Yes, I came with Jaikeer. I insisted."

"Why?" Again, he could only utter one word. His mouth had dried up.

"I wanted to hear the Song of Teaching, and I wanted to see you, Taryn."

"Me?"

She was nodding again. "Yes, you."

Someone wedged partially past Taryn, and the tray of cups, saucers, and two whistlepots disappeared from Camfel's hands. She raised those hands up to touch his face. A shiver spilled from her caress to run through his body. She was *here*. It was all he could think.

"Camfel." His voice broke as his heart seemed to expand.

"Taryn." Her voice was husky with something he'd never heard before, and he wanted to hear it again and again.

Taryn leaned down just a bit as she rose on tiptoe and firmly pulled him close. Their lips touched for the first time.

Gelwood's voice broke through Taryn's focus. "Ha! I knew it when we met her!"

Taryn slowly released the kiss and looked at his father and mother peeking around the corner of the kitchen door. He could feel the heat of a blush darken his skin and straightened up, tucking the Southern archeologist to his side in a one-armed embrace. He felt her adjust and sneak one arm around his waist in return.

"You've met already?"

Laughter from all around him answered his question. Embarrassment threatened another blush as he realized how silly his question was. Of course they had met. She'd been in the kitchen with them. She'd brought out a tray of something. Tea? Yes, tea. He turned around, keeping Camfel at his side.

With his free hand, Taryn waggled a finger at the crowd in the living room. They burst out laughing as they came forward to give the reunited pair hugs.

Taryn whispered warnings of brotherly retribution in Ani's ears. His sister chuckled and smacked his shoulder playfully. Melli and Gelwood came out of the kitchen with two more trays of tea, and soon the conversational tone was restored.

Hours later, all the guests except Camfel and a woman diplomat from The Necklace Islands, had left his parent's home. The diplomat excused herself to retire to one of the extra rooms upstairs, and in the quiet that followed, Camfel filled Taryn in on the days since he'd left her at The Necklace Island cave site on his way to find his own Stone.

# CHAPTER THIRTY-EIGHT

The next morn, harrumphing at his reflection in the mirror, Taryn draped the towel over his head and stalked back to his room. At least his hair had passed the bristle stage and was now just long enough to lay down so he could sculpt a part. Why didn't his hair grow back faster? Was there a tonic that would encourage faster hair growth? There probably was, but with his luck, it would grow hair all over his body, not just the hair on his scalp. Better to ignore it for a few more months and see how long it would be by then.

Maybe he wouldn't cut it at all, what with being a Stone Singer. Wasn't the length of hair one of the signs of a Lrakiran Stone Singer? Ani's was certainly long enough, matching or exceeding the length of Diani's and Layson's. Taryn paused outside the doors to his guest rooms. Mihalas's hair brushed his shoulders and Jaikeer usually wore his in a braid to keep it out of the dirt during his excavations.

Then the vision of Camfel filled his mind. Her cropped

cut accentuated the length of her neck and the width of her cheekbones below those mesmerizing eyes. As much as Taryn liked to run his fingers through longer tresses, he knew he liked the short style the Southern archeologist wore. It was perfect for her. Pragmatically, he decided that hair length was a personal choice and not indicative of any increase in power, strength, or beauty. An agreeing hum sounded in his head.

He chuckled at Chandaron's response. Whipping the towel off his head, he knocked on the doors of his guests. "I'll have the morn meal ready in ten." There were cheerful greeting comments from both Singers. They had gotten several more hours of rest than him.

He padded barefoot to his room and closed the door. The room lighting had a distinct purplish tinge. He walked over to the chest of drawers and placed both hands on the large crystal, tracing the crevices and edges, familiarizing himself with the physical feel of his Stone. *Soon*, he thought.

*Yes, soon, my Singer.* Chandaron's music filled him. *You are rested, and I have given you the Song. You will learn while you sing, as it should be. Ingest enough nourishment, for the Song ahead will be long.*

Taryn smiled at the sense of eager expectation that infused the tune. He was still in awe of the fact that he had and could communicate with a living crystal—not one, but six, having spoken to the three Lrakiran Stones and the other two Stones of Teramar. In all his imagining, he'd never considered the possibility of such an alien life-form. And to know he was one of six intermediaries between the people of two planets and the guardian Stones was nearly overwhelming. He now appreciated Ani's hesitation to accept her position.

He had quickly become comfortable with the voice in his head. Noticeably different from the three Lrakiran Stones, Beyleden, and Ellashin, Chandaron's voice carried humor and joy.

Taryn paused in his dressing to contemplate that information. Had he known or heard that each Stone had its own personality before becoming a Stone Singer? Certainly not before the blade bonding. He looked deep into the Chandaron Stone, willing the life light, as the Lrakiran Singers had called it, to answer his question. All he got in response was the opening measures of the Song of Teaching. He laced up his boots, slid the purple crystal blade into the boot sheath, and put a hand on the cool surface of the Stone. Its life light pulsed in time with his heart.

*Patience, Singer. Eat and then prepare with the others.*

He heard voices on the other side of his door.

"Taryn? We've brought the morn meal and tea," Melli sang out.

He wondered how many other people were with her and hoped he wouldn't be surrounded in his own home.

Jaikeer and Mihalas left their rooms at the same time as Taryn, and the three made their way to the kitchen. Taryn breathed a sigh when only Melli and Gelwood were present. A snippet of thought wondered where Camfel was, then he was thrust into a chair and a large plate was set before him. Without his crutch, Gelwood edged around the table adjusting chairs so Jaikeer and Mihalas could sit, and the two grinned in response. Already these two young men seemed like the siblings he'd always wished for. He silently corrected himself. He had a sister, so he was not an only child.

Gelwood limped around the table piling hash and vegetables onto the three plates. Melli appeared at Taryn's elbow, sliding four cushawk eggs on top of the hash and used the spatula to point at the bowl of fruit in the center of the table. He acknowledged her invitation to take what he desired from the bowl, but he waited until his guests had been served. Melli then followed up with a large whistlepot of her cinnamon tea.

"Take care, it's hot," Taryn announced as he blew across the liquid surface.

An exclamation by Mihalas forewarned Jaikeer.

"Reslo yearns for your tea, Mistress," Jaikeer said. "He extolled its virtues . . . and warned me."

Melli snorted. Gelwood patted her hand and blew across his own cup, barely hiding a smile. Mihalas dipped a spoon into his mug and blew several times before cautiously sipping. He set the spoon down, outstretched his palms, and executed a short bow of acknowledgement. "Excellent. It is of your own recipe?"

"Yes," Melli said.

"Might we discuss some trade? After the Song, of course."

Melli blushed a little and took another hefty swallow. Taryn watched in amusement as the Singers flinched. "Yes, we would be agreeable to a discussion." She glanced at Gelwood, who winked at her.

"You may have two outlets by the end of this," Gelwood said.

The rest of the meal was eaten while preparations were discussed. Gelwood had brought a produce delivery vehicle from the grocery, all washed and decorated for transporting the Stones and the Singers to the central square. Mroz, Yenne, Reslo, and

Renloret were already at the square putting the finishing touches on the pedestals and moving the chairs from the dance hall to encircle the ceremonial space.

After the dishes were washed and put away, the three Singers bundled up the Stones and placed them in the bed of the delivery vehicle. Then Melli insisted on inspecting their attire. Taryn was not inclined to argue, though he was a bit embarrassed as she turned them around several times and straightened a seam here and there. After a few brotherly jokes that caused Melli to glare at the trio, they settled down, and Melli gave each a motherly hug before joining Gelwood in the driver's compartment.

During the short drive to the central square, Taryn asked how the other two new Singers felt about being chosen by an alien life-form to be its interpreter.

Mihalas answered first. "Honored, intimidated, and somewhat frightened at the prospect of now being a leader without much experience. My government held a special secret council, and I translated the Stone's song for them. Now I hold the unique position of being the Stone Singer of The Necklace Islands. The officials will wait to see what the Song of Teaching says before presenting Ellashin and me to the people of The Necklace Islands."

"Do you have blade skills?" Jaikeer asked.

The islander laughed. "Oh, yes. I achieved the top rank last year. I competed to a tie in the short blade. The winner was decided by knife throwing. That has not happened many times. Perhaps I cheated because I practiced throwing knives at fish in streams." He winked and laughed again. "Flowing water makes for a difficult aim."

He pointed at Taryn. "You took many awards at the last Northern Championship. I did not remember your face or name until you left to find the Chandaron Stone. I apologize. Why did you not go against the woman in the short blade singles final?"

Taryn smiled. "Northern competition rules limit the number of events and weapons divisions a person can enter. Plus, we didn't want to compete against each other. We shared the championship in pairs. I medaled in long saber, while Ani took top marks in hand-to-hand and, of course, in singles short blade."

The Islander nodded solemnly. "I watched the replay of the singles short blade final. Magnificent technique. Is your technique similar?"

"To be honest, we used to be very similar when we were younger. Then Reslo and Ani's mother decided we should concentrate in different singles events. And under separate training, our styles began to diverge." He waggled his eyebrows. "I concentrated more on the other two areas so I could score high. There are more championships in the future. Once our governments are informed about the Stones and a whole other planet of people, perhaps we can compete wherever we want."

The Islander approved of the idea with a single nod, then he turned to Jaikeer. "And you, Southern friend?"

Jaikeer shrugged. "I have done well enough. Three years ago, I took my second championship in long saber, but I have not practiced much since then, until very recently." He reached over to his side and caressed the hilt of his red crystal blade. "There is not much income in the blade ring for one more interested in old bones and ancient pot shards."

Mihalas clapped a hand on Jaikeer's shoulder. "I think we have done well enough to be chosen to protect the Stones."

Taryn remembered the tremendous increase in speed and accuracy when he used the Chandaron Stone's blade during the fight at the Wharton mine. He cautioned them about using the crystal blades in competition. The two Singers gave him solemn acknowledgment.

The vehicle puffed to a stop and settled outside the ring of benches and chairs. Renloret, Yenne, and Reslo were wiping off the last of the chairs. The pilot straightened up and waved in greeting and then bent back to his work. Taryn studied the triangular setup of pedestals. Each pedestal was solid wood, perhaps sections of trunk cut from a single massive tree. Ani was nailing loops of yellow fabric around the top of one of the pedestals, and Kela was intent on sniffing them. Ani attached the last fabric loop and waved as Kela barked and danced around the trio of brightly decorated pedestals. Each was draped in similar style and in the color of one of the Stones: red, yellow, or purple.

While they had slept, Taryn, Jaikeer, and Mihalas had received instructions on how to present the Stones and their Singers to the Star Valley residents. The onlookers would arrive at the central square in about an hour, and the Stones would already be in place atop the appropriately colored pedestals, with additional fabric draped over them. The Singers would wait inside the dance hall until all were seated.

All the governmental representatives would be side by side on the hall porch waiting for the start signal. They would open the double doors and lead the Singers to the pedestals before taking assigned front row seats. The new Singers would follow, single file, in order of blade bonding—Jaikeer, Mihalas, and Taryn.

Taryn rubbed at his scalp.

"Nervous?" Jaikeer asked, his own voice shaking just a bit.

"As much as any blade ring competitor," Taryn replied.

"Aye," Mihalas agreed as he fiddled with the hilt of his yellow blade. "A good way to explain the way my heart beats."

Taryn realized that both Jaikeer and Mihalas carried their blades in the scabbards they had found with them. There had been no scabbard with the purple blade, so he'd carried it in his boot sheath. Should he have a scabbard made? He shoved the question away, reminding himself that it was not how the blade was stored or carried but how it was used that was important. He felt the warm tone of the Chandaron Stone agree with his thought.

"Well, best get it started." Taryn hollered at Renloret, Mroz, and Yenne to leave off cleaning the chairs and help move the Stones to their respective places.

An hour later, Jaikeer peeked through the crack in the dance hall door. "How did they know to come?"

"Mother just said they would come at the appropriate time and we were supposed to be ready." Taryn closed one eye and peered out as well.

"It's almost time," Ani said as she joined them. She was dressed in her championship blade ring uniform. The dark green fabric fit like a layer of skin. Subtle designs woven into the fabric showed the shape of her leg muscles and torso. Her arms were bare, so everyone could see the light scar lines that told, in Lrakiran script, that she was the Northern blade ring champion, as well as The Blood, savior of the Lrakiran people, and the Anyala Stone's Singer. Matching green laces accented her black leather knee-high blade ring boots. The soft leather soles were silent against the wood flooring. A pulsing iridescent green glow showed between the hilt and the top of one of her boot's full-length calf sheath where the Anyala Stone's blade was nestled. She wore her hair loose, and it swung side to side at hip level, accenting the predatory toe-first walk.

Jaikeer and Mihalas stared at her. That walk had silenced a full stadium of onlookers when she accepted her wreath and medals almost three years ago. Back then, there had not been the green glow at her knee, but it was the same stunning vision. Her face was smooth and calm, and confidence shone through her Anyala Stone green eyes.

"Ready to sing?"

The trio of new Singers saluted her and lined up. She prowled past them, looking each directly in the eyes for three heartbeats before taking her place behind Taryn. What was the signal for the ceremony to start? As Taryn started to ask her, a wild harmonic howl sounded. Kela was the signal.

The doors opened, and the representatives saluted in the manner dictated by their individual cultures. Then in measured steps, they began the procession.

Kela sat in the center of the triangle, howling his own song. The government officials found their seats, and the Singers took positions behind their covered Stones, looking out at the circle of people. Ani had paused at the circle edge to allow the Teramaran

Singers time to find their places. Taryn was not sure he'd ever heard the Star Valley residents be so quiet, but then he noticed that all eyes were on Ani—just as the stadium full of people had been at the blade ring championships. They were seeing her in real time as the continent's first female champion. This was not a recording of the ceremony three years ago. Their champion was here. Taryn could see curiosity in most of the faces before him. Keci's six-year-old daughter, Ryken, gave him a little wave and a grin before her father pulled her hand down and settled the youngster on her chair.

Ani passed him on her way to join Kela in the center. A few breaths later, the beautiful howls diminished and then stopped. Kela trotted by, his tail high and waving. Taryn wondered what kind of conversation he was having with Ani. The canine turned around and sat next to Northern's vice chancellor in a space specifically provided for the animal.

Taryn counted three breaths. What was next?

Renloret strode into the triangular opening wearing what Taryn knew was his Lrakiran pilot's uniform. The pilot walked slowly, tracing the triangular outline within the surrounding circle of onlookers. He saluted each of the Singers in their cultural manner, saving the last salute, in Lrakiran style, for Ani. Then he turned to face the Star Valley residents and government representatives. He raised his hands overhead, brought them down to shoulder height, and rotated slowly, looking into each person's eyes. "We begin with a story from many thousands of years ago."

The audience shifted in their seats, and Taryn felt them relax. They recognized the time-honored method of storytelling.

"In a faraway place, seven unique entities were given charge of a people they would come to cherish. They were instructed to keep the people safe, for there was greatness ahead, should the people desire to make the transition. Only the entities were informed of the exact nature of the transition, and they were to guide the people toward it over many generations. A symbiotic relationship was developed and treasured. The people learned to protect the entities and they, in turn, guided, enhanced, and encouraged the people's growth and development in all matters."

Renloret paused. Taryn saw Ani frown. Evidently, she had not been told of the pilot's exact part in the ceremony. She did not move from her assigned position in the middle of the triangle, though she turned to watch the pilot as he drew in the audience. Her frown smoothed away and a smile flitted across her lips. Perhaps the Anyala Stone had spoken to her. Taryn shifted his attention to Renloret. He had moved to face another section of the audience.

"The people prospered under the guidance of the entities until a warning light entered their eve sky, a harbinger of disaster and destruction. At first, the comet was too small for the people to notice, but the seven guardians watched it grow brighter with apprehension. Its approach was unwavering, and the guardians knew they could not change its path or that of the massive asteroid that followed. They began to plan for ways to keep the people safe. With the help of their interpreters, known throughout the land as Singers, the guardians searched out two new homes and prepared the people for long journeys."

Renloret moved to face another section of the audience. Taryn was as enthralled as everyone else. Even the youngest babe seemed to be listening. He recognized the resemblance between this story and the First Song.

"One thousand years ago, the people were gathered and then divided. The seven guardians and their Singers sang a great song—the greatest song ever sung, a Song of Saving. A strong and powerful song it was—so powerful the people were transported to the chosen sanctuaries, far away from the coming destruction. The guardians divided as well, and three each followed their half of the people to new homes to continue guiding and caring for their charges. The seventh stayed to care for and heal the lands of origin so the people could return when they were ready to move forward." Renloret stopped suddenly, lowered his arms, hung his head, and was still.

The audience inhaled. Taryn could feel their fear, their questions. They all knew something terrible had happened. Renloret's head rose to look at the sky. His arms reached out to the sky in a beseeching gesture. The audience looked up as well.

"The new homes were suitable, with one exception. One lacked a particular set of minerals usually found in the places the guardians had looked. But the people had already been sent, and there was not time to find another safe and appropriate place. Based on the timeline when the population on that location would experience the effects of that lack, the guardians proposed a plan, and the Singers agreed. The First Song of Lrakira was written as a warning to that population. It included a warning about the effects the lack of this mineral would have on the people and instructions on how to cure the people of Lrakira when the time came."

There was an audible exhalation as the audience again relaxed. There was hope for the people in the story. Renloret moved to face another section of the audience. "The time has come." He paused.

Taryn watched the section of the audience the pilot faced. There were murmurs and shifting of positions in seats. Curiosity, not fear, was on every face. Renloret continued.

"The people of Star Valley have already played an important role in the healing of those people by being the birthplace of the prophesied child whose blood would provide the cure. We of Lrakira are grateful beyond measure."

Taryn heard whispers of "Didn't Ani go to Southern to save her parents' village? Was Lrakira the name of the village?" The words Southern and Lrakira were passed among the audience faster than Taryn's ears could discern. He did not have a problem with that. The connection was close enough to the truth and to the story that had been told months earlier. This part of Renloret's story was now verified, however thinly. The audience settled once more and were attentive to Renloret.

"Ancient things recently discovered on Southern, The Necklace Islands, and on Northern describe the circumstances of the guardians' choices and solutions. It was decided to honor Star Valley's part in the saving of Lrakira with these ancient things debuting their full story here, this day, this sun-time.

"Citizens of Star Valley, as hosts for this unique event, I present Northern's vice chancellor, Zabion Eknerah, here representing your government. I introduce Thrayo Dway, of Southern's government, and Pinmah Nyairfee, representing The Necklace Islands." Renloret's voice seemed to fill the entire valley.

The three stood, saluted, and sat again. Murmurs of welcome were voiced. The pilot continued. "They are here to witness, along with you, what will follow. I cannot tell you exactly what will happen, nor what to expect. Do not be afraid of the displays of light, color, and sound you will experience. There is no danger to any of us. I have seven more introductions to make before the *performance*. Please pay close attention. You will soon learn more about the guardian Stones and their Singers.

"From Southern, Jaikeer Bricka, a regional blade ring champion, famed archeologist, and now Singer of the guardian Bayleden Stone."

The covering fabric slid from the Stone. There was an audible gasp as the audience saw the huge red crystal for the first time.

"From The Necklace Islands, Mihalas, last year's top champion in The Necklace Islands blade championships, fisherman, and now Singer of the guardian Ellashin Stone."

Fabric slid again. The audience gasped again. Taryn slowed his breathing. He was next.

"From Northern, Taryn Avere, multiple division blade ring champion at Northern's last continental competition, sheriff of Star Valley, known as The Balance on the planet Lrakira, and now Singer of the guardian Chandaron Stone." Quick murmurs of surprise flitted across the audience as people recognized that Lrakira was not a village on Southern's continent.

Taryn pulled the purple covering aside, allowing it to drop

to the ground. He gasped along with the audience as the sun sparked and flashed off the Stone's many facets, its life light pulsing bright. The crystal blade in his boot sheath heated up in preparation for being pulled free. Chandaron's song thrummed low in his head. It was beginning.

He stepped around the Stone to stand facing the center and made eye contact with Jaikeer and Mihalas as they also moved to face the center, where Ani stood, their backs now to the audience. They nodded. Taryn dropped his hand to the hilt of the crystal blade as the other two placed hands on their blade hilts. They released their blades in perfect synchrony and held them aloft. The audience gasped as one.

Renloret's voice cut through the song beginning in Taryn's head.

"Lastly, I introduce Anyala Chenakainet, known as The Blood on the planet Lrakira, and now Singer of the guardian Anyala Stone."

Taryn sucked in a breath as he realized Renloret had used the term *planet* twice—first in his introduction of Taryn and now in his introduction of Ani. The flush of surprised whispers indicated that some members of the audience noticed. He wondered if Sarinne was present and what she was thinking. He had not noticed her in the crowd. It wouldn't matter much longer anyway because the Song of Teaching was about to commence. Ani drew the green blade from her boot sheath. It glowed as intensely as the three Stones in the triangle.

Renloret's voice seemed to echo. "Listen. Learn. Rejoice in knowledge now shared between Lrakira and Teramar." Renloret's last words carried undeniable command.

The Chandaron Stone began to Sing. Taryn faltered over the first words in the ancient Lrakiran language, but then they slid into Northern as they flowed across his lips. The Chandaron Stone blazed, throwing swirls of purple around Taryn and his blade in tornado-like ribbons. Purple joined yellow and red ribbons high above the trio of Stones. He heard Jaikeer's Southern words, so close to the ancient language of Lrakira, and then Mihalas's voice came in with the lilting softness that permeated The Necklace Islands language. Oddly, the combination of languages did not sound discordant. They were compatible. Each was singing to their own, tapping into their consciousness, embedding the Song of Teaching.

The ribbons of color danced to the beat of the song, wrapping and writhing around the Singers. Taryn saw tendrils fly out to touch Ani. She raised the green blade above her head, looked skyward, and began to sing in Lrakiran. A flash of green pierced the display and shot high, disappearing beyond sight. Ani's voice was amplified somehow. She was calling to the Anyala Stone, connecting to the Lrakiran Stones and their Singers.

Within measures, Taryn saw shades of green, amber, and blue vining their way along the green of Ani's blade and branching from the blade to entwine with the red, yellow, and purple of the Teramaran Stones. Pieces of red, yellow, and purple danced upward retracing the path of the Lrakiran colors. Two worlds were connected. Taryn felt the cool power of the Anyala Stone, the steady calmness of the Pericha Stone and Diani, and the clear, bright playfulness of the Kita Stone and Layson. The six Stones mixed introductions into the song and then wrapped Ani and the Teramaran Singers in glorious color.

A crescendo seemed to take his soul away to fly with the ribbons of energy. He touched each person within the encircling audience and then beyond to thousands, then tens of thousands and more, far beyond ordinary sight. The song vibrated every cell in Taryn's body. He lost himself in the song—becoming the song. He heard color sing.

# CHARACTER/TERM LIST AND PRONUNCIATION GUIDE

Abren (ah-**bren**): Lrakiran word for open.

Ani (**ah**-nee): Northern's 1st female blade ring champion, Renloret's rescuer, The Blood.

Anyala Stone (ahn-**yall**-ah): largest of the Stones of Lrakira, green.

Awarna (ah-**war**-nah): Capital city of Lrakira and home location of the Anyala Stone.

Bell: Lrakiran time equal to an hour.

Bayleden (**bay**-leh-den): Teramaran Southern Stone, red.

Belladine (bell-ah-**dye**-neh): Southern for "the color of warrior blood".

Brenlee (**brin**-lee): infant, Keci and Nonnash's sixth daughter.

Caason Sector (kah-**ah**-sun): collection of planets populated with reptilian-based people. Scale-like skin, large oval pupiled eyes, and tails. Prefer warmer climates. A gentle scientific people with a long history of traveling the stars.

Cabithayin (ka-bi-**thay**-in): The Necklace Island village near where the Ellashin Stone was found and the home of Mihalas.

Camfel Tondon (**kam**-fell **tawn**-don): Southern archeologist who translates hieroglyphs on Southern cave walls, business partner of Jaikeer Bricka.

Canta (**can**-tah): Southern city, has aerospace center where Reslo works.

Chandaron Stone (**Chan**-dah-ron): Teramaran Northern continent Stone, purple.

Chignan (chig-**nan**): transportation hub at junction of three rivers and rail lines serving mining district in western mountains of Northern.

Chime: Lrakiran time equal to a minute.

Cranite (**cray**-night): Lrakiran moon.

Craudlin (**craw'd**-linn): mineral used in production of Treyder's coma device only found in sufficient quantities in Mount Piffital mines.

Croshin (**crow**-shin): Teramaran lice-like insect.

Cushawk (**cuss**-hawk): a Teramaran medium-sized farm bird raised for eggs and meat.

Cyralist (**sigh**-rah-list): bulbous hourglass shaped stringed instrument on Teramar.

Daneeha (da-**nee**-ha): Star Valley sheriff's secretary.

Denert (**deh**-nert): smallest Lrakiran moon.

Diani (dee-**ah**-nee): Pericha Stone's Singer.

Digoson Mountains (**dee**-go-son): mountain range north of Awarna, home of Anyala Stone.

Dinshinga (din-**shin**-gah): a commercially distilled liquor from Lrakiran desert.

Doven (**dough**-vin): village multiple hours north of Saedi City, Northern, Teramar.

Dowhe Nou (**dow**-he **now**): youngest elder of Necklace Island where Ellashin Stone is located.

Drigwan (drig-**wan**): small vole-like rodent, native to Northern, Teramar.

Ear/sun-guards: protective insertables or coverings to prevent hearing loss or damage to eyes.

Ellashin (**el**-ah-shin): Teramaran Necklace Islands' Stone, yellow.

Erid (**air**-id): largest Lrakiran moon.

Eteel (eh-**teel**): bass player and master composer of Star Valley Bashers, dance band on Teramar.

Fairaden (**fair**-ah-den): medical assistant on original research team, married Treyder.

First Song: also known as The Prophecy of The Blood and The Balance, is the first song in the oldest book on the guidelines for the Stones and the Singers of Lrakira.

Flitter (**flit**-er): term used for multiple species of songbirds on Lrakira.

Fresjen (**frees**-jen): lead communications officer on large Lrakiran ship hiding behind planet Kriswen.

Garrend (**gair**-end): fictitious name Ani gives to Renloret.

Gednium (**ged**-nee-um): small purple fruit native to Northern, Teramar.

Gelwood Avere (**gell**-wood ahv-**air**-eh): Taryn's father, grocery store owner.

General Wistoff: Northern military officer bribed by Senator Nelham to supply fourteen soldiers for coma device experimentation.

Geth (geth): previous Singer of Necklace Island Stone, Ellashin.

Grarr (grrr-ar Think growl and roll all the Rs): The Slerdonian communications officer, a telepathic alien with four legs, tail, and kreline-like face.

Gravitas plague: resulting from a thousand years without trace minerals that causes women to die when get pregnant.

Grundel (grun-**dell**): chef of Wharton mining dining hall and investor in Treyder's scheme

Hand-lights: handheld artificial lighting, like a flashlight.

Highcraft (hi-craft): Northern term for master craftsman, the very best. Usually associated with sword blade creation or manufacture.

Hopper: small rodent native to Northern, Teramar.

Ishan-Druneeaabe (ee-shan drew-knee-ah-**ah**-beh): white haired and skinned alien with heavy forehead ridges arching above opaque singularly colored eyes – no apparent pupils. A knot of cartilage protrudes between pupil less eyes.

Isul Treyder (**eye**-sul **tray**-der): genius mechanical engineer, a bit crazy.

Jaikeer Bricka (jeye-**kear brik**-ah): Southern archeologist, Southern Stone Singer.

Doctor Jarden (jar-**din**): alias of Doctor Isul Treyder.

Jinma (gin-**mah**): a type of stylized stretching exercise.

Juleen (Jew-**leen**): Singer Diani's granddaughter, destined to be next Singer of the Pericha Stone after Diani.

Karvlet (carve-**lay**): Singer Layson's husband.

Kela (**kay**-la): telepathic canine, Ani's companion, native to Teramar.

Keci (**keh**-see): farmer in Star Valley, Northern, Teramar.

Kita Stone (**kit**-ah): blue Stone of Lrakira.

Kiver (**keye**-ver): language specialist on rescue mission with Renloret, dies in crash.

Kreline (**creh**-lean): large predator on Teramar's Northern continent.

Kriswen (**cris**-win): gas giant, fifth planet in Teramaran solar system.

Kursal Ceri (**curse**-all sir-**eye**): blade ring opponent known to Ani and Taryn.

Layson (**lay**-son): Kita Stone's Singer.

Leeshob (lee-**shob**): Mroz's herding canine.

Liander-metal crystal (lee-**an**-der): rare crystal having metallic characteristics. Can be melted and forged in shapes without losing its crystalline properties. Can only be forged once. Cannot be broken or shattered. Usually used in small quantities in jewelry.

Lrakira (ulrrah-**keer**-ah) (L is barely pronounced, and first r is rolled): second of six planets in Lrakiran solar system.

Luris seed (**lur**-iss): a citrusy seed used as a spice on Northern, Teramar.

Mahzali (mah-**zahl**-ee): last Singer of Bayleden Stone before Jaikeer.

Makoshan (mah-**ko**-shahn): name of Melli & Gelwood's daughter, died in premature birth, means "gift of the heart" in Northern language.

Manthra (man-thraw): Large oval-shaped grain on Teramar. Often ground into flour or cooked as a cereal.

Melli Avere (**mell**-ee ahv-**air**-eh): Taryn's mother, maker of fine teas.

Mihalas (Mee-**hall**-us): fisherman, new Necklace Island Singer of the Ellashin Stone.

Milit/milits (**mill**-it/**mill**-its): Northern term for military personnel or soldiers.

Moon-cycle: Lrakiran month.

Moon-time: Lrakiran night.

Mount Piffital (**pif**-i-tall): specific mountain where mining operations are taking place, near Wharton, Northern, Teramar.

Mroz (mer-**rose**): bar owner, part-time coroner, Star Valley, Northern, Teramar.

Musky dam weaver: a large rodent native to the mountainous regions of Teramar's northern continent. It weaves dams and nest mounds from branches, leaves, and mud, glued together with a saliva-like substance secreted from two glands on either side of its muzzle. These glands emit a distinct musky odor.

Necklace Islands: a ring of thousands of islands predominately on the equator of Teramar. Looks like a necklace or belt from space.

Nelham (**nell**-ham): senator, head of space protection committee, Northern Teramar government.

Newsline: electronic or paper news conveyance available on Teramar. A newspaper or newscast.

Nonnash (**no**-nash): Keci's wife, mother of six daughters, Star Valley, Northern, Teramar.

Northern: Large continent on Teramar north of the equator.

Olbers (**ole**-bears): Name of Teramar's sun. Last name of German physician and astronomer (Heinrich Wilhelm Matthaus Olbers, 1758-1840); discovered many comets and asteroids.

Ovline (**ahv**-line): a four-legged domesticated ungulate similar to cattle.

Pericha Stone (pair-**ee**-cha): amber Stone of Lrakira.

Pinmah Nyairfee (pin-**mah** nye-**air**-fee): representative from Necklace Islands for witnessing Teaching Song.

Prakwel (**prah**-quell): Daneeha's husband

Pren (**pren**): name of commander of private guards who protect Treyder's secluded laboratory and mining operations in village of Wharton.

Remembrance Ceremony: usually a joyful celebration of life occurring on or near the one-year anniversary of a person's death. Similar ceremonies are held on both Lrakira and Teramar. (For readers: If you are curious about the sword dance that proceeds the Remembrance Song at the end of the ceremony you can Google "Morris Longsword Dances" or "Morris Rapper Dances" to learn about the dance forms on which it is based).

Renloret (wren-lore-**ay**) (t is not pronounced, think French): Lrakiran pilot of rescue mission.

Reslo Chenak/R'Schlonick Chenakainet (**rehs**-low **chen**-ack / ruh-**schlawn**-ick chen-ah-kah-**nay**): Ani's uncle, Yenne Chenakainet's brother.

Ryken (**rye**-kin): seven-year-old girl, Keci and Nonnash's third daughter.

Saedi City (saw-**ee**-dee): capital of Northern continent on Teramar.

Saltren (**sal**-tren): a type of gin, often served over ice with a sprinkle of cinnamon, found on Teramar.

Sancharos Peaks (san-**chair**-ose): mountain range on Lrakira, home of Kita Stone, Renloret's home.

Sarinne Flaymatov (sah-**reen** **flay**-mah-tahv): Lrakiran communications officer in original research team to Teramar.

Selabec (**sell**-ah-beck): Anyala Stone's Singer, mother of S'Hendale/Shendahl, Ani's Grandmother.

Sharnel (shar-**nell**): lead of Lrakiran rescue mission, 2nd pilot to Renloret, dies in crash.

S'Hendale/Shendahl (say-hen-**dale**/shen-**doll**): Ani's mother, head medical researcher, former Singer of the Anyala Stone – Lrakira.

Sheren leaf (**sheer**-en): a peppery leafed vegetable similar to arugula.

Sheriff Driton (**dry**-ton): sheriff in neighboring valley on Teramar.

Sholoret (show-low-**ray**): Lrakiran surgeon, finds and removes coma device.

Silteene (sill-**teen**): a rare and expensive fabric woven on Lrakira.

Slerdon/Slerdonians (**slur**-don/slur-**dough**-knee-onz): planet of telepathic beings, have no voice box, four legs, two arms and hands, fur-covered, kreline faced with fangs, three toes on paws and hands.

Song of Finding: specific song sung by a Stone to assist a new Singer in finding that same Stone.

Song of Healing: a song sung by a Singer or Singers while using a Stone's crystal blade to promote healing of an injury.

Song of Saving: a specific song sung by the seven Stones and Singers to safely transport the people from their planet of origin to Lrakira and Teramar, where they would stay until the origin planet was healed.

Song of Teaching: a specific song by six Singers and six Stones to inform the people of Lrakira and Teramar of their shared past and to begin preparing them to return to their planet of origin.

Song of Transition: A song sung by the Lrakiran Stones when no Passing has occurred and a new Singer takes the place of a *retired* Singer. The new Singer must carry the blade to the Stone and physically touch the Stone with blade in hand to transition or Pass on the Singer title.

Song of Welcome: a song sung by a Stone to welcome a new Singer.

Southern: Large continent on Teramar south of the equator.

S'Roadoss (sah-**row**-ah-dose): renewal ceremony of Stone and blade bonding for Lrakiran Stone Singers usually held every three years.

Star Runner: smallest interstellar ship in Lrakiran fleet. Carries between 1 and 15 crew and passengers.

Star Traveler: largest interstellar ship in the Lrakiran fleet. Carries up to 1,100 crew and passengers.

Star Valley: Ani's home village on Northern, Teramar.

Stone Singer: liaison between Stones and their charges.

Stubin Dalkey (**stew**-bin **doll**-key): general in Northern continent's military, alien-phobic.

Sun-cycle: Lrakiran time designation equal to a year.

Sun-time: Lrakiran time designation equal to a day.

Swark (swark): largest land predator on Lrakira, considered to be vicious, mate for life, litters of three to four cubs every four years, both parents participate in rearing of offspring.

Tacara (ta-**car**-ah): starchy root native to Teramar.

Tailings: a mining term for the waste dirt and rocks left behind after the desired minerals are extracted.

Taryn Avere (**tair**-in ahv-**air**-eh): sheriff of Star Valley, Ani's best friend.

Tel-com (**tell**-com): communication devices, either audio and/or visual, Northern, Teramar.

Teramar (**tair**-ah-mar): first of five planets in Teramaran solar system.

Tezak Ganevek (**tay**-zack **gan**-eh-vehk): Star Valley doctor, coworker of Ani's mother.

Theyech (**thay**-ech): Renloret's older brother.

Thrayo Dway (**thray**-oh duh-**way**): representative from Southern government to witness the Song of Teaching

Tianet Mountains (tee-ah-**nay**): remote mountain range on Southern continent, Teramar.

Time Song: sung by the Stones of Lrakira to twist time around the Olbers solar system and Teramar. Designed to age the people forward at least ten years so The Blood would be of the correct age to have the necessary hormones to create a vaccine to cure the gravitas plague killing the women of Lrakira.

Traseevat (trah-**see**-vot): Lrakiran word for thank you.

Appendix

Trimag (**tree**-mag): Lrakiran high commander of planetary safety, supporter of Renloret.

Tri-pronged sueders (**sway**-ders): four-legged ungulate similar to deer or elk.

Udi root (**oo**-dee): a spice common to Northern, Teramar.

Valik (**val**-ick): previous Singer of Northern's Chandaron Stone.

Vaquin (vah-**quinn**): strong Teramaran liquor, blue in color.

Viken (**vike**-in): Teramaran ringed moon.

Vishon (vee-**shawn**): a fishlike creature native to Teramar.

Tivi (**tiv**-ee): Renloret's great grandmother, former Singer of the Kita Stone.

Wharton (**whar**-ton): mining village deep in western mountains of Northern.

Whirjerata (whir-jer-**ah**- tah): fruit on Southern Teramar, bears fruit every three years.

Whis'jeras (whiss-**jer**-ass): fruit on Lrakira, bears fruit every three years.

Whistlepot (**whis**-ill-pot): a small stovetop kettle with a spout that sounds a tone when water is hot enough to produce steam.

Yantel (yan-**tell**): Star Valley sheriff deputy.

Yenne Chenakainet (**yen**-nay chen-ah-kah-**nay**): Commander of Lrakiran research team, Ani's father.

Zabion Eknerah (**zab**-ee-on **ehk**-nair-ah): Vice Chancellor of Northern's government.

Zocanel Province (zo-**can**-ell): one of the provinces on the northern continent of Teramar.

# ABOUT THE AUTHOR

Allynn Riggs began telling stories before she could write them down, and after being nagged and cajoled by a determined collection of fictional characters for many years, she surrendered and shifted careers to share their stories. *The Stone's Blade* series began innocently enough as a short story written when she was fourteen. The characters of Ani, Kela, Taryn, and Renloret have never left her imagination or dreams and waited patiently until she was ready to share their worlds with you. *The Blades* is the third installment of the four core books of *The Stone's Blade* series. Others may be added depending on character requests.

When Allynn is not writing, she avidly participates in and teaches square dancing and hunts big game. The mother of three grown daughters, Allynn resides in Centennial, Colorado, with her dance partner and husband, Bob.

To contact Allynn directly: email her at info@AllynnRiggs.com For more information and interaction check out her social media platforms:

**Websites:**
www.AllynnRiggs.com and www.timberdark.com
**Blog:**
TimberdarkWriter.wordpress.com
**Facebook:**
www.facebook.com/TimberdarkPublications
**Goodreads Author:**
www.goodreads.com/AllynnRiggs
**LinkedIn:**
www.linkedin.com/in/allynnriggs/

Thank you for reading *The Blades*. Gaining exposure as an award winning independently published author relies mostly on word-of-mouth. If you have the time and inclination, please consider leaving a short review of this and the other books in the series wherever you can.

www.ingramcontent.com/pod-product-compliance
Lightning Source LLC
Chambersburg PA
CBHW020632020726
47494CB00001B/156